Torch

The Unbreakable Bonds Series

By Jocelynn Drake and Rinda Elliott

Praise for *Shatter*

"I absolutely loved this book. Snow and Jude were everything I hoped they would be and more. Jude is the exactly what Snow needs and I adored watching these two strong men fall for each other. It was incredibly sexy, emotional, and kept me flipping the pages."

—Riley Hart, Author of the Crossroads Series

"This is a 5+ star read… This is about as close to perfection as they come for me."

—Gay Book Reviews

"For *Shatter* the authors took: a great suspense story, an ERMERGERD sexy-alpha-male-getting-dominated romance, and a heartwarming friendship story, and dropped them in a blender… creating a sexy smoothie with bite. Yum!"

—I Smell Sheep

"I really liked reading *Shatter* I can certainly rave over Jude for ages and how he and Snow meshed. I also liked watching the interplay between the characters because one of the things I love is when the main characters have close relationships outside of their romantic interest. In this particular series I don't think any of the main group of friends would still be living without the others. I really hope Drake and Elliott can write quickly because I NEED to see what happens next."

—Bookpushers

Praise for *Shiver*

"I love it when a new to you author leaves you wanting more! I really enjoyed this first book in the Unbreakable Bonds series and can't wait to see where it goes next."

—Prism Book Alliance

"Shiver was everything I hoped for and more. I didn't want to put it down. I loved these characters. It is an alpha-male hot mess (I mean that in the best possible ways). In m/f romance, a caveman mentality is a big turn off, but if you pair that up with another caveman alpha-male…fireworks!"

—I Smell Sheep

"I just flat out enjoyed this. The relationships, suspense, mystery, and hot smexy times…it all boils down to fun. I had fun while reading this and look forward to a continuation of the series."

—Gay Book Reviews

"I believed in their emotional ties and in the growing romance between Lucas and Andrei. The sex is hot. The pacing is good. And I liked the overall story… I would recommend for fans of m/m romantic suspense. I am curious to see what the authors have in store for the next installment."

—Red Hot Books

"This book was filled with angst, excitement, action and a whole lot of emotion. I loved how Lucas and Andrei slowly grew together, and Andrei discovers his true sexuality. How Lucas realizes he's let in Andrei without him noticing and without a whole lot of effort. The amount of feelings that these two authors have managed to write into and action filled book is amazing."

—Love Bytes

The Unbreakable Bonds Series
Shiver
Shatter
Torch

Unbreakable Bonds Short Story Collection
Unbreakable Stories: Lucas

Also by Jocelynn Drake

The Dark Days Series
Bound to Me
The Dead, the Damned and the Forgotten
Nightwalker
Dayhunter
Dawnbreaker
Pray for Dawn
Wait for Dusk
Burn the Night

The Lost Nights Series
Stefan

The Asylum Tales
The Asylum Interviews: Bronx
The Asylum Interviews: Trixie
Angel's Ink
Dead Man's Deal
Demon's Vengeance

Also by Rinda Elliott

Beri O'Dell Series
Dweller on the Threshold
Blood of an Ancient

The Brothers Bernaux
Raisonne Curse

Sisters of Fate
Foretold
Forecast
Foresworn

Also by Rinda Elliott writing as Dani Worth

The Kithran Regenesis Series
Kithra
Replicant
Catalyst
Origin

Crux Survivors Series
After the Crux
Sole Survivors

Copyright

This book is a work of fiction. Names, characters, places, and incidents are products of the authors' imagination or are used factiously and are not to be construed as real. Any resemblance to actual events, locales, or organizations, or persons, living or dead, is entirely coincidental.

TORCH. Copyright ©2016 Jocelynn Drake and Rinda Elliott. All rights reserved under International and Pan-American Copyright Conventions. By payment of the required fees, you have been granted the nonexclusive, nontransferable right to access and read the text of this e-book onscreen. No part of this text may be reproduced, transmitted, introduced into any information storage and retrieval system, in any form or by any means, whether electronic or mechanical, now known or hereinafter invented, without the express written permission of Jocelynn Drake and Rinda Elliott.

Cover art by Stephen Drake of Design by Drake.

Edited by Flat Earth Editing

Dedication

We'd like to dedicate *Torch* to Devon Monk and Riley Hart for their invaluable support and feedback during the creation of this book.

Acknowledgements

Rinda — A big thank you to Devon Monk and Riley Hart for beta reading our Rowe and Noah and for coming back with such enthusiasm and wonderful suggestions!

Thanks to Hope and Jessica of Flat Earth Editing for making the production of *Torch* such a blast. And for your eagle eyes! And for your Barbies!!!!

Thanks to Rachel Vincent, my long time critique partner for being there for any crazy thing I can think up and for hosting Jocelynn and me in an incredible week-long writer's retreat so we could plot MORE BOOKS. Thanks to Rachel's husband for co-hosting and providing such fantastic meals. I still want an office in the Vincent basement.

Thanks to my husband for his continuing support while I chase after this career dream.

And as always, a big thank you to Jocelynn. I absolutely love this world we've built together and I love working with you!

Jocelynn — As always, it was exciting to return to the Unbreakable Bonds world to hang out with our boys. I want to reiterate all the thanks that Rinda gave as well as extend a big thanks to Rinda for being so patient with me when I'm a stubborn handful. She made writing this book an absolute joy.

I would like to thank my husband for being so understanding when it comes to the strange and long hours required to get this book into the hands of readers as well as helping to answer some of my odd questions.

I also want to give a little nod to the original Warehouse, settled on 1313 Vine. It feels like a lifetime ago now, but it was the first place where I felt at home, safe to be myself—not an easy thing for a hard-core introvert. Swathed in black, leather and chains while industrial music thumped from the speakers, the occupants of the Warehouse found a place in the world to simply be for a few hours. I'm just sorry that Lucas, Snow, and Rowe rolled into town after it was already gone.

The Warehouse…1313 Vine…it isn't very pretty…

Chapter 1

Fuck, he was getting old.

Well, maybe he wasn't really *old*, but watching all the tiny women scurrying around Lucas's new nightclub in their barely-there outfits, trying to catch the eye of a bunch of overdressed men…ah hell, Rowe was definitely feeling old even if he wasn't yet forty.

Leaning against the low wall overlooking the main dance floor, Rowe sipped his drink—at least the bourbon was older than him—and tried to relax, even if it wasn't his kind of place. His best friend had a talent for high-end, trendy clubs that served complicated drinks and played loud, obnoxious music, but this…this was familiar.

Aptly named The Warehouse, the entire club had an industrial feel to it with its exposed metal beams, concrete floor and bare pipes. Even the music perfectly matched, the classic industrial tunes blasting from the speakers. The club reminded Rowe of the places he'd hit with Snow and Lucas while in the Army and the few years they'd lived in Baltimore together.

A smirk curled one corner of Rowe's mouth. Lucas was getting nostalgic now that he was closing in on forty as well.

Tonight was the exclusive grand opening—an invitation-only affair that quickly became the hottest ticket in town. Lucas had given some of the local radio stations a handful of tickets and Rowe had listened for weeks to the strange antics they demanded of people in order to win one.

Of course, those tickets didn't get a single one of them up to the second floor. Lucas had created that guest list personally, and as far as Rowe could see, it included only their family, friends, and some close business associates. And, oddly enough, Geoffrey.

Lucas had filled Rowe in on the special task Geoffrey had helped them with when it came to tracking down Dwight Gratton, the man who murdered Rowe's wife Melissa and nearly killed both Ian and Snow. Rowe was willing to guess this was Lucas's attempt to show gratitude. If Geoffrey's hang-dog expression was anything to go by, it wasn't working very well.

Rowe watched the delicate man approach him with his martini glass in hand. He was pretty in a big-eyed, elfin kind of way that left Rowe feeling like he was a slow, clumsy troll.

"You're a friend of Snow's, right?"

"Yep."

"Any chance there's trouble in paradise?" he asked, his voice lifting with desperate hope.

"Between Snow and Jude?" Rowe's gaze drifted over to the pair in question where they stood on the deck. Jude and Ian were in animated conversation and Snow stood quietly, his eyes on Jude and his hand resting on the man's back as if he just needed to be touching him. "Nope. Sunshine and roses."

"But it's been nearly a year."

"Still in love," Rowe said, though he'd never expected to say those words about Snow. But once Snow had given his heart, he'd been all in and would be for life. Hell, he'd bought a damn *home* with Jude after only a few months.

Geoffrey groaned loudly, slouching against the low wall as well. "It's not fair."

"Yeah, they're nauseating to be around."

The young man gave him the evil eye and started to walk away, but Rowe grabbed his shoulder and turned them both so that they were staring down at the writhing crowd on the first floor.

"Look down there," Rowe instructed.

"At what?"

"Just look."

Geoffrey huffed and stood silently for a minute, his gaze shifting over the people.

Rowe leaned closer so he could speak directly into Geoffrey's ear. "Did you notice that eventually everyone looks up here? They're looking at you and wondering who you are, how you know Lucas Vallois, and why the hell you're so special. Right now, every last person down there wants to be you."

When Rowe pulled away, he noticed that Geoffrey was standing a little straighter, his chin lifted and his shoulders were back. Yeah, he got it now.

Geoffrey glanced over at Rowe, a wicked grin on his lips. "Oh, you're good. You're very good."

"Go get 'em, tiger. I think you've got your pick tonight." Rowe patted him on the shoulder, feeling the slim, delicate bones. "You should come in to Ward Security, take a self-defense class. First one's free."

Nodding absently, Geoffrey headed toward the stairs.

Rowe wandered to an empty pub table half hidden in the shadows. The placement allowed him to see most of the second floor, and be away from anyone who might want to engage in painful small talk. By his count, he needed to stick around for another thirty minutes and then he could slip out. It had become a complicated dance with his friends. He didn't want to be out. He didn't want to be social. It had been nine months since Mel's death and he didn't want to date—couldn't imagine dating—not that they had started pushing about that, but it was coming.

For now, he showed up to most things they invited him to and worked to hold the smile on his lips. As long as he put forth a little effort, they stayed happy and didn't nag him about not locking himself away in his house with his dogs, shunning daylight like some clichéd vampire. He was grateful and he *did* enjoy himself, but after a couple of hours, what had once been fun became work. Nothing was quite as fun without Mel's laugh and mischief. But then, nothing would be quite as fun as it once was without her.

The ache she'd left in his heart had eased; it wasn't the breath-stealing stab of a broadsword now. But it lingered, felt permanent—a constant reminder that she was not coming back.

Rowe sipped his drink, his eyes slowly sliding over the occupants of the second floor. The music wasn't as loud up there, allowing the little groups of people to talk without needing to shout. Of course, that wasn't stopping Lucas from using sign language with his assistant, Candace. Rowe had watched the woman working with Lucas for more than three years now. Lucas claimed he signed with her only in his clubs so he didn't have to yell. But Rowe took a special pleasure in pointing out that Lucas had started signing with Candace when they were in his quiet office.

A loud, easy laugh pulled Rowe's attention from Lucas and his eyes snagged on a man his friend had briefly pointed out as the architect for The Warehouse. He was talking to another of Lucas's business partners and Rowe found that he suddenly couldn't look away from the man's mouth. He had full lips that were pulled into a half smile. His front teeth pressed into his lush lower lip, tugging at it as if he were begging someone to come along and suck on it.

"He's cute."

Rowe jumped at Andrei's voice, splashing his drink across his hand. He didn't even hear his employee approach and Rowe had been sure that he was the only person Andrei Hadeon couldn't surprise. Fuck, what was wrong with him? Rowe put his glass down on the table and wiped his hand on his pants, carefully schooling his features for a second while trying to get his frantically pounding heart under control. There was no point in trying to hide that he'd been surprised. Andrei wouldn't have bought it for a second.

"Who's cute?" he asked, looking up at Andrei. The younger man was standing right beside him leaning against the wall while he sipped water from the bottle in his hand. Seriously? He'd gotten this fucking close and Rowe hadn't noticed it?

A slow smile spread across Andrei's mouth and his dark eyes absolutely sparkled with mischief. Yeah, the architect was cute—not that Rowe was at all willing to admit that aloud to anyone—but Andrei was gorgeous with his dark hair, high cheekbones, and dark complexion. There was a rumor floating around the office that he'd once been offered a modeling contract, but the whispers had largely died down after Andrei pulled the last person to utter those words into an intense and painful sparring match.

"I think Harrison is single," Andrei continued. He paused, screwing the cap back onto his bottle before putting it on the table. "I could introduce you if you'd like."

"You're not funny," Rowe grumbled.

Andrei shrugged, a smile playing on his lips, but if he had anything else to say, the man kept it to himself. He just stood there with Rowe, watching the crowd. If anything, the silence seemed to pull at Rowe, wearing him down despite his best intentions. The fact was, the architect wasn't the first man he'd caught himself staring at, and not the "I think he's going to kill someone" staring. More of the "I wonder what he tastes like" staring. It had cropped up a lot over the years, but more often the last couple of months. And every time, it reminded him of one man in particular.

"How…" Rowe paused and licked his lips. His voice was barely audible over the music, nearly drowned out by his own pounding heart. "How did you know for sure that you were interested in more than women?"

If Andrei was at all surprised by Rowe's question, his face gave nothing away. He continued to stare straight ahead, watching the crowd. "I think I've been bi almost as long as I've been sexually active, which would be since I was sixteen, but it was easier to pretend it wasn't there. I didn't fit in too well as a kid, and I didn't see any reason to make it worse. But to actually know it…to face it…Lucas did that for me."

"What do you mean?"

"Before him, it was just about getting off." Andrei's smirk turned a little self-deprecating. "A guy's mouth could do that just as easily as a woman's. Matters even less when your eyes are closed. Not that I'm proud of it." Rowe watched that smile change to something softer when Andrei's eyes landed on the man in question. "With Lucas, it was always about more than just getting off. Things changed. My eyes were wide open every second with him. I wanted to know him, spend time with him, make him happy." He looked at Rowe. "I take it you're questioning some new…inclinations?"

"I don't know what I'm feeling—but it isn't new." Rowe frowned. "Don't say anything to them."

Andrei stiffened. He turned to face Rowe, his dark eyebrows beetling together over his nose. He'd even stepped a hair closer so he could lower his voice. "Why not? They're your friends. They care for you."

"Yeah, and I don't want some kind of weird intervention where we all sit around drinking and discussing my sex life. It could be nothing. It's been me and my hand for almost a year now. Maybe I'm just…frustrated."

"Fine," Andrei announced after an extended silence, snapping Rowe's gaze back to the other man. "I won't tell them, but two things…"

"Oh hell," Rowe muttered and then motioned for Andrei to continue.

"Don't forget that you've got a killer support system and knowledge base if this isn't just frustration."

Rowe drew in a deep breath and held it. Yeah, he couldn't fault Andrei on that one. "True."

"And second," Andrei stopped, waiting for Rowe to meet his eyes. "Be happy, whatever it takes. You deserve to be, Rowe."

And that was the hard part, wasn't it? Being happy. Since Mel's death, Rowe couldn't quite find his way back to happy. Not really. Some moments were less bad than others. And some ripped the air straight out of his lungs, leaving him shaking and sobbing. He really didn't think happy was on the menu for him any longer. He'd be fine if he could find his way back to content or maybe even at peace.

Lucas came up behind Andrei and clamped his hand down on Andrei's shoulder. "You two better not be discussing work over here," Lucas announced. "This is supposed to be a party."

"Just talking a little shop," Rowe quickly said.

Andrei grunted. "I don't think we hired enough security for the size of this place."

"Everything is running smoothly." Lucas's hand tightened on Andrei's shoulder as if he were trying to massage away the tension there. "We kept the size of the opening-night crowd manageable."

A frown still tugged at Andrei's mouth and his eyes locked on Rowe. "Between the two levels, the deck, the parking lot, and the fact that the neighborhood is still questionable, I think we need more eyes. It's better to stop something before it starts than break it up after it's already erupted."

Rowe's smile was smug as he looked at Lucas. "You should listen to him. He's pretty smart," Rowe said, pointing to Andrei with his glass.

"Yeah, he is," Lucas agreed easily.

"Would you mind if I raided the roster for a few weeks?" Andrei pushed on, ignoring both their comments. "Let us borrow two people while we look to add some more bodies. I think I know of a couple who would be interested, but they would need to be interviewed and trained up."

Rowe scratched his chin. He couldn't make light of this. After everything that had happened to them, he knew they were all still being extra cautious. They needed to be. "Remind me when we get into the office tomorrow. We'll look over the assignment lists and see who we've got where."

"Thanks." Andrei turned and pressed a lingering kiss on Lucas's mouth. "I'm going to make a quick pass around the first floor one last time and then I think I'll be ready for a drink."

Lucas turned and watched Andrei smoothly cut through the sparse crowd, pausing to shake a hand here and there, a smile on his lips while still watching for trouble. The man was just as skilled at working a room as Lucas, and he made it look easy.

"You are so lost over him," Rowe announced after an extended silence where Lucas simply couldn't look away from Andrei.

"Have been since the day I met him."

Rowe snorted. God, the man had changed over the past year with Andrei. It was like his wall had come down...well, some of it had come down. When he was around his family, he was a little looser, a little quicker to smile, and far more willing to admit that Andrei had become the center of his world.

"Have you proposed yet?"

"Why? Your date coming up soon?"

Rowe flinched and Lucas laughed loudly, the sound filling the second floor.

"Did you really think I wouldn't find out about that stupid pool between you, Snow, and Ian?"

"Hey! Sarah, Jude, and Rebecca have thrown in too. The pot's up to $600. It'd be $700, but we haven't been able to corrupt Candace yet."

"I think Snow is closer to proposing than me," Lucas said, obviously attempting to deflect the conversation away from his relationship failings.

"Nah," Rowe said with a shake of his head. "They're still enjoying the newness of living together now that Hurricane Anna has backed off." Jude's mom was wonderful, but the woman was a freaking force of nature when she swept in with her mothering. Of course, Rowe didn't know a person who needed it more than Snow. "Can you imagine what'll happen when Snow and Jude get engaged? She'll explode in a shower of pink unicorns and rainbows."

"True."

"So that just leaves you and Andrei."

Lucas rolled his eyes, but he was still smiling. "Andrei isn't even officially living with me. He's still got his apartment."

"Even though most of his clothes are at your place now."

Lucas shrugged.

"Have you at least told him?"

"What?"

Rowe groaned, wanting to shake Lucas. The man wasn't this dense. "That you love him."

"He knows."

"That's a no."

Lucas frowned, looking more than a little uncomfortable. "I start to and…the moment never seems quite right."

Reaching over, Rowe placed his hand on Lucas's broad shoulder, giving in to the urge to shake him. "Let me tell you this, as someone who has loved and buried the other half of his soul, *every* moment is the right moment."

Lucas nodded, the lightness evaporating from their conversation. But then, any mention of Mel tended to do that. Rowe hoped that it would stop soon and they'd hold their smiles when they thought of her. She would have hated to see anyone sad on her account. The woman had hated to be serious.

"I'm guessing that you caught the news about Jagger yesterday," Lucas said after nearly a minute of silence.

"Fucker," Rowe snarled. "How the hell did he get off?"

Boris Jagger was Cincinnati's top crime boss with ties to both drugs and sex trade in the city. Unfortunately, Rowe, Snow, and Lucas had suffered a run-in with Jagger several years ago. The good thing was that they'd managed to save Ian.

After a deal had been struck and money had changed hands, Rowe had always thought they'd never cross paths again. But something had gone wrong.

Jagger had loosed his favorite butcher on them. Dwight Gratton was dead, but Rowe had a sick feeling in his stomach that it wasn't over. Gratton had been hired to kill Lucas and Rowe after he was done with Snow. They just had no clue as to why they were on Jagger's shit list again.

"How could the feds have fucked up the case?" Rowe demanded, raising his voice. Lucas frowned at him in warning and Rowe huffed, but lowered his voice when he spoke again. "They had to have gotten something on him in relation to that sick auction you stopped." While Rowe had been off mourning his wife, his friends had helped stop an auction of underage kids. The police had been able to get the missing children home to their families.

"They likely had problems getting anything to stick after two of the witnesses ended up dead."

Rowe quickly downed the last of his drink, letting the liquor warm him against the chill trying to sink into his bones. "You know he's not done." His voice was now rough and bourbon burned.

"You don't know for sure Jagger started this. Gratton could have been lying to Snow to fuck with his head. Jagger has no reason to go after us."

Rowe stared at the other man in shock. Lucas was not one to stick his head in the sand and pray that it would all blow over. Lucas faced shit head on. Hell, he usually led the charge into the fire. But then…for the first time in his life, Lucas was in love and he was terrified of risking Andrei's life. Especially after coming so close to losing him.

The noise from the second floor spiked above the screeching guitar blasting through the speakers. Lucas started to say something, but Rowe grabbed his friend's arm and pulled him forward, swapping places so that Lucas's back was against the wall and Rowe was closest to the stairs leading to the first floor. His heart pounded hard in his chest, but the same calm he always felt in dangerous situations swept over him, clearing his mind and giving him the sense of peace he couldn't find in day-to-day life. Killers and thugs he could handle. This was familiar territory.

The noise grew, punctuated by screams as people rushed for the front exit. Just as Andrei reached the top of the stairs, Rowe caught the first whiff of smoke.

"Fire!" Andrei shouted above the noise. His eyes drifted to Lucas for only a heartbeat before locking on Rowe once again. "Get everyone on the second floor out using the rear emergency exit. I'm going back to oversee the first floor evac."

Rowe nodded, but Lucas was already stepping forward, reaching for Andrei.

"Andrei, no—"

The bodyguard spun around and grabbed Lucas by both shoulders, slamming him against the wall. Hard. "Listen to me. You will leave here now. Get everyone out safe. You will be safe and smart so I can do my job without worrying about you." Andrei paused for a second, frowning. "I almost lost you here before."

Rowe stared open-mouthed at Andrei as he held Lucas pinned against the wall for another breath before he charged down the stairs. Someone had hit the main lights in the growing chaos, but that only made the smoke more visible. Looking back at Lucas, Rowe's heart lurched at the fear etched in his friend's face. Mel's death had done that. They all felt a little more vulnerable, a little more fragile now.

"Ian," Rowe said, snapping Lucas from his worries. As he expected, Lucas's expression closed up and the man straightened. He was a mountain again. A titan of old.

"Last saw him on the deck with Snow and Jude," Lucas said. "I'll clear that area, direct everyone to the exit." He pointed to the brightly lit exit sign on the right near the back of the building. "You clear the bar area. There's also a small storeroom behind the bar."

With a nod, Rowe set off quickly. People were scattered about looking confused and afraid, but too few were actually moving toward the exits. Luckily all it took was him barking "Fire!" or "Exit now!" and they took off. He caught a brief glance of Jude, Rebecca, and Ian heading to the exit. Snow would be close by along with Lucas. At least they had three medical professionals on hand. Snow, as a doctor, always kept first aid gear in his car and Rowe was sure that Jude and Rebecca, as paramedics, would likely do the same.

Smoke burned his eyes and tickled the back of his throat. The air was growing thicker and hotter by the second, but he couldn't leave yet. After checking the back room to see that it was empty, he ducked behind the bar, grabbed a white towel and ran it under cold water before pressing it to his face. An immediate feeling of relief washed across his cheeks and nose. But the towel wasn't going to filter the smoke from the air for long. Only another minute or two—that was all he needed.

Crouching as low as he could, Rowe hurried back across the second floor to the stairs. A little, nagging voice was screaming that this was wrong. So very wrong. Rowe had worked in enough bars as a bouncer to recognize an accidental trash can fire or even a grease fire in the kitchen—and this was neither. He was also surprised that no one had bothered to pull the fire alarm and the sprinkler system hadn't kicked in. Other than his footsteps on the stairs, the only sound was the random sharp snap and crackle of fire eating away at the building. As he reached the ground floor, the lights popped off, plunging the place into darkness.

Dropping to a knee, he blinked against a flood of tears. The smoke was burning his eyes, making it nearly impossible to see. The air became a little clearer as the smoke rushed up to the second floor, but the heat was baking him, drying the sweat on his skin as soon as it rose. He hesitated halfway between the exit and the back of the building. He wanted to see where the fire had started, get an idea of how it started, but he didn't have a damn flashlight on him and it was too fucking hard to see. Getting lost in the dark of a burning building was a really bad fucking idea.

Rowe growled. He had no idea how long he had been in there, but his friends were probably losing their minds. There wasn't anything he could do now. Turning for the main entrance, he stopped at what sounded like a cough. He froze. Was it the culprit? Coming out of hiding at the last second?

Backpedaling to the deeper shadows by the stairs, Rowe drew the gun he had nestled against his lower back and waited. He blinked rapidly, spilling tears from the corners of his sore eyes, trying to clear his vision. He couldn't linger more than a few seconds.

A figure moved in the darkness, heading for the entrance. His large body was hunched low, but he stopped suddenly, dropping to his knees, coughing loudly. Rowe couldn't see his face, but he recognized the tenor of his cough.

"Andrei!" Rowe called, holstering his gun.

"Rowe!" Andrei croaked back, his voice rough and fractured.

Rowe rushed over and pulled Andrei's arm around his shoulders. Together, they hurried the last few feet to the entrance and clear air. Firm but gentle hands grabbed Rowe's left arm, guiding him away from the building, but he kept Andrei close as they both gasped and coughed. The chilly night air bit at his face and crept through his damp shirt, but he welcomed the cold after the suffocating heat of the nightclub. The world was blurry, but he could make out flashing red lights drawing close and the shadowy figures of the crowd from inside the bar.

His skin pricked and every instinct demanded that he draw his gun. The fire could have been an accident, but his gut said there was an arsonist lurking in the crowd, watching them, possibly poised to use the chaos as cover to strike.

A new set of sirens rent the air, joining the fire trucks. Cop cars were bearing down on them and Rowe relaxed. Whether the threat was real or imagined, they were safe…for now.

Lucas spotted them as soon as they were no more than a dozen paces from the entrance and quickly ushered them over to Snow's makeshift care center.

"Ash!" Lucas shouted but there was no missing the tremble in his voice.

Snow gave quick instructions to Jude, who was treating a woman with a long cut on her arm and then he pulled Andrei in front of the headlights of his Lexus.

"I'm fine," Andrei rasped, coughing harshly. It was a little hard to believe him when his face was streaked with soot and sweat. Little burns pockmarked his black shirt. "Got everyone out."

"Shut up," Snow snapped. He placed the earpieces of his stethoscope in his ears and placed the metal disc to Andrei's chest. "Breathe deep."

A hand landed against Rowe's neck and he looked up into Lucas's worried eyes, now more gray than green in the harsh streetlights.

"Are you okay? Jude is finished—"

"I'm good." Rowe cut him off. "Sweaty and smoky, but good."

"You got him out."

Rowe looked at his friend, unsure if it was a statement or a question. "We got each other out."

"Good." Lucas's hand tightened on the back of his neck and he pulled Rowe a little closer. "I need you both."

Snow stepped back as he finished his inspection of the bodyguard. "Some smoke inhalation. I'll put him on oxygen as soon as the ambulance is here and we'll need to keep an eye on him for a day or so. For now, it's probably best if he doesn't talk to give his throat and vocal cords a rest."

"That's fine," Lucas declared as he released Rowe and stepped in front of Andrei. "I need you to listen and not speak."

Andrei straightened, lifting one eyebrow. The man looked like hell between his sweat-matted hair, puffy red eyes, and soot-streaked face, but Rowe was pretty sure Andrei could still take Lucas in a fight.

"*I love you.*" Lucas murmured the words, voice low, though the crowds of people weren't paying attention to them.

Rowe thought about stepping away to give them more privacy, but Snow turned to him and held his chin, tilting his face toward the light. He jerked his head out of Snow's hands, frowning, then caught the look on Andrei's face. His eyes widened, making Snow look as well.

Lucas cupped Andrei's cheeks, his thumbs moving over his face, smearing the soot. "I love you so fucking much. I should have told you that every day for the past year. God knows I've thought it a hundred times each and every one of those days, but I was too much of a coward to say it. Not anymore. You will never doubt how important you are to me."

Andrei opened his mouth to speak.

"Ahh!" Snow interrupted with a wicked grin. "No talking."

Andrei smiled back at Snow before flipping him off. The surgeon chuckled and walked back to Jude, who was checking on Geoffrey.

"I love you too, baby," Andrei uttered huskily, pulling Lucas into his arms.

"Get rid of that damn apartment."

Rowe shook his head at Lucas's uttered order and stepped closer to them. "Don't you realize you're supposed to do all that heartfelt stuff in private?"

"Get out of our fucking bubble, Ward." He looked back at Andrei like the man was all he saw.

"I'm sorry about our place," Andrei said softly.

"I only care that you're okay."

Giving them what relative privacy he could with the crowds around them, Rowe turned to find Ian standing a couple of feet away, a smile on his lips.

"It's about time," Ian muttered when Rowe was standing beside him.

Rowe heaved a fake sigh. "Another one bites the dust."

Ian shrugged. "It was bound to happen." He snorted. "Besides, that dust was bitten a long time ago. It was just lodged behind a wall of stubborn."

"Are we talking about the same Lucas Vallois?"

Ian wrapped an arm around Rowe's waist and leaned against him. Despite the fire and chaos, the young man still looked his usual handsome self. Rowe hesitated for only a second before wrapping an arm around his shoulder and pulling him in tighter. Fuck the soot. He needed this as much as Ian.

"Yes, even grumpy Lucas Vallois can find love," Ian teased.

"I guess it's your turn."

The young man snorted again and Rowe couldn't blame him for his skepticism. He'd shown interest in someone, a cop who had haunted Ian's every move for a time, one who'd been conspicuously absent from their lives for months. Rowe was reluctant to ask what happened with Hollis. Lucas wasn't a fan, but Rowe had always thought the cop was okay. Even Snow had come around some.

"Was this an accident?" Ian asked after they'd stood there in companionable silence, watching the police and fire department descend upon the crowd and building.

"Don't know yet."

"But..."

Rowe tensed, weighing his words before speaking. "Probably not."

"Was it *him*?"

Rowe's gut twisted at Ian's question. He could feel the young man balling his shirt in his fist as tension hummed in his slender frame.

"Come by my office tomorrow. We'll talk...without Lucas and Snow."

Ian drew a deep breath and slowly released it before he nodded once. "Tomorrow."

Chapter 2

"Gidget!" Rowe poked another button on his phone and snarled when it made a harsh beeping noise. He hit another. "Gidget!"

A throat cleared near the door of his office and he looked up to find Gidget standing in the open doorway. He frowned, taking in the pale cast to her face and the dark circles under her normally bright eyes. "You feeling okay?"

She nodded, but didn't come farther into the office. She smoothed her hands down her long skirt, then tugged on the hem of her pink top. "I'm fine." Her eyebrows came together as she frowned. "Why do you bother to use the phone at all when your yelling comes right into my office?"

A low growl rumbled from Rowe as he picked up a stack of contracts that he needed to look over and moved them to another part of his desk. He just couldn't deal with the day-to-day nonsense, not right now. "I still don't understand why we changed the set-up. These phones are annoying."

"You'll get the hang of them." She crossed her arms and leaned against the doorjamb. "What did you need?"

"I'd like everything you dug up on Jagger and Gratton back in January."

"I heard he was acquitted." Her lips tightened, her eyes narrowed and she abruptly stood up straight. "That man needs to be strung up by his balls."

Surprised, Rowe lifted his eyebrows, but nodded. "He does. So get me whatever you dug up before."

Gidget gave a little shrug. "Sure. I can have that to you in a couple minutes. Anything else?"

Rowe paused, looking down at his hand gripping the edge of his now-clear desk, his knuckles growing whiter. "Yes. I want you to keep digging. Cross-reference all of Jagger's activities—anything you can pull from the CPD and the FBI—against all of Lucas's existing business and new ventures, as well as Rialto and any of our own clients." Rowe paused and licked his lips. It was on the tip of his tongue to ask her to hack into the UC Hospital records and check Jagger's activities against the list of Snow's patients over the past couple of years, but he swallowed the words. Hacking the police and Feds gave him a little thrill. Hacking the hospital just left him feeling dirty. He'd wait, save it for when they got really fucking desperate.

"Rowe..."

His head snapped up, her wavering voice pulling him from his thoughts. "We're fighting this bastard in the dark, Gidge, and we're losing. It can't continue. It won't. Can you do this for me?"

"Sure," she whispered. "Andrei has me looking into that new security system for the Lyntons. Want me to push that aside?"

"No." He shook his head and dug his fingers into the short beard he'd let grow. Just hadn't been interested enough in shaving it off. But sometimes it was itchy. "And don't tell him I have you digging into Jagger again. He's got enough on his plate right now with the fire."

"I feel so bad for him. I know he and Lucas worked really hard to get that place just right. Sorry I couldn't make the opening last night."

"I'm not. Go ahead and stay on the Lynton thing, but start digging on the other when you get time. I'll work on it myself, too." He gave her a tight smile, but the dismissal was clear. As she turned to go back to her office, Rowe walked over to the door and closed it.

"Ian, did you drown in there?" He called out as he headed to the back of his office to the private bathroom.

Ian splashed cold water on his face, then stared into the mirror. Water dripped off his eyelashes and he blinked, before pulling a paper towel free from the dispenser. He buried his face in it.

Rowe was a devious man. The moment Ian had stepped into the bathroom to wash his hands, his friend had started shouting for Gidget. Ian hadn't thought anything of it and had looked forward to saying hi to the lovely woman, but the moment Rowe had mentioned Jagger, Ian's entire body froze. He'd shut off the water so he could hear Rowe's request. Hell, just the mention of his restaurant in the same breath as Jagger had nearly knocked his legs out from beneath him.

But he could do this. There was no doubt that Jagger knew about his restaurant. The entire city knew he was the chef and part owner. But Jagger had kept his distance and as far as Ian saw, so did all of his goons. Jagger was his past, and he needed to focus on the present.

Only…his present sucked. The restaurant was the only thing going well in his life. He worried for his friends and hated that his past was hurting them. As for his personal life…

It was time he got laid.

It had been so long and unlike his friends, he wasn't comfortable picking up strangers. He loved sex, craved it. Now. It had taken him a long time to embrace it, but once he'd worked past his fears, he'd enjoyed it. He missed feeling close to someone, missed the slide of another body onto his, missed the sweat—the kissing. Hard arms around him. He was so fucking lonely; it had become a physical ache in his chest that never eased. And to watch his friends pairing off made it worse. And that made him feel rotten because he loved them. They were his world. He was glad they were finding happiness and he was already nuts about the men they'd chosen.

He wanted one of his own. The problem was, he had a particular need: to feel safe enough to let himself go with someone. That took time and he hadn't had a lot of that lately. Not since he opened his own restaurant. There had been a waiter he'd found attractive…but he knew better than to sleep with someone who worked for him.

Then there'd been the detective.

His chest tightened at the thought of Hollis Banner before the usual disappointment flooded in behind the strange twinge. Ian had thought there'd been something between them. Just a spark, but it had felt important somehow. Like thousands of possibilities existed in its nucleus. Neither had made a move and though Ian wasn't the type to sit back and wait for someone to step forward first, the big man had made him nervous enough to pause. Thankfully, it was nervous mostly in a good way. His damn heart had picked up its pace every time they were in the same room together.

But the cop had obviously not been as interested because he never did more than eat in the restaurant and make small talk...and then he'd disappeared.

Or he had been interested and learning about Ian's past with Boris Jagger had ruined everything. It had for Ian. He wanted nobody who knew the truth of his past, who would think him broken or fragile.

Ian lowered the towel and stared at his face. He wasn't broken and he wasn't fragile. But he did have issues and though he wanted to go out and find some random stranger for sex, he knew he wouldn't be able to go through with it. He'd tried, and that had been a lesson in humiliation he wasn't willing to repeat. He supposed he could call Sam, a friend who sometimes came with benefits, but he'd learned from experience that when he had this particular ache, he needed something a little harder and lot hotter than his sweet friend.

It was hell being both attracted to and afraid of big men.

"Ian, did you drown in there?" Rowe's voice came through the door followed by a hard knock. Once it would have come with laughter, but Rowe rarely laughed these days.

Familiar guilt chased away his need for sex. Guilt that he'd been the one to walk away from the car accident that had taken Rowe's wife. His friend. He missed Melissa so badly and couldn't imagine what it was like for Rowe. He only knew that his friend had changed and he missed the pranks, the jokes. They all did. They all worried. Snow baited Rowe constantly now and it hardly ever worked.

"Ian?" Concern laced his voice this time, though he sounded farther away.

Ian tried a smile at his reflection, took a deep breath and went back into the office. He sat in the chair across from Rowe and crossed his legs, flicking off a piece of lint from his brown slacks. "Sorry, was lost in thought in there." He eyed the red scruff Rowe kept on his face more often than not these days. It suited his rough friend. "Have you always been this sneaky?"

"I have no idea what you're talking about," Rowe deadpanned, but there was a faint crinkle around his eyes, a ghost of the playful Rowe they all loved.

"You waited until I was in the bathroom to call for Gidget. Why?"

Rowe huffed, acting as if he was put out, but Ian didn't buy it. "She won't tell Andrei about the research request, but she would mention to Andrei that you were here talking to me, in private. Andrei would tell Lucas, who would then be all over my shit about stressing you out. Let's just say I'm circumventing another Vallois temper tantrum."

A smile rose on Ian's lips. He was long used to Lucas's overprotectiveness. It was one of the things he loved most about the man. Of course, Ian had learned years ago how to properly navigate Lucas and Snow's protective urges. "It's only because he cares and worries." Ian paused and bit his lower lip, debating for a heartbeat whether to continue. "He's worried about you, too."

Rowe waved his hand, brushing off the comment as he looked back down at his empty desk. "Yeah, whatever. He worries too much. I'm fine."

Ian didn't believe a word of it, but he dropped the subject, going back to what he'd overheard while in the bathroom. "Why the new research? And Rialto? What's my restaurant got to do with Jagger?"

Rowe shrugged, but when he looked up at Ian, his expression had softened. "Hopefully nothing. But there has to be a reason for his current hard-on to see us dead. It didn't come out of nowhere. Something happened. We crossed his fucking path without knowing it."

"And if we know why, then we can fix it."

Rowe's expression changed and he looked away from Ian. He was hiding something.

"Say it," Ian snapped, his voice growing colder. He could accept their overprotectiveness, but he hated when they hid stuff from him. "Really, Rowe. Just tell me."

"There's no fixing this." There was a ruthless, almost cruel edge to Rowe's words, something he'd never seen before in the man, bringing up a rush of guilt that nearly choked Ian. Rowe would never be like this if Mel had survived. "But knowing the reason could give us an angle on how best to hit Jagger to end this once and for all."

"You don't think that fire was an accident."

"I don't." Rowe fiddled with a pen on his desk. "Lucas is going to send over the final investigative report when it's ready, but the fire inspector spoke with him and gave him his preliminary findings. There was an accelerant found and not one of the more common ones like gasoline. It also looks like the entire sprinkler system was taken out, which had been checked by the inspector just earlier that day. This fucker is a professional."

"But how do you know this was Jagger? Lucas has had other attempts on his life and businesses that have nothing to do with Jagger."

"Other than the impeccable timing of everything, we don't. But until then, and I want no arguments, I'm going to send one of my guys with you again." He held up a hand when Ian opened his mouth. "I said no arguments."

"Of all my friends, you've always been the first to remind everyone that I'm a grownup."

"Yeah, and I also insisted on Lucas having a guard when he was in danger. And he has a hell of a lot more training than you do." He leaned forward. "Speaking of which, why don't you start coming back in for more? I know you slowed it down because of the restaurant and I get it, but I have the gym and trainers here and it's free."

"I'm not taking advantage of you like that."

Rowe's mouth fell open and true anger darkened his expression. "Since when is that taking advantage? What the hell is up with you?"

Ian sighed and ran his hand through his hair. "Sorry. I'm just tired." And horny. He kept that to himself. Especially since he knew for a fact Rowe hadn't been physical with anyone since his wife's death.

"You were rubbing your leg." Rowe cleared his throat, looked away for a long moment before he looked back. "It still hurt?"

"Sometimes." Ian hurriedly changed the subject. He hated talking about the accident and the pain he still carried from it. Mostly he just hated seeing the grief white-wash Rowe's skin when the subject came up. "Do you have solid proof that I'm in danger?"

Rowe shook his head. "No, but the timing? Jagger being acquitted this week. We were all in one location in public and relatively easy to access. The timing is perfect for all the shit to start up again."

Ian held his breath a moment, then decided because it was Rowe, he could speak his mind. Sometimes talking about his years with Jagger got Snow and Lucas too worked up. Rowe had always been more of the "get angry and use fists," then "let it go" type. "There is no reason for Jagger to go after me. He liked me young and small. I'm too old and too filled out for him so there is no way he's looking to get me back and if he were for some crazy reason, he'd just have me plucked off the street."

"We know he sent Gratton after us."

"Then there had to be another reason and it can't have had anything to do with me."

Lips twisting in a grimace, Rowe leaned forward and crossed his arms on his desk. "Ian, the man wasn't ready to give you up at eighteen. You don't look much older than that now."

Ian glared at him.

"Sorry, but you haven't changed that much. Yeah, you seem older and your face has matured, and yeah, you've filled out some, but you're still the small, slim, cute guy he…liked."

"You forget, he did give me up. And stop calling me small. I only seem that way because Lucas and Snow are so big and because you've got some kind of gym fetish going on. Plus, you're like an inch taller than me."

Rowe flexed his arm. "But I'm a lot bigger."

Shaking his head, Ian scowled. "I don't want a bodyguard. Not yet. Let's wait and see what Lucas finds out about the fire." He jerked in his seat when someone yelled and he realized that a new training session had started. He stood and walked to open the door so he could look over the rail to the sparring mats below. He had to get out of that office, get some fresh air. Talking about Jagger and Gratton had stirred up too many ugly memories, leaving his stomach queasy and his palms sweaty. He was fighting back an onslaught of ghosts from his past and he was not reliving those moments.

The bodyguard Andrei hired nearly a year before was obviously settling well into Ward Security. Ian had spent a lot of time with Sven in the months after the accident and he really liked the quiet, wall-sized man. His long, thick blond hair was up in a haphazard bun, his matching beard trimmed into a point on his chin. He wore basketball shorts over compression pants and a tight black T-shirt that showed off the massive muscles in his shoulders and arms. White teeth flashed in a grin as another man rushed him, showed off some fancy spin move before trying to take him down.

Sven had the guy on the floor in seconds.

All of Ian's earlier horniness returned. "Got any gay bodyguards who happen to be really nice guys, Rowe?"

"I'm not running a damn dating service here. No matter what Lucas and Andrei think." Rowe came around the desk and leaned against the other side of the doorjamb. "You ever hear from that cop?"

"Not since the last time he came to Rialto to eat. He acted really strange. Stared a lot."

Rowe snorted. "He always did that. Ian, the man likes you."

"It was different the last time." He couldn't explain it. Hollis had sat there, eating his favorite bolognese and barely said a word. He'd looked...sad. If Ian hadn't been so busy that night, he would have sat down and tried to cheer the man up and had, in fact, been planning to take him a dessert and do just that, but he'd been gone when Ian had come out with the dishes of crème brûlée in his hands.

"I'm surprised," Rowe said, breaking into his thoughts. "I thought he would have called. Checked in if he was off doing something for work."

"Why would he? It's not like we ever got together."

Ian watched another guy try to take Sven down, but the man stood firm and solid. Like a massive tree trunk. Sweat had started to darken his shirt and strands of silky-looking blond hair had pulled free of the bun. Ian sighed. After spending time with Sven, he knew he wasn't the man's type. He had no idea what type Sven went for because he'd been the epitome of a professional bodyguard, silent, unobtrusive, yet willing to step in and help. Especially in the kitchen. But there'd been no spark between them. Not like he'd had with…

He broke off the thought and scowled. It really was time he went out and started meeting people. He didn't want to live alone forever.

Realizing Rowe had been silent a long time, Ian finally looked at him to find him staring.

"What?"

"You wanted to get together with him. The cop. I could tell, Ian. And it's not like you to wait to ask someone out once you…once you…"

"Once I what?" Ian didn't mean to snap the question and he immediately felt bad. "Sorry again."

A heavy hand clasped his shoulder. "It's a miracle you want to be with someone at all, Ian, so don't ever apologize for being picky."

"Picky is a nice way of putting it," he muttered as he watched Sven turn toward someone new who'd just crossed the large open expanse of the first floor. When the black hoodie came down to show golden curls, Ian smirked. He couldn't help it. "Geoffrey been coming here long?"

Rowe walked to the rail and leaned his elbows on it. "He's never been here before, but I told him to come in and try a class for free last night."

Ian joined Rowe and couldn't stop his grin as Geoffrey stared up at Sven with his mouth open. "There's no way Sven will spar with him. The kid looks frail."

"That *kid* is your age. Besides, I heard Sven was real gentle with you, carrying you around and all." He smirked. "Snow said he thought the cop was going to find a reason to arrest my employee."

Ian couldn't stop the heat that climbed his neck. Yeah, he'd enjoyed that quite a bit and from the look on Geoffrey's face, it was possible he'd found someone besides Snow to fixate on. He didn't bother to respond to Rowe, just watched as Geoffrey pulled off his hoodie to reveal a black tank over loose black sweats. With his arms over his head, the tank lifted, showing a strip of golden skin at his abdomen.

"Huh," Rowe grunted. "He's got some definition to him. Color me surprised. I thought he was some rich club kid."

"He is." Ian eyed his arms, shocked to see Rowe was right. He had a small set of pretty tight abs and his arms were slim but defined. He'd been curious about Geoffrey after hearing about the escapade his friends had taken him on last winter. "Very rich, by the way."

"Like Lucas?"

Ian shook his head. "No, but apparently he created some app and sold it before he hit twenty. He's some kind of gamer or something." He chuckled. "One who gets on Jude's every nerve—not that I blame him."

He was stunned when Sven nodded and walked with Geoffrey to the exercise mat. They stood talking for a few minutes and while he couldn't hear the words, Ian had taken enough beginner self-defense classes with Rowe and even Lucas to know that Sven was teaching Geoffrey about the basics of stance and how to lower your center of gravity. Of course, Ian wasn't too sure how much of it was sinking in because even from the second floor, Ian could see Geoffrey had this dazed expression as he stared up at Sven like he was some kind of Norse god. Not that Ian could blame him.

As if to snap him out of it, Sven grabbed for Geoffrey and even from here, Ian could tell he held back. But in the blink of an eye, Geoffrey easily dodged his large grasping hands. Sven reached again and Geoffrey slipped away, moving like a jackrabbit on crack. The young man giggled, almost bouncing on the balls of his feet. Sven reached a third time, aiming wider to catch Geoffrey. But this time, Geoffrey didn't try to dodge. He delivered one lightning-quick hit to the center of Sven's chest before grabbing his left wrist. Geoffrey twisted around and dropped to his knees, pulling Sven's arm over his shoulder.

The quick hit and sudden movement pulled Sven completely off-balance, sending him flying head over feet to land with a heavy thump on the mats. Sven didn't move for a breath, looking utterly stunned that the delicate man had bested him so simply. Geoffrey—never one to miss an opportunity—straddled Sven, his small hands braced on the other man's massive shoulders.

"Poor Sven," Rowe said from behind his hand as they watched the big guy just lie there and frown at the smaller man perched on his groin.

Ian kind of wished he was the one sitting on the man's crotch. To hell with their lack of attraction. Enough kissing and he could make it work. Kissing just flat-out did it for him. And he knew Sven was a nice guy…

Rowe's laugh was enough to pull his attention back to his friend because the man laughed so rarely these days.

"You do not need to be looking at my employee like that. Time to go out and find yourself a friend."

"I could say the same for you," Ian retorted without thinking. He instantly felt a hot wave of shame sweep through his chest.

Rowe didn't say anything for a long time, just watched the activity below. He finally cleared his throat and when he spoke, his voice came out sandpaper rough. "Well if you need a wingman, let me know. It's not like I haven't done the same for the others. We'll just not take them with us. You're never going to get laid with those two mother hens." He paused. "I really did think that cop was interested in you."

Ian just shrugged. "Doesn't matter. It's pointless to talk about Hollis. I think he moved away."

Rowe frowned and smoothed down his beard.

"No," Ian said, voice firm as he pointed at his friend. "I know that look on your face. Do not look into it. I don't want to know where he is. He missed his chance and that's all there is to it."

Again, Rowe remained silent, but a spark had returned to his eyes that made Ian both happy and very, very worried.

Chapter 3

Rowe frowned as he drove toward the end of the street and saw that his front porch light was out. It could be a coincidence. He hadn't changed the bulbs when he set up the security system after buying the house. But after Lucas and Snow...and Mel...there were no coincidences for him. He slowed, removing the gun he kept in the center console.

The bright lights of the truck splashed across the front of the small, red brick, single-story house, elongating shadows but revealing no one as he parked. Rowe's heart sped up and he found himself praying that someone was waiting to kill him. He didn't like the waiting, not knowing how the next assailant was going to strike or when or even why.

Switching the lights off, Rowe pocketed the keys with his left hand while tightly clutching the gun in his right. As he opened the door, the snick of a lighter echoed in the silence followed by the soft glow of a flame as it was applied to the tip of a cigarette. The light caressed features that looked hauntingly familiar, but he couldn't place the face from what little he could see of it. At least it answered the question of whether someone was waiting for him.

The flame disappeared, but the cherry-red glow of the cigarette remained.

"Don't shoot, Ward. I didn't travel sixteen fucking hours from Berlin to be shot by your crazy ass."

The voice was rough and tired and older than he remembered, but it speared straight through his chest. Fuck. He had heard it only a handful of times since leaving the Army, but he knew that voice.

"Keegan?" Rowe called, stepping slowly out of the truck cab. He kept his gun held out to the side, but his finger rested on the trigger guard.

The cigarette ember rose in the air and the shadows shifted as the figure stepped back toward the front door. A high-pitched squeak was followed by the front porch light flaring on as the person screwed the light bulb back into the fixture next to the front door.

Squinting against the light, the man stepped forward and pinched off the flame of his cigarette, then field-stripped it as he grinned at Rowe. Rowe drank in the sight of his old friend. His shaggy brownish-blond hair grazed his slumped shoulders—so much longer than the regulation cut Rowe was used to seeing him with. It threatened to hide vibrant blue eyes that had never truly left Rowe's memories. New lines cut across his forehead and stretched around his eyes and mouth. He looked worn, as if life had tried to beat him into the ground and very nearly succeeded.

But it was still Noah Keegan. His best friend in the Army after Lucas and Snow returned to civilian life. The only other person in the world he could even think of to watch his back. The only man he'd ever known to come up with crazier shit to try than himself.

And the one man who'd first made him question his sexuality.

"What the hell are you doing here?" Rowe asked, still frozen to the spot as he stared at a ghost from his past.

A half-smile tugged at one corner of his mouth and a little of the man Rowe knew sparkled in his eyes. "Hoping an old friend's got a rack and a beer to spare for me."

Slamming the truck door shut, Rowe shoved his gun into the pocket of his coat and joined Noah on the porch. A closer inspection didn't make him look any better. His jeans and sweatshirt were badly wrinkled from hours of travel. He looked dead on his feet and considering what they both survived during their years as Rangers, Rowe knew Noah had to have been running far longer than sixteen hours without sleep.

Something swelled in Rowe's chest, a sort of elation he hadn't felt in a long time. Fuck, it was good to see him.

Rowe gripped Noah by the back of the neck and pulled him into a tight embrace. Noah hesitated for only a breath before he wrapped both arms around Rowe and hugged him back. A shudder ran through the length of Noah's long body and something in Rowe ached to think that his friend was suffering.

"It's about fucking time you came to see me," Rowe mumbled into Noah's hair.

"I was never sure you'd welcome me."

Rowe jerked away, stunned at his friend's words. They'd gone through an awkward period, yeah, but he'd thought they'd smoothed through it, repairing their friendship through emails, raunchy birthday wishes, and some hilarious phone calls. He stared hard at Noah, trying to pick up his meaning through his expression.

"Face it, Ward. If I hadn't caught pneumonia, you'd never have taken one to the chest," he paused, tapping his knuckle against Rowe's sternum, just over his heart. "Ending your damn career as a Ranger."

"Fuck that," Rowe growled, batting Noah's hand away. "Life didn't go how I'd planned, but I wouldn't change how it worked out." As soon as the words were out of his mouth, he knew they were wrong. He would have changed the fact that Mel was gone. And now that he was staring into Noah's face, he would have done more to see his friend.

But the bullet that ripped through his chest? No, he wouldn't change that. Considering that when Noah and Rowe were in the same squad, Noah had been at his back at all times. If Noah hadn't been sick that day, that bullet would have ripped through his friend first, probably killing him.

Rowe shook his head, shoving that ugly thought aside. "Let's get inside. The neighbors are probably waiting to see if we start making out."

Both of Noah's eyebrows jumped toward his hairline and his mouth fell open. "Something you want to tell me…"

"No," Rowe snapped, and then sighed as he dug his keys out of his pocket. He'd naturally thought of the time he'd caught Jude and Snow making out while leaning against his front door. Rowe had taken a lot of pleasure in jerking the door open and sending them crashing to the floor, followed by the slobbery attack of his dogs as they scrambled cursing and snarling back to their feet. It was the best damn laugh he'd had in months. He was used to being around Lucas and Snow and while he and Noah had joked along similar lines, he wondered if they'd screwed up too much that last week before he was injured. "It's a long story."

As soon as Rowe got his key in the lock, he heard the pounding from the other end of the house. The flea brigade had likely been sleeping on his bed again, waiting for him to come home. Rowe quickly slipped inside and tapped in the code to disarm the security system before his dogs—two Rottweilers and one German Shephard—launched their large bodies at him.

"Damn! Did you adopt them from Satan's rescue shelter?" Noah complained above the yipping and barking, staying in the open doorway.

Rowe looked up from where he was kneeling on the floor, giving attention to each dog while at the same time trying to avoid getting a tongue up his nose or across his eyes. "What? They're just babies."

"Babies my ass," he muttered, but allowed Rowe to introduce him to each dog. There were a few quick sniffs before they attempted to lick and tackle Noah as well.

Rowe pushed back his feet, brushing off the dog hair and drool. "Why don't you grab a shower before you fall over while I let the mongrels out?"

"Sounds like heaven to me."

"Bathroom is down the hall. First door on the right. You can take the spare bedroom across from it."

Once the dogs were settled in the backyard and he made one last check of his voicemail for any work-related issues, Rowe walked to the bathroom with a couple of beers in hand and slowly nudged the partially open door wider. Then he hesitated. He hadn't thought twice about entering the bathroom because they'd been in each other's pockets for years and got used to talking anywhere it was convenient. But now, he couldn't help but think of the last time he'd seen Noah naked. Rowe clamped down on the memory hard, shoving it aside. There was no revisiting that.

Steam filled the small bathroom and Noah's clothes were scattered across the floor. He resisted the urge to poke at them, to discover where his friend had been and more importantly why he was now on his doorstep. He'd notched it up to too many years of poking around in things he shouldn't.

"Here," he grunted, slipping a cold beer inside the shower past the curtain, careful not to look.

"Fuck," Noah groaned, accepting the bottle. "If I'd known I'd get this kind of service, I'd have camped on your front step years ago."

"Just so long as you don't expect me to wash your back." He nearly choked over the thoughtless remark, then silently cursed. He needed to stop second guessing his every move. They'd patched things up long ago.

A low chuckle lifted above the sound of pounding water. "It wouldn't be the first time."

Rowe leaned his butt against the sink and smiled before taking a drink of his beer. Noah sounded like…Noah. His friend. "That was only because that no-star motel you found had only two minutes of hot water and if we hadn't shared, you wouldn't have left me any."

But that night had been a real eye-opener for Rowe. He'd noticed men before but never like he had with Noah, and that shared shower had strung a wire of tension between them that had never loosened. It had in fact, kept stretching until it snapped one night in Prague.

"And after your comment earlier, I'd thought something had changed…"

Rowe forced a laugh, but didn't say anything as his mind raced. A massive wave of disjointed memories crashed over him. He remembered smooth, sweaty skin, full lips, and the rough burn of whiskers abrading the tender skin of his inner thighs. Noah's moans from so many years ago echoed in his ears and he barely swallowed back an answering groan. One stupid night they'd given in to that taut attraction and it had been hotter, fucking better than anything he'd ever known before.

And Rowe had run. That next day, he'd panicked and insisted they forget what happened. Sure, Noah had shrugged and laughed in his usual, easy-going manner, chalking everything up to booze, but Rowe hadn't been blind to the pain flashing in his brilliant blue eyes. Of course, shortly after that, Noah had gotten sick and Rowe was shot, ending his career as a Ranger and separating them. It had taken them years to get back to the easy friendship they'd built before that stupid night.

Rowe sucked down half of his beer, realizing that Noah's words held a faint hopeful hint. But they couldn't go back down that road. He had his friend back and Rowe wasn't going to fuck that up—not when he was still too emotionally wrecked over his wife for anything else.

Of course, this all assumed that Noah was even staying. Rowe hadn't seen Noah in years. His appearance could just be a pit stop on the road to wherever he was headed next.

"So, it's not that I'm unhappy to see you," Rowe started slowly, his eyes focused on the nearly empty bottle in his hands. "But what are you doing here? Last I heard you were still a fucking Ranger."

Noah's laugh echoed through the bathroom. He still sounded tired, but his voice was lighter than it had been outside. "Real smooth, Ward." The bottle poked out the shower and Rowe took it, dropping it the wastebasket.

"Stuff it."

"Do you mind if we save the questions for tomorrow? Because I'd really like to know why you're living in suburban hell."

Rowe grunted. Yeah, the questions could wait. He was tired too and there were things he just wasn't in the mood to talk about.

Noah peeked around the curtain, his features sharp with his hair slicked back. "If it helps you sleep, I'm not with the Army anymore."

Rowe pushed away from the sink and smiled to himself. "I'm not sure that helps, Keegan."

"It was an amicable split. I'm not AWOL. They're not after me, you paranoid fuck."

"Whatever. I've got to let the dogs in. Raid the fridge if you're hungry. I've got a friend who's a chef. Plenty of leftovers."

"Thanks, Rowe. I mean it. Thanks."

Rowe shuffled out of the bathroom on another grunt and checked on the dogs, seeing that they had enough water to get them through the night. He pulled on his jacket and played with them for a while in the yard, keeping Daisy busy with fetch while Vlad and Igor played tug. The slobbering trio still reminded him of Mel, but their own quirky personalities kept drawing reluctant chuckles from him when he thought it would just be better to get rid of them. They kept him floating on the really bad days.

And right now, they were a good distraction from the ghost in his bathroom. Damn. Noah Keegan. They'd seen each other briefly nine years before, but the last time they'd spent any time together, things had grown awkward. Then he'd stopped by the hospital to check on his partner, tease him about getting freaking pneumonia and get their friendship back to normal, before Rowe was due to go back to Serbia for a very short job.

Rowe hadn't even gotten out of Germany. They never found the sniper that shot Rowe and three other American soldiers that day. Rowe was the only lucky one to survive. But even though they were stuck in the same damn hospital, Keegan hadn't been able to visit Rowe before he was shipped stateside again.

It never crossed Rowe's mind that Noah might feel guilt over Rowe's injury. There had been nothing Noah could do to stop it and he likely would have been killed along with the others. Just the thought made Rowe rub his chest, remembering how thankful he'd been that Noah hadn't been there. Losing him would have been devastating. The similarities between then and what he'd lost this past year hit him, raising questions he didn't want to answer, so he moved away from that thought.

So had guilt kept his friend away? Or was it what happened in Prague? Of course, Noah hadn't said one word about it so it was very likely that he'd completely forgotten and moved on with his life. They'd both had their share of one-night stands.

He snorted and scrubbed his hands over his face. That had been no one-night stand and he'd known it then. It was why he'd panicked. He watched the two Rottweilers tug at the same toy, playfully growling at each other. Daisy was flopped across the deck, waiting for Rowe to head to bed. He'd hated how he and Noah had drifted apart. While in the Army, he and Noah had found trouble just as easily as he had with Snow and Lucas. Hell, Noah had helped to fill a massive void in his life after Lucas and Snow left. Sure, Noah was as much of a troublemaker as Snow, if not worse at times, and his antics had very nearly gotten Rowe court-martialed once, but Noah always had his back.

But when Rowe was forced to return home, his focus has been entirely on getting his feet under him again. Surviving and just not fucking up had been his main focus. And then…time simply got away from him. Snow and Lucas kept him busy, and then he started his own business, and then…he met Mel.

The past wasn't important. What bothered him now—what he needed to know—was why Keegan showed up out of the blue, looking as if he'd crawled out of hell on his hands and knees. He didn't have the edgy, twitchy look of a hunted man. Just a really, really tired one.

Glancing at his watch, Rowe was surprised to find that it was already after midnight. He'd expected to see Noah stick his head out to say good night or grab some grub. He went back inside, tossed his jacket over a chair and ordered the dogs to bed. He silently followed the thundering herd down the hall. A couple of steps from the guest bedroom the low rumble of snoring reached Rowe's ears.

Rowe barely stifled a groan when he peeked in the room and was greeted with the sight of Keegan's bare ass. Not that it was the first time he'd seen it. Some things simply couldn't be helped when spending nearly every waking moment with a person for almost four years. A shadow of the same heat that he'd experienced in the bathroom ghosted through him, but it faded fast under the weight of concern and relief he felt just looking at Noah's limp, exhausted form. Apparently Noah had dropped on the bed after showering and immediately passed out buck naked.

Standing at the foot of the bed, Rowe let his gaze travel over Noah's long, muscular frame in the dim light slanting across him from the hall. New scars stretched across his back and there were a few that could have only been put there by bullets.

With a shake of his head, Rowe grabbed the far corner of the plain navy-blue comforter and pulled it over his friend. Maybe everything would make a little more sense by the light of day. Right now, he was just too damn tired to try and figure it all out.

Rowe awoke with a start, his hand immediately sliding under his pillow for the gun he kept there. Otherwise he remained perfectly still, holding his breath while straining to hear what had awakened him. In the distance, he heard the rattle of a garage door slowly lowering. He opened his eyes and glanced at the clock. 3:20 a.m. His neighbor Sam Bell was leaving for work.

But that knowledge didn't slow his heart. He knew it had only been the sound of Sam pulling his car out of the garage that woke him, but his brain was still wondering if Noah had left. Would he slip out in the darkness and just disappear?

Silently cursing himself, Rowe released the gun and slid out of bed. He stepped around the dogs in the darkness and soundlessly padded down the hall to the guest bedroom. He paused and flipped on the bathroom light so that the glow would illuminate the dark room. When he peered inside, he found Noah lying in the same position. He hadn't moved a muscle.

Rowe rubbed his eyes, trying to settle his fragmented thoughts. He was exhausted but wide awake. Without making a sound, he moved to a deep shadow on the side of the bed closest to where Noah had dropped and sat on the floor with his back against the wall.

He would just sit there a few minutes, reassure himself that Noah wasn't going anywhere and that he was safe, and then he'd be able to return to his own bed. He gazed at Noah's sleeping face, remembering how he'd done the same before—years ago— confused about why the man brought forth such strong urges. Urges Rowe had always been able to brush off before. Noah was a good-looking man, so his attraction to him wasn't surprising, but it hadn't been only about that. He'd genuinely cared for him.

"Why are you lurking, Ward?" Noah's low, rough voice rumbled across the room even though the man had yet to move.

Of course Noah knew he was there. The man was a former Ranger. You didn't survive that job by sleeping soundly, no matter how fucking tired you were.

"It's my house. I'm allowed to lurk all I want," Rowe replied, ignoring the petulant tone of his voice.

"I'm not going anywhere."

"I know," he snapped, but the words settled something deep in his chest, releasing some hidden tension so that his eyelids finally felt heavy.

Sliding his right arm across the bed to the empty space beside him, Noah started pulling at the sheets. "Get in the fucking bed so I can sleep."

"I'm not sleeping with you."

"Get in. The damn. Bed."

"Keegan."

"Ward. Now."

Rowe pushed to his feet and shuffled across the room to the other side of the bed. "Could you at least put on some underwear?"

"No."

Rowe huffed but still climbed under the sheets beside his old friend. "You have protection?"

Noah groaned. "Not tonight, honey. I've got a headache."

"Fucker." It was all Rowe could do not to laugh. Damn Noah.

Before Rowe could say another word, Noah pulled a Glock out from under this pillow and held it out to Rowe. "If you're asking me if I'm armed while I'm in *your house*, you keep it. I'm too tired to shoot anyone tonight."

Rowe wordlessly accepted the gun and put it under his own pillow before settling the blankets more comfortably around him.

Silence fell back over the house and Rowe felt himself relaxing to the sound of Noah's steady, even breathing. He was edging toward sleep when Noah's whispered words washed over him.

"I'm sorry about your wife."

Rowe breathed through the first dull ache, concentrating on the steady thump of his heart. In the darkness with the sound of Noah beside him, the pain didn't seem so impossible to survive this time.

"You would have liked her."

Noah lifted his head, turning it so that he was facing Rowe. His dark eyes reflected the faint light from the bathroom. For a moment, he looked so sad it took Rowe's breath away. "Anyone who's smart enough to love your goofy ass is definitely someone I would like."

"Thanks."

Noah snorted, his eyes falling shut again. "Sleep, Rowe. Or I'm taking my gun back and I'm shooting you myself."

Closing his eyes, sleep claimed Rowe fast and for the first time in more months than he could count, he fell asleep with a smile on his lips.

Chapter 4

Rowe awoke wrapped in a cocoon of sheets and blankets. Early morning sunlight was attempting to peek around the blackout curtains on the one window in the guest bedroom, giving him just enough light to see that Noah had already gotten up. How had he not heard it? Not stirred in the slightest when the other man moved?

Shoving out of the blankets, Rowe hesitated, trying to decide whether to take the gun with him or leave it under the pillow he'd used. He was home; he was safe. But then safe was relative now and there was a former Ranger supposedly lurking around his place, friend or not. With a barely stifled groan, Rowe got to his feet without the gun, and shuffled to his bedroom for his phone. A quick pass through his email revealed that nothing had blown up while he'd slept. In fact, it was after eight. He'd slept like the dead for five hours. That was more sleep than he'd gotten any other night during the past year.

Before he even reached the kitchen, the scent of coffee hit his nose and he sighed. But Noah was nowhere to be found. Not in the kitchen, bathroom or living room. It was then he realized the dogs were missing as well. Panic swelled in his chest, threatening to overwhelm him. He rushed to the door off the kitchen leading to the deck and backyard. It was the last place…

His breath left him in a rush as his eyes fell on Noah standing near the edge of the deck, dressed in jeans and a sweatshirt. In one hand, he clutched a travel mug, while he launched a tennis ball with the other toward the back of the fenced-in yard, sending Daisy running after it. The two Rottweilers were sprawled across the deck in the early morning sun, looking as if they were exhausted.

A fine trembling wracked Rowe's frame and he gritted his teeth for control as he came down from the surge of panic. He had to get a handle on this. Mel's death left him constantly struggling to keep his balance, waiting for something new to rip his world apart. With Noah there, he trusted his friend even if he hadn't seen him in years, but he was afraid to hope that his appearance would last more than a couple hours. And did he even want Noah to stick around? Jagger was gunning for him and his friends. Rowe didn't want to think about putting Noah's life in danger, too.

Unless he chose to help...

As a former Ranger, the man had the training to protect himself and he probably had a few tricks up his sleeve that Rowe might not have heard of yet. Of course, Noah might have other plans.

"Enough," Rowe growled to himself. This indecision was eating him alive.

Opening the door, Rowe stepped out onto the deck, wincing at the brisk air biting through his T-shirt and flannel sleep pants. Noah looked over his shoulder from where he was prying the ball loose from Daisy and smiled.

"Morning," he said before hurling the ball across the yard and sending the German Shepard off like a shot. However, her pace was a shade slower this time. She was wearing out. With any luck, Rowe would be able to cancel one of the dog walker visits. Right now, it didn't look like the trio would be moving much for at least a few hours.

"Sleep well?"

"A few hours." Noah shrugged and turned sideways so he could look at Rowe and keep an eye on the dog that had just reached the ball. "When my body figures out what time zone I'm in, I'll catch a few more Zs."

"You said last night that you flew in from Berlin? Were you there long?"

Noah gave a shrug of one shoulder that told Rowe absolutely nothing.

Rowe pushed one hand through his disheveled hair and snorted. "I just can't believe you're here. I mean...what's it been?"

"Last phone call? Almost two years. Last email? Ten months. In person? Nine years when we met for beers in Vienna while your friend was checking out some investment."

"Yeah, but who's counting?" Rowe joked but Noah lost his smile.

"I am." Noah knelt down in the wet grass and scratched Daisy behind her ear. The dog dropped the ball, her breathing heavy as she leaned into his large hand. "I should have come to see you sooner." Noah's voice had become softer and he paused like he wanted to say more, but was holding back the words.

"Why drop by now?"

Noah frowned as he got back to his feet, turning to face Rowe fully. "You really want to do the twenty questions before you have your first cup of coffee?"

"I'm not particularly looking forward to it, coffee or not," Rowe grumbled.

"Which part? Asking questions or supplying the answers?"

Rowe snorted, reaching behind his back for the doorknob. He was less than thrilled about the prospect of talking about Mel's death and what life was like without her constant shining presence.

He slipped back into the kitchen with Noah following behind him. The dogs were content to lounge in the yard a while longer. Rowe texted Andrei that he'd be in the office late and then fixed a mug of coffee. Noah was right behind him, freshening his cup before sitting down at the dinette.

"I left the Army," Noah admitted as soon as Rowe's butt touched the chair. Rowe held his mug with both hands, but didn't drink it. He stared at his friend, seeing him a little more clearly in the daylight. He looked less exhausted and beaten than he had the night before, but there was something worn about him that pissed Rowe off. The Noah Keegan he'd known then was a source of boundless energy and optimism. It was more than time that had dulled that vigor.

But even with the passage of thirteen years, he had to admit that the added age agreed with him. His boyish good looks had smoothed into a quiet strength and dignity. There were flecks of gray in the short beard that lined his jaw and chin, giving him a slightly more distinguished appearance. But he still had those damn bedroom eyes that had earned him endless offers from both men and women when they were out. And for all Rowe knew, those offers had been turned down with a sweet but gentle smile.

"Why?"

A little smirk twisted Noah's lips, his eyes locked on the travel mug in front of him. "Lost my love for it. It had become a job and not one that I enjoyed…not for a long time. And then I woke up on my birthday last year and realized that I would have completely forgotten it if it hadn't been for that disgusting video greeting that you sent."

Rowe chuckled at the memory. It had been particularly raunchy last year.

"And I realized that you were the only person left who gave a shit about me." Noah paused, lifting his gaze to Rowe. "It's not like I ever planned on the marriage, house, kids thing, but I thought I'd have friends who cared and a life where I saw them frequently. I thought I'd be able to bullshit about work and catch the game on Sunday. Maybe a few less bullets and a few more laughs. But I couldn't do any of that stuck as a Ranger, moving from war zone to war zone. Who'd want a life like that with me? I got out, traveled around for several months, tried to figure out what the fuck to do with myself, then came here."

He tried not to stare at Noah as he spoke, but Rowe realized that he wasn't seeing fatigue brought on from days of travel, but that Noah was eaten from the inside out with years of weariness that came from a lack of joy and purpose in his life. Rowe swallowed back a knot of guilt. If he hadn't gotten shot, he'd have been there for Noah, helped him when he got lost. Hell, he should have known something was wrong, reached out to him sooner. But he hadn't. There was nothing to be gained from dwelling on what he should have done. He was with Noah now.

"What's next?"

Noah shrugged and took a big gulp of coffee. "Not exactly sure. I just thought I'd go back to the last person I knew who gave a shit and try to figure it out from there. The only thing I do know is that I want to build a life that isn't based on secrets and lies." Noah frowned and opened his mouth as if he wanted to say something then closed it again. Sliding to the edge of his chair, he pinned Rowe with his piercing blue gaze. "Look, I know I just kind of dropped in on you and I'm sorry. I wasn't planning to stay long...I just—"

Rowe reached across the small table and wrapped his fingers around Noah's forearm. "You're welcome here as long as you want."

"Thanks."

Releasing Noah, Rowe took a drink of his coffee, trying to fight off the chill that was still biting at his arms after being outside. "Well, you might not be so grateful after a bit."

"I think I can put up with you and a few dogs."

Rowe frowned. He had to tell Noah, particularly if his life was going to be in danger while in his house.

Noah eyed him for a long moment, then shook his head. "Fuck, Ward. What are you into now?"

"Give me a minute," he grumbled, pushing to his feet. "Let me grab a sweatshirt. It's ball freezing this morning." Rowe started down the hall toward the master bedroom, both hands shoved into his hair. How the fuck was he going to tell him about the mess that he'd gotten into with Snow, Lucas, and Ian? And the fact that this mess had nearly gotten them all killed at one point or another? And had led to the death of his wife?

Halfway down the hall, Rowe jerked to a stop at the sound of his cell phone ringing. He patted his pockets only to realize that he'd left his phone on the table...with Noah. Fuck. He wouldn't...

The second ring stopped in the middle and he heard Noah's warm voice drift down the hall.

"Hello....No, Rowe's busy at the moment....Who's this?"

Rowe spun on his heel and started to jog the short distance back to the kitchen. Noah looked up as he came back into the room, flashing him an evil grin as he jumped from his own chair and moved so that the table was between him and Rowe.

"Damnit Keegan," Rowe snarled. "Give me the phone!"

Noah held up one finger as if to silence Rowe. "I really think you should tell me who you are first," Noah said to whomever was on the phone with him, still grinning like an idiot at Rowe. "Me? I'm the man he's drilling into the mattress this morning and if I'm lucky, later tonight."

"Holy fuck!" Rowe groaned, watching as Noah hung up with whomever he was talking to and dropped the phone on the table. "What the hell were you thinking? I use that for work! Who was that? One of my fucking employees? A client?" Rowe snatched up the phone as soon as he could break from his horrified paralysis. He shouldn't have been surprised. They'd pulled shit like this on each other all through their years in the Army, but this was different.

"No idea. He wouldn't say. Real asshole."

"Fuck." Rowe quickly thumbed in his security code and went to the call history all while praying that it hadn't been Lucas. Snow and Andrei might laugh it off and give him shit later, but Lucas…geez, the man could be way too serious when he was worried about his friends.

Before he could reach the recent calls, Lucas's picture flashed across the screen as another call came in.

"Fuck me!" Rowe dropped the phone as if it had burst into flames in his hands.

Noah leaned forward to look at the screen. "Yep, that was him. Want me to answer it?"

Rowe smacked his hand away. "No! You've done enough. Fuck! I'm not awake enough to deal with this shit." He stood there for a second in indecision before grabbing Noah by the shoulders and pushing him toward the hall. "Go. Do whatever you have to do to get ready to go. We have to leave the house in less than fifteen minutes."

"Wait! Why? Who is that?"

"A very good friend and I really don't feel like answering his questions right now because of you."

Noah grabbed the doorjamb and locked his elbows so Rowe couldn't shove him into the spare bedroom. "What the hell do you mean 'very good friend'?"

Rowe's breath caught in his throat and his mouth suddenly went dry at the fire that sparked in Noah's narrowed eyes. It felt…possessive. His eyes dropped to Noah's parted lips, following the tip of his tongue as it passed over his bottom lip. Muscles cramped as Rowe fought the resurgence of heat—all too familiar because he'd fought it for years with this man. He stared, caught in those slitted blue eyes that looked back at him with the same heat.

His phone rang again. He shook his head.

"I'll explain everything after we leave," Rowe said, giving Noah another shove but he refused to budge.

"No. Who's Lucas? What the fuck has got you so panicked?"

"A friend. It's okay. We just got to go. He's probably not at the office yet, which means that he can be *here* in twenty minutes. We've got to move now if I'm going to avoid him banging on my door wondering who the fuck is on my phone."

"You gonna buy me breakfast?"

"I'll buy you fucking pancakes if you just move your ass."

Noah chortled as he surged into the bedroom, leaving Rowe to stumble after him. Catching his balance on the doorjamb, Rowe hurried down to the master bedroom for the world's fastest shower.

It was stupid, really. The damn phone was still ringing on the kitchen table. He should just answer the phone and talk to Lucas, explain that his old friend was a goddamn lunatic and he was just teasing about the comment. But those answers would just generate more questions and it was bad enough that he still had to answer Noah's questions. Rowe was also starting to chafe under his friends' protective hovering. He appreciated their concern, but it was getting old…fast.

🐾🐾🐾

Rowe didn't breathe a sigh of relief until he and Noah were a few miles down the winding back roads that would take them toward the nearest interstate on-ramp. He sent a quick text to Lucas, informing him that everything was fine, before he shut off his phone. Right now, his main concern was Noah. He needed to tell him a few things, particularly about the threat that was still hanging over his head and could too easily extend to his friend.

"So…" Noah said, breaking the silence that had filled the cab of the truck for the past several minutes. "Who's Lucas? Some homophobe?"

Rowe winced. "Oh fuck, no!" Geez, Noah couldn't be more wrong. He needed to start talking before Noah made some more horrible assumptions. But the problem was that he'd never been able to really explain his friendship with Lucas, Snow, and Ian. They were his family, his brothers. The people he'd die for. Rowe glanced across the seat at Noah lounging in the truck with his shoulder propped against the door, an expectant look on his face. Well, maybe Noah would get it. They'd been pretty tight once.

"Do you remember me telling you about some friends I made while with my first squad? Before entering Ranger training."

Noah grunted. "Yeah, quite often actually. You were close."

"Lucas and Snow."

"Wait." Noah sat up straight, his chest pulling against the seat belt as he leaned forward a bit. "*This guy* is the same Lucas?"

"And Snow." Rowe slowed the truck for a red light. Balancing his left elbow on the door, he rested his head on his hand. "After I recovered from surgery, I found them again. They helped me get on my feet. They're…my brothers. I'd do anything for them, and they'd do anything for me. It's just…they've been a little overprotective this year."

"Yeah, but they know you're fine, right?"

Rowe groaned and hit the gas as the light turned green, signaling to pick up the on-ramp that would take him farther south. They were all far from fine with Jagger gunning for them. "Lucas knows that some unknown person answered my phone. Fuck only knows what he's thinking. He's probably got Andrei trying to track the damn GPS chip."

"Who's Andrei?"

"Lucas's boyfriend and my employee." Rowe paused and snorted, a smile starting to tug at one corner of his mouth. "A good friend too."

"So Lucas…is gay? And he's worried that…what? You're having wild, headboard-breaking sex with a gay man in your house?"

Rowe couldn't help but snicker at Noah's incredulous tone. Maybe he was overreacting, but it was very likely that he wasn't the only one overreacting. The laugh helped to relieve some of the tension in his shoulders and put a ghost of a smile on his lips.

"No, they're just worried. We've had some bad things happen and I haven't been thinking clearly…"

"Since your wife's death," Noah supplied when Rowe's voice drifted off.

"Yeah." His hands tightened on the steering wheel and he shifted in his seat, forcing his brain to focus on the pale gray ribbon of road stretching in front of him. The traffic wasn't bad for the last lingering bits of morning rush hour. With any luck, the IHOP would be quiet for a Friday morning. He could really use a fucking cup of coffee. He hadn't had a chance to drink much of the one he'd poured at home before Typhoon Noah blew through.

"Look, if you're going to stick around for a while, you're going to meet Lucas, Snow and Ian. They're a big part of my life."

Out of the corner of his eye, Rowe saw Noah give a shrug as he settled back in his seat. "That's cool. I can play nice with others."

"I'm sure you can, you fucking ground pounder."

"Ex-ground pounder, thank you very much."

"Whatever."

"So then…that whole 'guy you're drilling into the mattress' thing probably didn't go over well," Noah said nonchalantly but Rowe could hear the laughter bubbling in his voice.

Rowe laughed. "You're such an asshole." He turned off the next exit and slowed to a stop for the red light. Leaning to the side, he pulled his cell phone out of his back pocket and thumbed it back on. Now that he was sure that Noah was cool, he felt more comfortable in confronting a seething Lucas. However, Lucas was not the first one to call.

Within seconds of the phone powering back up, a call rang through and Rowe grinned wide. This was gonna be better than

Lucas. Putting his finger to his lips, Rowe answered the call and put it on speaker so Noah could hear too.

"Rowan, you shit," Snow growled.

"Good morning, sunshine!"

"Bastard," Snow snarled. "I pulled the night shift. I was in bed two hours before Lucas was lighting up my phone. Two. Hours. What the fuck?"

"What's wrong? Something happen?"

Snow's loud sigh filled the cab of the truck, followed by the rustling of fabric, indicating that he was likely calling from his bed. "Who was at your house? Lucas was growling about someone at your place and that you're fucking some guy."

"Jealous?"

"Hell yes! You promised me your virgin ass," Snow snapped back. The doc was still quick even if he was running on zero sleep.

"Fuck, you've got all the ass you can handle right now."

Snow made a low noise, almost like he was purring, and Rowe rolled his eyes as he turned at the light and into the main flow of traffic. If there was ever a man he thought would be a permanent bachelor, it was Dr. Ashton Frost, but Jude had proved that to be so damn wrong. Rowe had never seen the doc so happy.

"That's true," Snow conceded. "Seriously, Ward. Are you good? Having a stranger answer your phone after the fire? You can understand why Lucas would be worried, right?"

"I'm good. An old Army friend stopped in town for a visit. It was just a joke."

"Fine, then grow a set and call Lucas so he'll stop waking me up!"

"Yeah, yeah. You working tonight? Thought I might bring him around. Get this shit out of the way."

There was a long pause and Rowe actually looked down at the phone to make sure the call hadn't been dropped.

"Are you fucking him?" Snow asked softly, sounding far too serious for Rowe's comfort.

"No! He's going to be in town for a while. He's bound to meet you assholes eventually."

"Whatever. I'm off. Too many long nights recently."

"Cool. Catch you later."

"Rowe."

"Yeah?"

"Fucking call Lucas."

Rowe sighed. "I will."

"Your ass is still mine," Snow muttered right before hanging up.

Rowe glanced over at Noah, who was just staring at the phone with a strange, unreadable expression. Snow was something of an acquired taste. He'd mellowed a bit since finding Jude but few people would have noticed. The doc didn't pull punches and he certainly didn't censor what he was thinking for anyone. That was never going to change.

Pulling into the restaurant parking, Rowe threw the truck into park and turned off the engine. "Go inside and get a table. I've got to call Lucas and tell him it was a fucking joke. It'll just be a minute."

"You think you can untwist his panties in only a minute?" Noah said with a smirk.

"No, that's Andrei's job. I'm just keeping him from sending out the search teams."

Noah opened his door with a nod. "Good luck with that."

Chapter 5

Noah sat in the booth and immediately ordered a pot of coffee while waiting for Rowe to join him. He needed the caffeine because his brain was struggling to process the information that he'd been given on the drive to the restaurant. Dropping his head into his hands while resting his elbows on the table, Noah swallowed back a groan.

When he'd come up with the brilliant idea to go see his best and only friend in the world, to check on him after the death of his wife, he'd conveniently forgotten that Rowe had this whole other group of incredibly close friends who were essentially a family to him. Rowe had told him about Lucas and the others on some of their calls, but Noah had been so excited by the prospect of seeing Rowe again that he'd overlooked these men. What the fuck was he doing? Rowe definitely didn't need him hanging around, complicating his life.

Not to mention that Rowe obviously had something else going on, something bad, if he was worried about protection in his own home. If Rowe and his friends had everything in hand, maybe his best option was to grab his bag after breakfast and head out…somewhere.

The thought of wandering aimlessly like he'd been doing for months filled his heart with lead. He just…couldn't.

Noah's head jerked up at the sound of Rowe loudly dropping into the booth opposite him. The server followed right behind him, pouring a cup of coffee for each and then leaving behind a fresh pot along with a bowl of little servings of creamer. The scents of frying bacon and hot syrup made his stomach growl. The place had only half a dozen diners spread around the restaurant, mostly of the blue-haired variety sipping their coffee and flipping through the paper. Noah had taken the seat with his back to the door, leaving him with little to look at besides a framed picture of a rooster…and Rowe.

His friend looked up from the menu in his hands and smiled. "Relax. Lucas is over his shit fit. Apparently Andrei needed some stitches last night when his latest job got rough. He's still pissed over that."

"They been together long?"

Shrugging, Rowe looked down at the laminated menu filled with pictures of pancakes, waffles, omelets, and breakfast meats. "More than a year. We have a pool going on when he'll finally propose."

Rowe's mouth split into that insanely gorgeous grin and it was like getting punched in the gut. It was that same smile that had broken Noah so many years ago. Maybe it was worse now after the passage of so much time.

His friend had gotten sexier with age. The little lines around his eyes and the laugh lines framing his mouth left Noah wanting to cup Rowe's face and nibble along his lips until he finally coaxed a sigh from him, gaining entrance to his mouth once again.

Noah didn't even need to close his eyes to remember the sound of that sigh, the brush of his lips, first tentative, then giving way to desperation and hunger until Noah found himself pinned to the floor under Rowe's heavy weight.

Panic slammed through Noah and for a moment he struggled to draw a breath. *What the fuck was he doing?* Rowe had a life with these close friends; he was struggling to get on his feet again after losing his beloved wife. Rowe had obviously moved on from that one night years ago, never given it another thought. Noah could only offer him more complications and chaos. He never should have sought Rowe out.

The return of the server helped to pull Noah from old memories that were best left forgotten. They both placed their orders and she left with the menus, leaving Noah flinching under Rowe's direct stare.

"Spit it out, Keegan," Rowe said.

His head jerked up and he stared at Rowe, his mouth suddenly gone dry. "What?"

"You've got that look. You're either constipated or you've got something to say."

"Nice."

"Talk."

Noah looked down, turned a little container of cream over with his fingertips, keeping his eyes locked on it rather than the intensity of Rowe's bright green eyes along with that damned smile. It had turned his head the very first day he'd met Rowe.

"I was thinking about that last trip," Noah started slowly, waiting for Rowe to stop him but praying that he wouldn't. The words were painful to say, but it was better to have them said and clear the air. Noah had to know that he didn't have a shot in hell with Rowe if he was ever going to let go of the hope of a second chance.

Rowe said nothing, just continued staring.

"We got so fucking lost in Prague that night, looking for that stupid absinthe bar some local drunk told you about."

"Noah…"

There was a breathless note of pleading in Rowe's voice, as if he were begging Noah not to continue, but the words had started and he couldn't cut them off. Not yet. "We stayed in that weird B&B with all the ceramic cats. You kept saying they were staring at you."

Rowe huffed a soundless laugh. "They *were* fucking staring at me."

Noah lifted his eyes back to Rowe to see his expression had softened, the smile still curling the corners of his mouth. "I had rug burn on my elbows and shoulders for two days after that night."

Rowe's expression closed off in the blink of an eye, both hands tightening around the coffee mug. "Keegan, don't."

"Don't ever think about that night, huh?" He struggled to keep his tone light when his muscles clenched tight in anticipation of the hard smack down he expected from Rowe.

"Sometimes. More often now since…" Rowe mumbled, letting his voice drift off.

Noah fought the urge to press him, his heart pounding like an addict shooting a speedball. Did Rowe mean since the death of his wife or since Noah had come into town? He really didn't want to crawl into this dark corner of their past, but the words kept falling from his mouth. After that night, they never talked about it. Rowe just ran, telling Noah to forget that it ever happened. Two days later, Noah had ended up in the hospital with fucking pneumonia.

"Did you...ever again?"

Rowe shifted in the booth, his eyes locked on the coffee in front of him. He shook his head, lines in his forehead running deeper. "With another guy?" he asked, his voice dipping rough and low as if he were afraid someone would overhear them from their remote location. "No. I...no, I haven't."

A shout of joy bubbled up in Noah's throat but he swallowed it back. He knew he shouldn't feel happiness that Rowe hadn't explored more of his sexuality, but he couldn't help it. Some little possessive voice whispered in the back of his brain that Rowe was his. He could accept the love Rowe had with Mel. That was different. She'd made him happy for years. He'd given up on the idea of something more with Rowe a long time ago. But now...no, someone else wasn't getting a shot at him.

"Look, Keegan..."

Noah forced out a laugh and tried to relax in the booth. Or at least look like he was. He could hear it in Rowe's tone. The man was about to lay down something heavy and it was better if he cut him off now. Though...he knew he wasn't going to give up as easily this time. If he could walk up to the man after so long and still feel that heavy kick of desire, whatever they had between them was worth more of a try.

"Breathe, Ward. I'm just giving you shit." Noah paused, licked his lower lip as he flashed a wicked grin at Rowe. He loved the way Rowe followed the movement with hungry eyes, a flush staining his cheeks before Noah quickly pushed on. This he could work with. He'd back off for now. "Nothing has changed between us."

And just like that, Noah could see the tension flow out of Rowe's shoulders and out of his body. They were out of dangerous territory and back on firmer ground.

"It was just nice to discover that you could do something else with that mouth of yours besides get me into trouble," Rowe joked.

Noah threw his creamer at Rowe who just laughed, raising his hands to protect himself as the little container bounced off his chest and spiraled over his shoulder. A chuckle escaped Noah as well. "You're an ass."

"Yeah, you love my ass."

Noah groaned and Rowe just sat looking pleased with himself. This was a glimpse of the man he hadn't seen in too many fucking years. Let him have his laugh. Noah didn't mind.

A few minutes later the server delivered their food and they were content to lose themselves in a shared meal. Noah smiled to himself, feeling better simply being near Rowe again, as if the world was suddenly a little closer to being balanced. They let their conversation drift to lighter topics like football, the coming college basketball season, and the latest tech for security.

"You finally going to tell me what the hell's going on with you?" Noah demanded when their bellies were full.

Rowe's shoulders stiffened at his words and for a breath, he thought his friend was going to deny it, but Rowe sighed and his shoulders slumped.

"There's a man…Boris Jagger. He runs the local crime family, mostly drugs, extortion, and sex trade. Lucas, Snow, and I ran afoul of him some years back. It took some doing, but we got square." Rowe paused and raised his right hand, rubbing his thumb and index finger together to indicate that it had taken a lot of money to reach "square." Rowe stared down at the table, the paper napkin bunched in his left hand. "It's been quiet. Not a peep from this guy for years and then…out of the blue, he sent his demented muscle after us. The fucker killed Mel, Melissa— my wife. He almost killed Ian. He framed Snow for murder and planned to kill me, Snow, and Lucas."

"I'm assuming the bastard is six feet under."

Rowe grunted. "For nearly a year."

"But…"

"Jagger's not done. He wouldn't just drop this. Not if he went to the trouble of sending this fuckstick, Gratton after us." Rowe lifted worried eyes to Noah, who had to grind his teeth together to stop himself from reaching across the table to comfort his friend. "It's been quiet awhile, but Jagger's been wrapped up in a pretty nasty court case with the feds until recently. He was acquitted just days ago, and I feel like he's now free to direct his attention back to us."

"New attempts?"

"Not like being shot at, no. But Lucas's new club went up in flames two nights ago. It was arson. And we don't have a freaking clue as to why he even started with us recently. There's no reason for it. We went our separate ways." With a low growl, Rowe shoved a hand through his short red hair, leaving it sticking up in different directions.

"I'm in," Noah announced. He knew there were bits that his friend was holding back, but he wasn't doing it because he didn't trust Noah. It was likely that it had something to do with his friends and he was protecting their privacy as much as he could. Didn't matter. Rowe needed someone watching his back. He was still getting over the death of his wife and his friends were in danger from this Jagger. He wasn't doing enough to keep himself safe and Noah could easily do that. Hell, after being around him less than twenty-four hours, he realized he'd do just about anything to protect the man. Those old feelings hadn't disappeared at all. Maybe they never would.

Rowe shifted in his seat so he could pull his wallet out of his back pocket. "I wasn't telling you so you could risk your neck in this shit. I just wanted you to know if you decided to stay. If someone is looking to put a bullet in my brainpan, you need to know that you're gonna get hit with the splatter. It's only right."

Noah mirrored his movements, grabbing his own wallet. "I know you weren't looking for help. Unfortunately, you've got it." He threw a twenty on the table while Rowe did the same. It more than covered breakfast, but they were each too stubborn to let the other pay.

"Keegan."

"Don't Keegan me!" Noah slid to his feet and stepped in front of Rowe's bench. Placing one hand on the back of the seat and the other on the table, he leaned down, trapping his friend in the booth. "You can't look me in the eye and honestly tell me you can't use my help."

Rowe paused, looking up at his friend. "You learn anything interesting after I left the Army?"

"You know I did."

That slow, wicked grin spread across Rowe's lips and Noah felt his heart speed up. He was sure Rowe had no clue how sexy he was when he tapped into his devilish side—which was most of the time when Noah had been around him.

"Would you like to see my toys?" Rowe said in a low, rough voice that sent Noah's heated blood straight to his dick. Rowe could fucking obliterate all common sense from his brain with just a goddamn grin. The man had two channels—sex and violence—and for a moment, Noah couldn't decide which toys Rowe might be talking about.

"Tease," Noah muttered before pushing away from Rowe to lead the way back out of the restaurant. Too bad the man was joking.

Chapter 6

Rowe leaned against the back wall of the elevator, his hands in the pockets of his leather jacket, trying to ignore the uneasiness twisting in his stomach. He couldn't understand why he was so unnerved about introducing Keegan to his friends. Well, other than the fact that Lucas was probably still in a mood and Snow...*fuck*...Snow was just a lot for anyone to adjust to. It wasn't that the man didn't have a filter—that was Rowe's problem—it was that Snow took pleasure in pushing a person until they finally punched him. Ian wasn't an issue. Everyone loved Ian upon meeting him.

Glancing over, Rowe took in Noah's dark slacks and deep-blue button-down shirt that seemed to enhance the startling blue of his eyes. His blondish-brown hair hung loose around his face, nearly hiding the frown tugging at his full lips, making him look like some renegade California surfer. Fuck, ever since breakfast, Rowe had found himself staring at Noah's mouth and remembering that night he wasn't supposed to be thinking about at all. He'd felt those lips on every part of his body but they had simply rocked when wrapped around his cock. He shut his eyes and willed his body to settle.

Common sense said that Rowe had nothing to worry about. Keegan was ex-army. The man had likely easily passed through dozens of dangerous situations, thinking fast on his feet and sneaking through far too much with that easy grin. Keegan could handle this.

But Rowe didn't want Noah faking this. As soon as he'd agreed to bring Keegan over to meet the boys, it had become important that Noah like his friends and vice versa. He wanted Keegan to be a regular part of his life; he wanted to pull him into this family he'd made.

Why he wanted that so much was still in question, but the feeling was there. Strongly there.

"Whose place is this again?" Noah asked, breaking the silence that had stretched since they stepped into the elevator.

Rowe lifted his eyes back to the numbers, watching as they climbed higher. "Lucas's."

"His boyfriend live with him?"

Giving a half shrug, Rowe looked over at Noah, one corner of his mouth tugging higher. "They're working on it."

"Why do you look so amused by that?"

"Because it annoys the hell out of Lucas." Andrei confided in Rowe that he'd moved several boxes of his stuff over from his old apartment to Lucas's penthouse the past couple of days. Lucas wanted to hire a mover to get Andrei completely moved in now, but Andrei was taking it slow since he was already paid through the end of the month. With Lucas's frustrating need to take charge, the slow move was driving him insane. Rowe personally felt that maybe Andrei got off on making his boyfriend squirm.

When they reached the top floor and the silver doors slid silently open to reveal a small hallway with a pair of white double doors, Noah gave a low whistle, drawing Rowe's gaze back to him.

"Penthouse?"

"Oh yeah. Lucas likes being king." Rowe snickered.

"Fabulous," Keegan groaned.

Rowe paused, narrowing his eyes on his friend. Apparently he wasn't the only one who was worried about this meeting. "You're going to love them. They're crazy, but that makes them fun."

"Hell, if they're anything like you, I'll be surprised if I survive the night."

Rather than knocking, Rowe pulled his keys out of his pocket and used one to unlock Lucas's door. He strolled in as if he lived there as well, shrugging out of his jacket. Something in him relaxed just a little walking into the gorgeous penthouse. Lucas didn't have it set up as someplace too fancy—he'd created a space for comfort and Rowe loved it. Too often it was his second home, with Snow's place being his third. He'd crashed enough on their sofas and in their guest beds after a night of hard drinking. He didn't venture to Ian's too much simply because the young man was likely to be found at Lucas's or Snow's as well.

"Vallois!" he called, his loud voice echoing through the large, open room. His eyes skimmed over the familiar furniture, but now there was the occasional brown box stacked against the wall with something scrawled along the side in Andrei's familiar handwriting. The great move-in was progressing. About fucking time.

"Upstairs," a voice immediately answered. Both men turned toward the young, slender man with brown hair and a warm smile. "He'll be down in a minute. Something about Andrei and work."

Rowe inwardly cringed at those words. He was hoping that it was a matter of Lucas being busy with work and Andrei not happy about it, rather than the other way around. With Noah showing up for the first time in thirteen years, Rowe had taken a personal day, leaving Andrei to handle things back in the office. But the worry was shoved from his mind as he watched Ian pull a serving platter out of Lucas's cabinets.

"Are you cooking?" Rowe asked on a moan. He drew in a deep breath, scenting the air while wandering into the kitchen. "I thought we were ordering in, giving you a night off?"

"And lose an opportunity to use you guys as guinea pigs? Not a chance."

"Smells fantastic," he said as he walked into the heat coming from the oven.

"Damn, Ward!" Noah laughed behind him. "You just ate. I don't remember you being such a bottomless pit."

Rowe wrapped one arm around Ian's shoulders, drawing him close while at the same time reaching for the oven door to peek inside. "There's always room for Ian's cooking."

Ian rolled his eyes as he looked up at Noah over Rowe's shoulder for a second before smacking Rowe's hand and carefully shutting the oven again. Rowe let Ian pull away from him and approach Noah, who was smiling at Ian.

Unease twisted deep in his gut and he struggled to wipe the confusion from his face. Something felt...wrong. Like he suddenly needed to stand between Ian and Noah.

"Hi. Ian Pierce."

Noah stepped forward and took his hand with a smile that made Ian's cheeks grow redder and Rowe knew it had nothing to do with the heat from the oven and everything to do with those damn dimples. "Noah Keegan. I'm assuming that you're the chef that Rowe said is amazing."

"I don't know," he hedged. "Rowe just likes to eat and hates to cook."

"Whatever," Rowe grumbled, turning his attention back to the oven. Pulling the door down just enough to peek inside, he glanced over what looked like flaky golden rolls of bread that smelled sweet and heavenly. "You're amazing and you know it. You've got the most popular restaurant in the entire city."

Ian grabbed an oven mitt off the counter and smacked Rowe on the back of the head. Rowe yelped and jerked back from the oven, rubbing the back of head.

"Get out of there!" Ian snapped, waving at the oven mitt at him like a sword as if to beat him back farther. "I don't want you screwing this up. It's the first time I've made them. Andrei's mom finally gave me some new recipes. You don't even want to know what I had to promise that woman."

"That's not dinner, right?" Rowe took another step back, holding his hands up in surrender. You didn't fuck with Ian when he was cooking.

"No, it's a dessert."

A low moan slipped from Noah, drawing Rowe's eyes back to his friend. He pointed to the fresh blueberries sitting beside the sink. "Oh god, you're making *papanași cu brânză de vaci și affine*. I never thought I'd have that again."

"Oh, you've been to Romania?" Ian asked.

"Some." Noah gave a shrug, his eyes locking on Ian again. "I've spent most of my time stationed in Europe and the Middle East."

"Well, don't get your hopes up too high. Like I said, it's the first time I've made it," Ian said. "I also made this fried dough using the same sweet cheese—"

"You made *plăcinte cu brânză dulce*?" Noah moaned again. Stepping forward, he leaned both his forearms on the counter in the middle of the kitchen and pinned Ian with a hooded look that had Rowe grinding his teeth. "For *papanași*, I'll get on my knees for you. If you can make *sarmale*, I'll propose marriage right now."

"Keegan!" Rowe snarled in warning, but Ian just laughed, the light sound filling the penthouse.

"What?" Noah blinked wide innocent eyes at him. He turned his gaze on Ian and smiled. "I'm sorry. Are you married already? If so, he or she is a lucky son of a bitch."

"No, not married," Ian quickly said, taking a step closer to Noah, "but I don't know if there are too many men in Cincinnati with an appreciation for cabbage rolls."

"Someone who can make good *sarmale* and *plăcinte cu brânză dulce* is worth marrying in a heartbeat," Noah said in a low, velvety voice and it looked like Ian was just going to melt into a puddle before Rowe's eyes.

"Awww, Rowe, did you find yourself a hot Romanian lover too?" intruded a new, deeper voice. Rowe looked up to see Snow followed by Jude entering the room from the door off the balcony. Snow's silver-streaked hair was mussed like he'd been running his fingers through it. But more than likely, the man with the easy smile and big, dark eyes next to him had been doing it.

Finally. Someone else to rein in this flirting. Snow was practically a caveman when it came to protecting Ian from anyone who might be considering hitting on the young man. There was no way he was going to tolerate Noah flirting with Ian. He wanted Keegan to get along with his friends, but every warning Rowe gave only seemed to encourage Noah.

"Never, Doc. You know I'm holding out the hope that you'll come after me," Rowe said, muscles loosening some.

Snow lifted one brow in surprise as he stared at Rowe for a second before looking speculatively at Noah. His fingers tightened on the hand he was holding, bringing it to his lips. "Intriguing offer. I know I said your ass was still mine, but my chasing days are over." He looked at Jude and the two locked gazes in a way that made Rowe feel as if he'd disappeared.

It was still a shock to see Snow so devoted to another person the way he was to Jude. He'd always been loyal to his friends, but when it came to Jude, it was like he held nothing back. Of course, it had been a long, hard road for Snow to find someone that he could trust with his heart. Fuck. Rowe was happy for his friend. Really, really happy.

"Noah Keegan," Rowe said. "This asshole is Dr. Ashton Frost, but we just call him Snow because of all that white stuff that cropped up early on his head. And that," he continued, pointing to the muscular, dark-haired man beside Snow, "is Jude Torres. Despite hanging out with the doc, he's all right."

Jude stepped away from Snow with a smirk. "There's no accounting for taste, Rowe. Always good to see you." He turned his attention to Noah and extended his hand. "Nice to meet you."

"You were a Ranger," Snow said, not moving any closer or extending his hand.

"Yes."

"Why leave?"

Noah shrugged and flashed Snow an easy-going smile. "Just wasn't as fun without Rowe around to blow shit up."

A grudging half-smile twisted Snow's lips while he placed on arm over Jude's shoulders. "I'll give you that."

"That's right. You ran with Rowe in the Army for a while." Keegan's smile became sly, his gaze darting to Rowe and then back to Snow. Rowe nearly groaned even as his heart rate picked up at that look. "He told me this crazy story about this time when you were on leave for forty-eight hours. Where were you again?" Noah paused, scratching his chin as if digging around in his brain for the threads of the story, but Rowe knew that tone. Noah knew exactly what he was saying. The fucker was slowly stringing Rowe up. "Munich, I think. And you were passing yourself off as this American playboy at a nightclub using Snow's name—"

"Lucas's name," Snow quickly corrected with a chuckle. "We'd gone to a bar in the Ritz and Rowe was putting the tab on someone else's hotel room. He'd commandeered this huge booth and had a blonde bimbo on one side and this blond twink on the other arm, all while claiming to be Lucas Vallois. I'm surprised we didn't get killed that night."

"What are you complaining about?" Rowe snickered. "If I remember correctly, that *twink* got on his knees under the table and blew you right there. You were too wasted to stumble to the damn bathroom."

"And at that point, the cops were called," announced a newcomer in a low, cold voice that froze all the people in the room. Rowe twisted to find Lucas standing on the edge of the living room. They'd all been laughing so hard that no one had heard his approach.

Whenever Lucas Vallois entered a room, he instantly dominated it. He was a few inches shorter than Snow, but the man simply had a presence that was bigger than life. It also didn't help that he'd chosen to dress in black slacks and a black V-neck sweater that clung to his wide shoulders and chest, making him look like a stylish shadow of death. Rowe loved Lucas completely, but there were days when he just wanted to strangle the man. He was too poised, too controlled at all times. But that control had enabled him to keep Snow from self-destructing for too many years.

It was part of the reason he'd needed to leave after Mel's death. He'd known that Lucas would try to keep him from imploding and Rowe hadn't been sure that he didn't want to implode. He'd needed to completely fall apart if he was to ever put himself back together again. He hated thinking about those weeks before he'd been forced to come back to help his friends fight Gratton.

Rowe held his breath as Lucas stared at Noah for several seconds, his face a hard, unreadable mask. "Rowe is the reason I have not returned to Munich," he continued and Rowe rolled his eyes.

"And I thought," Snow started and Rowe tensed, waiting for the other man to throw more fuel onto the fire, "it was because of the guy on his knees, sobbing desperate 'I love yous' in the hotel lobby after you'd fucked him."

A bark of laughter jumped from Rowe and Lucas seemed to relax, though he was still fighting his smile. "There was that too," Lucas muttered, wringing peals of laughter out of Ian who was still puttering around the kitchen.

"All that fuss and I was the only one who didn't get some that night," Rowe moaned.

Lucas gave a wave of his hand as he crossed the room to stand in front of Noah. "Rowe has undoubtedly made up for that one poor night over his many other outings," Lucas said, as he extended his hand. "Lucas Vallois."

"Noah Keegan and yes, he has."

"You'll meet Andrei shortly. Rowe is just going up to get him."

Rowe lifted an eyebrow, bristling at Lucas's imperial tone. "I am?"

"Yes," Lucas hissed, suddenly turning back to face Rowe. Lucas let the anger show this time. Fuck, he was seriously pissed and Rowe almost found himself taking a step backward. "Not only was he shot at last night *and* injured, but he's been dealing with other cases that have had issues all this evening. Maybe you could go assist him."

"I don't know. I've got a guest. I really shouldn't leave him alone," Rowe teased simply because he couldn't help himself. Making Lucas lose his temper was just too much damn fun.

"Don't worry about me. I'll just help Ian in the kitchen," Noah said, taking a step toward the massive island in the center of the kitchen area.

"You don't cook," Rowe snapped before he could stop himself.

Noah grinned at him. "Maybe he'll let me lick a spoon."

"No—"

Ian interrupted quickly, grabbing Noah's elbow. "I'd be happy to let him help me. He's had *papanași* before. He can give me some pointers."

Rowe's mouth fell open as he looked expectantly from Lucas to Snow, but neither man seemed inclined to stop Noah. *Really?* Were they that oblivious to Noah's ridiculous flirting? Did they not care? Both men were ready to stomp a mud hole in that damn detective who had been sniffing around Ian for months. Hollis was a cop so you had to figure that he was likely a good guy. What did they know about Noah? Other than the fact that he was Rowe's friend—well, that should have been a big fucking warning sign right there.

Throwing his hands up in the air, Rowe pounded up the stairs to the second floor where Lucas kept his office. Andrei sat behind the desk, a laptop open in front of him and the phone on speaker. George MacPherson's gravelly voice filled the room as he relayed to Andrei the events of the evening. When Andrei's eyes caught on Rowe, Rowe motioned for him to not mention that he was there, allowing Rowe to flop on the sofa at the opposite end of the room and watch the young man work.

The truth was that Rowe had met few people he was more impressed with than Andrei Hadeon. He'd thought he'd hired a former fighter with a cool head and quick reactions. What he'd gotten was a man who knew how to strategize, control chaos, and handle employees as well as picky clients. He'd also discovered a damn good friend he could lean on when shit hit the fan. He knew that if everything went to hell, he would just as quickly call Andrei as he would Lucas or Snow.

"That's fine, George," Andrei said evenly and his fingers flew across the keyboard, the sound of clacking filling the room under his voice. "You handled the situation just perfectly. I'm emailing Gidget now to get a copy of the police report for our records. And if Mr. Pottsfield gives you any problems about that broken vase, just remind him of the waiver that he signed when he hired our services. But I wouldn't expect him to say a word. You saved his life. Daniel will be there at 7 a.m. to relieve you for two days."

"Thanks, boss. I'll pop by the office tomorrow for a new magazine and to fill out the paperwork."

Andrei flinched, his eyes jumping up to Rowe as he ended the call. Rowe chuckled. He knew Andrei felt uneasy about sliding into Rowe's position when he'd left town. Even after the Gratton incident was concluded, Andrei continued to fill in for Rowe for another three months as he tried to get his footing after the loss of Mel. And now that Rowe was back, his employees were still coming to Andrei for answers and in truth, Rowe liked that.

"Problem?" Rowe asked, reclining on the couch with his hands behind his head.

"Break in at Pottsfield's house. George handled it, but it required a discharge of arms, and resulted in some broken items. George and the client weren't harmed. Cops have the assailant in custody."

Rowe shifted to the edge of the couch and smiled. "And you? Come on, let's see." He wagged two fingers at Andrei. "Let's see the gunshot wound that's got Lucas frothing."

"Is that what he told you?" Andrei swore and pushed to his feet. Coming around the desk, he lifted his charcoal gray T-shirt on his left side, revealing a long, red cut with about a dozen stitches pulling the flesh back together. "Damn client lied about the severity of the threat and I was more outnumbered than I'd expected. The bullet just grazed me and I got my bell rung. Nothing I couldn't handle."

Rowe rubbed his head, leaving his red hair standing up on end in messy disarray. "Still...bullet wound does take you out of the field for a few days."

"That's not a bullet wound!" Andrei jerked his shirt back down.

"It's a wound caused by a bullet."

"Rowe!"

"Sit. I want to talk to you about something."

Andrei glared down at him, his arms folded over his chest. His long hair was loose, crowding around his face so that his dark eyes looked nearly black. Rowe noticed that the Romanian was wearing his hair even longer now and it was likely due to Lucas's influence. Lucas made no effort to hide the fact that he loved Andrei's hair.

"If you're about to fire me again, you can shove it. You need me."

"Will you just sit? I'm not going to fire you, but it is fucking serious."

Andrei instantly relaxed, while confusion cut lines around his mouth. He sat on the far end of the sofa, turning to face Rowe with his left arm along the back. "What's up?"

"I want to know how you'd feel about doing less fieldwork."

Andrei stiffened, looking as if he were preparing to jump back to his feet. "How much less?"

Rowe inwardly cringed. "About 90% less."

The glare returned to Andrei's face and the muscles in his jaw flexed as if he were grinding his teeth. "Is this bullshit because of Lucas? He's not my fucking dad."

"No, I swear, it's not. Well, not directly."

"Rowe—"

"Listen. When I needed a break, you stepped up in a big way. You not only kept everything running, but profits even improved. Not a single client bitched or canceled. The fact is that you've got a great head on your shoulders for business and I'm wasting you in the field when I should have your ass in the office."

Andrei's mouth fell open in surprise and Rowe could only chuckle. "Oh," was all Andrei could manage.

Lounging back against the couch, Rowe smiled. "You know we need to expand. Clients are traveling more and staying out of the country longer. That means they need to take extra security with them. Gidget's been on my case to set up some servers overseas so we can start offering more personal information security options. And then fucking Lucas is gaining more notoriety with every new million that bastard makes and he's not making it any secret that he uses Ward Security. That's bringing us more business. We need to build and hire. To do that, I need someone I can depend on to fucking corral all this chaos and you're my first choice."

"What did you have in mind?"

"Be the COO for Ward Security."

Andrei launched to his feet and took a couple unsteady steps back as he struggled to catch his breath. "Are...are you serious? Chief operating officer? That's...that's a big deal. Rowe, I just got my bachelor's degree from that shitty online college. I'd need a master's for that. Did you tell Lucas what you were planning?"

"No," Rowe said sharply and then got to his feet. He walked over and peered down the hall, relieved to find that no one was there to overhear their conversation. He closed the door and turned back to Andrei who still looked stunned. "I didn't tell Lucas because this new job works for him. It'll mean some long hours, but it keeps you out of the field most of the time and you'll be home every night. For someone in a serious relationship, that's kind of fucking important. But I didn't want him strong-arming you into something you didn't want. You know how bullheaded he gets when he wants something."

"I...I don't know...I don't have the right degree. I'm just some fighter..."

Rowe walked over and grabbed both of Andrei's shoulders, forcing the young man to look him in the eye. "I don't give a damn about a degree. You've got real-world experience. You know how to handle people. You can read people, read a situation, and strategize. That's what I need. And if you've ever got a question, you've got me and Lucas always. Between the three of us, we'll figure it out."

"Okay."

"That's it? Okay, you'll do it?"

"Yeah, I'll do it. I've been thinking I need to start looking to get out of the field. I was going to ask if you'd let me do some more training classes, but this works even better."

"Great!" Rowe tightened his grip on Andrei and pulled him into a quick bear hug before releasing him. "We'll work out the details during the next week. We, technically, need to run this past Lucas since he's a major shareholder," Rowe paused and rolled his eyes, earning a chuckle from Andrei. "But I'll leave it to you to tell him our plans. I don't see him being a problem."

"Nah, probably not."

"Let's get downstairs before Snow decides to throw Keegan off the balcony for flirting with Ian," Rowe muttered.

"Keegan? This friend you mentioned to me before. Army Ranger, right?"

"Former Ranger, but yeah." Rowe pulled open the door and started down the hall.

"He could be a useful hire," Andrei ventured, following him.

"See. Already thinking like a COO." Rowe was about to say more when boisterous laughter exploded from the first floor, bouncing off the high ceilings.

"Doesn't sound like Lucas or Snow is having any problems with your friend," Andrei said, breaking through Rowe's shock.

Rowe picked up his pace, hurrying down the stairs. He didn't know why he should have been worried. Keegan was good with people, but then Lucas, Snow and Ian weren't people. They were family. They were nosy, annoying, obstinate, intrusive, frustrating, and overprotective...and he loved everything about them.

Stopping several feet from the group with Andrei right behind him, Rowe was stunned to find Noah sitting on the couch next to Snow, while Ian was perched on the arm of the sofa closest to Noah and Jude was sitting on the other side of Snow. They were all listening with wide grins as Noah regaled them with the story of the time he and Rowe pulled a prank on the press corps by weakening all the chairs so that they started randomly breaking, sending person after person crashing to the floor during an important press conference.

Mid-sentence, Noah stopped and turned his head to look directly at Rowe as if he'd just sensed that he'd returned to the room. He sent him a quick wink before diving back into the story without missing a beat. Something unexpected fluttered in his chest and Rowe cleared his throat. It had always been like that with them. Like they were in tune on some cosmic level.

Andrei stepped around Rowe, clapping him on the shoulder as he passed and approached Lucas. Rowe watched as Andrei leaned over the back of the chair where Lucas was relaxing and kissed his neck, nuzzling him for a moment. Lucas reached up, threading his fingers through Andrei's dark hair, holding him close as his eyes slid closed, soaking in the affection. Andrei reached a part of Lucas that they rarely saw. The distant man relaxed and was more easy-going.

"Ian, is the *papanași* ready?" Andrei inquired as the laughter died down.

"Oh crap!" Ian jumped to his feet and scrambled back to the kitchen. "I totally forgot. I was so wrapped up in Noah's story."

"Here, Ian. I'll give you a hand." Noah smoothly rose to his feet and followed Ian.

Rowe looked expectantly at Lucas and then Snow, waiting for one of the two men to growl or bark, but neither blinked an eye at the big man as he strolled into the kitchen. *What the fuck?* He couldn't be the one overreacting. That was their job.

Swallowing back a groan, Rowe flopped on the couch in Noah's spot and tried not to glare at the coffee table in front of him. Everything felt off-kilter and wrong. He had no business getting jealous over his friend and Ian was wonderful. It had to be the strange melding of his past and present. His brain was trying to play catch up. Too much had changed in his life over the past year. That had to be it.

"Noah said he's staying with you for a little while," Lucas began, his deep voice pitched low so it wouldn't carry over the noise in the kitchen.

Rowe grunted, scrubbing one hand through his hair. His friend's tone pulled his thoughts from more trivial matters.

"Does he know?"

Rowe looked up at Lucas, lifting both eyebrows, pretending ignorance. "Know what?"

"That you're a magnet for mayhem and chaos," Snow chimed in.

Andrei snorted. "Rowe has always been that way. I would imagine his friend knows."

"That someone is hunting you," Lucas interrupted before Rowe could retort, putting them unerringly back on track.

His heart stopped for a breath. For a short time, he'd managed to forget about the danger stalking them all. He'd laughed and the tight band of pain that always seemed to be present eased around his chest. But there was no avoiding it. Jagger wanted them dead and every moment Noah stayed near him, the higher the risk that he was going to end up dead along with them. He didn't want to put Noah in danger, but it was too late. Noah wouldn't back off at this point for anything. "Yeah, he knows."

Chapter 7

"There is too much food in my belly," Rowe said in a groan as he leaned back in his chair. He grinned when Andrei burst into laughter in the kitchen where he was washing dishes with Noah. The two had really hit it off and Noah volunteering to clean up had probably made a friend for life in Andrei—even though Lucas insisted the cleaning service would take care of things.

Andrei never listened because he hated getting up to a messy kitchen. It was a pet peeve Rowe shared. He often had cleaned up after Mel's disastrous attempts to...he broke off the thought, trying not to think about all the times he'd argued with his wife over who was cooking or cleaning. The pain that lashed into his gut still had the power to steal his breath. He rubbed his eyes with his right hand, focusing on Noah and his low rumble of laughter, letting the happy sound seep into him, hoping it would sink deep enough to keep the memories at bay for the night.

He looked toward the wall-sized window, taking in the familiar lights of the Suspension Bridge and downtown Cincinnati. He loved this city—had never expected it to take hold of him as it had. He'd grown up in Missouri, traveled throughout Europe with the Army and his friends, lived with Snow and Lucas in Baltimore for a time before they relocated to Cincinnati. He'd expected it to feel like any other place, but they'd settled here, met Ian, and...Mel. He'd really felt like he belonged. It was home, more than any other he'd ever tried to have.

Noah laughed again, drawing his attention back toward the kitchen. His friend stood in front of the sink, head tilted back so his hair was off his face. He had the most infectious laughter— deep and sometimes raspy. It rumbled down into low chuckles that made Rowe blink. Because those rumbles were sexy. Really sexy. He remembered thinking that before. Long ago. And had his upper arms always been that big?

A hand landed on his arm and squeezed. He blinked at Ian, who stared at him with wide, brown eyes. A grin split his lips, making him look younger than his twenty-six years.

Noah and Andrei started arguing in the kitchen, their words peppered with so much laughter, they could barely form sentences.

"Your friend is fun." Ian leaned close and searched his eyes.

Rowe looked at him, really looked at him, and he could suddenly see his charm. His blond-streaked brown hair was ruffled, and the top couple of buttons on his shirt were undone, showing smooth skin. He hadn't shaved and light brown whiskers shadowed his jaw and upper lip. He looked sleepy and sated—from food—but it worked for him. No wonder Noah had been paying extra attention to Ian tonight. While Lucas and Snow still saw him as a young, wounded creature in need of protecting, Rowe saw the twenty-six-year-old man he was. And for the first time he saw that his friend carried very real sex appeal.

Why that made him so goddamned uncomfortable all of sudden, he didn't know. No, that wasn't true. He knew very well why he didn't want Noah with Ian.

"How long is he staying with you?" Ian asked.

Rowe shrugged. "No idea. He's starting over."

"And he came to you first?" One corner of his mouth went up. "You don't find that interesting?"

"Find what interesting?" He looked around but Lucas, Snow and Jude weren't paying attention to them as they talked quietly at the other end of the table. "We were really close when we served together. Shared an apartment for a time, too."

"So you know your friend is gay." Ian plopped his elbow next to crumpled napkin and balanced his chin on his palm.

Lucas's phone rang and he excused himself to take it in the other room. When Rowe looked across the table, he met Snow's gaze. The other man shot a glance into the kitchen. When he looked back, he raised an eyebrow, then grinned in a way that only Snow could get away with. It was wicked, dark, and from the grunt Jude made, sexy as hell to the paramedic, who threaded his fingers with Snow's on the table. Snow turned to his boyfriend and the heat that passed between them in just one glance made Rowe squirm in his seat.

When Snow, still staring at Jude, pulled their hands under the table with a smirk, Rowe kicked the doctor under the table. Chuckling, Snow raised his hand above the table and wiggled his fingers. Jude narrowed his eyes and leaned back in his chair. The smile slid off Snow's mouth as he locked gazes with Jude.

"You guys," Ian said, waving a hand in front of his face. "Shit. Hot. Stop showing off in front of the single guys." He turned back to Rowe. "So, is Noah single? What's the scoop?"

"Huh? Scoop?"

"The scoop on Noah," Ian pressed, lowering his voice as if he were afraid that the man in question might hear him. However, considering the noise he and Andrei were making in the kitchen, there wasn't a chance of him hearing Ian. "Think he'd go out with me if I ask him?"

That captured Rowe's attention. "You want to go out with Noah?"

Ian smacked his shoulder and glared at him as Rowe hadn't bothered to lower his voice. "Why wouldn't I? He's gorgeous. He's nice. Funny."

"How do you know he's gay?"

Snow, Jude and Ian all went silent and stared at him, then Snow rolled his eyes. "How can you have such shitty gaydar when all your close friends are gay? It's like some sort of defect you share with Lucas. You should both be ashamed."

Rowe looked over at Ian who was regarding him like he was a strange bug that had crawled onto the table.

"Really? I mean, he's not…flamboyant, but how can you not know?" Ian asked.

Snorting, Snow leaned over the table, light blue eyes sparkling with amusement. "Hell, you don't even know when a guy is hitting on you. And they do. A lot."

Rowe's breath caught in his lungs and he stared at Ian without really seeing him as he thought back to all the years he'd spent with Noah and not knowing. His friend had to have gone out of his way to hide whatever he did sexually with other people. Tension had snapped between them for a long time before they'd given in, but until then, Rowe had always believed the attraction was more on his side even as he'd fought that part of himself. He blinked, bringing Ian back into focus to find the younger man nodding at him.

"They do. All you have to do is flash that pretty smile."

"I do not. Shut the fuck up." Rowe shoved Ian away from him.

"What are we talking about?" Andrei asked as he came to the table, carrying fresh drinks. Noah held some as well.

"How Rowe's pretty smile brings all the boys to the yard," Snow quipped.

Noah set down the drinks, stood in front of him, and grasped his chin roughly in his right hand, tilting Rowe's head up. His fingers were cool and damp from carrying the glasses, but his touch gentled almost instantly, allowing him to rub his calloused thumb along his jaw in a caress that no one else could see. That quick touch and devilish smirk were shorting out Rowe's brain and sending all the blood rushing to his cock. "Damn thing should come with a warning label," Noah said before releasing him. He sat on Rowe's other side and clasped his shoulder. "It took me forever to get used to it, then I spent half my time pulling the craziest shit I could come up with to coax it out."

Rowe's mouth fell open and he closed it with a snap. He needed to pull his shit together. This was Noah. But that was part of the problem. He knew what Noah tasted like, the softness of the skin on the inside of his hips, and the timbre of his moans just before he came. The memories came rushing back, leaving Rowe shifting in his seat.

Ian snorted beside him. "See? Clueless."

Rowe stared at Noah, beating back thoughts of the one night he needed to forget about. "You're serious?"

White teeth flashed as Noah laughed. "The first time you smiled at me, I was speechless. You don't remember?"

"No." Rowe frowned. "We met in a group of people."

"Well, I remember." He patted Rowe's shoulder again. "No worries, Ward." He winked and leaned across him to talk to Ian. "You did a fantastic job on those desserts. Are you planning to serve them at your restaurant?"

Before Ian could answer, Lucas cleared his throat.

Rowe glanced over to find his friend waving him from the room.

He stood and followed Lucas into the hall. "Yeah?"

"Is he in?" Lucas asked.

"Noah? Yeah, I've told him what's going on. You can trust him. Why?"

"That was the fire inspector about the investigation." He walked to his bar and pulled down a red box with a gold label.

Rowe whistled. "Must be some kind of news if you're pulling out the Michter's Limited Edition."

The others noticed Lucas pouring and filed into the living room. Even Noah picked up that something was going on. He looked at Rowe and nodded toward the patio door as he walked up close. He leaned down to murmur in his ear, "Should I duck out for a few?"

"Nah, it's cool if you stay."

Nodding, Noah stayed standing beside him, accepting the glass of whiskey from Lucas. He looked down into his glass and the curls that fell to his chin slid forward, covering one eye. They looked soft and when he turned to look over his shoulder, fragrant peppermint hit Rowe's nose as his hair swung by. Fuck, the scent hit him like a slap to the face. It seemed he had something else to add to all the things he'd never noticed about his friend.

Appreciating Noah's solid, warm presence by his side, Rowe sipped the expensive whiskey and watched as his friends settled into pairs. Lucas perched on the arm of the recliner where Andrei sat, the latter's hand on his back. Snow sat on the couch and Jude stood behind it, his hands on Snow's shoulders. Ian sat next to Snow, leaning in as usual. He'd always been tactile—with all of them—and the first thing Rowe had loved about Jude was his lack of jealousy where Ian was concerned because Ian snuggled into Snow often. Jude accepted their affection for Ian fully just as Andrei had. His friends couldn't have picked better men for lovers.

And it seemed Noah might actually be interested in Ian and that affection could be returned. He should be happy because Ian deserved someone like Noah, who would make him laugh and treat him like gold. The whole idea just caused a painful knot in his stomach he didn't understand at all. Noah was dragging up old memories and feelings he thought long buried, making them feel new again.

"This is the report from the investigator. The fire has officially been ruled as arson. The fire spread was not normal. There was an accelerant, a chemical that never should have been present in the club."

"So whoever did this didn't even try to make it look like an accident." Rowe walked to Lucas and held his hand out for the paperwork.

Lucas passed him the report. "I'd say the pyro didn't care. He didn't even bother to cover his tracks well. The alarm and the sprinkler system were both tampered with so they wouldn't work."

Rowe scanned the pages, glancing over mentions of first responders' notes, the condition of the building, the origin of the fire. There were witness reports, lab results, but not the kind of detail he was hoping for. It was impressive how quickly the report had been pulled together, but then the building was owned by one of the most powerful men in Cincinnati. People generally worked fast to keep Lucas happy. "Okay if I take these? I have someone who can get us deeper details."

Nodding, Lucas picked up his snifter of whiskey. "I made those copies for you. Knew you could get more off that." He started to smile, but it never took. "Whoever did this knew that we'd be there. It's not in the report, but the investigator who called said the fire was created and fed in such a way to spread fastest to the second floor." He nodded toward the papers in Rowe's hand. "So you don't need to dig deeper. We know what we need to."

"No, I'm looking for signature moves, something to tell us who did this."

Ian stood up, his slim body shaking with anger as he tightened his hands into fists at his side. "We know who did it. Take us all out in one fell swoop? You don't think this is tied to what happened to us in January?"

Jude came around to settle on the couch. "Gratton is dead. So I'm assuming you guys think this has something to do with

Jagger." He pulled Ian back down between him and Snow, his hand massaging the back of Ian's neck.

"Of course it does." Ian crossed his arms between them. "Gratton was insane and took it to personal levels. This sounds like Jagger hired someone to take us all out at once."

"Along with a lot of other people, too."

"He wouldn't care about that." Ian cleared his throat. "He doesn't care about people. He's incapable of it. The man is a true sociopath."

Rowe's stomach churned as he thought back to the eighteen-year-old Ian he'd first met. Lucas and Snow had talked about a sweet kid they'd met at an awful party and he'd talked them into taking him to another of the parties so he could see for himself. He'd heard the rumors about Boris Jagger, but nothing had prepared him for what he'd seen. The whole night had ended in disaster after Snow had walked in on some kid in one of the bedrooms with a guy three times his age and decided the old guy no longer needed his face. Jagger's thugs had taken Snow out to teach him a lesson and got schooled by Lucas and Rowe instead. But Rowe had been there long enough to meet Ian. They'd basically purchased him, though Ian didn't know that and they hoped like hell he never found out.

He stared at their sweet, young friend, cradled between Snow and Jude, and couldn't help but feel thankful he'd gone to that party.

To this day, Rowe left nasty surprises for Jagger in various forms, but he could never quite manage anything that would get the feds clearly locked on the dirtbag. He was sure he never left a trace, but he wondered if it was his fault they'd come back into Jagger's sights.

"We need proof this was Jagger," Lucas said.

Noah cleared his throat. "That's something I can help with. Rowe and I spent years sneaking into places we weren't supposed to be in and getting dirt that we should never be able to find. We can get your proof."

Looking over his shoulder, Rowe found Noah grinning at him, his bright eyes dancing with mischief and what were likely to be devious thoughts. "Are you asking me to do something illegal with you?" Rowe asked in mocking tones.

Noah threw his arm around Rowe's shoulder and drew him close, pressing his temple against Rowe's. "I'm asking you to help me break several laws, preferably in alphabetical order if we can manage it."

Rowe looked over at Lucas and blinked wide eyes at his friend. "Please, Dad, can we skip the legal bullshit this time around?"

Lucas didn't even crack a smile as he glared at Rowe and Noah, but the low snickers of his friends could be heard in the room. "Don't get fucking caught."

Noah snorted behind Rowe, his arm tightening around Rowe's shoulders so that Rowe's back was pressed against Noah's front. "As if."

Yeah, he and Noah were good, and now that Lucas had taken off his fucking "play by the rules" shackles, they were going to nail Jagger to the goddamn wall.

Chapter 8

Noah balanced a bottle of water on his belt buckle and crossed one ankle over the other on the arm of the brown couch. The thing was sinfully comfortable, so he'd stretched out when they came inside after taking out the dogs. He'd enjoyed the dinner at Lucas's quite a bit, but he'd had a little too much whiskey and now laziness seeped into his frame. He wasn't tired enough for bed, though. Rowe's friends…they were incredible. His friend had a true home here in Cincinnati and the men he called family were the kind of people Noah would want on his side any day.

"So, Ian huh?"

He opened one eye to peer at Rowe, who sat in the matching recliner at the end of the coffee table, then remembered why he'd shut his eyes in the first place. Rowe had his bare feet propped up on the coffee table and he'd changed into a white T-shirt that had been washed so often, it could barely be considered a shirt, and soft, gray pajama pants—ones that had been driving Noah crazy because they rode low on his hips. He'd wrestled with his dogs outside and his shirt had kept riding up, showing pelvic muscles that made Noah's mouth water. Between the pants, the whiskey, and those damned bare feet, Noah's libido had kicked into high gear. It didn't help that the intricate Maori tattoo that covered his upper chest, shoulder, and part of his arm kept peeking out. Made Noah want to tug off his shirt to reacquaint himself with the way those black lines circled Rowe's left nipple. His memory had been supplying him with that image longer than he cared to admit.

Rowe had given him plenty to think about at Lucas's with all the warning looks when it came to Ian, but there was something else. The soft catch in Rowe's breath when he'd put his arm around Rowe's shoulders and drew him close. The way Rowe's pupils had blown wide when he'd grabbed his chin. He been so damn tempted to kiss the man right there, draw out the moan he could still hear in his dreams. But that would have only gotten him slugged by Rowe or his friends. From what he'd seen, Rowe was playing straight to his friends and Noah wasn't about to be the one to expose Rowe. Well...expose Rowe's secret.

Daisy, Rowe's German Shephard, huffed and moved her head where she'd rested it on Rowe's thigh. She was the same color as the recliner he sat in. Rowe had said he bought furniture that matched his pets so the dog hair would blend, but the man had lint rollers stashed all over the house. One of his dogs was passed out on a cushion in the corner of the living room and the other, he thought maybe Igor, had his chin on Noah's leg.

"What about Ian?" Noah asked. He needed to get his mind of Rowe and his damn tattoos.

Rowe lifted his water bottle, his throat moving as he swallowed a couple of times. A drop slid down his strong neck to leave a dark splotch on his shirt. He lowered the bottle and met Noah's eyes, his gaze guarded. It hadn't been in the past and seeing it now tightened Noah's chest. Every damn time. "He the type you usually go for?"

Both eyes open now, Noah turned his head enough to fully look at his friend, his hair flopping over to tangle in his eyelashes. "Type?"

Rowe growled and leaned forward. "What's with the cryptic responses, man? Does he have the looks that normally turn your crank or what? You go for that slender, pretty sort?"

"My crank," Noah muttered with a low laugh as he brushed the curls out of his face. "I don't have a specific type, Rowe. I've been with different types of men. Chemistry happens."

Rowe nodded. "Yeah, I get that." He laughed, but it sounded kind of strangled like his voice had to be forced through a tight knot. "You saw some of the women I hooked up with in the past."

"I did. Some I didn't get at all because your type seemed all over the place." Noah snorted. "Not that I got any of them. I've never found myself attracted to any woman, so I'm not the best judge."

"Never? I can't believe we never talked about this. Not once?"

He shook his head, resisting the urge to laugh at Rowe's incredulous tone. Of course, Noah had worked hard to hide his sexuality from Rowe until the final few months of their time together in the Army. It just seemed like the safer choice. He'd had bad experiences sharing his orientation before and well, Rowe meant more than all his other friends combined, so he'd held his truth to his chest. "I tried, especially in high school. But they never really worked for me."

"Why'd you try? If you knew you were gay?"

"You really need to ask with all the time you've spent with your friends? We're still not accepted, still looked down on by quite a huge section of the population. Hell, some seem to think homosexual and pedophile are synonyms." Noah growled. "Remember when you were a teen? You wanted so badly to just fit in. All your friends were scheming their way into the girls' locker room and you were spending every second thinking of the most disgusting things you could imagine to keep from popping wood in the boys'."

Rowe grinned. "Did you?"

"What? Pop wood? All the fucking time." He picked at the torn label on his water and managed to keep from admitting he had popped some not too long ago. In the backyard. When Rowe had bent over and those pajamas had framed his taut ass. Rowe had the tightest, most perfectly round ass. He'd been reminded of all those years in the Army when he'd ducked into bathrooms or turned in early just to jerk off after Rowe had inadvertently revved him up.

"Did you have a boyfriend in high school?"

Noah shook his head. "Nah. But there was this one guy when I was a senior. Fuck, I wanted him. Sophomore and with that damned September birthday, I'd hit eighteen already, so he was a big no-no. But he was so beautiful and he had this shy way of looking at me. Tortured me the entire year."

"I knew plenty of guys who dated younger girls in school. He had to have been what, sixteen?"

"Something like that. It was dangerous for guys over eighteen to date younger girls. I even knew one who angered the parents enough for them to bring him up on statutory charges. But to be a gay eighteen-year-old still in high school in

Alabama? Dangerous doesn't come close to an accurate description."

"I guess I never thought about it that way." Rowe shrugged, his eyes on his own bottle of water. "So you never even got a kiss, eh?"

Noah grinned. "Can't say that. Damn kid cornered me behind a row of porta potties after a football game. Luckily, it was dark and most everyone had already left."

"He laid in wait to make his move? Brave guy."

Nodding, Noah lifted his head to drink some water. "Kid kissed like a fucking dream."

Rowe barked out a laugh, startling Daisy, who barked in return. He leaned over and patted her head. He was quiet for a few minutes after that.

Noah closed his eyes, enjoying the quiet, the warmth of Igor against him. Maybe he'd get a dog whenever he figured out what he was going to do with the rest of his life.

"Noah?"

He looked at his friend again.

"About Ian. He's...well, he's not really the type you hook up with. That's not really his thing."

Noah didn't say anything, just waited to see where this was going. Was Rowe warning him away from his friend? Granted, the young man was sexy as hell, but if Noah had answered Rowe with complete honesty, he would have had to say his type was a lot more...Rowe. But he had liked Ian and if he wasn't so wrapped up in hope with this one, they could have had some fun.

"It's just that Ian needs—" Rowe cleared his throat and shifted, obviously uncomfortable. He stood up and paced around the coffee table, the frown tightening on his face until concern formed in an uncomfortable knot in Noah's stomach.

Noah swung his legs around and sat up. The changes in his friend when he compared Rowe now to Rowe then, came to him in phases. They'd shared a lot during their time in the service, lived through situations that would have flattened weaker men, and Rowe had managed to keep that upbeat spark, that ability to find trouble in the most creative ways imaginable, and that general, sexy as hell, good nature even when he was screwing up. He was more reserved now, more cautious and quick to worry and Noah understood the reasons why and they broke his heart. The old Rowe didn't hesitate or debate or weigh his words. He just dove right in and told you exactly how he saw it, anyone's feelings be damned.

What surprised him was though he'd been crazy attracted to the Rowe of their past, this new Rowe stirred him in ways that were already starting to worry him.

Vlad, picking up on Rowe's agitation, sat up and watched him pace. He let out a soft whine.

"Rowe? What's wrong?"

"I don't know." Rowe's voice came out rusty and he cleared his throat. "I honestly don't. Ian has some things in his past and normally I'm the one of our friends who insists he's cool and ready to date." Rowe stopped and wrapped his hands around the water bottle he'd been sloshing onto the floor. Daisy stooped to lick it up. "It's just that you aren't planning on moving here, are you?"

Noah shrugged. "I don't know. Like I told you, I don't know what I want to do next. I might decide to stay here. What does that have to do with me finding Ian attractive?"

Green eyes locked with his and his entire body became as rigid as a steel pole. "You find him attractive?"

"Yeah," Noah said slowly. "I thought that was pretty obvious. The man is gorgeous. All your damn friends are. It's kind of ridiculous, really. But he was the single one."

"So you liked him because he was the only one available?"

He studied his friend with narrowed eyes. "No, Rowe. Homosexual men don't instantly imprint on the only available gay man every time there's one around."

Rowe released a loud sigh. "I know that. Those men you met tonight are more family than anything else. I spend a lot of my time with them. A lot."

"I like Ian because he seems really great."

"And because he's pretty."

Noah grinned, wondering if Rowe was even remotely aware of the body language he was throwing off. This wasn't just a warning. This…this was something else. "Well yeah, of course. I don't get why there's a problem." He set his bottle down on the coffee table and stood, ready to mess with Rowe. "The man has a right to date, Rowe. He seemed receptive to the idea of going out. And what does it matter how long I'm here? If it's just that you don't want me going out with your friend, I won't. You know that, right?"

"I do. And no, that's not it. He's a nice guy. So are you. If I were going to pick someone good enough for Ian, it would be you."

"Then what's the problem here? And I didn't say I wanted a relationship. Sometimes a guy just wants to get laid."

Rowe flinched, looked away from him. "I vaguely remember that feeling," he muttered.

Noah walked around the coffee table and put his hands on Rowe's shoulders. "How long has it been?"

"I'm not fucking talking about this."

Noah ignored him. He kept his voice low as something twisted in his gut at Rowe's expression. "You haven't been with anyone since your wife, have you?"

Red seeped up Rowe's neck. "No, I haven't." He suddenly glared. "Is that what you wanted to hear?"

"Wanted?" Noah let him go and clenched his hands into fists. This was no longer funny. "Why would I want to hear that? I lived around you and even fucking lived *with* you. Your sex drive would shame most porn stars. You think I don't remember how often you picked up women? Ever think that I might be worried you've closed yourself off to something you liked an awful lot?"

"Hey, I have a few memories of my own, Keegan." Rowe stepped into his space. "You don't think I remember you *never* picking anyone up? Why are you all up in my face about my lack of a sex drive when you don't have one?"

"Oh, I have a sex drive. And I sure as fuck did back then, too. I just didn't share it until—"

That night in Prague filled the air between them like a solid wall.

"And how do you think that makes me feel, huh? I've always thought we were friends. Good friends. How do you think it feels to know you kept such a huge part of yourself secret from me?" He crossed his arms. "So back then, were you picking up pretty boys like Ian? In secret?"

"You are so far off the mark. So far off the fucking mark. And clueless." A laugh erupted from Noah before he could stop it. One of those self-mocking ones that share more than you want someone to hear. Rowe was no dummy and he went still.

"Noah?" he asked, voice suddenly hoarse.

"Seeing a little more now, Ward? Why do you think that night happened?" He tucked his hair behind his ear, suddenly wishing he'd had a little less to drink earlier. He was putting too many cards on the table too fast. He'd get burned on this hand, but it was too late to back down now. He sighed, then met green eyes with a pointed look. "No, I didn't go after many pretty boys back then. I went out and found any damn tattooed redhead who would let me put my hands on him. Is that what you wanted to hear?" He stepped right up to Rowe's face. "But this wasn't about me; this was about you. It's been nearly a year and the Rowe I know never went this long without. I know you're heartbroken and I even get it. Fuck, I can't even imagine the pain you've been feeling and my heart aches for you. From everything you ever told me about her, your wife sounded pretty damn perfect."

"I don't want to talk about her. I can't talk about her." Rowe grabbed a handful of his shirt. "Explain the redhead remark."

Noah shoved his hands off. "Fuck, no."

"You wanted me back then? More than just that one night? Why didn't you tell me?"

His eyes flew open wide. "Tell you? And risk destroying our friendship?"

"It wouldn't have."

"How can you be so sure? Back then you were a straight man who really didn't want to face that he just *might* be bi. If I'd given you an inkling of the desire I felt then, you would have backed off in a big, damn hurry. And first and foremost, I like you. Really like you. You're the best friend I've ever had and I don't want to mess that up."

"You don't know that it would have messed anything up. You don't know everything about me—don't know that I would have run."

"You did run! After that night, you fucking ran and I was sure I lost us."

"I didn't run! I-I-I just needed some time to think. I hadn't expected…"

This time, Noah went still, afraid to move because it felt as if the entire world was falling away beneath his feet. Rowe had dropped a massive bomb and his brain had locked up, unwilling to try to unravel all the possibilities both past and present. He narrowed his eyes. "Explain."

That mutinous, stubborn expression that sent all Noah's blood south came over Rowe's face. "You. Explain. First."

And in that moment, Noah suddenly didn't give a shit. They'd managed to keep a friendship alive long distance for thirteen damn years so if one kiss could change that, they didn't deserve to have friendship. He reached out and slid his hand around the back of Rowe's neck and yanked him close. Without another word, he slammed his mouth over Rowe's.

Shock froze every muscle in Rowe's body. Noah didn't push for entry into his mouth at first, merely pressed his lips against Rowe's. Several impressions hit him at once. Noah's lips were softer than he remembered, but still firm and…holy shit, pliable. He smelled faintly of spicy cologne, sweat, and whiskey. And that heady peppermint he'd smelled earlier—from his shampoo. The mix was surprisingly appealing to his senses and made him step closer to the delicious heat coming off his very…very masculine body. Hard muscles instead of soft breasts met his chest and there was just so much heat. Rowe hadn't been this close to another body in so long, he sucked in a breath of shock. And awe.

Noah felt good.

Damn good.

The lust that swept through him made his heart pound, his balls draw up, and his blood flow south.

Noah's tongue touched his bottom lip and before he could stop it, a soft moan came from his throat. The noise worked like a green light to Noah, who clutched him close and pushed his tongue fully into Rowe's mouth. He met that hot slide with a stroke of his own, shock curling his toes into the carpet.

Noah groaned and clenched his fingers in Rowe's hair, pulling him even closer, kissing him even deeper.

Holy shit, holy shit ran in a continuous refrain in Rowe's mind as he had to fight the urge to push the man to the floor and crawl on top of him. It was just like before—the heat, the desire, the incredible urge to rip off all their clothes to get skin on skin. He realized he held Noah's hips hard and when the other man thrust against him, he felt the hard ridge of dick.

He froze, and this time shock uncurled his toes as he jerked back. Panting, he stared at his friend of sixteen years, taking in his flushed cheeks, his swollen lips, the heady desire narrowing his eyes. Eyes that flicked down and widened when he caught sight of Rowe's crotch.

He glanced down and saw that his pajama pants spectacularly showed off the spike his dick had become. Guess he had his answer to whether or not he was bisexual. All those years of wondering and thinking about it, trying to figure out if that one night had been a drunken fluke. Here was solid proof that his crank—so to speak—turned for a man.

And it turned hard.

For Noah fucking Keegan.

Chapter 9

It was time to face facts. He was hiding from Noah.

Sure, when he'd gotten up he'd breathed a big fucking sigh of relief when he'd discovered Noah was already gone, he then retreated to the spare bedroom he'd set up as his home office—he did have piles of paperwork to go through. He had reports to review regarding different client cases, Lucas's own arson issue to research, and little bits of news rolling in from discreet sources regarding Jagger. Several of his clients had heard about Lucas's fire as well as the issues at both George and Andrei's jobs. People who hadn't been affected were calling in for a little handholding and reassurance that they were safe. No one had canceled their contract…yet. But if shit kept raining down, it was coming.

Even with all the madness, Rowe had completed the majority of the paperwork hours ago.

Now Noah was back and there was no missing the fact that he was doing something in the kitchen. The sound of pots and pans being slammed around had stopped for the most part thirty minutes ago. Rowe managed to sneak out to piss once while Noah was taking the dogs out and now he really needed to get out of his office. He couldn't keep hiding.

But what the fuck was he supposed to say?

He'd kissed Noah.

Well, technically Noah had kissed him, but there was no denying that after that first second of shock Rowe had most definitely kissed the man back. He'd opened his mouth and tangled his tongue with Noah's, tasting him, swallowing down his groan. He'd shivered and let the other man's heat wash over him.

Fuck, he was getting hard again just thinking about it. Rowe shoved away from his desk and got to his feet, running both hands through his hair. What was the issue here?

That he kissed a man?

That he kissed Noah, one of his best friends?

That he kissed someone other than his wife and loved every fucking second of it?

Yes, to all of the above.

He couldn't…he wasn't….

Before he could even pull together a coherent thought in his head, loud knocking on the office door echoed through the silent room.

Rowe jumped, twisting around to face the door, his heart pounding erratically in his chest.

"Hey, Ward!" Noah shouted through the wood.

Rowe lurched forward, moving to lock the door to stop Noah from coming in, but halted at the last second. How freaking guilty would that look to lock his friend out of his office? He was hiding.

Turning on his heel, he slunk back to his desk and silently slid into his seat. "Yeah," he barked, trying to sound busy. He rolled his eyes at himself. Really, this was fucking ridiculous. If Snow had been in the room, the man would have laughed himself silly already and Rowe wouldn't have blamed him.

"I made dinner if you want to crawl out of the cave you've been hiding in," Noah said and there was no missing the taunt in his voice.

Rowe clenched his teeth against a growl. He'd skipped lunch and was starving, but he hadn't figured out what the hell to say to Noah yet. Rowe was the one out of the group who wasn't supposed to be kissing men. He was the straight one. Sort of. Mostly. Hell, he didn't know. At least that's what he'd been telling himself for years. That had been really fucking easy when he'd been married to Mel.

"I'm in the middle of some reports. Later," he called back, hating himself.

"I made spare ribs."

Rowe groaned loudly, not caring that he could be heard through the door. He lived for ribs. The messier the better. Meat just falling off the bone.

"You remember that time we were on leave for a month and you, me, Worth, and Bohman rented that house in Barcelona? Worth made those ribs you swore you were going to marry."

"Oh God." Rowe leaned forward and hit his forehead against the desk. "To this day, those are still the best ribs I have ever eaten. I cried, Noah, cried freaking tears when we were done."

"I got the recipe."

Rowe was out of his chair without a second thought, throwing open the door to find Noah standing with his wide shoulders against the wall next to the doorframe. He was aiming for nonchalant. His arms were crossed over his chest, stretching the cotton of his long-sleeved shirt. His expression seemed almost bored, but Rowe knew better.

"Fucking liar," he growled even as the scent of barbecued meat filled the air.

"Got it."

"Worth swore he'd take the recipe to his grave."

Noah's lips rose into a wicked grin and Rowe took a half step backward, his heart picking up its pace. "Worth just needed the right kind of incentive to cough up the recipe."

"You blackmailed him."

Noah shrugged. "I blackmailed him."

"Your comrade in arms. Your squad buddy. The man who watched your back for two years. You blackmailed him!"

Shoving away from the wall, Noah dropped his arms to his side and started toward the kitchen. "If your conscience is giving you issues, then don't eat the ribs."

"Bastard," Rowe muttered but followed Noah down the hall to the kitchen. Nerves still gnawed at him, but his hunger was winning out over his anxiety, and ribs—even if they weren't Worth's ribs—tended to overcome all of his reservations pretty damn fast.

As he walked into the kitchen, he found two full slabs covered in barbeque sauce, along with a mound of steak fries and a bowl of coleslaw. A rumble came from his stomach at the sight and there was no hiding it. Edging up to the ribs, he dipped his finger in the sauce and tasted it. His eyes rolled back as the flavors exploded on his tongue. Holy crap! Noah wasn't lying. It was Worth's family recipe.

"Oh man, I could fucking ki—" Rowe's entire body froze as he realized what he was about to say, stopping the words just a little too late. He knew he'd said those exact words at least a dozen times to Noah in the past over trivial, stupid shit, but now...now it was different because he had kissed Noah. Again. And if he was really honest with himself, he wanted to do it again for a hell of a lot longer.

Noah fell back against the counter, cackling madly, causing Rowe's cheeks to grow ruddy with embarrassment.

"Grab a plate, Ward," Noah said when he could catch his breath. "It was a fucking kiss. The world didn't end and nothing has changed between us."

Rowe snorted, sat, and started digging into the food. Relief untangled frazzled nerves, but it didn't explain away the short, sharp pain that knifed through his chest at Noah's easy words. Didn't matter. He and Noah were good. He also had ribs.

They ate in relative silence. The kitchen filled only with the sounds of happy moans and random comments. Noah talked a little about running to pick up a rental car so that he was no longer dependent on Rowe. He drove around the city, getting a feel for the area, and stopped to pick up a few odds and ends. He'd also purchased a new guitar. Rowe remembered many nights listening to Noah strumming music from the next room, his low voice murmuring random lyrics. Rowe suspected that his friend was also giving him some space to get his head on straight. Fuck knows he needed it.

Rowe leaned back in his chair and groaned, his hands resting lightly on his full stomach. He'd thought he'd never get Worth's ribs again. They were as good as he remembered. Now he was so stuffed he wasn't sure he'd make it to the couch to pass out for a couple hours with ESPN blasting out from the TV.

"You ran," Noah said suddenly. He licked his lips, a smile slowly spreading across them as he pinned Rowe under his narrowed gaze. "You ran...again."

Rowe flinched at his words. He should have known that Noah would pull something like this, the sneaky bastard. Fill him up with food so that he was relaxed and reluctant to move. "I didn't fucking run." Noah arched one of his golden eyebrows in question, prodding Rowe to continue. "It was a tactical retreat...to higher ground."

Laughter burst from Noah, loud and joyous, filling the small house in a way that hadn't occurred since Rowe had moved in.

But that was Noah. Joy fell from the man like leaves from a tree, touching any who passed closed enough to him. Rowe couldn't stop the smirk tugging at his mouth no matter how hard he tried.

"Tactical retreat? To higher ground? Is that what you call it?"

"Yep. Gave me the chance to access the intelligence I'd garnered about my opponent."

Noah's expression changed, losing its easy amusement to a seriousness that Rowe rarely saw. He leaned forward, resting his forearms on the table between them. "Never opponent. Nor adversary. Nor enemy."

Rowe huffed. "That's not what I meant."

"But it is how you see me. I'm not trying to change you. Just trying to get you to face something that's already there."

"That I'm gay?"

Noah's eyebrows jumped a little higher and Rowe couldn't blame him. Anger had crept into his tone, making him sound defensive when he didn't need to be. This was Noah. His best friend. He scrubbed a hand over his face, trying to get a handle on his emotions. Noah scrambled everything in his brain, making him crazy.

"I was going to go with bi," Noah said, his voice becoming lighter, almost teasing, as he tried to lift the mood. "I don't doubt that you loved your wife, that you were genuinely attracted to her."

"I'm not talking about Mel," he snapped.

Noah continued as if Rowe hadn't spoken. "I'm just saying the hard dick I felt pressed against me last night indicates that it's not just pussy that turns your crank."

"I don't know. I've looked, but never really wanted to take it further. You're the only one…" Rowe started to say and then his words drifted off.

Noah fell back in his seat, thrusting his hands through his loose hair so that it was pushed back from his face. Thick muscles strained the sleeves of his T-shirt, but it was his stunned expression that drew Rowe's eyes.

The air between them grew thick, leaden—like a mass of rain-heavy clouds had risen.

"Say that again," Noah commanded. His voice dipped low and turned rough with lust.

Heat suddenly coursed through Rowe's veins, adding a new tension to his frame while sending blood from his brain to his hardening cock. "What?"

"Am I the first man to ever turn you on? To make your dick a fucking steel pole in your jeans?"

Rowe swallowed twice against the tightening in his throat. "Yeah."

Noah moaned and Rowe felt himself grow even harder at the sound. He fucking loved that sound. Noah's left hand tightened in his hair while the right slid down his chest. Unfortunately, the table was between them and Rowe couldn't see what he was doing. He could guess from the way Noah shifted in his seat that he'd adjusted himself. He wanted to shove away the table that separated them, but instead he continued to hold the edge, knuckles growing whiter by the second. It was safer with the table between them.

"That turns you on?" Rowe asked, unable to take his eyes off Noah.

"The idea that I'm your first anything turns me the fuck on," Noah growled. "Keep talking. What else?"

Rowe was pretty sure that they'd both lost their minds as they sat at the eat-in kitchen table, the remains of their meal between them, his cock straining against the confines of his jeans, but he couldn't stop himself. Noah stretched out in his chair, his golden brown hair shining in the light, face flushed, and lips parted—the man was a fucking wet dream. He couldn't remember the last time he'd seen anything quite so sexy. And the idea that he could turn this man on was too much of a temptation to pass up.

"You're the first man to stick his tongue in my mouth. The first man to suck on my tongue."

Noah groaned and his hips lifted slightly, muscles straining in his arms and neck. "So many things I want to do with that tongue," Noah murmured. "What else?"

"You're the first man I've ever made hard."

A low, dirty chuckle rumbled from Noah. His piercing blue eyes captured Rowe's again. "I can guarantee you that's not true at all. But I'll give you that I'm probably the first man who's gotten rock hard at your dinner table just thinking about sucking your dick. That I want to get on my knees, spread your cheeks, and tongue your ass until you fucking lose your mind."

"Fuck, Noah!" Rowe groaned, pressing the heel of his palm into his cock. He nearly came just from his words and the blistering images passing through his brain. His ass muscles clenched and unclenched over and over again at the thought of Noah's intimate touch.

When he was sure that he could stand without his knees buckling, Rowe grabbed his plate with shaking hands and carried it to the sink. He dropped it in with a loud clatter and smacked on the water. They needed to stop before he gave in and they did something they'd both regret.

Rowe never heard Noah move, but a wall of heat was suddenly there, pressing against his back. Hot breath brushed against his bare neck and he could feel Noah's hands burning through the jeans at his hips.

"We have to stop," Rowe bit out. He held onto the edge of the counter so he couldn't give into the urge to turn and continue what they'd started last night…what they'd started so many years ago.

"One more. Give me one more."

Rowe closed his eyes, but he couldn't halt the words. "You're the only man to suck my dick. Only man to make me come so hard I thought I was going to die." Because that's what had happened that night. Kisses that lasted so long, their faces had been rubbed raw and Noah taking him down his throat.

Noah shivered, pressing his body even closer so that he could feel his hard length against his ass. Rowe bit his lower lip, fighting the need to push his ass back against him, the desire to have no clothes between them, just the feeling of sweat-slicked bodies.

"I'll do it again," Noah offered in a harsh voice. "I'll happily get on my knees right now and suck you off."

Rowe moaned through clenched teeth, closing his eyes tight. Noah was temptation, pure and simple. Everything about the man was seductive.

"And then what?" Rowe forced out, trying to get his brain working again.

"What do you mean?" Noah panted.

"What happens afterward? What's left of our friendship?"

"People have sex all the time without complications. It's just pleasure."

"Is that all it would be? Pleasure? Because friendship is all I've got to offer you, Noah."

Pressed so close, there was no way Rowe could miss the way Noah's muscles tensed at Rowe's words. There was something else…something Noah wasn't saying behind this haze of lust he was so artfully weaving.

They both jumped when Rowe's cellphone suddenly vibrated in his back pocket. Never had Rowe been so grateful for the distraction. Noah stepped back and Rowe reached for his phone. He answered the call without even looking at it.

"The alarm never went off!" It took Rowe only a moment to recognize Thomas Lynton's frantic voice as he shouted.

Rowe started for his office. He could feel Noah following close behind even if he couldn't hear the other man moving ghostlike through the house. "What's going on? What happened?"

"Someone broke into the house and set it on fire!"

His words stopped Rowe dead in his tracks. "What? Did you see the culprit?"

"No, we heard breaking glass. Andrei went to investigate. He never saw the person but a quarter of the first floor was on fire when he came back to get us out. There was no burglar alarm! Not even a smoke alarm!"

"Did you get out safely with Marilyn?" he demanded, swallowing down his horror and focusing on the problem at hand. "Did you call 9-1-1?"

"Yes, the police and fire department are on their way."

"Where's Andrei?"

"Nearby. He's searching around the house. Looking for signs of the culprit."

Rowe swallowed a curse of frustration. Twenty-four hours hadn't even passed when he offered to take Andrei out of the field and give him a safer position, and the man was back in freaking danger. "Thomas, I want you and your wife to go sit in your car. Lock the doors but don't start the engine. Stay there until the police and fire department arrive. I'll be there as soon as possible."

"There were no alarms!" Thomas shouted again and Rowe couldn't blame him. This was becoming a frightening trend. There had been no smoke alarms going off at The Warehouse when the fire started. And last year, when Dwight Gratton broke into Snow's townhouse, the burglar alarm never sounded. He'd not even been notified when Thomas called 9-1-1. That alone should have pinged his systems and alerted him and others within the company. This wasn't a cheap-ass security system he had running in his clients' homes and businesses. It was one of the most advanced in the industry. And someone was finding a way around it.

"I'll get to the bottom of this, personally," Rowe promised before ending the call.

He looked up to see Noah waiting for him to say go, ready to jump into the mess. And sadly, Rowe didn't even hesitate to take advantage of his eagerness or years of experience. "Fire at a clients' house. Andrei is already on site."

"How many?"

Rowe hurried over to the gun safe tucked in his office closet. He tapped in the code, unlocking it. "Unknown. Cops and fire department have already been called."

"So you're saying be subtle."

Rowe smirked, grabbing his Kimber Ultra Carry, along with a holster that would allow him to tuck it in the small of his back. Not his favorite gun, but the small size and black matte finish meant that he'd be able to easily hide it.

"Subtle would be nice."

Noah nodded, backpedaling out of the room. "I'll be ready in two." He disappeared down the hall at a brisk jog, his bare feet making a soft sound on the floor. The dogs scurrying after him were noisier. Rowe paused as he slipped a spare magazine in his back pocket while his phone went in the opposite pocket. Noah had tried to keep his expression blank and professional when Rowe ended the call, but he could see the excitement in his eyes, the way he balanced on the balls of his feet as if he were trying desperately not to bounce with glee. He didn't want to admit it, but he was excited to have Noah at his back again.

Less than thirty minutes later, Noah parked Rowe's truck behind the line of police cars and fire trucks. Noah had allowed the GPS on his phone to guide him to the ultra-posh Village of Indian Hills address while Rowe was stuck on the phone. He called several other bodyguards to check in on their status before calling Gidget to find out what the fuck was going on with their security system. She was checking on it, but it didn't make him feel any better.

Rotating red and blue lights splashed across the nearly bare limbs of the maple trees that filled the lawn leading up to the Lyntons' house. Exterior spotlights made the immediate area around the home bright as day, while the shadows within the woods surrounding the massive European-style manse deepened.

Rowe hesitated as he stepped down from the truck, his hand still on the open door. Thomas Lynton's house sat on five acres of land and most of it was densely wooded. Was the arsonist still lurking close by, enjoying the show? He'd had little interaction or even reason to research pyros—though he knew a few while a Ranger—but they weren't known for using guns to pick off their victims as they scrambled from the fire. But even knowing that, Rowe couldn't shake the feeling of eyes watching him.

Fighting the urge to check his gun, Rowe shut the door and started walking toward the long, winding driveway with Noah just a step behind him on his left. A smile pushed its way onto his lips. Thirteen years had passed and they fell into their usual stance as if it were only yesterday. Some things didn't change no matter the time or the distance.

Two cops stood at the end of the drive, already positioning their bodies to block his path, but he just grinned wider as he spotted a familiar figure striding toward him like a hurricane about to wipe a small beach village off the fucking map.

Detective Natalie Metcalfe was just over six feet with rich, dark skin and eyes that were pinned directly on him. She took shit from no one and Rowe knew from talking to his clients that she was well-respected by the residents of Indian Hill for her dedication and honesty. As the lead detective for the Indian Hill police department, she'd earned her place.

A large number of Rowe's Cincinnati clients lived in Indian Hill, so he'd had more than his fair share of dealings with the local police—and Detective Metcalfe in particular—when things went wrong. When it came to work, she had a take-no-prisoners approach that Rowe respected, but that didn't stop him from trying to antagonize her. Hell, he'd tried to recruit her more than once, but he had a feeling she wouldn't be able to handle his need to color outside the lines at times.

"I'm sorry, sir. You're—" one of the cops started to say as Rowe and Noah drew close, but Natalie talked over him, raising her voice to slice through the cold night.

"Oh no! His ass is mine."

Both cops jerked around, their hands automatically going to their weapons for a second before they relaxed. Well, relaxed enough to not look as if they were preparing to draw down on the detective out of fear. They still took a few steps back toward the nearby squad car.

"Evening, Detective Metcalfe. It's good to see you again."

"You can cram the sweet talk," she snapped, coming to a stop directly in front of Rowe so that he was forced to tip his head back to meet her gaze. "I was just about to head home for dinner with my husband when this shit was called in."

Rowe shook his head. "Criminals can be so inconsiderate."

She narrowed her eyes on Rowe for another couple of seconds, not even cracking a hint of a smile before her gaze lifted over Rowe's shoulder for Noah. "Who's this?"

"Noah Keegan, ma'am," Noah said, reaching around Rowe to offer his hand.

"New employee," Rowe added. It was mostly true. Keegan had offered to help. Rowe hadn't done anything so formal as to offer a job, get him to sign paperwork, contact HR, yadda, yadda, yadda. But that was all just details.

"There a reason your new employee is giving me the evil eye, Ward?" Natalie demanded as she shook Noah's hand.

"Nervous tic, ma'am. I was kicked by a mule as a child," Noah quickly returned.

The detective released his hand and took a step back from the two men. "Uh-huh. And fell down a well?"

"And ate paint chips," Rowe added for good measure.

"Then he'll fit right in with your brainless crew," Natalie muttered. She motioned for Rowe to follow her back up the driveway.

"Speaking of..." Rowe started, ready to get down to business now that the ice had been broken...as much as it could be anyway. "Andrei?"

"The EMTs just finished with him." She pointed to the ambulance parked off to the side. Their flashing lights had been turned off and it looked like they were packing up to leave. More importantly, they were packing up to leave *without* a patient. "Lyntons are fine. Physically, at least. There were some florists and catering staff on premises as well. All questioned, but with all the party set-up going on, no one is quite sure they saw someone who wasn't supposed to be there. What the hell is going on, Ward?"

"I wish I knew," he mumbled.

"This is not the first fire you've dealt with recently."

Rowe shook his head. She was referring to The Warehouse fire three nights ago. This one was decidedly less dangerous than the first. Was it possible that this was something entirely different? Could it have been just a break in and the burglar started the fire by accident?

"The department didn't get a call from your company on this one. Lynton called us. What's going on with your security system?"

"My people are checking on it," he said without really thinking about it.

He paused near the end of the driveway where it opened into a circle before the lavish house. A tall fountain surrounded by a low stone wall stood empty in the center of the circle. His hands on his hips, he slowly surveyed the scene. The ambulance was preparing to leave and the firemen were rolling up their last hose. There was a white van off to the side of the house near the back with "Artfully Decadent" written on the side. The catering company had been checked out by Ward Security in the past and was popular for lavish parties. Only thirty minutes had passed between Thomas's call to Rowe and their arrival. The couple along with the other party prep staff had gotten out safe and the house fire was out. That meant that the arsonist was either a complete idiot when it came to starting fires, or it wasn't intended to consume the entire house as well as the occupants. It was meant for something else.

"Are you done with the Lyntons, Detective?"

Rowe was vaguely aware that Natalie had stiffened beside him. "Your Ranger senses tingling?"

Noah snorted behind him and Rowe fought the urge to roll his eyes. "Maybe. Can you spare someone for a possible escort?"

"Yes."

"Let me get the Lyntons out of here and you see if you can speed along the fire department and the catering company."

"Rowe..." Natalie growled in warning.

"It might be nothing. Worst-case scenario, we got people out of here a little earlier on Saturday night."

Rowe hurried over to where Andrei was standing beside the driver's side door of a shiny hunter green Jaguar. His usual button-down shirt and suit jacket were missing. Now stained with soot and sweat, his dirty T-shirt clung to his muscular chest, but it wasn't nearly as eye-catching as the leather jackass rig with the glock nestled under his left arm or the large white bandage wrapped around his left forearm. A cold wind swept through, rattling the dead leaves still clinging to the trees. Somehow, Andrei didn't shiver, but then Rowe figured the man was still running on adrenaline.

"Rowe!" Thomas demanded, half leaning out the window of his car.

"Thomas, are you and Marilyn okay?" Rowe countered, cutting off what was likely to be an angry and justified diatribe.

"Yes. Yes, we're okay." He reached over and patted his wife's hand. "Andrei here was hurt a bit."

"Just a little scrape," Andrei interjected, trying to play down the injury.

"He was saving Snickers and Puddles," Marilyn chimed in. She leaned over her husband so that she could see Rowe. Clutched in her lap was an extremely large and fluffy cat, while a second one pawed at the back window closest to Andrei.

Rowe reluctantly tucked all that away for a later date when he could spend many minutes teasing and tormenting Andrei over the fact that he had to hunt down some cats for a client while trying to get them out of a burning building. Right now, they had more important things to worry about.

"Thomas, do you have someplace safe to stay tonight?"

The older man nodded. "We have reservations downtown—"

"Good. I'm going to have a cop follow you and check everything out."

"You don't think someone…"

"Honestly, no." Rowe stopped and heavily sighed. He wasn't about to tell Thomas that he and his wife were likely targets only as an attempt to ruin Rowe, or worse, kill Andrei to get at Lucas. "But I just want to be cautious tonight while I do some digging. I'll be in contact tomorrow."

"You send Andrei home and let Lucas take care of him," Marilyn admonished, leaning across her husband again. "He's been through enough tonight."

"Yes, ma'am." Rowe backpedaled, smirking briefly at Andrei, before he caught Natalie's eye. The detective was already nodding and shouting for a cop to follow the Lyntons.

"What's going on?" Andrei demanded as the Lyntons pulled away, followed by the catering van.

"Why were you here tonight?" Rowe asked.

"I was doing a security walk-through. They're having a party tomorrow and I was making some notes on the placement of the added security for the event as well as notes on some new surveillance cameras."

"Who knew you were going to be here tonight?"

Andrei shrugged. "Lucas, Gidget." He paused, frowning at Rowe. "Troy in accounting, I think. I'm not sure. I don't normally announce my schedule."

"Lucas on the guest list for the party tomorrow?"

"Yes. We both are along with Snow and Jude. The Lyntons are doing a fundraiser for the hospital."

"Was the party always scheduled for tomorrow?" Noah demanded.

Andrei opened his mouth to speak but stopped as the fire truck started to rumble past them, drowning out anything he would have potentially said. Rowe gazed around to find that there were only a few squad cars left in the driveway and they'd all turned off their lights. The detectives and the forensics crew would be on site for another few hours, trying to turn up a few clues.

"Yes, as far as I know. Sunday is the only date I've ever heard."

Rowe frowned and met Noah's confused stare. "So either the arsonist was given the wrong information about which night to start the fire…" Noah started.

"Or the guy is a fucking idiot," Rowe finished.

"Can we just say it's both?" Andrei griped. "I—"

Whatever Andrei had been about to say was cut off by the sharp crack of gunfire splitting the silent night air. Rowe jerked as pain sliced across the meat of his shoulder. Andrei was on him in a heartbeat tackling him to the ground and then rolling him to safety behind the low stone wall surrounding the empty fountain. Rowe was vaguely aware of the shouts of cops, but he was more stunned by the speed at which Andrei had moved. He'd seen Andrei move to cover clients before—seen it with Lucas even—but it was different to be the focus of the whirlwind of blinding movement.

Once they stopped moving, Rowe became aware of the searing pain in his shoulder. The bullet hadn't gone through his shoulder, but had torn through flesh. Fuckers. He was going to need some damn stitches.

He felt Noah crouched beside him, his body pressed against Rowe's uninjured side as if he were trying to use his own larger frame as a shield. "Where are you hit?"

"Shoulder. It's not bad. Eyes on shooter?" he barked, reaching behind his back with his uninjured arm and pulling out his gun.

"No," Noah growled. "But best line of sight would be between one and two o'clock."

Andrei shifted beside him, pulling at the new hole in Rowe's coat to look at the wound. "We can try to flank."

"Cops?" Noah asked.

Andrei looked up over the low wall he was crouched behind. "Six. Seven. Clueless."

"They gonna let us play?" The former Ranger sounded more than a little eager to bound over the dry fountain and head straight into the dark woods after an unknown number of assailants.

Rowe snorted. "No fucking way."

As if she could just sense that Rowe and his boys were trying to figure out a way to join into the mix, Natalie ran over with her weapon drawn. "You alive, Ward?"

"It's a fucking scratch. You gonna let us help you?"

"Hell no! I'm just here to tell you to stay out of police business."

"Can you temporarily deputize us or something? You're short on manpower."

"No I can't do that! This isn't some stupid movie." She stared at him for a second like he'd lost his mind. "And even if I could, there's no way in hell I would, you maniac."

"Metcalfe! We're trained for this shit!"

"And I said no. I don't want you shooting my men and I don't want to deal with the temptation of shooting you myself if you get in my way."

Before Rowe could argue, a squad car to the south of them in the driveway exploded in a ball of flames, knocking all four of them back against the fountain. Even from several yards away, Rowe could feel the wave of heat from the flames. Luckily, no one had been in it at the time. Everyone had left the cars to go searching for the shooter.

"Son of a…" Natalie's words drifted off as she glared at the orange and yellow dancing flames in disbelief.

"There's at least two perps here. The arsonist brought backup. You gotta let us help!" Noah jumped in. Over the snap of the flames, the sound of men shouting and rushing back out of the woods filled the night. All the cops that had gone after the shooter were returning.

"Damnit! Don't kill anyone."

That was enough for them to start moving. Noah stripped out of his dark winter coat and tossed it at Andrei. "Your T-shirt stands out," Noah quickly said.

Andrei nodded and he quickly pulled it on. "Got a plan?"

"Keep your head down," Noah suggested as he peered over the edge of the fountain wall.

"Don't get shot," Rowe snapped.

"The woods run all the way to the back of the Lyntons' property and meet up with the road to the north and the east," Andrei continued, ignoring their remarks. He'd worked the Lynton case on more than one occasion and had thoroughly studied their property as a result.

Rowe shoved to his feet, clenching his teeth against the pain that shot through his arm at the movement. He paused behind the bulk of the fountain, waiting for another shot at him, but it never happened. The shooter had moved on thanks to the cover offered by the arsonist.

"We head in at one and two o'clock. Noah cuts north. I'll head northeast. Andrei, cut east. We go until we hit the main road. Call in if you spot anything."

Noah flashed Rowe the most excited, wicked grin—one that sent his heart beating harder from more than just adrenaline. Fuck, the man really got to him. He couldn't help but return the look so he didn't miss the flash of heat that came and went in Noah's eyes.

And then they were off at a jog, breaking cover and cutting across the driveway and the lawn to the tree line. The dancing light cast by the car fire quickly dimmed as they were surrounded by trees. After a few more steps, there was only thickening darkness and the soft crunch of dead leaves underfoot. The air was sharp and cold, slipping through the new hole in his coat to chill the blood slicking his arm. The wound throbbed with each heartbeat, causing him to grit his teeth.

He wasn't as worried about the shooter putting one in his head now. The explosion was obviously cover so he could get away. Rowe would have preferred to get his hands on the fucking arsonist, but he'd take the sniper and then possibly lean on the bastard to get info on the firebug before dragging his sorry ass back to the cops.

Rowe's heart picked up as he glimpsed Andrei moving off on his right, disappearing in near silence into the shadows as he headed east. The man had to be part cat to move the way he did. Noah, on the other hand, stuck close to Rowe's side, moving just a step behind him on the left.

"I thought you were going north," Rowe griped, ducking under a low tree branch.

"Changed my mind."

Rowe paused to slowly step over a fallen log. The thick ground cover of dead leaves hid all sorts of dangers and he didn't want to risk twisting his ankle while hunting down a shooter in the dark woods. "What the fuck do you mean you changed your mind? You can't do that."

"Of course I can," Noah whispered, sounding as if he were fighting back a laugh. "This isn't the Army."

"I'm your fucking boss. You do what I say."

There was a soft shuffling of leaves as Noah followed behind him. "Then I quit."

"You can't quit," Rowe growled. "Not in the middle of a damn job. That's unprofessional."

"Fine, boss. You going to punish me when we get back to the office? Bend me over your desk and spank me?"

Rowe sucked in a sharp breath as the image filled his brain and he choked. He stopped in the middle of the woods, grateful that it was too damn dark for Noah to see that his face was likely beet red. No, he had no desire to spank Noah, but the vision of him bent over, moaning and begging Rowe, had come in far too clearly. Blood seemed to switch gears suddenly, rushing from his arm to his groin so that something else throbbed painfully. They didn't have time for this.

"I wouldn't be averse to the idea," Noah murmured, voice low. "Just so you know."

He glared at Noah, hoping his friend could at least see that as he resumed their trek through the woods, picking up their pace.

"Why did you follow?" Rowe demanded when he was sure that he could speak clearly.

"You're a magnet for trouble and this person already took a shot at you."

Rowe nearly groaned. Fucking Noah was playing the odds that Rowe's luck was going to continue to run bad—not that he could really blame the man. His luck had been pretty piss poor recently.

Pushing the rest of the world to the farthest reaches of his brain, Rowe let years of training and instinct take over. With the gun held tightly in his right hand, he carefully moved through the woods, shifting from deep shadow to deep shadow while scanning the area for movement. There were no sounds but the soft rustle of leaves as they moved and the wind brushing against the trees. It was still early enough in the season that most of the leaves had yet to fall, blocking out what little moon and starlight that would have brightened the woods. But Rowe didn't mind working in the dark.

Noah moved next to him, falling into their familiar pattern of easy stop and start. A small part of Rowe was worried over his friend's safety but it was overwhelmed by a greater sense of peace and relief to have Noah at his side again, as if some piece had been missing over the years and he suddenly had it back.

After several minutes, he paused, leaning against a tree. His shoulder felt like it was on fire and his sleeve was wet, sticking to his skin.

"Shoulder?" Noah asked without looking at Rowe. His eyes continue to scan the immediate area.

"It's fine."

Noah snorted softly. "So I'm sewing you up tonight and not the good doctor?"

"Only cuz you'll let me drink while you're doing it. I've got a brand new bottle of whiskey that's calling both our names at home."

They started again, Rowe frowning as they moved. They'd covered a good distance already and should be near the edge of the Lynton property and the road. Noah called a sudden halt and Rowe nodded. A soft noise lifted just beyond the tree line. A car engine and it was getting closer.

To his left, a shadow broke from the trees, running at a dead sprint, cutting through the trees like a deer on speed. Rowe and Noah ran after the figure, not bothering to shout halt. The fucker was not going to stop just because he asked nicely. Noah pulled ahead of Rowe, his longer legs eating up the distance despite the debris of dead limbs covering the ground. But the other figure was smaller and faster.

The shooter disappeared from sight a couple seconds later. Noah and Rowe followed, breaking through the tree line to find themselves standing on the top of a hill with a sharp drop-off. Their quarry had slid down the hill and sprung to his feet before launching himself into the back seat of a dark four-door sedan.

The second the perp landed in the back of the car, the vehicle sped off in a rush of squealing tires and smoke. With few lights on the road and no lights turned on in the car, Rowe was only able to make out the vague shape of a dark sedan. Not even enough for the color or the make.

Fuck!

Chapter 10

"Well? Whaddya think about the place?"

It was hard not to grin at Rowe as he stood before Noah with his fists propped on his narrow hips, a look of pride shining on his newly clean shaven face. Noah longed to close the two feet of distance between them and kiss the man senseless. Slide his tongue over Rowe's lips and into his mouth, swallowing down that low groan that would shoot straight to Noah's cock as he pulled Rowe in tight. He'd liked the red scruff on his chin a lot but wondered how that smooth skin would feel against his. But they had just gotten back to normal after that first unexpected kiss. No reason to upset their balance all over again. Even if Rowe had kissed him back and obviously wanted to do it again. He couldn't risk it. Shouldn't.

Damn he needed to get his mind off this. He'd decided to try and squash his hopes of something with Rowe when he'd seen how much the situation was getting to him the night before. They'd returned after the excitement at the Lyntons' and Rowe had been unable to meet his eyes when he'd doctored his shoulder. And something in his expression had taken a bite out of Noah's heart. His best friend wasn't an option. Not yet. Yeah, there was now a lot of fucking confusion. He was tempted to continue to press because he was sure Rowe was interested, but Rowe was still going through a lot of shit. He was being threatened. His friends were being threatened. And his wife had died less than a year ago. Noah needed to keep his hands to himself when it came to Rowe.

Maybe dinner with Ian was a good idea. Ian had texted that morning, asking if Noah would be interested in grabbing dinner and seeing some of the city. He'd teased that Noah might need a break from Rowe. The man had no fucking idea.

Of course, it didn't hurt that Ian was nice and funny and sexy as hell. Would it be so wrong to have a night out with someone who also found him funny and sexy too? Ian was at least in the realm of possibility, where Rowe…fuck, he didn't know what the hell Rowe was, but he was supposed to be untouchable. Right now, all he wanted to do was touch and lick and suck…and Noah couldn't be around temptation twenty-four seven and not finally crack. The back and forth was killing him.

And for now, they were stumped about the fire. The perps had escaped and the Lyntons' house now belonged to the cops for their investigation. Detective Metcalfe promised to be in contact, so they were stuck on the outside. There had been nothing to do but go home—particularly since Rowe refused to go to the hospital for stitches.

Now they were at Ward Security. Rowe said he wanted to show Noah around, make sure he had the proper gear if he was going to be accompanying Rowe on jobs, and at least get some of the paperwork out of the way. Noah just smiled and nodded. He knew the truth of it was that Rowe needed to get out of the house and feel like he was doing something productive—even on a Sunday—rather than twiddling their thumbs while they waited around for the fucking arsonist to strike again or their sources to turn up some useful information.

Rowe had taken him on a tour of the building, showing off all the interesting toys he'd accumulated for security, surveillance, and protection. Some legal…and some things not quite so legal. Noah watched as he talked with the few employees in the office on a weekend morning, marveling at the man's easy nature with everyone he met. Rowe was a natural people-person. He could talk to anyone about anything, which was probably part of what made him so damn dangerous. His big grin and big personality knocked a person's defenses down before they even realized it. Upon meeting him, you couldn't help liking him. And it didn't hurt that he genuinely cared about all the people who worked for him.

"The place is great," Noah conceded.

"Great? That's it? Great?"

Noah laughed, leaning back against a worktable used to take apart and clean weapons. The rubber soles of his shoes squeaked on the slick lacquer floor as he crossed one ankle over the other. "You've done good, boy, and you know it. This place is amazing. You've won. You've got the most toys."

Rowe snorted, some of his good humor dissolving. "But not the best." He dropped his hands from his hips, tightening them into fists at his sides. "Someone is getting around my security system." He paused again and shook his head. "It was bad enough when Gratton got into Snow's house, but then Lucas's club and now Lyntons' home?"

"You know who the target is," Noah said firmly.

Rowe's frown deepened. He waved at Noah, motioning for him to follow. "Let's go up to my office."

Noah nodded, falling into step behind his friend. There weren't many people around the building, but he could understand Rowe's preference for keeping quiet that he and his best friends were in the sights of an arsonist. Shit like that didn't instill confidence in the longevity of the company and Rowe also didn't need any of his own people going rogue in an effort to protect their boss.

At the top of the stairs, they turned toward Rowe's office but Rowe sharply stopped when a woman in a long floral skirt and soft yellow sweater stepped out of the next office down. She was pale and wisps of brown hair hung down around her thin face from where it had fallen out of the bun loosely piled on the top of her head. She jumped and gasped when she spotted Rowe, her eyes going wide.

"Rowe! What are you doing here?"

"Showing Keegan around," Rowe said. He shifted to the side so that Noah could step forward. "Noah Keegan, this is Jen Eccelston, but I just call her Gidget. She's my software/tech genius. Gidget, this is Noah. A good friend from the Army and he's going to be joining us."

"Good to meet you," Noah said, shaking her hand. She smiled at him, but it didn't reach her eyes. Something was bothering her. There was no missing it, but she was trying damn hard to hide it.

"Welcome to the team. Rowe's a great boss," she said, stepping back toward her office again. "Are you going to be working in the field?"

"He's going to be helping me with some special projects for now. I'll need you to get him set up in the system. He needs full access to everything."

"Oh...okay, I'll get started on setting him up—"

"Whoa! It can wait until Monday," Rowe said, holding up both hands as if to slow her down. "Why are you even in today? Where's Eric? I haven't seen him in the office in months."

Something crossed Gidget's face, cutting lines across her brow and tightening around her lips before it passed almost as quickly as it appeared. She shook her head several times before her mouth finally formed the words she'd been searching for. "Eric is with my mother. I...I wanted to come in. The fires. People could get hurt and..."

Rowe walked over and touched her arm. "Go home. Rest. Go see a movie with Eric."

"But people are getting through the security system and I need to figure this out."

"I know. I need to hire another white-hat group to work through the system again." Rowe shook his head, his expression turning grim for a second before he forced a smile on his face for Gidget. "The first group missed something. We'll figure this out."

"Rowe, I'm so sorry—" Gidget's voice wavered and Rowe quickly cut her off.

"Hey, no sorries. You know this isn't your fault. We'll figure it out and fix it."

Gidget nodded, chewing on her bottom lip. Her eyes ventured up to Noah and then just as quickly darted away, gaze sticking to the floor.

"Get out of here. Spend some time with your son. We'll have plenty to keep us busy on Monday," Rowe repeated.

Gidget nodded and slipped away from Rowe, heading back to her office. She paused in the doorway and turned her head toward Noah, but didn't quite lift her eyes back to his face. "It's good to meet you, Mr. Keegan."

"Likewise, Ms. Eccelston," he murmured before following Rowe into his office.

Noah closed the door behind him and turned back to watch Rowe prowling behind his desk. It was hard to imagine Rowe spending any kind of time behind a desk. The man was better with his feet on the ground and a gun in his hand. "How long has Gidget worked for you?"

Rowe's head snapped up and he stared at Noah with a look of confusion digging two lines between his eyebrows before his expression cleared, as if he needed a second to translate his words. "Oh, Gidget. God, I'd be lost without that woman. She's been with me for years. Hired her within six months of setting the company up. Knows more about computers and hacking into different systems than anyone I've ever met. She's been torn up about this whole fucking mess since the club fire. She designed a lot of the systems. Takes pride in being able to protect people." Rowe flopped down in his chair and roughly rubbed both of his hands over his face. "Don't think it, Keegan. She takes this shit personally. Thinks she's the smartest hacker on the planet. The fact that someone is outsmarting her is tearing her apart."

Noah bit back a sigh. Maybe he was just being paranoid.

Strolling across the office, Noah slumped into one of the chairs in front of Rowe's desk and propped his feet up on a bare spot. He'd let the Gidget thing go for now. They had other, more uncomfortable things to discuss.

"So…coincidence is off the table," Noah slowly drawled, earning a glare from Rowe.

"Fucker."

"You know you were still clinging to that flimsy pathetic straw."

"Yeah. Yeah. Lucas and Snow were on the guest list at the Lyntons' and they were both at the night club. They're a target. It's not a coincidence."

"Were you on the guest list?"

Rowe rolled his eyes. "I might run with those deviants, but I don't make that kind of money. No, I wasn't invited to the party."

"Let's assume Jagger has it out for you, Lucas, and Snow. Does he want Ian dead?"

Rowe growled but didn't immediately answer. "I…I don't know," he admitted softly. "My brain says no, but I can't overlook the fact that Ian was at the club. He could have been killed that night if we hadn't acted fast enough. He was in the car…with Mel." He stopped and swallowed hard. "He could have died that day. Almost did." With a shrug, he sat up straight and turned to face Noah across the desk. "Maybe Jagger is scared and wants to kill him. Tie up some loose ends. Maybe that's what we've become for him. A fucking loose end."

Noah straightened as well, dropping his feet to the floor with a heavy thump. His stomach twisted at Rowe's sickening words but he tamped down the rush of panic that tried to quicken his heart. Rowe and his friends were not loose ends. But they had to stay logical and calm. They had to stay ahead of Jagger and this fuckstick he'd hired.

"The CPD and FBI have been coming down hard on him recently," he murmured, talking as much to Rowe as to himself.

"Yeah, but that's been going on for a while now. At least a few years. Why come after us now? If any of us were going to sing, we would have done it a long time ago. We've all got lives. Too much to lose if we let ourselves get tied to Jagger now." Rowe shoved back to his feet and started to pace away from his desk, but he didn't get more than a couple steps before he stopped again. "Besides, this feels different," he ventured, his voice barely over a whisper.

Noah leaned forward just enough so he could hear Rowe. "What do you mean?"

Rowe cocked his head as if he were a dog straining to hear something distant. "Two witnesses came up dead before they could testify. Double-tap to the back of the head. Professional." He made a gun sign with his right hand and lifted it to the back of his own head. It was a sickening image Noah prayed he'd never see in real life.

A shiver ran through Noah, bringing him to his feet as well. "And you're thinking if Jagger was so desperate to have you dead, why not call the same hitman?"

Rowe nodded. "But this shit—calling in Gratton to destroy Snow's life, stalk Ian, and kill my wife. The arsonist attacking Lucas's place, nearly killing all of us. Hell, if the fucker had been a little more careful, he might have killed Andrei last night and that would have fucking destroyed Lucas. For almost a year now, we've been looking over our shoulders and waiting for the other shoe to drop. This…this…"

"Feels personal," Noah finished.

"Yeah." Rowe's shoulder slumped and his entire body sort of sank in, as if he was deflating right before Noah's eyes. He couldn't stand to see Rowe like this. The man he came to know in the Army was filled with boundless energy, ready to take on whatever was set in front of him, no matter how impossible the odds.

But this wasn't the same Rowe. This Rowe had experienced loss and he was worried about losing again.

"Come on."

Rowe's head popped up and he frowned at Noah. "What?"

"Let's get a couple sniper rifles, a few hand grenades, and some of your other toys. We'll put one between Jagger's eyes and call it a day."

Rowe stared at Noah for a second and then exploded with laughter, rocking back so that his ass was seated on the edge of his desk. "Oh yeah, because that would be just so damn easy," he replied, his words dripping sarcasm.

Noah rolled his eyes. "I never said it would be easy, but I figured it would at least be fun and would relieve a little stress."

A soft snort slipped from Rowe. "Most people go for sex as their source of fun and stress relief."

"You offering?"

Rowe didn't answer right away, then he smirked. "Please. You couldn't handle all this." He ran his hands down his chest. Noah couldn't stop his eyes from following Rowe's hands as they molded his shirt to his hard, muscular chest and flat stomach. Couldn't handle it? Fuck, Noah was more than willing to die trying.

"And you're terrified by how much you might love it if you try," Noah said with more heat than he'd meant to.

They stared at each other for a moment. Neither breathed. Their teasing had suddenly taken a turn into too much truth for either of them to handle. Everything within Noah screamed that he walk over to Rowe and kiss him. Pin him on the top of the desk and touch every damn inch of the man while exploring every bit of his mouth with his tongue. He wanted Rowe panting and begging and writhing beneath him.

Rowe's cheeks turned red and he looked away first, clearing his throat. "I've thought about it...killing Jagger," he clarified quickly. "He's not an easy person to get close to. Too much security. And even without the security, he's got the police and feds still watching him."

Dropping back in his chair, Noah placed his hands behind his head, trying to appear relaxed when he felt anything but. Disappointment tightened his chest. "Okay. So we go after the arsonist and we keep an eye on Jagger. Maybe an opportunity presents itself."

Noah sat up at the knock on Rowe's door. Rowe called for the person to enter, running his hand through his hair so that it was left standing up in all directions.

A young man stuck his head in the small opening and he looked in, starting a bit when his dark eyes fell on Noah before shifting on to Rowe. "Hey, boss. You got a sec?"

"Come on in, Quinn."

The man's eyes darted back to Noah for a heartbeat before he pushed the door the rest of the way open and walked in. He was slender, all knees and elbows, in his baggy Deadpool graphic tee and worn jeans. His hair was shaved on the sides while the remaining hair on top of his head was dyed black with red tips.

"Noah, this is Quinn, our other hacker."

Noah shifted in his seat, starting to rise, but the man nearly jumped out of his skin so Noah kept his seat. The kid—and he was more kid than man by all appearances—was skittish as hell.

"Noah Keegan," he said, softening his voice as he extended his hand.

"Quinn Lake," he replied, shaking his hand. "Whoa! You're the Ranger, right?"

Noah looked over at Rowe, raising one eyebrow in question. He didn't mind people knowing that he was a former Ranger, but he wasn't a fan of how it seemed to be spreading so quickly around the city.

Rowe threw up his hands in helpless defense. "Wasn't me!"

"Andrei mentioned that you were partnered with Rowe once. Said you were joining the team," Quinn added.

"Quinn, did you want something other than to make me look like a slave-driving ass?"

"You don't need help with that," Noah muttered and Rowe simply flipped him off, keeping his eyes locked on Quinn.

"Oh, yeah," the hacker said with a sheepish grin. "I developed this system to scan for the use of certain key words including both the Warehouse fire and the one in Indian Hill."

"What? On social media?" Noah inquired.

Quinn snorted. "Tip of the freaking iceberg. I've got social media, chat rooms, and even parts of the dark web covered. Those government drones can't touch my skills. I can wrangle all of the Internet."

Noah directed his gaze back at Rowe who looked completely undisturbed by his employee's boast. "Sounds real legal, Ward." The hacker didn't even blink, pride still pulling his grin wide.

"Not even close," Rowe admitted, not even sounding the least bit remorseful. But Noah couldn't blame him, considering his life and the lives of his friends were on the line. "Whaddaya got?"

"I found a chat room filled with a bunch of anarchists and firebugs. Lot of angry chatter and boasting, but not much matching up to actual events, except for the Warehouse fire and then again with the Lyntons'."

"Could be just repeating news?" Rowe ventured.

Whatever skittishness Quinn felt upon seeing Noah had been replaced by a new energy. He was practically bouncing on the balls of his feet.

"Nope. This douche nozzle knows details like the cop car explosion. Indian Hill PD never let that info out to the news."

Noah met Rowe's gaze. His friend gave just a casual shrug, but it was all an act. There was a light in Rowe's green eyes, a little tilt to the corner of his mouth that Noah came to associate with trouble, getting the blood rushing south when he really needed to get back in control. Rowe was ready to launch himself off the edge of his desk and out the door. They just needed a where.

"So...the arsonist is bragging online. Can we track him?"

"A little..." Quinn frowned, wrinkling his nose as he seemed to shrink in on himself just a bit under Rowe's direct gaze. "I tracked the IP address and it looks like he always posts from a terminal at You Are Toast."

"What the fuck is that? Some vegan hipster bullshit restaurant?" Rowe growled.

Quinn groaned loudly and rolled his eyes, causing Noah to bite his lower lip to keep from laughing out loud.

"No, it's an Internet café that also has some gaming terminals for groups."

Rowe's eyes narrowed and he looked over at Noah for support. "What? Was that even English?"

"Could you sound any older?" Noah teased and Rowe just grinned back at him. Before his friend could add any smartass comments, Noah continued, "Our guy could be hiding out in the area and using the computers to brag about his exploits."

"Where's this café?"

"Edge of Covington and Peaselburg."

"Peaselburg?" Noah repeated.

Rowe shrugged and pushed to his feet. "Lot of Germans in the area. You'll get used to it."

Noah tried to ignore the strange flutter in his chest at Rowe's words. While his friend had certainly acted like he wanted Noah to stick around, it was the first time he'd said anything that made it sound as if he wanted Noah to remain in the city far longer than just a visit. And the truth was, he liked the idea. He liked the thought of living in the same town as Rowe, of being able to meet up and have drinks, watch the game, to know his best friend was just a short distance away at any moment.

"Text me the address," Rowe continued, pulling Noah from his daydreams of something permanent. "We'll go check it out. Maybe we can set some eyes on the place."

"Got it, boss," Quinn said and was out of Rowe's office in a shot.

Rowe turned to Noah, his hands shoved into the pockets of his jeans. He rocked back on his heels, a sly grin splitting his face. God, the man was fucking sexy.

"You wanna see if we can find some trouble?" Rowe asked, waggling his eyebrows at Noah.

"Like you ever have to look hard for trouble," Noah muttered, remaining seated.

"I work hard to keep you entertained."

"Well, then. Let's not waste your hard work. We should go find a firebug."

"And squash the fucker…"

Chapter 11

The houses were too close together. That's all Rowe could think as he drove through Covington, following the directions given by his phone's GPS app. Most of the buildings were either brick or an old, heavily weathered siding that seemed to be hanging on with hope and rusted nails. Windows were covered with thick curtains, blocking out the outside world, and sagging chain-link fences marked off what little territory each owner could claim as theirs. Sidewalks were cracked and the curbs were lined with late-model cars, making the roads even narrower.

The whole area made Rowe feel claustrophobic. Everything was just too damn close. He'd even felt that when living in Hyde Park with Mel. The house was gorgeous and their quiet street had been filled with equally gorgeous homes and old trees. But the neighbors had been too damn close. He'd tried to tempt Mel into finding a house across the river in Kentucky or farther north where they could buy a full acre of land at least. Enough room to spread out and let the dogs run.

But a move north or south would have added a solid thirty minutes to their daily commute each way, and she'd already hated her commute. So they stayed in Hyde Park. With Mel gone, he'd moved to Kentucky to get away from the memories, but he couldn't bring himself to buy that plot of land without her. Didn't matter that the city still closed in on him.

"I think that's it up there," Noah said, jerking Rowe from his darker thoughts. Rowe spotted the small, single-story building painted black with the large front windows darkened. The sign at the top of the building was written in a frantic script, proclaiming "You Are Toast" beside the image of a toaster emblazoned with a bull's-eye. He couldn't stop from rolling his eyes at it. After spending nearly eight years in the Army, Rowe couldn't get into video games that mimicked battle. He still managed to get his high from covert operations provided by his day job.

They drove around a couple blocks before finding an open spot on the street big enough to handle Rowe's truck.

Noah unbuckled his seat belt, his eyes scanning the immediate area. "How we playing this?"

"Low key," Rowe said with a shrug. "We're just in to grab some coffee. That's all."

Noah chuckled. "Yeah, we'll start there."

Rowe didn't reply as he picked up his vibrating cellphone. He couldn't blame Noah for his skepticism. They'd been on plenty of missions, as well as just a few nights out for laughs, that had started "low key" and then went all to shit. Maybe Snow was right and he was a magnet for mayhem and chaos. Fuck knows he didn't ask for it…most of the time.

He glanced at the caller ID before answering the phone and immediately putting the caller on speaker. "What's up, Quinn?"

"Boss, are you there?" Quinn came back in a frantic voice.

"Yeah, I'm here," he said, raising an eyebrow at Noah.

"No, I mean are you there at the café?"

"Yeah."

"He's there. Right now!"

"The arsonist?"

"Yeah, he just logged into the chat room I've been monitoring. His first post went live thirty seconds ago. The IP address matches the café. He's there!"

Noah waved his hand at Rowe as if presenting him with proof to say, "and there's the shit that's about to hit the fan." Fuck. He really did attract it. He was cursed or something. But this could work for them…sort of. They had no idea what the person looked like, but there was good chance that this fucker knew what Rowe looked like.

"Hey Quinn!" Noah suddenly chimed in. "Most monitors have built-in cameras now. Can you use your tech voodoo to get a picture of this asshole?"

"I can try."

"Great."

Rowe couldn't stop the smile the tugged at the corners of his mouth. How they thought alike surprised even him at times.

"Quinn, we're going in. We're a couple blocks away. Don't engage this asshole unless it looks like he's going to log off. He needs to stay online until we get there."

"Gotcha, boss."

Rowe hung up the phone and looked over at Noah, who was struggling not to laugh.

"Low key, huh?"

"Fuck you. Let's see if we can catch this guy without shots being fired," Rowe grumbled, throwing open his door before climbing out. It would actually be better if they didn't pull their guns. Rowe had no intention of calling the cops in on this. Sure, it would help their investigation into the fires, but Rowe was after much bigger game than a little firebug. He wanted Jagger.

They walked briskly down the street, talking loudly about the fact that they were missing the Bengals-Steelers game on TV. Just two guys out, grabbing coffee. No big deal. Until they stepped inside the Internet café. Rowe stopped upon crossing the threshold and blinked several times, forcing his eyes to adjust to the lower light of the interior compared to the bright sunlight shining on the city. The front half of the café had the typical set up of wooden tables and chairs. There was a small scattering of people on laptops, paper cups beside them. A few people looked up at Rowe and Noah, but they all went quickly back to whatever they were doing, brushing them off.

A bar stood off to the right, a glass case displaying a handful of aged pastries that had probably looked appetizing when they were first put out a day or two ago. A shiny machine with an assortment of nozzles, making loud grinding and steaming noises. Behind it was a large chalkboard filled with the specials of the day and prices.

As they walked up to the bar, Rowe caught sight of a room on the left filled with long tables divided into cubes similar to what you'd see in a library. Each cube held a large monitor and keyboard. From what he could spot, another dozen customers sat at the computer screens.

"Can I help you?" demanded a bored-sounding barista wearing a shit-ton of dark eye make-up and multiple lip piercings. Yeah, this was so not the type of place Rowe would normally find himself in.

"One black coffee and a salted caramel mocha with an extra shot," Noah said with a wink. The kid blushed and Rowe suddenly had to fight the urge not to reach across the counter and strangle him.

"N-name?" he stumbled, gaze locked on Noah and Rowe ground his teeth.

"Just put Noah on both." Noah's grin grew and those goddamn dimples came into play.

"I've never seen you guys in here before," the barista ventured. Rowe watched him suck on his lower lip, his cheeks flushing. No, the guy wasn't suspicious. He was too busy fucking hitting on the guy who looked like a walking advertisement for sex beside him.

"A friend, Chris, told us to meet him here. Said he was going to be gaming for a while," Rowe said before Noah could say something that would reduce the kid to a useless pile of goo. Sure, he understood blending in, but Noah didn't need to get any fucking chummier than he was with the kid.

"Chris?" The barista's eyes jumped over to Rowe and surveyed the man, his smile growing. "Yeah, I think there's a couple back there."

Noah clapped his hand on Rowe's shoulder, adding just enough pressure to turn him away from the barista and toward the gaming room. "You good, boss?" Noah whispered in his ear, leaving Rowe dying to shove his elbow backward into Noah's stomach. Fucker knew he wanted to throttle the kid and was laughing.

"Keep your eyes peeled," Rowe grumbled.

"How will we—"

"Fuck!" Both Rowe and Noah's heads swiveled as one to the cubicle facing them not more than fifty feet away. A head had popped up, partially covered with a black hood from a hoodie, but they could easily make out the young face with big brown eyes and delicate features. Rowe's heart stopped as he looked at the young man. His appearance felt all too familiar. But before Rowe could think too much on it, the boy darted toward the back of the café. Rowe and Noah charged after him, pushing other gamers out of the way as they tried to get to their feet. People shouted after them, but Rowe ignored it, his eyes focused on the back door the guy had exploded through and into the bright sunlight.

Rowe followed into the light, blinking rapidly, still partially blind when he started after a dark blur. He could hear the scrape of Noah's shoes on the pavement behind him. Their target crossed the litter-strewn back alley behind the café to a tall chain-link fence. He jumped, his toe catching in one of the holes so he could lift himself over the top to land heavily on the other side. The man didn't even look back, but darted on between two buildings. They easily followed, catching the fence and launching over with relative ease. Noah's longer legs gave him an advantage and he was after the guy a half second faster than Rowe.

They followed, cutting through weed-choked yards and narrow alleys. People screamed and cursed behind them as they were carelessly knocked out of the way, but Rowe and Noah didn't stop in their pursuit. Getting their hands on this fucker meant getting a step closer to Jagger. At the very least, it could mean an end to the fires.

Darting up one street and through another alley, Rowe and Noah came to a sharp halt as they came out onto a heavy street. The light had changed against them and cars surged forward, filling all four lanes. Their arsonist bounced off the hood of a gray sedan. Tires squealed as brakes were slammed and horns blared, but the guy was immediately back on his feet and on the other side of the street. Rowe hesitated another second and then started forward. Noah roughly grabbed his shoulder and jerked him back to the curb.

"Stop! You'll get killed!"

Rowe growled, swallowing back his own curse. Noah was right, but the pyro was gaining ground on them. He could only hope that the asshole wasn't accustomed to running five miles a day. Rowe still had plenty of steam left. He was happy to run this guy to ground.

As soon as traffic lightened enough to leave a few gaps, they were running again, cutting through another side street to come out to…fucking nothing.

They stopped on the sidewalk, looking up and down the street, but it was empty. Directly in front of them was an open parking lot without a single car. There were a few houses, but there was no one on the sidewalk and no cars on the street. The delay at the busy street had cost them. The perp had disappeared like free doughnuts on a fucking Friday.

Rowe grabbed Noah's arm and shoved him up the street. "Check the cars parked on the street. Movement in the windows. I'll go in this direction."

They canvased the area for nearly twenty minutes before Rowe had to face facts. They lost him. The guy had to know the area better than they did, because he found a hiding place or had a car secreted somewhere to make his escape. There wasn't a trace of him.

With a growl, Rowe pulled his vibrating cellphone out of his back pocket as he stood in the middle of the sidewalk, watching Noah walk toward him. The phone had been vibrating almost non-stop since they'd left the café, but Rowe guessed it was Quinn calling to tell him that the guy was no longer online.

"You get him?" Quinn demanded without greeting.

"No. Fucker disappeared. You get a picture?"

"Yeah, it's not great. I'm still cleaning it up."

Rowe grunted. "Send it to my phone, then run it through the facial recognition software. I want a name by tomorrow."

"Sure, boss, but these things take time to run through the system. It could take—"

"Tomorrow," he repeated and then hung up.

"Quinn?" Noah demanded as soon as he was standing at Rowe's side again.

Rowe grunted, lifting his eyes to look up and down the street. Where could the asshole have disappeared to? Was he still watching them, waiting?

"Sorry—"

"Don't," Rowe immediately interrupted. "You kept me out of the hospital today. We saw his face and Quinn at least got a pic. He's going to run facial recognition. When we get a name, he'll be easier to track down."

The phone vibrated once in Rowe's hand and he immediately pulled up the text that Quinn sent over, holding up the picture so that Noah could see it as well.

"Ward..." Noah started, his name coming out low and unsteady. "The guy reminds me of Ian."

Yeah, that was Rowe's exact thought. Big, soft eyes, delicate features, sweet mouth even if it was pulled open in surprise. And young looking. Something about the eyes made Rowe think he was at least in his early twenties, but he could so easily pass for a teen. He did remind him far too much of Ian. This poor guy was likely another one of Jagger's victims, which made him a special kind of dangerous.

"I don't think he's the arsonist," Noah announced.

Rowe jerked his eyes free of the picture at last, shoving the phone in his back pocket as he started to lead the way back to where he'd parked the truck. "What the hell do you mean? The guy recognized me and ran. He's the arsonist."

"No, I think he's the shooter." Rowe stopped and looked over his shoulder at Noah, who was frowning as he stared at the broken sidewalk under his feet. He squinted against the sun as he lifted his eyes to Rowe. "That night in the woods, we saw the figure for only a couple seconds in the darkness, but the build is the same. So is the body movement."

Rowe quickly replayed the chase through the Indian Hill woods against their chase through the street of Covington. Noah was right. The two figures were incredibly similar. They hadn't seen the arsonist yet, and the two people could be similar in build and movement, but it wasn't too likely.

"You thinking they're a team?"

"One starts the fires and the other acts as protection or just a sniper."

Shoving one hand through his sweaty hair, Rowe scratched his head before swearing loudly as he resumed the walk back to the truck. They'd undoubtedly stirred up the hornets' nest now. They had a face, which was a start, but there was no way in hell the guy was coming back to the café now. He'd keep Quinn watching for more posts on the chat boards, but he wasn't hopeful that they'd catch another break.

"You gonna put a bodyguard on Ian again?" Noah asked as they climbed back into the truck.

"I have to."

Noah nodded. "Okay. I'll tell him at dinner."

"Dinner?" Rowe stopped in the act of turning the key in the ignition and glared at Noah as he leaned against the passenger door.

"Yeah, dinner. The evening meal. Comes after lunch."

"I know what the fuck dinner is. You're seeing Ian at dinner?"

"More like we're going to have dinner together," Noah smoothly corrected. He paused, readjusting the seatbelt strap stretched across his chest. "I'll try to wait to tell him about the bodyguard after dessert and coffee. Don't want to ruin his appetite."

"What the fuck! Why are you having dinner with Ian? Is this a...a...a date?"

Noah shrugged. "Maybe. You know, I can just stay over at Ian's tonight. Give you time to get your bodyguard in place. I'm sure he won't mind."

"Let me think about it," Rowe practically snarled as he started the truck. This was really turning out to be a shit day.

Chapter 12

Ian parked his new Chevrolet Volt in one of the open lots and eyed the ominous clouds hovering over the city as he slipped out of the car. It hadn't been too cold today and he'd hoped he and Noah would be able to take a walk after dinner. Looked like that was out. Too bad. He was looking forward to showing Noah more of his city.

A small crowd gathered outside the Thai restaurant, half the people with their gaze locked on their phone rather than talking to their companions. At least he'd been smart enough to make reservations. The food was excellent and since Noah had talked about Thai food while they were at Lucas's, Ian was sure he'd like this place.

Nervous anticipation made his hands sweat. He surreptitiously wiped his palms on his pants as he walked to the restaurant. He hadn't been on a date in so long, he wasn't sure he even remembered how. Not that this was necessarily a date. He'd phrased the invitation as a way to give Noah a break from Rowe, but he'd been clear that it would be just the two of them. That was a date, right? Maybe it was best if it wasn't. He didn't feel the gut-deep burn he'd felt around Detective Hollis Banner. On the other hand, he was attracted to Noah and the man made him laugh. Having Rowe's complete trust in him made him the perfect date material, too.

Who knew? If dinner went well, maybe he'd get laid soon.

Pausing at the corner, waiting for the light to change so he could cross the street, Ian straightened his beige Dries van Noten silk jacket, smoothing his hands down the black trim. He'd saved for a long time for it and it made him feel confident and sexy. He'd paired it with black jeans and his favorite black Chukkas. As he walked toward the front of the restaurant, he felt eyes on him and looked toward the crowd of people milling under a streetlight. When he spotted a tall man with messy, blond hair, his heart clenched and he picked up the pace, sure that was the missing detective in the back of the group.

But when he reached it, the man was gone. Ian stood there, staring into the shadows, feeling the burn of hot eyes on him as the hair stood on the back of his neck. Once again, he felt anger laced with regret. He should have just asked the detective out, and he would have if that accident hadn't happened. Not that it had been an accident. He realized he was rubbing his thigh. Phantom or real pain—he didn't know anymore.

"Hope that frown isn't for me."

He looked up and dropped the frown when he saw Noah standing close. His eyes widened because the man looked fantastic. His hair lay in a mass of curls that fell half over the right side of his face. He'd shaved, leaving his square jaw clear. He wore jeans and a navy blue shirt under a brown leather jacket. He had the kind of wide shoulders and arms Ian loved, nice and big. Like the detective. "No," he finally answered. "That frown was for someone else. Bad memories."

"Then let's make some new, good ones." Noah turned and placed his hand on Ian's back to lead him into the restaurant. "I can tell I'm going to like this place already just by the smell. You eat here often?"

Nodding, Ian smiled at the hostess. "Reservation for two under Pierce." He turned to Noah. "I do. They serve traditional dishes from north Thailand, so there aren't a lot of the sweeter choices. My favorite is the *nam phrik oong*."

"So you like the hot food."

"I do." Ian smiled up at him as they followed the hostess around the small, wicker tables. "You mentioned you like Thai food the other night."

"Love it."

After they were seated on the floor mats, their waiter showed up and asked if they wanted drinks right away. Noah ordered an American beer and Ian a Thai one. Noah grinned at Ian after the waiter left. "I thought you'd take me to your restaurant. From what I've eaten at Rowe's, I can tell you I wouldn't have minded."

"I'm there all the time and this place takes care of my craving for hot peppers. But I'd love for you to come by and try the food. Rowe has been eating there often since—" Ian stopped talking, his gut twisting up.

"Since his wife passed?" Noah nodded up at the waiter when he set his beer in front of him.

They placed their food order and Ian reached for his Singha, and took a long swallow. *Way to start a date off right, Ian.* Talk about one of the worst things that had ever happened to Ian. He missed Melissa badly and felt the deep stab of survivor's guilt every time he was around Rowe.

"How has he been? Really?" Noah shifted on the mat. "It's been a long time since I spent any time with him in person and he's changed, of course. Thirteen years will do that. But he's changed a lot."

"He has. He's quieter and before that happened, any time he was quiet, the rest of us got nervous."

White teeth flashed in a grin. "I remember that feeling. He'd fall quiet and then look at me with that grin." Noah shook his head. "My heart would pound like I was about to jump out of a plane, but I knew I'd do whatever mad scheme he cooked up." Noah paused, his blue eyes locked on the beer he held with both hands and his grin fading almost as quickly as it had appeared. "Does he ever talk about her with you? Talk about good memories or anything that involves her?"

Ian shook his head, swallowing against the tightness growing in his throat at the thought of Melissa. "No," he croaked and paused. He sipped his beer and started again when he was sure his voice was firmer. "We've tried a couple times, but he closes up, walks away. We were afraid that he'd disappear again so we stopped pushing."

"Would…would you tell me about her?"

Ian sat up straight, his hand convulsively tightening around his beer. Of all the things he'd thought they'd talk about, he'd never expected to hear that request from Noah. "I…I—"

"I don't mean anything really personal," Noah hedged when Ian seemed to hesitate. "She was just such an important part of Rowe's life, I hate not knowing her, not having really met her."

Taking another quick drink of his beer, Ian told himself that he could do this. He needed to talk about Melissa, keep her memory alive. "She was…insane," he started and then softly chuckled. "And so energetic. She was the only person I knew who could keep up with Rowe and his mad plans. And dirty." He laughed again. The words were coming so much easier, like a dam had broken around the memories. "She and Snow would get together and tell the raunchiest stories. She could make a porn star blush. She used to love trying to get Lucas to blush."

When Ian stopped, he found Noah watching him with a wide smile on his lips, but a heavy sadness in his bright blue eyes.

"In other words, perfect for Rowe in every way," Noah murmured, his voice low and rough.

"You're worried about him?"

Noah flashed him a bright smile that didn't wash the sadness from his eyes. "I don't think there's ever been a moment since I first met Rowe that I didn't worry about him. It's a full-time job in itself, but I'm glad he has you guys."

"We drive him nuts, checking in. I get to see him a lot more than the others because he comes to Rialto, but Lucas and Snow both started to smother him for a time. He puts up with it well."

"He loves them. Loves you all. I could see that right away."

Nodding, Ian picked up his napkin, then ran it through his fingers. "Those three are the most incredible people I ever met. We bonded immediately and I wasn't in the best situation. They…did things to help me before they really knew me. Big things. I owe them everything."

"I didn't get the feeling they felt owed. Not that I was with them long, but you're all tight. Really tight. And Rowe talked about them a lot when we were working together. He felt like they were family and from what I could tell, that's how they feel about you."

"They do." Their food arrived and Ian closed his eyes and inhaled the incredible aroma of dried chilies, pork and tomatoes. He was grateful for the distraction, hoping he could find a way to move their conversation in a lighter direction.

Noah took a bite of his curry and grunted. "Good. Have you come here with Rowe? He'd love this."

"Know a lot about him, don't you?"

He nodded. "Know a lot about him, but more importantly I know what the man likes to eat. I'm pretty sure he's all stomach.

I made us these spare ribs last night. When Rowe ate them, I thought he was going to fight the dogs over the bones."

Ian chuckled at the image, shaking his head.

"We spent nearly four years together," Noah continued. "That's how I knew about Snow and Lucas because he kept in touch with them often. I actually used to be jealous. Good thing I hadn't actually seen them because, damn." Noah sipped his beer. "You fit right in, so how are you the single one in the group?"

Ian grinned. "Because I'm the prettiest?" He couldn't hold the smile because it was just too ridiculous a statement. "I'm kidding. Rowe is the prettiest. He's just sneaky and only reveals the truth when he pulls out the big guns. That smile."

Noah didn't say anything at first—just dug into his curry. In fact, it was the first time Noah refused to look at him since they'd sat down. Little lines of tension dug in between his brows and around his mouth that hadn't been there before. "Damn smile," he muttered.

Ian watched him closely for long moments and when a faint hint of red crept up Noah's neck, he knew there was a lot more to the man's feelings for Rowe. And when he realized what he felt was relief, he shook his head. Of course, his response to just thinking Hollis Banner had been outside had been a pretty big damn clue that he was still hung up on the asshole.

He and Noah weren't happening—not when the man had a crush on his friend, which just made him feel so bad for Noah. There really were few worse things than falling for someone who had no chance of returning those feelings. But this put tonight in a whole new light. He decided to relax and enjoy the evening, but did feel a twinge of regret over not getting laid by this sexy man tonight.

"I just fucked up the date, didn't I?" Noah asked.

"No. But I know where you stand now and that's probably for the best. How long have you loved him?"

Noah reared back. "Whoa! Nobody said anything about love."

"You haven't seen him in years and you still have that note in your voice when you mention his smile? It's something close if it isn't."

Noah raked his fingers through his hair, tugging on a tangle when he got stuck. He sucked in a couple of deep breaths like a man just breaking above the surface of the ocean after a deep dive. "I'm attracted to him and I care about him a lot and yeah, for a time when we served together, I thought I was in love with him. But as you probably know all too well, falling for a mostly straight man is stupid."

"I never have. I've never fallen for anyone, in fact." He had never been comfortable enough with any of the men he'd slept with to open himself up like that.

"Not even one of your friends? That's hard to believe with this crowd. I told Rowe it was ridiculous—the amount of hotness in that penthouse the other night."

"I was pretty young when I met them and they took on the roles of brothers so fast, I never saw them any differently." Now that he knew where he stood with Noah, he decided to go all in. "That bad situation I mentioned earlier? I was a teenager when I got caught up with Boris Jagger and Rowe and the others got me away from him."

"I'm guessing the 'caught up' wasn't your choice?"

Ian toyed with his beer, his stomach suddenly souring, but then that usually happened when he thought about those years with Jagger. "No, it wasn't. And I was too scared to run away for a long, long time. I was luckier than some of the other boys. I ended up having more freedom. Jagger even let me cook, but it came with a price." He looked away for a moment, watching a family of four enjoying their dinner. "Everything with Jagger came with a price."

Noah flagged the waiter down and asked for beers for them both. He waited until the man left to speak again, but still lowered his voice. "If I'm understanding this, it's amazing you're even alive. Pedoph—men like Jagger—don't normally let those who could testify against them live."

"He was different." Ian's food sat like a heavy lump in his stomach. "The kids I knew were just let go once they were past their useful date."

Noah paled.

Ian nodded. "Yeah, you understand. But Jagger scared us into staying with him while we were young, told us what it would be like if we ran away. Some were so far under his influence, they turned around and worked for him instead."

"Seriously?"

"I knew several who did. He could be…charming when he wanted to be. Could make you think you couldn't get better or that you didn't deserve better. He could make you feel like you owed him for taking care of you. Most of those kids fell for his act."

"Not you?"

Ian slowly shook his head. "Not later, but I did at first. I was too in shock over being in that situation. Later, I saw right through him but pretended my ass off. I managed to make it so I cooked for his parties instead of being one of the party favors." He broke off before he could say most of the time. He was making that part of his life sound prettier than it actually had been. He looked at Noah, who watched him closely, blue eyes sharp. This man was too smart to know he didn't share everything and that he wouldn't—especially not with someone he didn't know. The only reason he shared now was because Noah had offered to help them. He laughed and it sounded choked, nervous. "The date is really messed up now."

Noah reached across the small table and touched his hand. "No, it's not—not because of that anyway. I'm impressed at how fucking strong you must be. You own a restaurant at what, twenty-five?"

"Twenty-six. And I'm only part owner. I have that restaurant because of Lucas."

"He strikes me as a smart man when it comes to money, so he obviously believes you're a good investment."

"I hope so," Ian murmured. "And he really is a genius. Google him sometime."

"Then he would only invest in something or someone he believes in."

"Or loves." Ian smiled. "I'm not sure what luck I stumbled upon, but the day those men came into my life was the best one ever."

"Yeah well, I think they're pretty lucky, too."

"Thanks. Too bad you're in love with Rowe. And what did you mean by *mostly* straight? Thought I didn't catch that, didn't you?"

This time, Noah didn't instantly refute it and Ian knew if he wasn't still, he was falling back in love. Sadness and worry flooded him. Noah was a nice guy. A really nice guy. And Rowe had been in a dark, dark place for a long time. He didn't want to see either one of them hurt.

"Has he told you that he still owns the house he bought with Melissa? That he closed it up after her death and left it locked up like some sad mausoleum?"

If he'd thought Noah paled earlier, it was nothing compared to now. He looked down at his food and cleared his throat. "No. Didn't know that. Fuck."

"He was devastated and we've been watching him all these months, hoping to see him pulling out of the grief. He's been showing signs of it, but never so much as he did the other night. He laughed with you. He smiles. We see glimpses of the evil schemer that we love." Ian patted the hand Noah still had on his. "Snow was so choked up with relief, he left the room twice. Thinks none of us noticed." He rolled his eyes. "We're happy you're here. You're good for him." He bit his lip. "But I have to say I'm worried that he won't or can't return your feelings. He's straight."

Noah's lips flattened into a hard, straight line as if he were fighting to hold the words in. He also refused to meet Ian's gaze.

"Right?" Ian pressed, unable to ignore the fact that his voice had crept a little higher either in shock or panic.

"I said mostly for a reason."

"Wait, what?" Ian leaned forward. "Did something happen back then? Or now?"

"Both."

"Really? Wow." He sat back, blinked and looked around because it felt like he'd entered an alternate dimension. Other diners continued to talk and laugh while eating. Servers flowed along the open paths, delivering food, taking orders, removing dishes, and replenishing drinks. All of them were completely oblivious to the fact that Ian's world was changing. He wasn't sure how he felt about this because while they were both great guys, he had a feeling this could come out painful for Noah.

"Don't worry, Ian. Rowe backtracked pretty fast and hard." A bitter note colored his voice and his smile held a hint of pain that made Ian more concerned. "I know better than to push him. He won't let himself…" Noah paused and grimaced like he was clenching his teeth, holding something back. "We're just friends."

Ian continued to worry while they finished their dinner and it hadn't stopped when they stood outside by his car, though he was briefly distracted by the news that he'd be acquiring a bodyguard again whether he wanted one or not. While he liked Sven, the big, sexy blond wasn't doing his sex-starved libido any favors.

He shoved his hands into his pockets and stared up at Noah. He really was so much Ian's type with his height and muscular build. "Too bad we're both caught up in someone else."

"Both?" Light from the street lamps flashed on Noah's teeth.

Ian shrugged. "A blockhead cop who disappeared."

Noah rested a hand on his shoulder. "If this man couldn't see what he had in you, he really was a blockhead."

"We never really hooked up anyway. It was just wishful thinking on my part and things happened. He got away from me." He touched the lapel of Noah's leather jacket. "How about just one? To see if there's a spark?"

Before Noah had time to answer, Ian rose on his toes and kissed him. He had to work back a groan of disappointment that nothing would be happening between them because Noah smelled and felt fantastic. The kiss was slow and sweet. Everything about it should have come together to be the absolutely perfect kiss, but it didn't make him want to throw the man down and maul him. He slowly let go and balanced back on his feet. They both chuckled nervously.

"So…friends?"

Noah nodded. "Definitely."

Ian unlocked his car but felt the need to warn his new friend again. "Be careful. I love Rowe dearly and want more than anything for him to find happiness and love again. If that's with you, I'll be thrilled. But he may still need time or be confused. I don't know what happened between you two in the past, but he's different now. Mel's death made him different. I can tell you have a nice, big heart. So, keep it safe."

Chapter 13

Noah sat in the driver's seat of the rental, his hands loosening and tightening on the steering wheel as he stared at the garage door in front of the car. He'd been sitting in the driveway in the dark and cold for over ten minutes, Ian's words of warning repeating over and over in his head. Ian was right. He knew Ian was right. He'd already decided earlier or he never would have gone out with Ian. He needed to give Rowe space and give him time to heal. No matter what he felt for Rowe, he'd always be his friend first and that's what Rowe really needed. Not more questions and complications.

But that fucking kiss. And that look Rowe had directed at him across the table after their rib dinner. It was like Rowe had wanted to eat him alive, and Noah would have welcomed it. Even now, forty-eight hours later, he could still feel Rowe's lips against his, questing tongue pushing and sliding along his. And had that been a sharp bite of teeth shorting out his brain?

A low growl rumbled from Noah as he shifted in the driver's seat. He reached down and adjusted himself. He was getting hard just thinking about it. Rubbing his hand roughly along his face, Noah sucked in a deep breath, trying to grab control of the desire that was racing like liquid fire through his veins. He could pull himself together and be the friend that Rowe needed.

Not letting his mind spend another second dwelling on the hard muscles that wrapped around every inch of the other man's body, Noah surged out of the car and into the house, where he found Rowe sprawled across the couch, his narrowed eyes already trained on the front door as if he'd been waiting for Noah to stroll in.

"Evening," Noah said stiffly. He knelt down and scratched each of the dogs that had come to greet him, taking the second to quickly survey the room. The TV was on, but it was turned to what looked like an infomercial for a high-power blender. Beer cans littered the coffee table, so it was a safe bet that Rowe had been drinking since his departure.

"Did you fuck him?" Rowe asked, his tone unemotionally flat.

Noah flinched at the words. He clenched his teeth and exhaled through his nose, trying to keep his head. Rowe was drunk and…well, he didn't know what else. If he didn't know better, he'd say that Rowe was jealous, but that would just make things a hell of a lot more complicated.

"Ian and I went to a Thai place. Great food." Noah forced a casual tone. "He's a nice guy. Killer sense of humor."

Rowe sat up, both his feet landing on the floor with a heavy thump. He shifted to the edge of the cushion, narrowing his eyes on Noah. "Did. You. Fuck. Him?" he slowly repeated, carefully enunciating each word as if the hours out of Rowe's sight had made him mentally deficient.

Something in Noah snapped. "What the hell do you care what we did?" He shrugged out of his jacket and tossed it into an empty chair. "From what I can tell, Ian's a grown man with a good head on his shoulders. He's allowed to have sex with whomever he wants. It's none of your goddamn business!" The dogs scattered as soon as he started shouting, running for cover in the kitchen.

Rowe shoved to his feet and Noah was relieved to see that he didn't sway. Maybe he wasn't as far gone as he'd first guessed. But that knowledge didn't do much to calm his temper.

"Ian's my friend—"

"And what the hell am I?" Noah threw up his hands. "Huh? What am I to you, Rowe?"

"It's not the same."

Noah's flinch came harder that time—like Rowe had physically hit him.

Rowe briefly closed his eyes and Noah could see the muscles clenching in his jaw as he gritted out his next words. "He's been through shit."

"Yeah, we all have." Noah immediately held up his hand when Rowe's face flushed and his mouth opened like he was about to tear into Noah with a blistering swell of rage. "And Ian has a right to go out and have a good time with whomever the fuck he wants without a keeper. He doesn't need you monitoring his sex life."

Rowe stared at Noah for a couple seconds in silence, his hands clenching and unclenching at his sides before he finally asked, "Did you fuck him?"

Noah roared, thrusting his hands through his loose hair in frustration. "No! No, I didn't fuck him! No! What the hell is wrong with you? No, I didn't fuck him!"

No one could drive him insane like Rowe could. In all his life, no one could get under his skin the way Rowe could. He drove him absolutely crazy in one second then made him die of laughter in the next. He took in the wary look in Rowe's eyes and the way he was chewing on his bottom lip in indecision, and Noah felt a sharp stab of pain in his heart. It didn't feel like they'd get to the laughter this time…maybe never.

"Did you kiss him?" This question came softer.

A heavy groan rumbled from Noah's lips and he dropped his hand. "Yeah," he admitted quietly, closing his eyes. Rowe didn't get it. Not that Noah could tell his best friend that he didn't really want Ian, no matter how funny or sexy he thought the man was. The only person he wanted was standing in front of him and he was untouchable. "Once. It was nice."

"Was it like this?"

Noah's eyes snapped open, shocked at the question. He had only a heartbeat to register that despite having alcohol in his system, Rowe was still frighteningly fast. And then Rowe's mouth was on his in a rough, searing kiss that sucked the air straight out of Noah's lungs. Rowe's fingers plunged into his hair, painfully twisting around the strands to hold his head captive as his tongue pushed into Noah's mouth. A shiver ran through the length of Rowe's body and he softly moaned, switching off Noah's brain completely.

The kiss with Ian had been sweet and tentative. They had both cautiously felt each other out, checking to see the other person's interest, careful not to push too far too fast. There had been a hint of a tease, a little promise of something more if the other person was willing to take the step forward.

But with Rowe? Pure fucking fire.

The second Noah's lips touched Rowe it threatened to blaze out of control and he wanted to let it consume him. Wrapping his arms around Rowe, Noah pulled him against his own body so that they were pressed tightly together from lips to knees. He ran his hands down Rowe's muscular back to cup the cheeks of his ass, pressing his groin against Noah's so that he could feel the hard outline of his cock grinding into his own. No running. No hiding. They both moaned in unison, the kiss growing hungry, devouring. Rowe sucked on his bottom lip, bit it, then licked deep into his mouth. Noah couldn't think, didn't want to think. He was so damn tired of fighting this when all he wanted was Rowe. He loved his tight, compact body, the hardness of his hands as they gripped his head with desperation, as if he was afraid Noah was going to suddenly push him away and walk out the door. Hell, he was pretty sure he'd never be able to walk across the room, at least not without Rowe attached to him.

"Fuck," Rowe groaned, breaking off the kiss long enough to slide his lips along Noah's jaw to his neck. "Why does this feel so damn good?"

A dozen answers surged through Noah's mind, but he pushed them all down. He didn't want Rowe thinking too much about the *why* of everything. Was it so wrong to just revel in the fact that it did feel good? Rowe had been in pain for so long. Noah had been alone and empty for too many damn years. Couldn't they just have this moment where it felt so fucking good that that rest of the world didn't matter?

He decided they could.

He ground his spike-hard dick against Rowe, pressing his hands hard down on Rowe's ass before slowly running them up his back. He didn't lessen the pressure, stroking firmly, knowing his hold was possessive as he wrapped his arms under Rowe's and clasped the backs of his shoulders. He held the man close, tilted his head and slashed his mouth over Rowe's

Oh yeah. The pleasure that bore through him made him see stars behind his closed lids.

Rowe pulled back, gasping in air loudly and Noah opened his eyes and met that shocked, green gaze. "You okay?" he breathed. Or at least, he thought that's what he said. His mind was scrambled and all he could register was heat and lust and the goddamn need to drag Rowe onto the nearest flat surface.

"You taste good."

He couldn't stop the crack of a grin at the hint of bewilderment in Rowe's voice. "Then come back for more," he whispered.

Rowe nodded and this time, he leaned in slower and pressed his lips to Noah's. If Noah thought he liked snarling, biting Rowe, slow, gentle Rowe sent his heart soaring. The moan that came from his throat was ragged, and Rowe swallowed it down with a clench of hard fingers on his hips. Gripping tight, he pressed his lips harder and Noah opened for him, let him do as he pleased.

He stroked his tongue into Noah, proving that wicked muscle was so incredibly good for something other than smart-assed quips. He flicked it against Noah's and chuckled when Noah made another incredibly embarrassing noise in his throat. Noah couldn't help it. This was everything to him—everything he'd been trying not to wish for. He'd never felt this kind of heat with anyone else and he'd convinced himself that one night of theirs had been a fluke and that Rowe had run because it had been bad and not terrifyingly good. He'd told himself a lot of bullshit, but this proved it hadn't been a drunken, foggy dream of perfection. It had been all too fucking real.

Rowe pushed against him and Noah's back hit the door. He kissed Noah until he no longer felt alone inside his own body and when he retreated, breathing heavily and staring with narrow, hard eyes at his mouth, Noah held perfectly still. Rowe never took his gaze away as he opened Noah's jeans and slid his hand inside to wrap strong fingers around his cock.

All the air left Noah's lungs and his eyes rolled back in his head. "Oh fuck," he said in a gasp. "Just go in directly for the kill, why don't you?"

"Expect anything different?" Rowe leaned in and kissed his neck, leaving his lips there as he ran his calloused hand up and down Noah's dick.

"It feels the same."

Rowe didn't ask what he meant and Noah knew he didn't have to. It was like before. Years ago. The night he'd given into need and Rowe had responded beyond his wildest dreams. Rowe was feeling it again now if his harsh pants and flushed skin were anything to go by. He blushed dark like every other redhead Noah had ever met and suddenly he wanted—no, *needed*—to see that flush around and against Rowe's tattoos.

"We need to lose some clothes."

Rowe nodded, let go of his cock and stepped back. His startled loud, bark of laughter made Noah straighten up. He followed Rowe's gaze and cracked up when he saw all three dogs sitting next to them, lined up like they were settled in for the show. "Yeah, no," Rowe said, voice gruff. "Not letting them watch." He held out his hand.

Noah didn't hesitate. He took it and followed Rowe down the hall.

Rowe didn't know what the fuck he was doing. He just didn't plan to fumble his way through this with his dogs as an audience. He hoped it wasn't visible on the outside because on the inside, he was shaking like this was his first time. In a way, it was. The one time he'd given in to his curiosity about the male half of his species, he'd been a lot drunker than he was now. He mostly remembered the overwhelming excitement he'd felt and later he'd attributed it to some twisted sense of the forbidden.

He'd had a few beers tonight but he'd also hit some of Noah's leftover ribs, so he was wide awake and his lingering buzz was fading fast. Add in a kiss that had shocked his libido from hibernation to overdrive and he was ready to try again.

With the same man.

That fact hit him hard. He'd looked at other men over the years, but only one had ever intrigued him enough to give in and here he was again. And this time, Rowe wasn't the same. He'd grown up, experienced life and loss, and he no longer felt that odd sense of something forbidden. He'd been around his friends long enough to know the truth. No, this was new. And exciting.

Rowe was very aware that he was leading one of his closest friends to his bed. Most of his shaking came from anticipation. Holy hell, he loved kissing Noah. The man's hand was hot in his and he'd felt amazing against him—hard muscles and his dick, damn. He'd had his own in his hand countless times and it hadn't been the same at all. He knew how good fingers felt wrapped around that sensitive flesh and to be the one causing those soft catches of breath felt amazing. He knew what Noah felt, and holding that warm, silky skin over steel…shorted out his brain. He paused at his door.

He wanted to explore every inch of Noah. He'd wanted that before but what they'd had was an over-stimulated night of crazy passion that had been brought on by holding it back so long. He remembered coming more than once in that explosive haze, but they'd never slowed down to explore.

Noah tightened his fingers and tugged, causing Rowe to glance over his shoulder. Noah lifted an eyebrow, silently asking if he'd stopped because he'd changed his mind.

"We're doing this," he gritted out through clenched teeth.

He pulled Noah into his bedroom. They got through the door and he turned to kick it shut before the dogs could follow, then grabbed a handful of Noah's shirt and tugged him close. They stared at each other—green locked with blue.

"Still doing okay, Ward?"

He studied the slightly wary look in his friend's eyes and hated it. He wanted nothing but that overwhelming heat, wanted him to stare at Rowe like he had earlier. Like he wanted to eat him alive. "Yeah. I'm working on instinct here, but I'm all in."

The wicked grin he got in return sent butterflies into his belly. "Instinct is how we all do this at first." Noah ran his hands down Rowe's chest, scraping his short nails through the T-shirt. "It takes practice to learn how to do it right. Practice with the same person." He kissed him. "Over." He kissed him again. "And over."

"Lots of practice," Rowe breathed before he spun Noah around, hooked his foot behind his knee, and sent him to his back on the bed. He crawled up Noah's big body quickly and fastened their mouths back together while he stretched out on top of Noah. Unadulterated pleasure surged through him and his plans of slow exploration vanished.

He rolled his hips against Noah, loving when Noah rocked up against him and spread his legs so Rowe snuggled in between. He groaned and Noah cupped the sides of his head, lifting to deepen the kiss, tangling their tongues together before thrusting inside Rowe's mouth in the same rhythm he moved his hips. Fuck, his smooth rolling movements drove every thought but one from Rowe's mind.

"Naked. We need naked." He rolled off Noah and tugged his T-shirt off and fumbled with the snap of his jeans. Noah moved just as frantically next to him. He struggled out of his pants and turned to see that moonlight streamed through the window and highlighted Noah's gorgeous, tight ass. He reached out slowly, ran his finger over one taut globe, then gasped when Noah rolled over and basically attacked him. He pressed their naked flesh together, ran his hand down Rowe's hip and opened his mouth over Rowe's neck.

Rowe stretched his head back, moaning when Noah sucked and bit at the long muscle down the side of his neck. His calloused hands ran all over Rowe's back, his sides. He dug strong fingers into Rowe's leg and hiked it up over his hip. Their dicks touched and Rowe cried out and shoved his hand between them to grab both in his hand. He stroked them together, relishing the throaty moans and other sounds coming from Noah. The other man was completely lost, writhing against him.

The heady power he felt in turning the big man to mush rushed through him like wildfire and he stroked harder and brought his face up so he could meet Noah's mouth. His lips were full and softer against his than he would have ever believed. His tongue slid into Noah's mouth and he tasted faintly of curry and beer, but mostly of that Noah flavor that Rowe hadn't realized he'd memorized. It was addicting and he flashed back to the way he'd lost it that time, the way he'd given in to a desire he'd worried would complicate his life too much, the way they'd been all over each other.

Like they were now.

Noah stroked over his skin, touching everywhere he could reach as he stayed open for Rowe's tongue. He sucked on it and

Rowe shuddered and squeezed his hand. He pulled back. "I want...I want..." He couldn't get the words past the harsh breaths escaping his mouth.

"What?" Noah kissed his jaw and groaned, thrusting his cock into Rowe's grip. "What do you need, babe?"

Rowe ran his thumb over the top of Noah's dick, feeling the slick pre-come. Noah sucked in a deep breath.

"Do that again," he whispered.

Rowe did and the strangled cry Noah released made Rowe latch on to his lower lip. He sucked it into his mouth, laved it with his tongue and suddenly, he knew exactly what he wanted. He let go, pushed Noah onto his back and crouched over the other man. Noah stared up at him, hair in wild disarray around his head, blue eyes dazed, mouth open as he breathed hard and fast.

Rowe couldn't look away for a long moment as something passed between them—something he'd felt between them in the past. It had sent him running then and a part of him felt that old rise of fear now. He shoved it back for now, planning to pull it out and explore it later. Instead, he moved down Noah's body, taking in the light smattering of chest hair over hard, sculpted muscles, the trail of darker hair under his navel. He stared at his cock. Noah was built thicker than him and he was so damned hard, the tip flushed red. Rowe's own dick jumped, his balls drew up and saliva filled his mouth.

Of all his most secret fantasies, this was the one he pulled out the most. Noah had taken him into his mouth all those years ago and he'd loved it so much—but he'd never reciprocated. He wanted to now. He leaned down and licked the bead of pre-come off the tip, tasting the similar bitter flavor of his own. Noah had gone still and he glanced up to find wide, blue eyes locked on him. He offered him a shaky smile. "I've never done this to someone before."

"You don't have to," Noah answered but the blatant need shining from his eyes said something entirely different.

"I do. And not just for you." He looked down as Noah's cock jerked. "I've waited years to do this to you."

"Oh God." Noah shut his eyes tight and dropped his head back to the bed. "It's going to be fast. Don't judge my manliness."

A smile cracked Rowe's mouth and he chuckled. Laughter during sex was something he'd always loved. Something he'd had with…pain slashed through him and he had to shut his own eyes. No, he couldn't think of her now. He opened his eyes and looked at Noah, who waited for him, who trusted him to pleasure him. It wasn't fair to this man underneath him. It took everything he had to push the memories of sex with his wife aside. What finally worked was leaning down and taking Noah into his mouth.

Faintly salty skin that was so fucking velvety slid along his tongue and he groaned and gripped the base with his fist. He licked, learning the grooves, the pulse of veins against his tongue, twisting his fingers in the saliva that dripped down—just the way he loved having done to him.

Noah yelled when he closed his lips and sucked. Yelled and grabbed the sides of his head. He didn't shove into his mouth and from experience, Rowe knew he wanted to, that the need to thrust hit hard when someone's warm mouth was wrapped around your dick. He appreciated the patience the other man showed, but he decided he didn't want Noah able to think at all, so he increased his suction and speed. Noah bucked and yelled again and Rowe felt the trembling in his thigh where he'd braced one hand. He sucked as he pulled to the end of Noah's prick, licked around the head and felt Noah's body tense below him.

Before he could go back down, Noah yanked him up, grabbed his own dick and cried out as he came all over his abdomen.

Rowe watched, fascinated, and so turned on he had to grab himself. He'd wanted to taste him, wanted to nuzzle his balls and explore, but like before, everything had moved fast. Noah laid there, sprawled out, covered in spunk and when he grinned, Rowe's chest tightened. "Thought maybe I'd give you more time before hitting your throat with all that. But just so you know, for a first timer, you rocked."

"I know what I like, so I did it to you."

"You are welcome to do everything you like to me. Anything you like." The seriousness of the words hit Rowe and he tightened his fingers and stroked himself.

Noah glanced down, watched the movement of his hand for a moment before he met his gaze again. "What do you want to do to me, Rowe?"

"What don't I want to do?" He chuckled but it was strangled and choppy because he was balanced on the edge of coming and just needed something, anything to send him over.

Noah tugged his arm, pulling him back up on top of him and that was all it took. The feel of all that hot skin against his and the slide of his cock through Noah's semen. He didn't even have time to be embarrassed as he cried out and spilled all over Noah's belly. He panted and stared at the mix of them both and it was the hottest fucking thing he'd ever seen.

"Fuck, Ward," Noah breathed. "Come here." He pulled him down for a kiss. This one was gentle and touching and Rowe felt that strange, inner jitteriness again as he softly kissed Noah's jaw before he rolled over to lie on his side next to him.

They were quiet as they looked at each other for long, long moments. Then Noah started to roll toward him and grimaced when he must have remembered what was all over his front. Chuckling, Rowe got up. "I'll get you a towel." He knew Noah watched his ass the whole way into the bathroom.

He turned on the water to let it warm and as he stared at his disheveled reflection in the mirror, memories of his wetting down towels for his wife hit him and he waited for the sword-slash of pain but it was only an ache this time. All he could think about was how much she would have enjoyed watching what he'd just done. He'd confessed his attraction to men before they ever married and they had in fact, bonded over a love of gay porn.

When Snow had once asked if he knew his wife liked it, he'd almost admitted that he was the one who'd signed them up for an online site, but he'd refrained. He never told them he suspected he was bisexual because once he'd fallen for Mel, he'd mostly put that aside. He never would have cheated on her, so watching porn and reliving memories of his night with Noah were his only outlet. And he'd been perfectly fine with that. He'd loved her with every fiber of his being and had been sexually fulfilled with her. And Mel would have never begrudged him a life beyond her.

He told himself that as he wiped his body clean, then wet down another towel for Noah. He walked back into the bedroom to find that Noah had flipped on a lamp and had been watching the bathroom door. The wariness in his eyes speared into Rowe because he wanted to see the joking, strong man he knew. The laughter and teasing helped to keep the growing panic at bay. Rowe forced a grin and tossed the warm towel at Noah, who caught it and slapped it over his belly.

"Thanks. That was getting cold." Blue eyes probed his as he dropped the dirty towel over the side of the bed. "You okay?"

Rowe didn't know how to answer that because his emotions were all twisted up in his throat, so he just smiled, but it was slipping off his lips almost as quickly as he could push it in place. He rested his hand on Noah's thigh. He ran his thumb along the soft hair there, completely unsure how to handle this after-sex situation with one of his best friends. He felt so out of his element, he couldn't find the right words.

Just last night Noah had talked about giving in to pleasure, that it didn't have to be more than that. But every laugh and touch and moan tangled up in his chest, like a length of twine tightening around his lungs so that he could barely drag in a breath. Could it ever be just pleasure with Noah? Could he really walk away from him after having such a shattering moment and not feel like he'd left behind a piece of his soul?

Fuck, did he even want to risk that? He was finally learning to function again after the loss of Mel so that he didn't feel like he was going to fall to pieces with every step. He couldn't risk his sanity, his heart, to another loss. Jagger wanted him dead and he would have no problem ripping through Noah just to get to Rowe. Oh God, he couldn't lose Noah.

"You need some time, don't you?" Noah asked softly.

He pretended he didn't see Noah's flash of pain when he nodded. And he hated himself for not saying anything as Noah stood and gathered his clothes. He didn't dress, just held them in front of his gorgeous, tall body and stared at Rowe for what felt like forever. Then, he gave him a half smile and said, "I really enjoyed that. See you in the morning."

He turned and left the room and Rowe sat in the same spot until he finally fell over with exhaustion. What the fuck was he doing?

Chapter 14

Noah stared at the ceiling of Rowe's guest room, listening to his friend move around the kitchen. Exhaustion pulled at every muscle, especially the big, blood-pumping one in his chest. He'd known all those years ago. He'd known that his attachment to Rowan Ward was stronger than any other he'd experienced. And he'd known the man could break him. Yet he'd been unable to resist coming here and yeah, he'd hoped for their friendship to move into this territory, but he should have been more wary.

He closed his eyes, once again recalling the vivid image of his dick sliding into Rowe's mouth. He turned and muffled his groan with his pillow.

Hottest damn thing ever.

It hadn't mattered that Rowe had no experience. He hadn't cared that he'd never done that before. No, that knowledge had made everything so much more intense. It had pulled deep emotion into the act and he'd been honored to be the first. He wanted to be the only. He'd watched himself moving in and out of that hot mouth and now he had trouble getting it out of his head.

The only thing to shove it aside was Rowe's expression as he left the room.

That had kept him up most of the night. Rowe's pain had hit him like a kick to the nuts, so his walk down the hall had felt more like a crawl. He hadn't known what to do, how to ease the pain and settle Rowe's mind. Noah had always felt strong enough, tough enough, to deal with anything that came his way, but he wasn't sure he could handle this. Rowe meant too much to him—it felt like he could be the other half of Noah's soul.

He forced himself to sit up and swing his legs out of the bed. He propped his head in his hands and stared at the hardwood floor. He should leave, but he wouldn't. Not when there was another chance of getting naked with Rowe. And definitely not when someone was attempting to kill him.

After a shower, he walked into the kitchen and felt his heart stutter at the sight of Rowe grinning at him from in front of the stove. The man wore a pair of black slacks and a loose gray sweater. He'd pushed the sleeves of the sweater up his thick forearms, his tattoo hidden. His auburn hair had been combed off his face and that fucking smile...the man was simply stunning. Noah held his breath, eyes locked on Rowe's mouth as his mind went right back to the image that had kept him up half the night. All he could think about was Rowe sinking to his knees now.

Rowe handed him a plate stacked with pancakes. He knew they were Noah's favorite thing to eat. Was this an apology?

"They probably taste like shit. I was short an ingredient."

"Thanks." Noah smiled, hating the nerves tearing through his body. He settled at the table, took a bite and it took a lot of effort to not grimace. He reached for the syrup. Lots of syrup.

Three minutes later, Rowe cracked up and dropped his fork. "Stop. This is worse than shit."

"It is." He spit his last bite into a napkin, chuckling. "I'm sure Ian could explain it better, but pancakes are a science. Pretty sure every ingredient has an important purpose."

"You would have sat there and ate all that, huh?"

Noah shrugged. "You made the effort to cook them for me."

Rowe stared at him for long, long moments, then dropped his gaze to his plate. More seconds passed before he finally spoke. "Are you going out with him again? You did say the kiss was nice."

He balled up his napkin and tossed it onto his plate, scowling. "Really? You think I'd do that after what happened between you and me last night?"

"No." Rowe grimaced. "But I honestly don't know what's happening with us. With me. Lots of things are confusing me."

"Rowe, look at me. Please."

Green eyes came up and locked on him and Noah felt a sense of relief to see that very real affection still shone there.

He leaned over the table, reached out and laid his hand over Rowe's arm. Warm skin, masculine hair...he stroked his hand over it. "Even if I was the kind of asshole to play friends against each other, I wouldn't be going out with Ian again. I like him. A lot. He's great. But there wasn't anything like that between us and we both realized it." *Because I'm nuts about you.* He kept that last part to himself.

Instead, he let go of Rowe, reached into the fruit bowl, grabbed a couple of apples and tossed one to Rowe. "Come on. I'm ready to start my first day working under you." He couldn't stop the wicked grin those words brought forth. And he was glad. They needed to reclaim friend territory. For now.

Rowe's eyes flew open wide. The heat that flared there raised an answering need in Noah. He stared, once again remembering that gorgeous mouth wrapped around his cock. Was Rowe taking his words literally? Imagining that? Stretched out on top of him, sliding those narrow hips between his legs…Noah had to close his eyes as desire tore through him like it would burst from his veins. Just the thought of letting Rowe inside his body had his knees shaking.

Rowe abruptly jumped up, grabbed the dishes and dumped the leftovers down the garbage disposal. He stacked the dishes in the plugged sink and ran water over them. "I'll do these later. Let's hit the road."

That awkward state stayed between them all the way to his office and throughout his introduction to the woman in Ward's HR department. Before he walked away, he dropped a heavy hand on Noah's shoulder and squeezed.

Noah watched him all the way down the walkway, the nasty pancakes a heavy lump in his stomach. He turned and went to fill out the paperwork, sure he was making a mistake the whole time.

"Hey, Noah."

He had just turned the paperwork in when Andrei spoke from the doorway. The man looked more sweaty and disheveled than he'd ever seen him. His white T-shirt had dark patches and his black basketball shorts clung to his muscled legs with moisture. Wet, black curls stuck to his cheeks. Either he'd been running miles or his last training session had been a bitch.

"You looking for a sparring partner?" Noah asked. "I could use the stress relief."

One dark eyebrow went up. "Your date last night didn't go as planned, I take it?"

Noah crossed his arms, surprised. "How'd you know about that?"

"You'll learn there is no keeping a secret in Rowe's family. And especially when it comes to Ian. Those men love him something fierce."

"He's lovable."

"So the date went really well, then?" Andrei chuckled. "Good for Ian. I could tell he liked you at Lucas's."

"Nah, it wasn't like that."

Andrei stared at him with probing dark eyes a long time before he nodded. "Fine then. I thought not. Come on. I'm supposed to give you a weapons training session."

Noah had barely enough time to sort through Andrei's apparent belief that he and Ian were a poor match before being slammed with the idea that he actually needed weapons training. He snorted. "We have met before, right? You know I've been in the Army all my adult life. Former Ranger even. There isn't a lot I don't know about weapons."

"Right?" Andrei shook his head. "I think it's Rowe who needs the stress relief. He nearly bit my head off."

Noah didn't know what to say to that, but his gut twisted up in knots because it was his fault Rowe wasn't dealing well with their situation.

Andrei suddenly grinned. "He didn't say what kind of weapons training. I got an idea."

Thirty minutes later, Noah whooped and held up his target. "This one won't be eating any more brains." He winked at Andrei through the hole his bullets had made through target's head. "I've never seen zombie targets."

"Rowe ordered them." Andrei pulled his in and pointed.

Noah cracked up when he saw the happy face right in its center mass. With weapons and targets in hand, they walked over to a weapons cleaning and storage area. Andrei quickly showed him how to mark the usage of ammo and the fact they were the last ones to use those particular guns before they started to clean their weapons.

"Have you worked for Rowe long?" Noah asked, his fingers moving over the metal with a practiced ease.

Andrei shook his head. A few stray tendrils slipped from where he'd pulled it back to crowd his eyes. "Just a few years. I was training to be a professional MMA fighter when I blew out my knee in the cage."

"Damn," Noah whispered, pausing to look at the younger man. Rowe wasn't the only one walking around the company with a dream-ending injury. "You couldn't come back from it?"

"Thought about it." Andrei paused for a minute, his long fingers tightening around the gun for a second. "But the injury would have been common knowledge. Every fighter would have been aiming for my bad knee for an easy takedown. One or two rough matches and the knee would get fucked up bad enough that I wouldn't be able to walk. Wasn't worth the risk. I was lucky Rowe found me. So instead of beating the crap out of people for a living, I'm protecting them."

"And beating the crap out of the people threatening your clients."

Andrei snorted. "Every job has its perks."

Noah matched his smile, feeling the last of the lingering tension ease from his shoulders. He liked talking to Andrei. The man had this easy-going nature to him, as if there wasn't much that could actually get under his skin. That kind of mellow demeanor helped him to push his worries about Rowe to the back of his brain.

"Do you ever miss it?"

Andrei looked over his shoulder at Noah as he slid home the lock for the weapons cage. "The cage?" He grinned and there was a little self-mocking in that look. "For the first year working here, yes. Every fucking second."

Noah chuckled. "But not now? What changed?" But even as the words left his mouth, he knew the answer. Andrei met Lucas.

"Found something that means more to me than being the best fighter in the world." Andrei turned and pushed back a stray, damp hair from his cheek. "Besides, Rowe lets me 'train' with the new recruits whenever I'm feeling restless."

A loud laugh jumped from Noah's throat. "Gee, thanks for the warning." A new tension crept into Noah's frame as he noticed that Andrei stood with his arms folded loosely over his wide chest, a speculative look in his eyes. He caught the bodyguard doing that a few times while at Lucas's penthouse, and each time it preceded something particularly insightful coming out of his mouth. The man was good at playing the role of the watchful guardian, sinking back into the shadows until you nearly forgot that he was there, but he was and he was taking in everything that happened around him. Noah wasn't sure he wanted to know what Andrei saw.

"You need to give him more time," Andrei said softly after nearly a minute of silence.

Noah didn't need to ask who Andrei was talking about and he didn't really want to know how Andrei even knew. For just a second, sympathy filled his dark brown eyes, showing Noah that he understood. And Andrei probably did. He couldn't imagine loving someone like Lucas Vallois was particularly easy.

"If I thought I had a real shot in hell with him, I'd give him the rest of my life."

Rowe swore under his breath and slammed the linen closet door shut. Out of fucking towels. Again. He sucked at housework. Sadly, he knew that he couldn't blame Mel's death on how things fell behind. She was never any better than him, and they'd had more than their fair share of arguments over the laundry, dishes, and…ugh, he shuddered to even think about it…the grocery shopping.

Unfortunately, he didn't notice that he was out of towels until he was already done with the shower—a shower that he'd spent the entire time trying to ignore his hard-on and the fact that Noah was just on the other side of the wall, naked in the guest bathroom shower. They'd struggled through some awkward small talk before Noah escaped for a shower before dinner.

When he wasn't imagining Noah standing under the hot spray, water rushing down the sleek muscled hills of his stomach, he was remembering last night and how much he'd loved the feel of Noah's dick in his mouth. It had been so warm and smooth and he'd loved the way it pulsed against his tongue.

He groaned and hit the tile with the side of his fist.

That memory didn't help at all.

He needed to get a handle on this shit. But first, he needed a goddamn towel.

Clenching his teeth as he stepped out of the steam-filled bathroom, Rowe quickly walked through his bathroom, cursing himself again for tossing the dry towel Noah had used into the laundry room that morning as if removing it would remove the memory of last night. The cold air chilled the drops of water racing down his body and dripping down his face from his hair. He paused at the bedroom door and pulled it open only a crack to peer down the hall.

The house was silent. No sign of Noah. No sign of the drooling trio either. Usually lined up outside the door, they kept their distance from the bathroom out of fear of a bath, but stayed close in the event of surprise food. Rowe took a second to roll his eyes at himself. He was sneaking naked and wet through his own home. It certainly wasn't like Noah had never seen him naked, but now just seemed like a bad time.

Steam still filled the guest bathroom and he smiled at the faint scent of peppermint. Before he could think about what he was doing, he plucked the white bottle off the shower shelf and brought it to his nose. His dick started filling with just one whiff.

This was getting out of hand.

He put the bottle back and snagged the last clean towel from under the sink before stomping back to his bathroom. He quickly finished drying off, brushed his hair, and slapped on some deodorant. Tightening the towel around his waist, Rowe frowned and forced himself to face his reflection in the partially fogged mirror. He was disappointed. Some small part of him had hoped for Noah to catch him hurrying naked through the house, to pin him against the wall and run his calloused hands over Rowe's wet skin.

"You're an idiot," Rowe muttered to his reflection. He was a mess and Noah was better off finding someone whose life wasn't a natural disaster.

Jerking open the bathroom door, Rowe stepped out, telling himself that he'd put on some clothes and pull his head out of his ass so that he could get their friendship back to familiar ground.

The lamp beside his bed clicked on and Noah grinned at him from where he was stretched out on his bed. He wore black sweats and a plain white T-shirt, his hair still damp from the shower. He'd pushed it behind his ears. Fuck, he was gorgeous. His hair probably smelled of that damned peppermint. All his plans flew the fuck out the window.

Noah cleared his throat and sat up. "I took the dogs out. They're currently crashed out in their beds in the living room." Blue eyes flicked down over his chest and stomach and his lids lowered when he reached Rowe's waist.

Rowe swallowed a curse as his dick jerked from where it was attempting to poke out from the towel. Heat crept up his neck, but he did nothing to try and hide it. What would be the point? It wasn't going anywhere until he did something about it.

"You acted like an ass today."

"I know," he answered quietly. "I don't know what to think about all this." He leaned against the doorjamb, crossed his arms. "There's so much going on and we need to figure out how to get to Jagger and—" he stopped and ran his fingers through his hair. "Damn, Keegan, what the hell are we doing?"

"We're just having some fun, Ward."

Something in his voice made Rowe look up. He sounded sincere but there was a thread of untruth or maybe fear in his voice and that worried him. Rowe was so new at all this, so emotionally locked up and the last thing he wanted to do was hurt Noah.

"This what you did with other guys? Just some fun?"

Noah lifted both of his eyebrows at Rowe, his grin growing. "I believe I remember you having some fun with women and not worrying about the next day."

"Is that what this is? What you want?" Yeah, he had plenty of one-night stands when he'd been single and young. But not once had he thought about what that person thought of him the next day. He never worried about whether the person was happy or whether she wanted to see the new Jason Statham flick at the theaters that weekend or what she wanted to eat for fucking breakfast. Rowe thought about all those things with Noah and more. "I'm terrified we're fucking up our friendship." Rowe took a step then stopped when Noah stood and crossed the room to him.

He shook his head, turned and pressed his forehead to the wood.

"Christ, you have a beautiful back." Noah's voice, husky and low, sent heat spiraling through Rowe. Hot, big hands cupped his shoulders, then smoothed down either side of his spine. "I love the way this tattoo wraps your shoulder and goes down part of your back. Makes me think about bending you over something and watching the muscles move underneath it." He kissed his shoulder. "I want to see it covered in sweat."

Rowe started to shake. That image didn't freak him out the way he thought it might. It sent a thrill through him that almost, *almost*, compared to what he felt when this man's hands were on him. The heat, the desire, shocked him. And *terrified* him. He closed his eyes as lips opened over the back of his neck. Shivers rippled over his skin as Noah kissed down the cord on the side of his neck, and opened his mouth on the muscle over his collarbone. Rowe shuddered, reached back to thread his fingers in that sinfully soft hair. He turned his head, met Noah's mouth, and began to drown.

So. Fucking. Good.

He didn't think about anything but the taste and feel of the man as he turned and cupped the other side of Noah's head. He ate at Noah's mouth, licking, biting and the other man groaned, reaching down to clench strong fingers on his hips. The towel fell and Noah slid his hands around to grip his ass and thrust against him. He kneaded the flesh and muscle, holding him tight to his body.

Rowe tore his mouth away to pull air into his starving lungs.

Noah didn't stop, his mouth moving down. He growled, turned and shoved Rowe onto the bed.

"Hey, now!" Rowe started to complain but all his words disappeared as Noah quickly stripped off his shirt and crawled over him, latching on to his nipple and biting down. He slid his hands back into that fall of hair and held on, gritting his teeth as pleasure ripped through him. Noah nudged his legs apart and settled between. His chest brushed against Rowe's groin, the hair rasping over his sensitive flesh. Rowe tilted his head back, loving the weight on him, the heat…the feel of his heartbeat against Rowe's dick. "Fuck, Noah!"

Noah didn't stop with that talented mouth. He bit into his pecks. "Love your tattoos," he murmured, running his tongue around the lines of black then kissing down his abs. He licked the head of Rowe's dick, then used strong suction to pull it into mouth, causing Rowe to cry out. Wet, tight, heat sent stars to flash behind his eyelids. He panted, doing everything he could not to thrust up hard into Noah's mouth. The man sucked him deep, rubbing his tongue over throbbing, sensitive flesh. The tip of his cock hit Noah's throat and he yelled again. "So good," he muttered. "It's so good."

He felt Noah moving his body against the bed and just the thought of him rubbing off on the comforter made him dizzy. He stroked his fingers through soft hair and over the stubble on Noah's jaw, running them around his lips to feel them stretched over his cock. Just knowing it was Noah sucking him did something crazy to him. Noah pulled off and pressed his lips to the tips of Rowe's fingers.

He looked up, mouth still on Rowe's fingers in a soft kiss that made Rowe's heart stutter. This was why it was different from every one-night stand and string-free fuck he'd ever had. Because it was Noah.

Blue gaze still locked with his, Noah sucked his finger into his mouth. All the air left Rowe's lungs and he couldn't stop staring. Noah let go of his finger, shuffled down and held his dick upright. It was so hard and red from all the attention. Still watching Rowe, he lowered his mouth around it again. His hair fell over one eye, brushed over the sensitive skin around the base of his cock, tangling in his pubic hair.

"Oh fuck," Rowe breathed. "Do it. Take it back in your mouth. Suck harder."

Noah grinned around his prick, then did what he asked, increasing the suction and the speed of his movements until Rowe couldn't breathe. When the air returned, all he could do was moan and thrust into that hot, hot cavern. Noah shifted on him and he felt the man rubbing on the bed again, only this time, his dick also rubbed against the side of his leg.

He couldn't believe how fucking hot he found that. Noah swallowed around the head of his cock and Rowe reached up to brace his hands on the headboard, stretching his head back, taking in the feel of Noah's mouth, Noah's body and all that slow, sexy movement. Noah cupped his balls, stroked his finger over his perineum and pressed and Rowe lost it. He shouted again as he erupted into Noah's mouth. He was only half aware of Noah swallowing and reaching down to grab his own dick. Hot semen hit his leg.

He lay there, stunned, his heart pounding so hard, he was afraid it was going to burst through his ribcage. Noah rested a cheek on his hip, also breathing hard. He had one hand on Rowe's thigh, his thumb moving in gentle strokes over the tender skin of his inner thigh.

Panic began to grow in his gut. A dark fist of pain that punched deep, then swelled and spread. He tamped it back, managed to lie next to Noah, who crawled up beside him and watched him quietly in the low light. Eyelids slowly covered blue eyes that saw too much while Rowe found all his words caught in that flow of pain. He couldn't do this. It was too much. Too fast. He was going to fuck it up. Going to lose Noah and just the barest hint of this man not being in his life the next day sucked all the air from his lungs.

When Noah fell asleep, Rowe quietly got up, grabbed a pair of sweats off his dresser and left the man sleeping in his bed.

Chapter 15

"Noah?"

He turned onto his back and blinked into the darkness. Several days had passed and they'd fallen into a pattern. He hung around with Rowe at work, even staying late like they had tonight when this blond mountain named Sven brought in takeout. They'd talk, crack jokes, laugh—just like they always had even if there was a new tension to it. And then when they returned home, somehow it would start. A look. A stray touch. Fuck, half the time Noah didn't have a clue what it was that set them off. He only knew that he had to be touching Rowe and he had to have Rowe's hands on him. But once their frantic passion was spent…Rowe was gone.

Tonight though, Noah had needed a break. Or…he'd felt that Rowe did. So, he'd turned in early to give his friend space. The pinched look hadn't left his face in two days.

"Noah?" Rowe repeated. He sounded gutted. Lonely.

Noah's heart sped up as he waited for whatever Rowe had to say, but he stayed silent.

Rowe stood next to his bed, wearing nothing more than a pair of boxers—Noah couldn't see their color in the darkness. Moonlight spilled through the open curtains, caressing the muscles of Rowe's chest, highlighting the intricate black lines and swirls that wrapped his shoulder and impressive bicep. The desire and need in his expression ripped into Noah.

Even as he knew his heart was going to break, he lifted the covers.

Rowe tugged off his boxers and crawled underneath. His mouth found Noah's in the darkness with unerring accuracy. He plastered his lips and his hard, muscled body against Noah's fast. He lowered the covers, cocooning them together underneath. Rowe slid one thigh between his legs and rolled on top of him. He moaned as he settled between Noah's legs and Noah swallowed the noise, held him close.

The most carnal sound escaped Rowe's mouth as he tentatively thrust against Noah, his naked body pressing into Noah's sweatpants.

He wanted to be naked so badly.

Thrusting his tongue into Rowe's mouth, Noah felt fire streaking through his veins and he gasped. Rowe's body was like a furnace and he spread his legs more, bucking up against him. He wrapped his legs around him and shuddered, reveling in the way Rowe's body started to shake as his thrusts became harder, more rhythmic. Their cocks rubbed together and Noah gasped, twisting his mouth to the side. "You gotta take off my pants."

"Yeah," Rowe breathed. He scrambled back to his knees and tugged Noah's pants off his hips. He had to move to the side to get them off both Noah's legs. He dropped them off the side of the bed and ran his hands over Noah's calves, up over his knees and slowly, slowly up the insides of his thighs. Moonlight flashed on his teeth when he shot Noah a wicked grin and came back over him.

"Oh fuck, you feel good." Noah opened his legs, cradled all Rowe's wonderful naked flesh against him. "What do you want to do?"

"Anything. Everything. I'm sorry I—" Rowe kissed his neck, latching on to the sensitive spot right under Noah's ear. "I just can't stay away." He nuzzled his jaw and brought their mouths back together. His tongue stroked into Noah's mouth and he chuckled when Noah groaned loudly into his mouth. He pulled back, balanced on one elbow as he threaded his fingers through Noah's hair. "I like it long like this. It's soft. Fucking love the peppermint shampoo you use." He kissed his chin. "I always thought it would be awkward."

Noah smiled, his heart pounding to find Rowe moving a little slower. More willing to talk for the first time in days, as if Rowe had missed him. "What would be?"

"To be with another man like this. I did wonder. All the way back in high school, I wondered what it would be like but I never tried—not when it felt good being with girls. I always thought it was more like curiosity until I met you." He rolled his hips into Noah's and his cock slipped down in the groove where his leg met his body. Sweat from their bodies made Rowe slide easily against him. "Oh fuck," he whispered, moving his hips faster.

"Do you want to fuck me, Rowe?"

"You do that? I always sort of thought—"

Noah grasped a handful of Rowe's tight ass and rubbed right back against him. "You thought what? That I only top?"

"Yeah. I'm not sure why, though. Just a feeling."

"I like it both ways." He stopped moving his hips, let go of Rowe's ass and reached up with both hands to cup his face. "It would probably be better if you topped first. It's what you're used to."

A strange expression passed over Rowe's face, but he only nodded.

"Rowe," Noah whispered. "We don't have to do anything that you're not ready for. There are lots of ways to get off."

"That's the thing, Noah. I don't just want to get off. I want you. I want on you and inside you and even under you." He pressed their mouths together, turning his head so their lips slid perfectly into place before he sucked Noah's bottom lip between his teeth. "Wish I'd pulled you into my room, though. I have supplies there. Bought them when I went out to lunch today."

The knowledge that Rowe had anticipated this between them drove him crazy and Noah growled and rolled them over so he could reach his duffle on the floor. He rummaged around inside with one hand blindly as Rowe sucked on his neck and rubbed his cock on Noah's hip. "Shit, Ward, hold on a sec. You're making me blind."

"Good because I'm already there. Hurry up!"

The laughter was welcome. It was such a part of their relationship, the very core of it, that it felt natural to have this between them along with the passion. And the passion. Fuck, intense didn't come close to the fire lit inside his body. His ass already clenched in anticipation of having all that raw sexuality unleashed on him and inside him. He finally found the box of condoms and the lube and he rolled them back to where they were, spreading his legs, cradling Rowe against him. On his back, his hands were free and he ripped into the box, got a condom and ripped open the package with his teeth.

"Yeah, I may be new at doing this myself, but I've watched it enough on video and heard enough from my big-mouthed friends to know we have to get you ready." Rowe pulled back, kissing down his chest.

Noah's eyes rolled back in his head when Rowe latched onto a nipple and sucked. At the same time, he stroked his palm down Noah's stomach, dancing his fingers along his abs.

"So fucking sexy," he breathed, following the same path with his mouth. He wrapped his lips around Noah's dick and sucked it deep into his mouth.

"Oh man, you are getting so good at that." He wanted to tell him to stop, that he wanted to feel the man inside him but Rowe rubbed his tongue on the head and he lost his ability to think. He could only feel the warm, wet heat, the vibration of Rowe's moan as he let Noah's cock slide close to his throat. When a lubed finger started rubbing around his hole, Noah gasped as every muscle in his body tightened and he bowed up off the bed.

"Yeah," Rowe breathed on a long moan as he licked Noah's hip and slowly opened him up.

The man knew what he was doing and Noah didn't want to ask how, didn't want to make him think of anyone or anything else. He only wanted that sharp, lovely mind on him and on his body. He writhed under Rowe's ministrations, reaching down to thread his fingers in Rowe's hair. It was silkier than it looked and he loved the feel of it between his fingers. He had to force himself not to thrust up when Rowe licked the head of his cock before coming back up his body. He stopped on his other nipple, licking and biting.

"I fucking love how responsive you are. To everything." Rowe rubbed his chest over Noah's, whispering into his neck. "Tell me your favorite things."

"Can't. Think." Noah turned and took Rowe's mouth in a hungry, desperate kiss. "More. Put your fingers in me deeper."

Rowe groaned and pulled his mouth back to kiss his shoulder as he worked his fingers deeper.

He realized Rowe wasn't tall enough to kiss him and slide his fingers deep and the strangest sort of protective feeling squeezed his heart. This strong, tough man wouldn't want to be protected, but he would want to be needed. No, he needed to be needed and as Noah nuzzled into the soft, red hair on Rowe's head, he knew that what he did with Rowe had everything to do with need.

And with love.

Ian had been right. Noah loved Rowe and he had for years. It was why it had nearly killed him when Rowe got shot, then disappeared. And it was why he'd stayed mostly out of his life when he'd heard about Melissa. Rowe's marriage had broken his heart. He'd almost come here when he'd heard of her death, but he'd waited, forcing himself to stay away, to not show up like some vulture. And then, when he'd realized how alone he was and how much he just plain missed Rowe, he hadn't been able to keep himself away. He hadn't expected this, but he had hoped.

Rowe added a third finger and Noah gritted his teeth. It had been a long time since he'd let anyone in his body.

"You okay?" Rowe asked. Moonlight spilled over his face, making his eyes shiny as he stared at Noah. He stilled the movement of his hand, but he still panted, still rubbed his cock against Noah's hip, almost as if he couldn't help it.

"More than okay," Noah answered. He reached down and wrapped his fingers around Rowe's dick, his heart slamming hard against his ribs when a hoarse cry escaped Rowe's mouth. He squeezed his hand, stroked the silky, hot skin. "Find the condom. I want you inside me now."

Rowe nodded, groped around the bed and actually growled before he stretched out and flipped on the small lamp on the nightstand. He blinked into the light, scanning the bed, found the condom and quickly put it on. Noah had to squint as he watched him. Rowe had the pale skin of a redhead and the flush of desire stood out on his chest and around the tattoo on his shoulder. His hair stood up in tufts on his head, his lips were swollen and soft-looking from all the kissing. His toned, muscled body came over Noah's and he could only stare up at him in awe. He was fucking gorgeous.

Hot, slightly sweaty skin rose over his. Rowe groaned and slid against him, his hand stroking over the light matt of hair on Noah's chest. "I think my heart is going to come out of my chest. I want you so fucking bad. Do you like it like this? On your back? Or do you want to turn over?" Rowe rocked against him.

"God Noah, I can't believe how good you feel, how hard you make me."

Noah pulled one leg back. "Come on. Now."

Rowe guided himself to Noah's entrance and slowly pushed inside. "Oh, oh, fuck!" he breathed, his head going back, the muscles in his arms flexing as he held himself up. He rocked in farther, pulled out and thrust back in, another sexy as hell noise coming from his throat.

Unable to pull his gaze from the man above him, Noah let the pleasure roll through him. He stretched up and placed his lips on the healing gash on Rowe's shoulder before pulling back. Rowe went still a moment, eyes wide open and locked with his. Then he smiled as Noah lifted his hips, groaning at the stretch of his body around Rowe's. Rowe thrust hard and hit his prostate, wringing a cry from Noah.

"Oh yeah, that's the spot." The sexy as hell grin that peeked through the pleasured expression had a wicked cast that made Noah's toes curl. Rowe relentlessly aimed for that place inside Noah and it didn't take long for Noah to writhe underneath him, clutching his hard, slim hips as they rammed against him. He lifted up and pressed his lips to Rowe's, loving the way the man opened for him. Their tongues tangled together as Rowe's hips slowed and he pressed deep inside Noah. He lowered himself completely onto Noah and the fluid roll of his hips as he moved in and out was the sexiest thing Noah had ever seen or felt.

He wrapped his arms around that muscled back and opened his mouth over Rowe's jaw. Rowe stretched back, giving him access and he sucked warm flesh into his mouth and picked up the pace of his hips. Rowe suddenly wedged one hand between them and wrapped it around Noah's cock and that one touch was all it took to send him over the edge. He shouted as his orgasm hit so hard and fast, his vision blacked out. He clamped down on Rowe's dick.

"Fuck!" Rowe yelled as he thrust a couple more times before going rigid as he released inside Noah. "So hot. So damn hot." He collapsed onto Noah, kissing him over and over. "I had no idea it would feel like that. You felt…fuck, that felt incredible." He pulled back, breathing hard, his expression suddenly serious. "You're good?"

Noah gave him a slow, sleepy grin. "More than good."

When Rowe sat up, obviously intending to start the cleanup, Noah shook his head and reached into his duffle for a T-shirt. He used it to wipe himself up, watching as Rowe tied off the condom. He stuck it in the shirt, dropped both on the floor and held out his arm. "Come back."

Rowe laid back against him and Noah couldn't stop himself from burying his mouth in that soft, red hair. He held him close and thought about what they should talk about but the exhaustion from his sleepless night before—from the months of accumulated fatigue—hit him and he tightened his arm around Rowe. Right before he dropped off, he felt Rowe leave a kiss on his jaw and climb out of the bed.

That woke him up. He pretended to sleep and watched through slitted eyes as Rowe picked up his boxers, stared down at him for a few moments before he walked around to turn off the lamp.

The stark confusion in his expression kept Noah up for hours again.

Daisy waited outside Noah's door and followed Rowe as he walked to his room and pulled on jeans and a sweatshirt. He found the Rottweilers passed out in the living room, so he snagged a warm throw blanket and quietly let Daisy outside with him. She seemed content to sit beside him, so he didn't bother throwing her ball. Instead he wrapped the blanket around his shoulders, sat in a lawn chair, and stared at the stars.

His mind was blown.

That had been incredible. Everything they did together was. Just like it had been before. And he'd attributed it to being drunk and excited over the newness of feeling a man's mouth around his dick. But it hadn't been. Rowe was into this and he wasn't an idiot. It had everything to do with the man. Not just any man would make him feel this way. What he'd felt for Noah all those years ago had been strong and he'd just walked away from him, then later set those feelings aside, perfectly happy while with his wife.

He missed her. So fucking much. Rubbing a hand over the pain in his chest, he shut his eyes and he could see her smiling at him as clearly as if it had just happened a second ago and not nearly a year. He did feel guilt for enjoying himself so much with Noah. Couldn't help it. But it wasn't the searing kind he'd expected and it was that more than anything else that kept making him crawl out of the warm bed with Noah. He felt like he should feel guiltier, but the emotions tearing him up had a lot more to do with an older guilt—for walking away from Noah. And then…there was the fear. Fear of getting close again. Opening himself up to that possibility of loss again.

He thought of Melissa and how she'd react to his situation. She'd be eager to hear everything that he'd experienced, everything that he'd felt. She'd lean forward, that wide grin splitting her beautiful face. Laughter filling her eyes. She'd prod him for all the dirty details and tease him when he finally blushed. They'd shared everything—the good and the terrible—over the years and it just seemed cruel that she wasn't there with him at that moment so she could hear about Noah. And as twisted as it sounded, he felt like she'd understand.

She could help him make sense of the emotions blowing his mind that had nothing at all to do with regret and everything to do with shock. And hard realizations. He liked being with Noah. No, he loved it.

But that kiss on his shoulder. It had been so tender and something Mel had done often when he'd been hurt on the job. He'd had a flash of loving Noah and losing him, too. Because it had felt so good being inside the man, he'd been able to shove that feeling aside, but it had hit him hard as Noah fell asleep—his strong arm wrapped tightly around Rowe.

He didn't know what to think or if what he was doing was making everything worse. All he knew for sure was that if Noah stayed, he would never be able to keep his hands off him. And that he was terrified to love him.

With his elbows on his knees, Rowe dropped his head into his hands and squeezed his burning eyes shut. "What the hell am I doing, Mel?"

Chapter 16

They were driving each other crazy and it was only a matter of time before one of them finally exploded. Attempting to work together was fast becoming ridiculous and he'd been at Ward Security for less than a week. Rowe had stuffed him into training for three days and then shoved him behind a computer—as if Noah knew a damn thing about hacker tech bullshit. He was happy when he didn't lock himself out of his own fucking email most days.

He belonged in the field. He had more than a decade of experience as an Army Ranger. He knew how to protect himself and others. But every time he tried to broach the subject with Rowe, the man muttered something and brushed it aside with some nonsense about meetings. There was a small voice in his brain saying that Rowe was just trying to keep him safe, which would have been touching if Noah wasn't insulted about Rowe's lack of faith in his skills.

The only time they seemed to be getting along was when they were in bed together. That had been absolutely brain melting, but lasted only until Rowe slid out of bed, leaving Noah feeling cold and alone.

When they'd gotten up to another awkward breakfast that Friday, Noah did the only thing he could think of to save their friendship: he lied. He made up some nonsense about needing to run some errands, buy clothes, get a new driver's license, health care, whatever. By the time, he finally stopped rambling, he was sure Rowe didn't actually believe him, but Rowe easily agreed to the day off. It gave them both the space they needed to get their heads on straight.

But now he was in Rowe's house, alone with only the dogs, and he realized that he wished he was in the office so he could hear the other man's voice or pop his head in Rowe's office randomly just to make him laugh. He was becoming pathetic.

With clothes in the washer and dryer, Noah bummed around Rowe's house, trying to figure out what to do with himself. He thought about checking his email, but the only ones he'd ever really looked forward to had come from Rowe. He had a few friends who occasionally wrote, so he'd have to plug in his laptop at some point. If it still worked. He'd knocked it around a lot.

He poked through the house, but there wasn't a lot to look at. Everything was functional and utilitarian. There weren't any personal knickknacks anywhere in the house and it made his heart ache. It was like Rowe had just been existing. Though, he had no room to talk. He hadn't had a real home in longer than he could remember. Not since he'd lived with his grandmother. His parents had been killed just after his eighth birthday and he'd been sent to Alabama where he'd pretended to be someone else all throughout high school. He'd loved his grandmother and had always felt welcome with her, but he'd never told her he was gay. He'd been too afraid of losing her love and of disappointing her. So, he'd had a home—but it hadn't been an honest one. The day he'd left the Army, he'd vowed to live the rest of his life honestly.

And here he was having sex with the one man he wanted above all others and he wasn't being completely honest with him. If he were, he'd tell him how he really felt.

After finding a huge pile of dirty clothes in Rowe's bathroom, he settled in to wash those along with his own. In between shuffling loads from the washer to dryer, he reacquainted himself with music on his new guitar. He'd once had dreams of being a songwriter, but lyrics had never come easily to him. The music did, though. He could play the guitar and the piano and he yearned for the day he had a stable place where he could have access to a piano as well. He'd never understood why, but when he picked up an instrument, it was like his brain came to life, electricity sparking and firing him up with creativity. He could see the notes in his head. There had been no time for music in the service and he planned to make it more a priority from then on out. He told himself it was better late than never and he spent the afternoon strumming chords and writing them down.

He hadn't played in a long time, but his fingers returned to the chords with a familiarity that felt more like home than anything in his life had in a long, long time.

Kind of like the way Rowe felt.

This past week with him had been the hottest time of Noah's life. But it was fast becoming the hardest as well. This morning's awkward breakfast conversation had been over yet another cooked apology from Rowe. This time something that resembled waffles but leaned more toward the cardboard food group. Rowe really shouldn't be allowed to cook.

His face burned as he remembered why Rowe had felt he owed him an apology and he quickly shoved that thought aside and instead lost himself in the music. One of the Rottweilers, Igor, he thought, seemed to love the music more than the others as he sat and tilted his head back and forth, making Noah grin. He was growing as attached to Rowe's dogs as he was the man himself.

Though if he were to stick with that honesty thing, he'd cared about Rowe a lot more than he'd fully realized or even accepted, for a long time. He'd actually been planning to visit Rowe years before while on leave and had bought plane tickets. He'd never used them because he'd gotten an email about Rowe's wedding. A fucking wedding.

He'd blurred the pain of that time in his memories, but he remembered being reckless and instead of using his plane tickets to see his friend, he'd picked up a guy and spent the next week in a sleazy motel, trying to forget he'd been stupid enough to fall for his best friend. All he'd gotten from the experience had been shame, regret, and the knowledge that sex with anyone other than Rowe didn't compare. And Rowe had been happily married. To a woman.

So what was he doing now? Setting himself up for the kind of heartbreak he might not come back from...

Shaking his head, he set the guitar down and put the last load of their combined clothes in the dryer. He took the rest to the couch, folded and set it inside a basket he'd found on top of the dryer. All the sleepless nights caught up to him and he stretched out on the couch, chuckling when Igor came and rested his head on Noah's leg. He really loved this dog.

He wasn't sure what woke him but when he opened his eyes, it was to find Rowe sitting on the coffee table watching him. He wore dark jeans and a brown blazer over a white button-down shirt. And ridiculously big construction boots. Noah grinned, forgetting all about the awkwardness of their morning.

"Fucking dimples," Rowe muttered as he touched Noah's cheek.

Noah lifted an eyebrow. "How was your day, dear?" His vocal chords sounded like they were coated with sand. He blinked at the darkness of the rooms beyond this one. He'd slept a lot longer than he'd planned. He hadn't come close to catching up on needed sleep since he'd been here.

Chuckling, Rowe kept his green gaze locked on Noah as he unlaced his boots and left them on the floor. He dropped the jacket on the table, then put one knee on the couch and turned Noah onto his back. He stretched out on top of him and instead of the kiss Noah expected, he crossed his arms on Noah's chest and propped his chin on them. He also nestled his jean-clad legs between Noah's bare ones. "I like finding you half naked on my couch. You think it's summer or something? Where's your shirt?"

"In the dryer with the rest of my things. These shorts are yours. I was out of clean clothes." Noah wrapped his arms around that tight, stocky body, touched that Rowe was openly cuddling him.

Rowe nestled his hips closer to Noah's and Noah knew good and well Rowe could feel him hardening against him. The loose basketball shorts weren't much of a barrier. Still, he didn't act. Noah brought one hand around and touched Rowe's hand and then immediately wished he hadn't because the memory from the night before slammed into him, causing heat to crawl up his neck. From the apology that filled Rowe's expression, he was remembering it, too.

Noah had humiliated himself by tightening his hold on Rowe's hand as he'd climbed from his bed… again. All the nights before he'd managed to pretend to be asleep, but last night he couldn't do it anymore. He needed that connection with Rowe. Yes, he'd said that it was just about fun and pleasure, but he'd been so fucking wrong. There was more between them and at times he was sure that Rowe was feeling it too. Yet, each night he'd walk away and it was like Rowe was deftly slicing away bits of his heart.

Prickly pain tightened the muscles in his chest and he wished he could go back and keep himself from giving into the need that was starting to threaten the tremulous relationship they were building. There was a lot of heat—unbelievable heat—but Rowe was keeping a part of himself separate and whether Noah liked it or not, it hurt. Hurt on a level he was all too familiar with because he'd felt the same twice before and both times had come from things Rowe had done. The second being his marriage.

Noah closed his eyes, his tongue frozen in his mouth because he didn't know what to say, how to breach the gap he could feel between them despite skin-on-skin contact. This back and forth passionate, tender, then remote Rowe was an emotional wrecking ball.

Rowe abruptly braced his hands on either side of Noah and stood. He ran his hands through his hair. "Sorry. I had a bad fucking day. Got called out on an emergency this morning that took forever and Gidget didn't get any further with her digging. It's like Jagger has better hackers working for him or something."

He paced across the room and back and when he looked back at Noah, the shields had gone back up in front of his eyes. "Did you eat? Andrei picked up burgers for us at work. He does that a lot when Lucas goes out of town."

And just like that, the awkwardness of earlier returned like an unwelcome relative. Noah sat up and snagged the brown throw off the back of the couch so he could cover up the hard-on that hadn't had time to go down. He felt like all the air had solidified in his chest. He watched as Rowe cleared his throat and again ran his fingers through his hair, sending all those beautiful red strands up and all over the place. "Do you want to invite him over?"

Rowe shook his head. "He filled in for Sven in some of the training classes and said he had a date with Lucas's big tub." He started toward the kitchen then abruptly stopped and stared down at the basket of clothes. He reached down and picked up a pair of socks, his gaze locked on them like he'd never seen them before. "You fold your socks like this?"

There was something in his voice that sent alarm skittering through Noah's entire system. He stood, the throw falling to the floor. "I do. But those are your socks."

When that taut body started to shake, Noah rushed toward Rowe, but his friend turned and the thunderous expression on his face stopped Noah in his tracks. "You did my fucking laundry? Why? You're not here to take care of me." He held up the socks that Noah had folded over at the openings instead of rolling them into balls the way he'd seen Rowe do it in the past. "And you fucking folded my socks like this?" His voice actually broke on the last word.

Noah stood still as a dark confusion filled his legs with lead. "Rowe?" he asked quietly.

"This is wrong. All wrong."

Daisy trotted up to Rowe, wagging her tail, her eyes locked on the socks and that's when Rowe made the most horrific, strangled noise in his throat. He dropped the socks and stormed out the front door.

Noah could only stand there, stunned. He had no idea what had just happened.

Chapter 17

Rowe stopped his truck at a red light and pounded the heel of his hand on the steering wheel. The knot of pain in the middle of his stomach took up too much space, making it hard to breathe. The last argument he'd had with Mel had been about the way she folded his socks—the exact way Noah had. Seeing the rows of his socks on top of the rest of his folded laundry had twisted up his guts. He liked them rolled all the way into balls and she said they fit better in the drawer her way. She was right, but he'd been stubborn. Over something so fucking small.

And now, he had lost it over that small thing. With Noah, who'd looked completely stunned. He had no excuse for acting the way he had. None. He kept seeing the anguish that had flashed in Noah's eyes before he'd slammed out of his house. He worried that image would burn a permanent brand inside him.

Damn. He hated hurting him.

But he also hated feeling like this. All twisted up and confused. Hot one minute and breaking into a cold sweat the next. This...thing with Noah scared the shit out of him. He'd had passion like this with only two people in his lifetime and the first time had been years ago with Noah. They'd burned up the sheets just one night and it had left him feeling so confused, he hadn't known how to handle it. Later, he'd met Mel and been deliriously happy. He'd loved her with all his heart. Fuck, he'd loved her. And it had nearly killed him to lose her.

He could love Noah just as much. He knew it.

The terror that sliced through his chest stole his breath. He needed to figure out what to do. He needed...he didn't know what the fuck what.

When he spotted the turn off for Newport, he knew exactly what he needed. A friend. He called and made sure Snow was home. It was time to come clean and get some blunt advice and the doc would be perfect.

Snow had recently purchased a home with his partner. Rowe supposed partner was a better word for Jude because boyfriend and Snow were two words that just seemed ridiculous together. Those two would no doubt end up married and honestly, Rowe was surprised they hadn't run off and gotten hitched. He supposed that had a lot to do with Jude's mother. And Ian. Hell, their younger friend had started planning a wedding for Lucas and Andrei before Jude had even sauntered into their world. For the longest time, Rowe had believed he'd be the only one of them to get domesticated.

The memory of Mel's laugh washed through him, numbing his fingers on the wheel. He'd never stop missing her. He wished he could shoot Dwight Gratton all over again.

Rowe headed toward the river and parked his truck in the empty house's driveway next door to his friend's place. He didn't want to block Jude when he got home. The houses along this street were part of a new development and Snow had been the first to snap one up before the flooring had even been chosen. Rowe didn't blame him. He was closer to the water this time and the place was really gorgeous—a bricked A-frame cottage with a wrap-around porch in the back and side. It wasn't nearly as big as Snow's last place, but that had been ridiculous. What single man needed three floors? The new house had enough room for kids, though, should they choose to have them.

That thought no longer shocked him. It cracked him up. Snow as a father. He'd always been fiercely loyal, protective toward his friends, especially Ian, and quick to dole out whatever force was needed in a situation. But he also loved just as fiercely. He'd make a great dad.

Rowe shook his head and opened the truck door. A strong gust of November wind hit him as he climbed down. With the recently cleared land across the road, there wasn't a lot to block it. He shivered and hurried to the front porch.

Snow opened the door before he knocked. He looked comfy in his loose, faded jeans, a red T-shirt and thick, white socks. Damn socks. Rowe frowned.

"It's that kind of visit, huh? Come in."

Snow had changed since he'd been with Jude. He still had the wicked sense of humor, could still be a complete ass at the drop of a hat, and he certainly didn't give a crap about proper social subjects—not that Rowe had ever cared either. But he smiled a hell of a lot more than he used to. He grinned now as he grabbed the beer Rowe had stopped to pick up and walked toward the kitchen.

Rowe paused to admire the wide, wooden staircase at the end of the entry. The house had two floors, all covered in dark hardwood. The walls, a warm beige stucco, complimented the exposed dark wood beams lining the living room and kitchen. The doors all over the house as well as the cabinetry in the kitchen were the same color and some of the doorways had black trim. The combination gave the entire home an elegant yet comfortable feel and it suited the men who called it home.

Snow grabbed a couple of beers, then set them on the island in the kitchen. "Hungry? Jude and I found this cool place with imported meat and cheeses. Some of this shit is amazing."

"I'm not hungry." Rowe jumped when something squeaked and scampered past his feet. "What the hell?" Rowe squatted and peered at the amber eyes peeking at him from the side of the island. "You got a cat. You."

"I know." Snow sighed. "I've obviously lost my mind. We went to lunch in Covington last weekend and Jude couldn't resist this little girl giving away kittens on the street."

"And you can't resist Jude. For shame, Doc. You're nothing but mush these days."

"Shut the fuck up."

The gray and black cat inched closer and made a high-pitched mewling noise that pierced Rowe's ears. He held out his hand, sure the creature wouldn't come close to him because he had to smell like his dogs. "What's its name?"

"It's a boy." Snow mumbled something after that.

"What did you say?" Rowe stood, unable to stop the welcome laugh building in his chest.

"Jude named that damn thing Sergeant. He thinks he has a sense of humor."

The laughter escaped. He couldn't help it because he'd repeatedly heard Jude refer to Snow as General. Personally, he thought the nickname fit the surgeon to a T. He'd seen him shouting orders in the ER a time or two.

"It's not funny." Snow came around the bar and handed Rowe a beer. The tiny kitten trotted to him and leapt, claws attaching to Snow's jeans. "Ow! Shit!" He set his beer back on the island and used both hands to pry the kitten gently off his leg. He held it up to his face and it mewled again. He shook his head and set it back on the floor. It immediately curled up on his sock-clad foot. He nudged it off and nodded toward the arched doorway into the living room. He strolled to the couch and folded one leg beneath him on one end. "Come on. Tell me what's wrong."

"Why do you think something is wrong?"

"Because you have a friend staying with you and you're over here. And from your expression, you're either upset or seriously constipated. Sit."

Rowe kicked off his shoes and sank into the soft gray couch. He chuckled over Snow's description, remembering when he'd used the exact same phrase with Noah at IHOP. Now that he was here, he didn't know what to say, how much to share. He stared at Snow, who stared steadily back with light blue eyes. He couldn't miss the worry Snow didn't bother to hide. It was the way his friends had been looking at him for nine months and he didn't blame them. His heart ached for the comfortable comradery he'd shared with them for most of his adult life. Around seventeen years of friendship with only a few of those away from them. The three he'd spent with Noah. And Noah was sitting back at his house feeling pain that Rowe had caused.

He picked at the label on his beer. He was shit.

"Why do I get the feeling I should be pulling down the harder stuff for this?"

Nodding slowly, Rowe set the beer on the coffee table. "You probably should."

Snow sat up straight. "Seriously? What's wrong? Was there another fire?"

"No. I mean, yeah, there was. But that's not why I'm here."

"There was another fire?"

"At the Lyntons' place. Andrei was there checking last-minute security for a party they were supposed to have."

"I hadn't heard. I've been pulling extra shifts and had to miss their party." Snow grimaced. "Lucas let him out of the house since?"

"Lucky for me, Lucas is out of town for a couple of days. But he needs to loosen the reins a bit on my COO. Can't imagine putting up with that bullshit."

"COO?"

Nodding, he picked his beer back up. "Yeah, he did a great job the last few months while I've been—" He cleared his throat. "Well, you know what I've been."

Snow nodded.

Rowe jerked in surprise when the kitten suddenly plastered itself on his jeans and started to climb. "Holy hell, its tiny claws are like needles!"

"He's not big enough to jump that high yet. We're all potential ladders."

Rowe pulled the animal off his leg and sat it on the couch between them. It sniffed at his hand a couple of moments before trotting over to Snow to paw at the hand he had resting on his thigh. He watched, surprised as Snow played with it. "You are truly and thoroughly domesticated. It's disgusting."

"Told you to shut up." Snow winced and pulled his hand away from the kitten.

"You're happy, Snow. Really happy. It's nice."

Snow gave him a long, steady look, concern pinching the corners of his mouth. "It is."

"I'm glad, Doc." He looked down at his beer. "So, I've been sleeping with Noah." He peeked at his friend to find him staring with his jaw hanging loose.

Snow slowly set his beer on a coaster on his coffee table. He nearly missed it because he hadn't looked away from Rowe. Without a word, he got up and left the room. There were rummaging noises in the kitchen and when he returned, he held a plate with a knife and a lime. He snagged a bottle of tequila and two shot glasses on the way.

Rowe opened his mouth but Snow held up his hand. "Just...wait." As he cut the lime into wedges, he shook his head. "Just fucking dropped that out of your mouth, you ass. I knew. I knew!" He stopped and pointed his finger.

"You knew what?"

"I knew you had interest. I've seen it. Plus all the gay porn."

"Hey now, no judgement, remember? Besides, what was all that bullshit you spouted about what turns us on versus action or something like that? More crap that just falls out of your mouth?"

"That stuff was true, yeah, but according to Melissa, you bought the movies and even signed up for an online subscription, too. That's different."

"You're so full of shit. And she told you that?" He knew that Snow and Melissa had been close. Hell, she'd been close to Ian, too. They probably missed her nearly as much as he did and if the harsh slash of Snow's lips said anything, he was thinking about her now. "So now you're saying that straight men can't enjoy gay porn?"

Snow closed his eyes a moment. "No. Shit…Ward, the world is not so fucking black and white and you know it. Everyone has their thing. Look at me. I spent most of my adult life mired in some kinky shit and now—"

"Now you're all vanilla and boring."

He snorted. "Yeah, no. Vanilla we are not. And there is nothing boring about sex with Jude." He pointed the knife at Rowe. "Don't distract me. I want to know what exactly is going on and why you look so upset about it." He set the knife down and handed Rowe a lime and a shot glass of alcohol. "I have the weekend off and you're going to take tomorrow off now. So drink up."

"I don't need to be shitfaced to talk about this." He thought about that look on Noah's face again. "I'm really messing this up so maybe I do." He took the shot, then bit the lime. It burned as only tequila can. He coughed, his voice gravelly when he could get words out. "What happened to the salt?"

"It's not good for you."

"And tequila is?"

Snow chuckled and drank his own. He put the kitten back onto the floor and sat back in the corner of the couch. "Spill. From the look on your face—"

"Which is not constipation—"

"Stop interrupting me. You're either upset because the sex is bad or you feel like you're cheating."

He shook his head. "Funny enough, I don't feel like I'm cheating. I haven't been with anyone else, but that's not the problem. I know she's gone. I fucking hate it. Every single day, I hate it. But my feelings won't change reality and I never planned to not have sex again. I just didn't plan...well, this."

"So the sex was bad."

"Hell no. It's good. Fucking fantastic, actually. But then it was before."

Snow cursed, held up a hand to keep him quiet, then poured them two more shots.

"I really hate tequila hangovers, Doc," Rowe mumbled, nerves making him clutch the glass tight. "They're like being shot through the space-time continuum into a displaced reality or something. I feel all funky."

"It just makes me adventurous." Snow drank his shot, his eyes snapping shut.

"Hey now. Just because I'm admitting to sleeping with a guy doesn't mean I'm ready to give up my ass to you. No matter how long you coveted it."

"Apparently, you've been giving up your ass a lot longer than you've ever told your friends!"

Snow's sudden shout took him by surprise and he sat up, eyeing his friend closely. "Why are you upset?"

"Because I didn't know!" Snow slammed his glass down. "Nearly twenty years we've been friends and this is the first I'm hearing about this. What kind of sense does that make? You thought, what, that we'd be weirded out by your bisexuality?"

"Of course not. Lucas is bisexual."

Snow snorted. "*He's so not*. You, on the other hand, are different." He sighed, handing another lime and shot to Rowe. "I have to catch up. Wrap my brain around this." He stopped and pointed the knife at Rowe again. "I can't believe you'd keep something like this from us. *From me*. So you've been with men in the past?"

"No. Not men. Just Noah and it was only once. I've always been curious, just never interested enough to try anything. I was always attracted to women, too...and that was just easier." Rowe threw back his drink, then sucked the lime. He flopped back against the sofa and scrubbed his hands over his face, wishing the tequila would kick in just a little bit faster. "But with Noah, everything is different. He stirs something in me—always has. I fought it for years in the Army, because I really enjoy his friendship. And since Mel…well, since Mel I've found a few guys attractive, but it was never enough to act on it. Until Noah appeared in Cincy." He paused, stared at Snow. "I loved my wife, Doc. Still love my wife, but a part of me has always cared about Noah. We have this sort of intense connection and it scares the shit out of me."

"You two had sex before you met Mel?"

"Yeah. Sort of. We did…stuff. But, I freaked out on him and took off. That's when I ended up hurt and discharged. You know the rest. But that night we spent together? It was a week before I got shot."

Snow winced.

"Yeah, I walked off. Left him. I know I hurt him. I suppose I knew it then, but I really do now. We've kept in touch over the years and even met up once while I was married. Just as friends—I never cheated. But it was awkward."

"If it was so awkward, why'd he come here now?"

"He's alone. Kind of adrift. You know how it is for some who stay in the service longer. He just needed to get his feet under him again. He came here looking only for friendship…but I think he hoped for more."

"Of course he would, Rowe. You're a great guy. Lucas and Ian both picked up on his attraction to you. Lucas, of course, who can't tell a gay man from a unicorn thought he had no chance. He actually felt bad for the guy."

"That's just it, Doc. I don't identify as a gay man. I've honestly always thought of myself as straight. I love women. Love everything about them. I just had…I don't know, leanings. But I know I'm not straight either now. For sure."

Snow cracked a naughty grin. "I understand why. Noah is fucking hot. And he's got this devil-may-care presence—kind of reminds me of someone." He winked. "Add in that he shares your secret weapon and you don't really stand a chance."

"What secret weapon?"

"Unexpected killer smile."

Rowe groaned and leaned his head back. "Those fucking dimples," he mumbled. He looked back at Snow. "Ian took him out on a date."

Snow lifted one still dark eyebrow. "And how did that make you feel?"

"Moving into psychiatry now, Doc?" Rowe countered a little sharper than he meant to.

Snow's lazy amusement disappeared and he sat up. "Wait. He went on a date. With Ian. A real date?" He picked up his cell phone off the coffee table and started thumbing through messages. "I'm sure I should have been in the loop with that."

Scowling, Rowe felt his hackles rise. "Noah is a good guy, so don't start that shit. Ian would count himself lucky to land a guy as great as Noah."

"Yeah, maybe." He sat the phone back down and ran his hands through his hair, making the gray streaked strands stand on end. "Just when I'd started to get used to the idea of that annoying-as-hell detective, he disappeared. You tried looking into that?"

"I did. There's nothing. I even looked for a death certificate. He's missing. My guess is working a job."

"That night we found Gratton's hideout, his reaction to seeing Ian's past was strong. Passionate. The man has deeper layers than I expected." He shook his head. "I can't imagine that made him not want Ian. Hell, you saw the way he looked at him."

"Something spooked him. Or he's somewhere he can't communicate because you're right. His interest didn't seem fleeting."

They were silent as Snow sliced off more lime wedges and poured.

"So...tell me about the sex."

Rowe snatched his glass, spilling some of the liquid on his jeans. "Fuck no."

"The man is built. Nice, thick arms like Jude's. I couldn't help but notice. And he has all that soft looking hair. You could really anchor him down and go to town. What was it you asked me once? Something about who tops?" The grin Snow flashed him was positively wicked.

Rowe eyed his friend, taking in the mischievous amusement, but also, the actual curiosity. He groaned because behind that, as always, was the deep caring that had always been buried inside the complicated man. Yeah, he wanted to know about the sex, not only because he was a fucking pervert, but because that would tell him how well the relationship was working. Snow categorized everything through sex. Rowe loved Snow. Always had. But he also really, *really* loved fucking with him. He waited until Snow raised his glass to his lips and answered. Truthfully. "I'm a switch-hitter, Doc. Was even with Mel."

Tequila sprayed out, and Snow choked hard before he threw his head back and laughed. It took him a few moments to get himself under control and when he did, whatever nasty comment about to leave his mouth was stopped by the phone.

Rowe picked it up off the coffee table and squinted at the screen. "Anna Torres. It's your mother-in-law. She call a lot?"

"Nah, not since we stopped house hunting." He answered the phone, his attempt to sound sober by slowing his words not working in the least.

Rowe had to cover his mouth.

"The big family dinner is where?" Snow asked. He frowned. "I thought you wanted us to get a large place so we'd throw one." He held his finger over his lips and hit speaker.

Anna sighed heavily. "I wanted you boys to get a home you both loved. I don't give a crap whether it's big or not. I never really planned to crowd our family into any place of yours anyway. I know you value your privacy."

Good, Rowe thought. *Good for her*. She paid attention to Snow. He really liked this woman.

"All unpacked?" she asked.

"We are. I hired people."

She made a sort of raspberry noise. "I wouldn't want strangers going through my things. I could have done that for you."

"Ah, but Anna, there are things we wouldn't want—"

"Are you drunk?" she interrupted.

"No, ma'am."

Rowe had to bite his fist to keep from cracking up over Snow's surprised response.

"Are you lying to me?" she asked.

"Yes, ma'am."

She snorted loud over the phone. "I know Jude had a late shift tonight, so which one of your friends is there?"

"It's me, Anna. Rowan."

"Oh hello, sweetheart! Are you taking care of yourself?"

"I am."

"Has Jude introduced you to his cousin, Mina yet? She gorgeous."

Rowe blinked at Snow, who just shrugged, blue eyes glittering with suppressed laughter. Anna was one of those women who believed everyone needed to be part of a pair—except for when it came to herself. "No. I'm not really ready to meet another woman right now."

"Oh." She was quiet a moment. "My nephew, Roger, is in town. He usually lives in New York. He's an attorney. Very handsome. Very gay."

Rowe's eyes flew open wide as he silently questioned Snow. Snow merely shrugged, snickering as he poured them more shots.

"I'm good, Mrs. Torres. Really."

"Anna, sweetheart. Snow?"

"Yes?" He smirked and handed Rowe his glass.

"You can bring Sergeant to dinner this weekend if you'd like. He's so little and sweet."

"Like hell he is. And especially not when you put him into the cat carrier. He starts squealing and hurling his body against the bars and every time, I expect him to start mutating into that creature from *The Thing*."

Rowe wondered if Snow realized how carefully and slowly he was pronouncing each word. An obvious drunken maneuver that never fooled anyone—least of all his sharp mother-in-law. And yeah, technically, she wasn't that, but for all intents and purposes, the title fit better than anything else. Her laughter sounded warm through the phone.

"You and Jude enjoy your weekend off. Sounds like it's off to an interesting start. Bye Rowe!" She hung up.

"She's all up in your business, isn't she?"

"I thought she'd be, but she really isn't. Once we stopped house hunting, she backed off. We do the family night dinner there, which is actually nice. Woman cooks as well as Ian. I...care about her."

Rowe made a sound of disgust. "You are just soooo completely and utterly housebroken, Doc."

"As I said before, shut the fuck up."

Two hours later, they had nearly finished the bottle of tequila and Rowe couldn't remember why they were both lying on the colorful living room rug. He also couldn't remember why he'd been so upset. Oh yeah. "I got mad at Noah for doing my laundry and folding my socks wrong."

"Dumbass."

Nodding, he crossed his legs at the ankle and eyed his feet. "These were my last clean pair, too." Shame washed over him despite the heavy tequila barrier. "Socks were just an excuse, you know."

"Yeah, I do. Rowe, if anyone would be happy that you're with Noah, it would be Mel. She'd only want you to keep living life to the fullest. That was her and you know it." He rolled his head on the rug, his mouth turned down. "So what's really going on here?"

Rowe didn't, couldn't, answer. Even through his spinning mind, that terror from earlier lurked, black and hungry. "I care about him...so much. I could love him, Snow. Really love him like I loved my wife." He swallowed the lump in his throat and whispered, "Scares the shit out of me."

Snow was silent long moments. "I thought it was something like that. We're all scared of giving our hearts, Rowe. Sometimes, we have no choice. Sometimes a person comes along who completes you in a way you can't imagine being able to breathe without them. We have to take that chance then. We have to revel in the good times. Cherish them. Being in love makes you feel so damn alive."

Rowe stared at him. "Who the hell are you?"

"I have no fucking idea." He stroked his hand over the cat's tiny head. "Rowe, I was crazy about Mel and miss her, too. Even trying to understand the pain you've been dealing with breaks my heart, but you didn't die with her."

"I know. I just can't go through something like this again." Rowe stared at the ceiling again.

"You know what I really miss right this moment? That I can't talk about how hot you and Noah must be together with her."

A fond smile twisted his lips. "Oh, she would have loved Noah. And if he was bisexual too, maybe we could have worked something out. But he's not." Bisexual. Rowe was most definitely ready to accept that he was bisexual. And that maybe, emotional attachment made him enjoy sex the most.

Snow groaned.

Rowe closed his eyes. "Please tell me you are not picturing that."

"Fuck no. Want me to lie? We're loaded up on honesty tequila, man. Even Jude said the two of you would be damn fine together. In fact, the other night—"

"Oh God, stop!" Rowe shot up and the room spun so fast, he leaned too hard to his left. He reached for the floor and his hand landed on Snow's stomach. Hard.

Snow grunted in pain and rolled, which made the kitten screech and hold on. Snow yelled, rolled back and Rowe took one look at the wide-eyed kitten holding on for dear life with its claws in Snow's chest, and lost it. He fell back, choking on laughter.

"It's okay, little demon. Mean old Rowe didn't mean to make me squish you." Snow patted the creature's head until it loosened its claws and curled back up on his chest.

Still chuckling, Rowe settled back into the rug and waited for the walls to stand still. The long, silky fibers of the rug cushioned his back nicely against the hard floor. "This thing is sinfully soft. I need to get one for in front of my fireplace."

"It's great for fucking."

This time, Rowe groaned. "You couldn't tell me *that's* what you use it for *before* I stretched out on it?"

"You've been on my couch and I've fucked there, too." Snow smirked and pointed. "You've leaned on that wall.

Wonder why there isn't any art on it? There are no sacred spots in this house."

"You have a one-track mind, Doc." He rolled onto his side and propped his head on his hand. "Is it still that good with Jude?"

"It's fucking mind-blowing. I can't get enough of him and don't see that ever changing."

"It's love then. One hundred percent love."

Snow nodded, blue eyes locked with Rowe's. "What I feel for Jude humbles me. He just…he shines light into all my dark corners. I'm the luckiest man on the face of the earth." As if he realized how uncharacteristically romantic he was being, he shuddered. Then he hiccoughed and tilted the bottle of tequila, eyeing the tiny bit left at the bottom. "But tomorrow, we're both gonna feel really, really fucking far from lucky."

"Arm wrestle for the last shot?"

"Nah. It's yours. I'd have to move and Sergeant is all comfortable."

Rowe dropped his head, groaning again. "I don't know if I like this new domesticated Snow."

"Hey, I've seen you brush your dog's teeth, so you have no room to talk." His face suddenly twisted in dismay. "Do people brush cat teeth?" He looked down at Sergeant. "Do they make brushes that small?"

He pictured Snow holding a tiny toothbrush and the resulting horrified expression of the tiny animal on his chest and lost it again.

Snow did, too. In fact, his laugh hit at the same time as a hiccough, which made him sort of giggle instead. It was the most undignified, unmanly sound he'd ever heard come from the surgeon. Rowe snorted, met Snow's gaze and they both cracked up. The kitten, disturbed by all Snow's shaking, jumped from his chest and pattered off. When its mews actually penetrated their laughter, he lifted his head and spotted Jude grinning in the doorway. He wore his black uniform and it matched the tousled mess of his hair and the close beard he'd been wearing that made him look kind of rakish. Yeah, rakish was the right word coming to his inebriated mind. He squinted at Jude's arms. They *were* nice and big like Noah's. Jude held the kitten close as he shook his head at them. "Tequila, General? Remember what we tried doing the last time you drank that?"

Choking, Snow slowly rolled onto his stomach on the rug and grinned up at Jude with the most sex-filled smile Rowe had ever seen.

Jude's eyes narrowed and he set the cat down and came toward them. When he dropped to his knees in front of Snow, Rowe thought maybe he'd have to hurry up and leave. He reached out, groping along the coffee table for his keys.

A hand shoved his off and he blinked at a blurry Jude.

"Like we'd let you drive like this, you dumb shit. Take one of the guest rooms; there are two." He looked back down and ran his finger over Snow's top lip. "In fact, you'd better take the one farthest from ours."

Chapter 18

The house was too quiet when Rowe walked in late the next morning. The dogs still rushed to see him, but there was an underlying anxiety to their greeting, as if they waiting for reassurance that everything was going to be okay. They were such sensitive creatures. But the heavy stillness made it hard for him to breathe.

Noah was there. The rental was in the driveway and the alarm was turned off. But there was no murmur of the television or thumping beat of music pouring out of one of the other rooms. No strumming of his guitar. No bangs or clangs or stomps of Noah moving around the house.

He'd gotten used to all of Noah's noises. The man sang in the shower and he cursed when he was in the kitchen. He talked to the dogs when they followed him from room to room. When he walked down the hall to the guest bedroom, he always hit that one spot in the floor that creaked, as if he felt the need to warn Rowe that he was moving through the house.

They'd lived together a few times while in the Army and Rowe had forgotten that he could always feel when Noah was moving around the same space as him, even when he was making no noise at all. And Noah was there in the house now…but it felt all wrong. Unfortunately, it wasn't the kind of wrong that he could so easily settle with a gun cradled between two hands. He'd fucked up in a big way and a night facing some hard truths with Snow had left Rowe a little surprised that Noah was still there. Any sane man would have said "fuck you" and been on the next plane out of Cincinnati.

But then, Noah was loyal to a fault.

Clenching his fists at his sides, Rowe drew in a deep breath to settle the butterflies high on crack in his stomach.

Rowe stopped in the doorway to the guest room and whatever breath he managed to take was knocked out of his lungs at the sight of Noah sitting on the edge of the bed, his elbows balanced on his knees and his head down. His packed bag sat on the bed next to him. Noah was leaving.

At that moment, every planned teasing remark, every argument that they could find a balance fled his brain. His throat tightened until he could barely swallow and his knees were threatening to dump his ass on the floor. He could fix this. They could fix this. "Don't leave," Rowe croaked out. He clasped the doorway with both hands, because he was pretty sure it would be the only way that he kept his feet.

A heavy sigh slipped from Noah, but he didn't look up. His long hair hung down, obscuring his face so that Rowe couldn't see his bright eyes, couldn't read his expression. And maybe he didn't want to. His sigh had said more than enough already.

"Rowe..."

"Please, don't leave," he repeated because it was the only clear thought running through his brain.

"I didn't want to leave without telling you. After Mel...since Mel's death, I know you've been anxious about me disappearing and I didn't want to do that to you." Noah paused and folded his hands together, fingers tightening around each other.

Rowe wanted to reach out and touch him, run his fingers through his hair, pushing it away from his face so he could read his expression. He wanted to press his face into Noah's throat and just breathe the other man in, let his heat wrap around him. He wanted to feel that little shudder that ran through Noah just before he finally surrendered to the one thing he seemed to want more than his next breath—Rowe.

"I'm not leaving town," Noah continued after several seconds of tense silence as if he were trying to get his own emotions pulled together. "I said that I'd help you and I will help. I'll stay in town until I know that you're safe."

"Where are you going? A hotel?"

Noah sat up so that Rowe could see his face. His skin was pale and dark circles underlined his eyes. He looked worn. Like he had when he'd first arrived. "Ian's. He said I could stay with him." Noah paused, his eyes narrowing on Rowe and his voice growing harder when he added, "There's nothing going on."

"I know," Rowe quickly replied.

Noah had made it abundantly clear that Rowe was the only person he was interested in. That didn't mean he didn't feel a sickening flash of jealousy at the thought of Noah staying at Ian's, knowing in some dark part of his heart that Ian could make Noah so damn happy. And Noah would take great care of Ian. But he...he just couldn't let go.

"If I'm staying there at night, I can protect him and give his bodyguard time off. It'll be safer for Ian."

Rowe clenched his teeth, swallowing back a growl. It was an argument that he struggled to fight. He wanted Ian to be safe, and there were few in the world who could protect Ian better, but he didn't want Noah staying anywhere at night other than under Rowe's roof.

"What about me? Who's going to watch my back?" Rowe asked, trying for teasing but he felt guilty as soon as the words left his lips.

"Rowe, I-I-I can't. I...just can't."

Noah surged to his feet and walked around the bed to the far side of the room as if he didn't trust himself being within arm's reach of Rowe. He crossed his arms over his chest, pulling the soft material of his knit shirt across his broad shoulders. A frown dug deep furrows in his face and he paced back and forth. Something demanded that Rowe cross the room and run his fingers over Noah's face until he finally smoothed away the troubled lines, tell him goofy stories until he laughed, but he couldn't. That path led to other terrifying things so he shoved his hands into his pockets and leaned his shoulder against the doorjamb.

"I—"

"No," Noah interrupted sharply. "I get it. I seriously do. You lost your wife nine, ten months ago, and every story I hear just proves how fucking amazing she was. I know it's way too soon for you to even think about moving on and I never want to replace her in your heart." Noah stopped, glaring at the bed, his hands tightening until Rowe heard several knuckles crack. "If anything, you're just looking for a good fuck and that's it. And if you were anyone else, I'd be happy to help. No strings attached. No fucking complications."

Noah lifted his eyes to Rowe and it was like being hit in the chest with a sledgehammer. Rowe had thought it was impossible for Noah to hide anything from him, but in that moment, Noah dropped his guard, letting all his pain shine in his bright blue eyes. This was so much more than sex for Noah and Rowe was slowly killing this man.

"But…it's you," Noah said, his voice a rough whisper. "And it will never be just sex with you. I—" Noah broke off suddenly, closing his eyes as if he were battling for control. Rowe rubbed his chest, suddenly both fearing and hoping for him to finish that sentence. "I need more from you, but you can't. I understand, but I also can't be your fuck buddy. It…it just won't work."

"You don't have to leave."

A harsh laugh broke from Noah. "Of course I do. You're a fucking drug. I can't say no to you. Every night I tell myself that I'm going to lock the door or kick you the fuck out of the bed, but then you're there and I'm lying to myself that it won't tear me up the next morning when I realize that it didn't mean shit to you."

Rowe shifted from one foot to the other, swallowing back a joke about being that good in bed. The joke was easier to think about, because the words really fighting to get out were the ones that denied that sex with Noah meant nothing to him. If it meant nothing, if Noah meant nothing to him, he wouldn't be so desperate to keep Noah sleeping in this bed, in this room, just twenty-three steps from Rowe's own bed.

A sad smile briefly lifted Noah's lips as he stared across the room at Rowe. Something in that look had Rowe's brain screaming desperately *No!* That look felt like a good-bye and he couldn't have that.

"We'll always be friends, I promise you that," Noah said, his voice low and rough. "It might take us a little bit to get back to exactly where we were, but we'll get past this and we'll be fine."

"Stay."

"Rowe—"

"I'll stop. No more sex," he quickly added before Noah could put him off with more logic. He was done with logic and good sense and smart decisions, because all of Noah's good sense was taking him away from Rowe and that so wasn't going to fucking work. He forced a cocky grin when he felt anything but. "You know, you're not that irresistible. I can keep it in my pants."

Some of the sadness faded from Noah's smile, but there was no missing the tension that continued to fill his frame or the fact that the entire length of the room still separated them. And that just felt wrong.

Pushing away from the doorjamb, Rowe slowly entered the room, walking around the bed so that he was just a few feet away from Noah. He tried to ignore the fact that Noah actually took a step backward, stopping only when the nightstand pressed against the back of his leg. He ignored the fact that Noah's entire body looked like a tensed muscle and one wrong move from Rowe would send Noah leaping over the bed to get away from him. A faint hint of cigarette smoke tinged the air and it sliced through Rowe. Noah had never been more than a social smoker, bumming a cigarette here or there as a night cap to an enjoyable evening of drinking in bars. But Rowe had been noticing the smell more often the past several days when they were home at night, as if the man were sneaking cigarettes when he took the dogs out in an effort to calm his nerves.

He extended his right hand to Noah, not even trying to hide the fact that his fingers were trembling. He couldn't lose Noah. Mel's death had destroyed his life, but Noah had given him balance and laughter again. He lifted him out of the abyss and made him feel alive. He had to find a way to meet Noah…at least part of the way. After years of loyalty, patience, and unwavering love, Noah deserved at least that.

But he was afraid. Was it too late? They were both so damn broken in their own way. Despite Noah's promise of friendship and returning to their "normal," had they already run past the point of fixing this?

"I'll stop. I promise." He could feel the cracks forming in his smile, slipping from where he'd pinned it to his cheeks. "No more sex…unless I can give you what you need." Noah took his hand and started to speak, but Rowe immediately squeezed his fingers and jerked him close. He wrapped his left arm around Noah's waist and nestled his face in his neck, taking his first easy breath since walking in the door. Noah hesitated only a moment before wrapping his free arm around Rowe, holding him tight.

"I've got to be fair to you." Rowe started to say that he didn't know if he could ever care for Noah the way Noah seemed to care for him, but there would have been no truth to those words. He simply couldn't face how easy it would be to fall for Noah. Standing there, he was already fighting the urge to brush his lips against Noah's neck, to snuggle into his warmth, and not because he wanted to fuck the man—well, technically that was always there—but because he simply wanted to be close to Noah. He wanted to hear his laughter, be free to reach out and simply touch his hand, to ask him about his day because he just needed to hear his voice.

"Can I ask…" Noah started and then Rowe could hear him lick his lips, "Is it just the grieving thing or is it also the gay thing?"

A snort escaped Rowe. "Is it wrong that I wish the gay thing bothered me? That I'd feel better if it bothered me?" Rowe felt more than heard Noah's laugh and it felt so good. The tension eased from Noah's shoulders and his fingers shifted so they entwined with Rowe's, locking them together so that Rowe could feel the heat gathering between their palms.

"You're so screwed up," Noah murmured, but there was a gentleness to his tone.

Rowe stepped back, but continued to hold Noah's hand. "After a lifetime of pushing this down and being with only women, I feel like this," he said, holding up their entwined hands, "should feel weird or awkward to me. But it doesn't. It feels…good."

He wanted to make this work. Give it an honest try because Noah deserved that.

They both did.

Chapter 19

"Shiver's on fire!"

Noah was already on his feet before the final syllable Rowe shouted finished rolling through the dark bedroom. He'd been lying on his back, waiting for sleep to claim him, cursing ever opening his mouth because sex with Rowe would have definitely helped him pass out. But Rowe had been true to his word. They ate and watched TV. Rowe told him about the random emergency at work and made some jokes. It wasn't hard to see Rowe was genuinely making an effort to get them back to their easy friendship, trying to heal the rift between them. By midnight, they went to their separate bedrooms and stayed there.

Until Rowe raced into his room—pants barely hanging onto his narrow hips and shirt clenched in his fist—to deliver his cryptic message. Noah dressed and grabbed weapons, trusting that he'd get more information once they were on the road.

They were in the truck and out of the neighborhood before he finally asked, "Shiver?"

Rowe swore and shoved his phone at Noah as he swerved around a car moving slower than Rowe's ninety and slamming Noah into the passenger door. Tires squealed and horns blared, but they managed not to hit anyone. "Shiver is another of Lucas's clubs. Gidget called hysterical and said she's getting reports that both Shiver *and* Snow's old house outside downtown are on fire."

Noah stopped in the act of trying to get comfortable behind his seat belt again, phone clenched in his left hand. "Old house? He doesn't live there?"

"Yeah, he sold it months ago. Living in Northern Kentucky with Jude—miles away. No idea if anyone is living there now." He pointed as his phone. "Pull up my contacts. Call Ian, Snow, Jude, Andrei and Lucas. Keep fucking calling them until someone answers!" He hammered his horn and raced around a little yellow Fiat moving way too slow for Rowe's liking. "It's

Lucas's night to be at Shiver. He likes to be there on Saturday. But he might have left before the fire started. Call the boys and find out if anyone has heard from him."

Cutting through downtown took another fifteen minutes. Noah growled softly to himself. Snow's phone was going directly to voicemail, but the surgeon could have easily been working. Jude wasn't answering and neither was Ian. Lucas's phone went directly to voicemail. He put off trying Andrei as Rowe swore softly next to him. Black smoke billowed into the sky and traffic had come to a complete standstill.

Rowe pulled the car into a nearly full lot and parked. "We're still two blocks away. Faster to hoof it."

"Got your six," Noah murmured, getting out of the car before Rowe even finished turning off the engine. He would follow Rowe into the fire and he would always have this man's back. Particularly since someone had already taken a shot at Rowe at the last fire.

His heart gave a little stutter to see the crowd of fire trucks, ambulances, police cars, and people dressed in skimpy clubbing clothes outside the building. Bright flames and smoke poured from the two stories and roof. It was utter chaos. Everything within him screamed to get Rowe out of the area and back to the safety of the truck. That many people gathered closely with tall buildings at all sides—there were too many places for a shooter. But there was no way in hell he was going to get Rowe out of there until he was sure none of his friends were in danger.

Rowe directed them around barriers set up by the police to slip between a pair of fire trucks with their ladders extended toward the roof. Noah stayed a step behind Rowe, his hands out and loose at his sides, ready to grab the first person who approached Rowe, but with everyone running around, dealing with crying, soot-and-blood-covered partiers, two men who acted like they belonged there were the least of their problems.

"Where?" Noah said in Rowe's ear when he paused to look around.

"The ambulances."

Positioned a short distance from the nightclub, the first two ambulances were seeing to a steady stream of clubbers with cuts and scrapes. Nothing that looked too serious. But the third revealed an all-too-familiar trio. Andrei paced at the back of an ambulance, shoulders and back painfully straight beneath his heavy wool coat. Dark hair hung loose around his face, but it did nothing to hide the rage cutting harsh lines around his mouth and eyes. The man was pissed and ready to tear into the world.

Inside the ambulance sat Lucas with an oxygen mask over his face while Jude checked his vitals. The millionaire looked tired and dirty, but otherwise fine.

"You okay?" Rowe barked as soon as his eyes fell on his friend.

Lucas nodded and started to lift the oxygen mask, but Jude smacked his hand away and met his glare before answering for him.

"He'll be fine," Jude said. "But we're taking him in. Between his concussion last year and the fact that he's favoring his ribs on the right side, we're going to run some scans."

Lucas jerked from Jude's touch and started to lift the mask again, but Jude easily batted his hand away.

"It'll keep Snow happy," Jude added, pulling out the big guns, and Lucas's spark of temper deflated in a second.

Noah turned his attention to Andrei, who'd stopped pacing the second Jude had started talking about Lucas's condition.

"You okay?"

"Fine," he snapped, and immediately turned his laser focus on Rowe. "What the fuck is going on? Do you have any leads on the asshole behind this?"

"We're getting close—"

"*Close?* Close isn't going to save him from being killed!" he roared, pointing at Lucas.

Rowe jerked back at the explosion from Andrei, but the other man didn't get any farther.

"Andrei," Lucas interceded. "I'm fine. Safe. Please, call Snow. Tell him what happened and that we're going to the hospital."

Andrei glared at Lucas as if he wanted to shout some more, but he nodded stiffly and walked away, pulling his cellphone out of his pocket. Lucas sighed softly, shoving a hand through his hair to push some of it from where it had fallen across his forehead. He took a couple deep breaths from the oxygen mask before lowering it again. Jude frowned, but continued with his work, making the occasional note on a tablet.

"The fire started on the main stairs to the second floor, seconds after Andrei had gone down. He left ahead of me to start the car and check some voicemails. We...we were separated. He's shaken up," Lucas explained softly, his voice ragged from the smoke.

Rowe swore softly and Noah felt a queasiness grow in his own stomach. He knew what Andrei was feeling because he'd seen Rowe trapped in similarly dangerous situations. At that moment, standing on the first floor as the smoke and flames filled the club, Andrei would have wondered if he was watching the man he loved die. That wasn't something you bounced back from after a couple minutes, even when you had that person safe in your arms again. The fear stuck like toxic soot, blackening and poisoning everything.

"George? I thought I assigned him to you," Rowe snarled.

"Here, boss."

Both Noah and Rowe spun around at the new voice to find a larger, somewhat older man standing just behind him. His rumpled suit was covered in soot and sweat.

"I was with Mr. Vallois the entire time," George quickly added, as if trying to head off Rowe's next line of questions. "Got him safely out the back exit after he finished giving some directions to his staff. Once Mr. Vallois was with the paramedics and Andrei, I was taken by the police to answer their questions."

Rowe sighed and stepped forward, clapping his hand on George's shoulder. "Thanks. Stick around for a bit and we'll talk. Then I'll take care of that one for the night," he said, giving a jerk of his head toward Lucas.

George chuckled and it was his last breath.

Less than a second after Rowe turned away from George to shout at Lucas in the ambulance, George jerked as a bullet tore through his back and out his chest. The sound of the shot followed like a muted explosion, sending Noah into motion. He roughly grabbed Rowe, pulling him to the wet, cold ground, covering him with his larger body as he shouted for Jude.

Footsteps pounded the pavement, but the noise was drowned out by the screams of innocent people as they realized a shot had been fired and there was still ample potential for more. Jude landed beside George's too-still body on the ground, shouting for someone named Rebecca. Noah stared at George's lifeless eyes. There was nothing Jude or any doctor could do for the man. The bullet had torn through his chest, likely destroying his heart. He'd been dead before he hit the ground.

And all he could think was that it had almost been Rowe.

He didn't want to let Rowe up, wanted to keep him hidden and guarded under his own body. Noah gritted his teeth against the tremors that swept through his muscles as he tightened around Rowe, feeling him move, the jagged breaths surging in and out of his lungs. He wanted to stay there and not let Rowe risk his life, but Rowe would never stay still. Never stop fighting. So the next best thing was to be at his side.

Swallowing hard, Noah closed his eyes for a second and dropped his forehead to the back of Rowe's head. "I saw the angle of the shot."

He'd only met George once during the past week in the office, but he'd struck Noah as a nice guy who took his job of keeping his clients safe very seriously. He'd spent several years on the police force, but had decided he wanted to do something where he could see the impact he was making on life. George didn't deserve to go like this. Noah was ready for blood and he knew that Rowe would be happy to avenge his employee.

Rowe's voice came back cold and slightly muffled. "Ten o'clock?"

"Yep."

"Roll to your left. We'll sneak around in the chaos."

Noah got up to his knees, still trying to cover Rowe as he got up to crouch. Out of the corner of his eye, he saw Andrei sneaking closer along the side of a dark blue sedan, his gun drawn. "Cover Jude and keep your boyfriend in the ambulance until we get this guy."

Following Rowe was like trying to keep up with a wild animal on its home turf. He moved fast and surefootedly, weaving around frantic people and vehicles with ease, all while keeping low to avoid giving the goddamn shooter a target. Noah stuck close to Rowe's back, eyes sweeping over the chaos, assessing potential threats and tossing them aside. No one would touch Rowe.

Smoke and crying continued to fill the cold night air. Outside the temporary barriers set up around Shiver, Rowe led the way through the panicked crowd to the buildings opposite the night club. The area was filled with restaurants that had been in the process of closing for the night, while the large windows of local shops already stood dark. But it was the second and third floors of one of these buildings that had their attention. Four buildings down from Shiver, a window stood open on the third floor, providing anyone peering out the window a good view of not only the fire but the ambulances stationed near the night club as well.

Rowe led the way down an alley a short distance from the building that likely housed their shooter, their heavy footsteps splashing through dark puddles. They were halfway through the narrow space between the two buildings when a lone skinny figure in a black hoodie stepped into the lamplight at the other end of the alley.

Noah instantly clamped his hand on Rowe's shoulder, jerking them both to a sliding halt. This was wrong. This was all really fucking wrong. Rowe was about to go charging forward, ready to kill the man with his bare hands if necessary, but Noah couldn't let him take another step.

He sucked in a deep breath, trying to put his finger on the overwhelming uneasiness. A sharp, chemical scent cut at Noah's nostrils, causing him to wrinkle his nose. He took a half-step back, his hand tightening on Rowe as he looked around. Even in the dim light of the street, he could see that the walls of the buildings on either side of him were wet. So was the ground, with standing puddles littering the ground. There had been no rain that day or the previous day.

"I take it you're looking for me," the stranger mocked at the other end of the alley.

"What the fuck is going on?" Rowe roared. He jerked against Noah's hold, trying to go after the man, but Noah refused to let go, his fingers twisting in Rowe's coat to hold him still.

The guy they'd chased out of the Internet café jerked back his hood so they could clearly see his face. His dark eyes were wide and his lips trembled as they stretched into a macabre grin. "He wants you dead. All of you. And I can do it. I can do what that fucking Gratton couldn't even manage." A soft laugh tumbled from his parted lips, sounding more of madness and twisted joy. "I'll even kill his fucking favorite."

"You won't touch—" Rowe started forward again, nearly getting free of Noah's grasp.

"Let's go!" commanded a new voice. They couldn't see the other speaker hidden around the corner of the building, but the guy nodded. He reached in the pocket of his hoodie and pulled out a ball.

Noah's stomach lurched at the sight. Even in the darkness, he knew the guy was holding a tennis ball bomb. When he was a kid, he had friends with access to the Internet and the *Anarchist's Cookbook*, which detailed how to make that quick and easy explosive. The guy needed to only throw it against a hard surface to get it to ignite. And suddenly the chemical smell filling the alley made sense.

"Fuck," Rowe said in a near whisper. Apparently he'd also figured it out. They'd run directly into a trap.

They turned as one and ran back the way they came. The man's cackle echoed down the alley above their pounding footsteps, but for only a second. Flames suddenly roared behind them as the tennis ball was used to ignite the chemical covering every inch of the alley. The fire consumed the oxygen in the narrow path and charged down the alley like a wild bull set loose on the streets of Pamplona. Blistering heat replaced the biting touch of cold hanging in the air.

Rowe rushed out of the alley and dove between two parked cars, tucking his body in to a roll as he hit the street. Noah launched himself over the trunk of a late-model Cadillac and hit the ground in a roll, praying that the street remained empty due to the night club fire. They didn't need to escape the fire only to get hit by a car.

Sitting in the middle of the street, Noah looked up to see Rowe stripping off his leather jacket and beating it on the ground to put out the tiny flames still licking at it.

"Your shoes!" Rowe barked.

Noah looked down to see that the soles of his shoes were actually on fire. How he'd not caught that was stunning, but then his attention had been on making sure that Rowe was safe. He pounded his feet on the ground, crushing out the last of the flames, the rubber soles squishing and sticking to the pavement like hot tar. Fucking shoes were ruined, but at least he and Rowe were still alive.

More shouts filled the night as people noticed a second fire burning in the alley down from Shiver. The worst of it had already burned itself out, but the various trash cans that had filled the alley were still ablaze. The fire department would need to come down and put out this fire before it spread to the interior of either of the buildings.

Dragging his jacket on the ground, Rowe collapsed next to Noah, leaning against the Caddy Noah had launched himself over. He dropped his head back and closed his eyes. Sweat trickled down his brow and dripped off his jaw. Noah couldn't remember ever seeing Rowe look so tired.

"I hate this fucker," Rowe mumbled.

"*Fuckers*," Noah corrected, settling against the car next to his friend. He kept his eyes open, watching as police and firemen raced to where they sat and the burning alley. Didn't matter. The danger was gone…for now. "There's definitely two of them. You heard the other voice."

"Doesn't make sense." Noah looked over to see Rowe's expression twist up before he opened his eyes. "Everything I've read about arsonists, every fucking thing, says these psychos work alone. Solo. No partners. No teams. No gangs. Solo. And that one"—Rowe jerked his thumb back to the alley—"that one is supposed to be the shooter. Not the firebug."

"A tag team of at least two is the only way they could start two fires plus set up this trap."

Resting his arms on his bent knees in front of him, Rowe clenched his fists. "This was our fault."

Noah jerked back from Rowe, turning so that he could clearly see his face. "How the fuck do you come to that notion?"

"We failed to catch the douchebag at Toast. He knows we're getting closer so he's getting desperate. He went after Lucas and

Snow tonight and set a trap for me. I thought we could use this as a chance to go after Jagger. I was wrong."

"Rowe—" Noah put his hand on Rowe's shoulder, but Rowe shoved to his feet, hand tightening on his singed jacket.

"We need to stop these fuckers now before somebody else dies. To hell with Jagger."

Noah swallowed down what comforting words he could scrounge together. Rowe was right. The arsonists were getting too fucking close and Noah didn't want to face the fact that what little success they'd had so far was basically luck. They were lucky to be alive and that kind of luck always ran out.

Getting to his feet, Noah prepared to face the barrage of questions that was coming their way from the cops, but his main focus continued to be keeping Rowe and his friends alive.

Chapter 20

Ian sat in his office doing the part of his job he enjoyed the least. Paperwork. He wanted to rush through it so he could get to the next thing on his schedule—planning his Thanksgiving dinner—because it was less than two weeks away. But even menu preparation failed to keep his attention. This first major family holiday without Mel was going to be a challenge for them all and again, he'd have to think about the fact he walked away from that wreck when she hadn't. He rubbed his thigh, wondering if the break had truly never healed or if he was cursed with phantom pain. A permanent ghostly reminder of guilt.

Sighing, he tried focusing on the numbers in front of him, feeling antsy and so unbelievably restless he wanted to crawl out of his own skin. He hadn't put up a fuss about Sven becoming his shadow again because lately he'd felt the prickly sensation of eyes on him. It came at odd moments, and a couple of times he'd felt it in his own home. And he kept the blinds shut most of the time now—ever since Snow had told him about Gratton watching him in his own bedroom.

He shivered, wishing not for the first time that his friend had kept that part to himself. He knew Snow had only told him to get him to shut his blinds at night, but he'd dealt with a return of fear that had taken him months to get past. He'd never let Snow know that or about the insomnia he fought so hard as a result.

His eyes burned now with exhaustion and he blinked as the numbers on the screen in front of him blurred. He rubbed his eyes.

Just knowing Dwight Gratton had been watching him…

There were several men in his past he wished to never hear about or see again and Dwight Gratton had been at the top of the list. He'd even surpassed Ian's fear of Boris Jagger and that took something since he'd spent two years of his life in hell with Jagger.

If he didn't love Lucas, Snow and Rowe so much, he would have moved far from Cincinnati years ago. Every instinct he had screamed *run* every time the man's name came up in the news and it had been often lately. But those three men who'd swooped in and changed his life meant everything to him and he couldn't imagine life without them. He had a real family that he would do anything to protect.

And it killed him that his past kept putting them in danger.

He heard a clatter from the kitchen and every hair on his body stood at attention. He opened his mouth to call Sven's name but his voice caught in the lump of terror lodged in his throat. The old, familiar fear slammed into him like a punch to the gut. He stood quietly and picked up the baseball bat he kept next to his desk. Rowe had given him a gun, but he hated the damn thing.

It could be Sven out there, but he'd noticed the man cleared his throat when he entered a room, a nice way to alert the person he protected that he was there. People gave up a lot of privacy with bodyguards.

He hated the way his hands shook as he quietly moved toward the open door of his office. He was stronger now, capable of taking care of himself and he would never, ever let anyone hurt him again. But sometimes…sometimes the fear was strong enough to leak through his barriers.

Just as he reached the door, there was a horrendous crash and a series of grunts. He ran through the maze of stainless steel to find Sven on top of someone on the floor near the back door. As he crept closer, Sven's head snapped back and he yelled before lifting one massive fist, obviously ready to pummel whoever was underneath him.

"No!" Ian yelled when he saw the prostrate man's furious face amidst the remains of broken plates.

Hollis Banner growled and yanked Sven down to head butt him before Ian could stop it. Sven let out a sort of roar. Ian panicked and jumped on his back. "No!" he yelled right in the man's ear. "He's a friend. A friendly! Cease fire!"

Sven stopped moving the second Ian's slighter body hit his back. Ian had noticed when Sven had guarded him all those months that he seemed to have an unnatural fear of hurting anyone smaller than him—though most people were. Smaller, that was. Even Hollis, who was several inches over six feet and muscled, didn't have the massive bulk of Sven. But Sven was especially careful around guys built like him.

"It's okay," Ian said, tightening his arms around Sven. "I know him."

Sven stayed perfectly still. "He shouldn't have been sneaking in the back door."

"You're right, he shouldn't have. But I get the feeling this particular cop doesn't care too much about polite rules of society."

Sven relaxed and Ian climbed off him and stood staring down at Hollis, who had blood trickling from his nose. Ian shook his head, scowled and stomped off to find him a towel. When he returned, Hollis and Sven stood glaring at each other.

"The fucker dove out of nowhere or I wouldn't be bleeding." Hollis took the towel and held it to his nose.

Sven's eyes narrowed and he took a menacing step toward Hollis, pottery crunching under his big boots.

Ian kind of wanted to just sit back and let them duke it out. He had a feeling Hollis could hold his own, but Sven was highly trained and normally, he hated violence of any kind. Stupid horniness was showing its ugly side.

And speaking of horny, Hollis looked good. Rough and a little strange with the darker brown hair, but it was just so good to see him. Ian stood silent, staring longer than he should have, taking in the battered leather jacket, the faded jeans and wishing for that messy blond hair.

"Can we talk in there?" Hollis nodded toward Ian's office. "In private?" He looked down and saw the baseball bat at Ian's feet and paled. "I didn't mean to scare you."

Ian picked up the bat and smiled at Sven to let him know it was fine. He led Hollis into his office, glancing over his shoulder to catch Sven picking up a broom. "I'll get that. It's okay. Really."

Sven merely frowned and started sweeping up the broken dishes.

Once he and Hollis stood in his small office, Hollis crossed his arms and stared. Ian stared back, liking the familiar aspects of the cop. Same tall, muscled body, same piercing stare. "I thought you'd moved."

"I took an assignment that means I have to hide, use a different identity. I'm not even supposed to be here now."

"Then why are you?"

A half smile tugged up the corner of Hollis's mouth. "It's not the first time I've checked in on you."

"So you're the one who's been watching me?"

Blue eyes narrowed, making lines crinkle in the corners of Hollis's eyes. "You've felt someone watching you? Is that why the bodyguard is back?"

"Maybe I'm dating him," Ian snapped.

The other side of Hollis's mouth went up in a full smile. "I don't think so."

"I could be." Ian realized he sounded slightly petulant and changed the subject. "I wish you'd let me know it was you watching me. It made me…uncomfortable." That was putting it mildly. "And just why have you been?"

"I've checked in on you several times, but I haven't been watching you." Anger darkened his expression. "But you're right to trust that gut feeling. Tonight I came in because I caught someone sneaking around the restaurant earlier. I waited until most of the staff left to see you."

A chill went through Ian. "What did he look like?"

"He took off before I could get a good look. Seemed small. I thought maybe it was a kid, but I wanted to warn you just in case. With the fires and everything going on, I needed to know you're being careful."

"So you broke your cover to warn me?"

"I didn't break anything. I snuck in and ran into the blond monster." He lowered the towel and frowned at the blood staining the white material. "That's what I deserve for wanting to see you so badly," he muttered.

Ian held his breath. "You wanted to see me badly?"

Scowling, Hollis tossed the towel into the trash can next to Ian's desk. "You won't want to use that again."

"Avoiding the question?"

Blue eyes locked on him and that wash of electricity came back with a vengeance making Ian dizzy with the force of it. He tilted his head back, letting Hollis see his interest and his heart slammed in his chest when Hollis's breath visibly picked up and his nostrils flared. "Yes, Ian Pierce, I wanted to see you. Badly. So much so I risked coming here when it could be the worst thing for you."

"But it sounds like you came just in time to scare someone away. Maybe you should come around more often."

Hollis shook his head. "I won't be able to. Not for a while." He cleared his throat. "I don't suppose I could talk you into moving in with Lucas at that penthouse for a few months, could I?"

"I've got Sven." Ian frowned. "Though we may be staying here to keep a closer eye on the restaurant since you saw someone out there. I love this place."

"No. It's not safe enough here."

"No?" Ian took a step closer to Hollis. It made his neck bend back more but he made sure the man was looking right at him. "What makes you think you can say no to me like that? We're not anything to each other, right? Acquaintances—and not very good ones at that—or you would have told me you were going to disappear."

"You know we're more than that," Hollis said, voice low.

"No. I don't. You eat here, you harass my friends." He sighed. "But you also helped catch Dwight Gratton. So I owe you."

"You owe me nothing." Hollis reached out, hesitated, then dropped his hand.

Ian's heart sort of stuttered to a stop. "You're afraid to touch me, aren't you? Too bad, Banner. It's just too damn bad you know so much about my past because that's a deal breaker for me. So, I don't know why you say we're somehow more to each other when, as I said, nothing has ever happened."

Hollis stared at him and then something twisted in his expression. He reached out again and this time, he didn't stop. He wrapped both hands around Ian's upper arms and pulled him into his bigger body with heady strength.

Oh, he felt good and he smelled like cool air and some sort of spicy aftershave and Ian wanted to climb his body and lock his legs around his waist. He settled for wrapping his arms around him instead and had to bury a smile in the man's coat when Hollis shuddered against him. He'd had a feeling all those months ago that they'd react to each other like this.

Hollis let go of his arms and put his hands on either side of Ian's face so he could lift it. He stared at him, at his eyes, then at his mouth and Ian got tired of waiting. He stood on his toes. "I'm going against my own rules here, but you say you're going to be gone months more, right?"

Hollis nodded.

"Then let's see if you're worth waiting for." He slammed his mouth onto Hollis's.

The big guy went completely still at first before a loud, rumbling groan spilled right into Ian's mouth as he opened his. Hollis tilted his head and their lips fit together like puzzle pieces. Ian loved to kiss and he clutched Hollis's coat and lured his tongue out to play.

He tasted like coffee and some kind of butterscotch candy and Ian briefly wondered if he'd hit a Starbucks recently, then he lost all train of thought when Hollis picked him up, turned them and braced him against the wall. He pressed his bigger body in to hold Ian up and now that he wasn't stretching up onto his toes, he could put his entire focus on the detective's wicked, wonderful mouth. Hollis tangled their tongues together and slid the fingers of one hand into his hair. The other he used to help prop Ian up to his height, by cupping Ian's ass. It was like being surrounded. And sort of…cherished. The man kissed him like he needed it—not just wanted it.

When Hollis kneaded his ass, digging into Ian's jeans, Ian was pretty sure his brain short-circuited. He moaned and wrapped his arms hard around Hollis's neck so he could anchor himself. He wrapped his legs around Hollis's waist and couldn't stop smiling against his mouth when Hollis moaned and gripped his ass tighter. He lowered his other hand to grip Ian's other ass cheek and he ground their bodies together.

Ian forgot all about his earlier fear and the worry about whoever had been skulking around his restaurant. He forgot about Sven. All he knew was the scratch of Hollis's beard on his cheek, the way the man melted into his mouth and molded all those thick muscles against his body.

And most of all, along with the incredible heat between them, Ian actually felt safe.

Ian had to pull back enough to get air into his starving lungs. "Whoa. Wow." He pulled Hollis's face into focus to find the older man looking at him like he was food. He liked that. Liked it a lot. He grinned and tightened his legs.

Hollis jerked and moaned again and the overly excited sound had a broken, thready quality to it that let Ian know the man was barely hanging on. Hollis shut his eyes. "You're okay," he whispered, voice gravelly. "Tell me you're okay."

He hated that Hollis felt he had to ask that, but he understood and if there was a way to keep this kind of desire and need in his life, he'd have to work to get past his resentment that Hollis knew of his past. And…he seemed patient. Hell, it had taken him over a year to fucking kiss him. Patience would be needed because, yeah, there were things Ian couldn't handle and there were times the fear wrestled for control.

"Ian?" Hollis leaned his head back, blue eyes locking with his.

"More than okay. Can't you feel that?" He thrust his hips into Hollis.

The man's eyes actually rolled back in his head and Ian couldn't stop the rush of delighted power he felt. "Oh, you are definitely worth waiting for and we are going to have a really, *really* good time together."

His phone rang and he had no intention of answering it—he couldn't even get his brain to fire enough to pay attention to whose ring tone it belonged to. Hollis's mouth came back onto his, tongue sliding deep into Ian's mouth and he thought about opening himself up to this man, letting him push his dick deep into his body and his moan nearly drowned out the next ring.

Back to back phone calls. He pulled back from Hollis, breathing hard. "Something's wrong."

"Feels pretty fucking right to me," Hollis said, his voice hoarse.

"No, I mean yeah, this is definitely right. But my phone keeps ringing." He patted Hollis's arm so he'd put him down and the rumbling chuckle that came from Hollis's throat made him shoot the man a hot look.

His phone rang again and this time, the ring was Snow's. He frowned. "Something is really wrong." He pushed away from Hollis and answered his phone.

"There was a fire at Shiver and Lucas is in the hospital. He's fine—just smoke inhalation. But we wanted you to know where we are and Rowe said to hang there because he's sending you another bodyguard."

Ian's knees went week and Hollis was there to hold him up. Thankful, he leaned back into the man's big body, loving the hard arm Hollis wrapped around his chest. "I've got Sven here."

"Apparently, he thinks there should be two. Hold on." Snow said something in the background, then came back. "Don't worry about coming here. They're releasing Lucas. Your second bodyguard's name is Royce. Rowe said to tell you that Sven knows him."

He thought about telling them about the man Hollis had chased off and decided not to give them anything else. Plus, knowing Snow, he'd turn into Ian's shadow. It had taken him months to get space from Snow when the man thought he was in danger before. When he hung up, he turned to Hollis.

"I like that you'll have more than one bodyguard. I'd stay with you myself if I could." He groaned and pulled Ian into his big body again. "I have to go. I don't want to."

"I don't want you to either." It was weird. He barely spent any time with the man but he felt like he knew him and the way he made him feel was unlike anything Ian had felt in his life. He wanted more. A lot more. "Do you know when you'll be free?"

Hollis shook his head, expression tightening. "Listen to me. Where I am, I hear things. And one of the things I've been hearing is that you and your friends are definitely a target of Boris Jagger's."

"We know that. Do you know why?"

"I'm working on finding that out."

Ian held his breath and stared hard into Hollis's blue eyes. "You're working undercover in Jagger's world?" The words came out as a whisper.

Hollis framed Ian's face with his big hands. "I hadn't planned on touching you but I can't seem to help myself where you're concerned. Are you fine with what happened here tonight?"

"You didn't answer my question."

"I need to know." He cradled Ian's face, stroking his thumb over Ian's bottom lip. "I need to know one hundred percent that you are okay with me touching you like this."

"I am." Ian understood then that Hollis had no intention of answering him and in his heart he knew. This man had taken a dangerous job because of him. He didn't understand that. It stole the air from his lungs and he started to shake. The last thing he wanted Hollis to think was that his shaking came from fear so he stood on his toes and pressed a soft, lingering kiss to the corner of Hollis's mouth. "I hope you finish your job soon because I want nothing more than for you to come back and touch me a lot more than this."

Chapter 21

They'd been home from the hospital for half an hour when Rowe stepped out of the shower. The hot water had helped the various aches and pains he felt from hitting asphalt more than once tonight, but he still winced when he pulled on his favorite pair of sweatpants. They'd been washed so many times, they were thin and soft and would settle under the big-ass road burn on his lower back. That raw skin hurt like a son of a bitch and he probably should have asked the doc for some kind of cream or something. But they'd all been focused on Lucas, who was thankfully fine.

He headed toward the kitchen, planning to grab a cup of coffee because he wouldn't be sleeping tonight, even if dawn was only a couple hours away.

George. His hand tightened around the mug and he took a deep breath as anger and grief swept through him in equal doses. He hadn't known George well; he'd been with the company less than two years. No family except for a sister in Charlotte, North Carolina and a few nieces and nephews. But he'd been a good cop at one time and died a good man. And this bullshit that was haunting him and his friends had killed him.

Trying to push aside thoughts of George, his mind instantly shifted to his friends, sending a new wave of pain through him. He'd never forget the anguished look on Lucas's face as he looked up at Shiver one last time before Jude shoved him back into the ambulance for transport to the hospital. He felt sick over Lucas's loss. Insurance would cover the properties, but Shiver, along with The Warehouse, held a special place in Lucas's heart and he ached for his friend.

Rowe also had a feeling Shiver's demise would make a lot of his already worried clients bolt. And something about that pyro kid's face was nagging him. It was too much. Work would clear his brain until the toxic mix of anger and worry bled out enough to sleep. Because he hadn't been doing enough of that lately either.

Not with the added confusion over Noah.

Trying to sleep earlier that night when he'd spent most of his time flashing back to what it felt like to be inside the tight, hot sheath of Noah's body hadn't worked. He'd ended up staring at his ceiling, listening for sounds from Noah, and remembering the peppermint smell of his hair. Or the way his wicked grin sent all the blood in Rowe's body to his dick.

Then that fucking broken look in his eyes when he'd found him packed and ready to leave smashed through the good images like a devil-possessed wrecking ball.

Rowe's heart felt caught in a blender.

He walked past Noah's room, glanced in, and was frozen in his tracks. Noah stood in front of the mirror as he slowly removed his shirt. He wasn't looking at himself, his gaze turned toward the floor in obvious exhaustion. Bruises covered his big body, too. One that was larger than Rowe's hand colored his side and Rowe flashed back to when Noah had taken him down—most of his body over Rowe's, but he'd grunted when his side hit the ground.

He hadn't even hesitated to put his body in the line of fire to protect Rowe.

And amid all that chaos, Rowe had lain there under his friend, reeling under the crushing knowledge that Noah had instinctively put him first, realizing he'd been wrong. He couldn't live in the same house with the man and keep his hands off him. And he didn't want him to leave.

Ever.

Fuck, he thought his heart would just flop out of his chest onto the floor right then. He didn't want to hurt Noah anymore and he wanted him. Really wanted him. And in order to move on, there were a few, hard truths Rowe needed to face. He had to work past the fear that gripped him every time he even thought of opening himself up again. He had to work past the guilt he felt for wanting to move on…and he had to work past the remorse he'd apparently been carrying around since he hadn't faced what happened between them thirteen years ago. Drunk or not, they'd connected—really connected—that night in Prague and he'd just brushed Noah off like he'd meant nothing. Rowe had never thought of himself as a coward and this incredible man deserved more.

He wanted to give him more.

He watched him struggle with the still-buttoned sleeves of his shirt, then sigh and chuckle softly when he'd realized what he'd done. Even with the bruises, Noah was a work of fucking art. Muscles rippled over those wide, massive shoulders and they flexed in his back. In the mirror, his abs showed lines of detail and they glistened with a sheen of sweat.

Rowe suddenly craved salt.

Noah's gaze came up in the mirror and locked on Rowe's from the doorway. He froze, white shirt tangled around his wrists. Rowe couldn't stop himself from moving forward and stopping when his chest was against Noah's arms and back. Wrapping his fist around the shirt, he effectively trapped Noah's wrists in the material. He opened his mouth over the place where Noah's neck met his shoulders, sucking the salty muscle into his mouth.

In the mirror, Noah's eyes closed as he tilted his head to give Rowe better access. Rowe licked over his skin, up his neck and kissed his jaw.

"You're breaking the rules, Ward," Noah said on a long breath.

"No, I'm not." Rowe nuzzled into that fall of soft curls, hating that he smelled smoke more than anything else.

"Certainly feels like it," Noah said with a sigh, but he wasn't pushing Rowe away. "Is this a 'we had a bad day so let's make it better with sex' thing or—" Noah broke off and moaned when Rowe kissed down his shoulder.

"We agreed no more sex…until I could give you what you needed." Rowe smiled against his skin, eyeing that bruise on Noah's side in the mirror. "We're probably too beat up for sex."

"There is no such thing."

Chuckling, Rowe helped unbutton and tug the sleeves off Noah's hands, then he carefully wrapped his arms around his waist. He put his chin onto Noah's shoulder and met his eyes in the mirror.

"Rowe…" he started and swallowed hard. Rowe held his breath, fearful of the words that were about to cross his lips. "I need a shower," Noah said, watching him closely.

"Come on," Rowe whispered, kissing his ear. He'd been given a reprieve, a second chance. And even though he wasn't sure he deserved it, he wasn't going to fucking blow it again. "I'll help."

He threaded their fingers together and tugged Noah into the hall and into the bathroom, watching over his shoulder most of the way, taking in the way Noah stared at him through narrowed eyes. He knew his friend was trying to decide whether to risk more of his heart and though Rowe didn't know what words he was ready to say, he knew what his heart had been telling him for a while now. For years, if he were to be honest. He'd wanted Noah thirteen years ago and having the man back in his life had only proved that those feelings had never entirely gone away. He'd loved his wife deeply, but apparently, he had room in his heart for this man, too. It was time to step up.

He'd show Noah how he felt.

Smiling, he reached for Noah's belt, letting his fingers slide against Noah's abdomen as he worked open his buckle. The man had fantastic skin—smooth and warm and the trail of hair there tickled Rowe's knuckles. He unzipped his jeans, hearing Noah's slight intake of breath, then knelt to tug them and his underwear down and off. He ran his palms up the soft, hair-covered skin of Noah's naked, inner thighs as he came back up. "I've got a thing for your legs. I'm looking forward to you wearing shorts in the summer." He leaned forward and kissed the center of Noah's chest.

Noah's eyes widened in surprise for a second and it took Rowe a moment to realize what he'd said. It was the first time he'd made future plans, plans that had included both of them. Hell, it might have been the first time Rowe had spoken of the future since Mel's death. Since that horrible moment, he'd not been willing to look ahead, to make plans for fear that it would all come tumbling down around him. But he did want a future and he wanted one that included seeing Noah every fucking day.

"Not feeling too beat up for sex, Rowe. Not caring about the rules now, either." Noah gripped his arms and pulled him close, kissing his lips. "You planning to get back into the water?"

Rowe nodded, stepped back, and pushed his pants to the floor. "Go ahead and get in. I have to get stuff first." He gave Noah his best, wicked grin and Noah's dick jerked and his hand actually shook as he reached in to turn on the water.

"Hurry," he said, voice raspy.

As he rushed into his bedroom to grab lube and a condom, he was aware Noah expected he'd be bottoming, but that wasn't what Rowe wanted tonight. He loved fucking Noah, loved the tight, hot clasp of his body, but he wanted something different tonight. He wanted to know what it felt like to have Noah inside him.

Noah was already under the water when Rowe returned and as he set the supplies on the back of the toilet next to the tub, he flashed back to the first night Noah had arrived when they'd joked about showering together before. Shaking his head, he stepped into the tub and pulled the curtain closed. He should have realized two years before they'd ever gotten together that they shared something a lot deeper than friendship.

"Changed your mind?" Noah asked.

"Huh?"

"You're shaking your head." Noah tilted his own back and let water run over his hair. He reached for the white bottle of shampoo. "It's been what, less than twenty-four hours since we decided not to touch each other anymore?" He lathered his hair.

Ahhh…that smelled so much better than smoke. Rowe smiled. "Did you really believe that would work?"

Smirking, Noah winked at him before ducking back into the water to rinse. "Nah. But I appreciate you trying."

"I was an idiot. I've been an idiot a lot when it comes to you." Rowe couldn't resist running his hands through the suds sliding down Noah's chest. "And no, I was shaking my head because I was remembering all the clues that we were more than friends all those years ago."

Noah swiped water off his face and stared down at Rowe. "You were always more than a friend to me." He slid his hands around Rowe's back and down to his waist.

Rowe couldn't help the flinch when Noah hit that raw skin.

Frowning, Noah turned him away so he could see. "Oh hell, Ward. Did that happen when I body-slammed you?"

"Better that than a fucking bullet."

"Doesn't the water hurt?"

Rowe shrugged and turned back to him. "I'm tough."

Chuckling, Noah moved his hands to clear skin and tugged Rowe into his body. "That why you flinched?" He didn't wait for an answer. Instead, he nuzzled Rowe's hair until he tilted his head back.

Their lips met and just as it did every time, heat roiled through him like a slow, enveloping river of lava. He groaned, tilted his head, marveling over how Noah's lips felt, how their mouths fit so well together. The hot water pouring over them made their skin slicker and the slide of his chest over Noah's made his dick throb. He still marveled over how much he loved the masculine feel of Noah's body against his—the hair on his chest, the hard muscles. Even the fact that Noah was bigger didn't bother him and instead, it made him feel strangely vulnerable in a way that he'd thought would make him uncomfortable—but didn't. That surprised him, too.

Strong hands carefully moved around the wound on his back and gripped his ass. Noah kneaded the globes and rocked against him. Rowe sucked his tongue into his mouth and grabbed onto his hair when Noah groaned loud and long. Noah's fingers moved on his ass, rubbing and sliding in the water and his finger brushed over Rowe's hole.

Noah went still, but didn't move as if he waited for some kind of sign from Rowe. Rowe grinned against his mouth and Noah chuckled when he felt it. Again, that warmth he felt with the laughter only intensified everything he was experiencing. Rowe wrapped his arms around Noah's chest, still mindful of that bruise as he squeezed. Noah nuzzled his cheek and hunched to open his mouth over Rowe's neck and at the same time, one finger stroked over the sensitive nerves of his ass.

The slam of lust and raw need that flooded him made him catch his breath, and he was nearly dizzy with it. He forgot about bruises and scrapes and began running his palms over every inch of Noah's skin. He loved the slick, wet muscles…the heat. He loved the noises Noah couldn't seem to stop making as he gripped Rowe's ass and when Noah brought one of his hands around to hold Rowe's dick, he saw fucking stars.

Moaning, he leaned back, water pouring over his face. Bombarded by sensations more powerful than he could have ever expected, Rowe thrust up into Noah's grip, hoarse cries escaping his throat.

"So hot, Rowe. You're so damn hot." Noah kissed his cheeks and sipped water from his lips. "I'm gonna lose my mind." He fumbled with something behind Rowe, then his other hand came back to Rowe's cock, this time covered in soap.

The slippery slide of his big hand brought back the stars and Rowe gritted his teeth and couldn't stop his body from bucking hard into Noah. He opened his eyes, working hard to blink back water that was starting to go cold and met those scorching, blue eyes. "Let's get out of here so you can fuck me."

Noah's free hand slapped the wall beside them. His eyes snapped closed.

"Noah?" Rowe touched the intriguing ripple of ab muscles.

"Gotta give me a second. I almost lost it when you said that."

Rowe grinned. "What? That I want you to fuck me?"

Noah groaned.

Rowe shut off the water and grabbed a towel. He slowly rubbed it over Noah's body. "I had this fantasy back when we were still working together. You remember the night we had to hide out in that freezing sandpit and you came over the back of me, trying to keep warm?"

"Oh yeah. That was a rough fucking night."

"In more ways than one." Rowe rubbed the towel over the curly brown hair surrounding Noah's dick. Then he held his cock in the palm of his hand and dried it, too.

Noah whimpered. "Oh man, ignore that noise. There goes my manliness again."

"Feel pretty damn manly to me, Noah." Rowe stroked his cock, relishing the feel of silky skin. "I thought about you taking me like that. From behind. It became a fantasy later."

"Really?"

Rowe looked up and Noah's pupils were blown wide. "Yeah. I want to do that."

Noah grabbed a towel and proceeded to dry Rowe off a hell of a lot faster, though he was still mindful of any place that looked tender. In between swipes of cloth, he dropped kisses and licks and Rowe nearly came out of his skin when Noah sucked on his nipple.

He barely managed to remember to grab the lube and condom when Noah practically dragged him down the hall. It didn't escape his notice that Noah steered them to Rowe's room and his heart clenched because it had to be in the hopes that Rowe wouldn't climb out of the bed afterward.

Fuck, he'd been an asshole.

He wouldn't do that to Noah again. He stopped him at the door, pressed him into the wall and kissed him long and deep and wet. He kissed him until Noah's heavy body melted into his and Rowe didn't sense any worry or trepidation. Then he took him to his bed. Not the guest one, but his own. Rowe was revved up more than he imagined he could be and part of it was nerves, even though he'd been honest when he'd told Snow he was a switch-hitter. He loved ass play and always had. Fingers, toys…he loved sex involving his prostate.

He'd never had a warm, real dick in there and just the thought of it being Noah buckled his knees. He didn't bother to pull down the covers. He just crawled up on top of the navy-blue comforter and lay on his stomach, turning enough to watch as Noah ripped open the condom and rolled it onto his dick. He came toward Rowe, lube in hand and his warmth was so damned welcome over his chilled skin, still partially wet from the shower.

Slick fingers probed his ass as a warm mouth opened over his tattooed shoulder. He'd noticed that Noah spent a lot of time on his ink, tracing it with fingers and tongue. He closed his eyes and basked in the kisses, the licks, the skilled movements of Noah's slicked fingers. Within moments, he was lifting his ass, bucking into the fingers, urging a deeper slide.

Noah bit his shoulder and groaned as he fucked Rowe with his fingers. He licked the spot he'd bitten. "You like this?"

"Love it," Rowe said, rubbing his dick into the comforter. "Want you. Want you badly."

"You smell and taste so good." Noah pressed his lips to Rowe's nape, making Rowe shiver. Hot fingers stroked him inside, twisted, and Noah's thumb brushed over his balls.

Rowe dug his hands into the bedding, clutching it tight in his fists. "Please," he finally begged. "Fuck Noah, you're killing me."

Fingers disappeared and Noah's hot, heavy body came down over his. He nudged Rowe's legs farther apart. Cool air hit his well-lubed ass, making Rowe tense in anticipation.

"You gotta relax," Noah breathed into his ear, raising goose bumps all over Rowe's body. "Relax and let me in."

His eyes rolled back into his head as he did as Noah requested. The lubed condom-covered head of Noah's cock poked at his entrance and Rowe wished for the condom to be gone. He wanted skin and heat and...absolutely nothing between them.

As Noah pushed inside his body, he slid his lube-free hand around Rowe's neck and cupped his chin. His thumb slid over Rowe's lower lip and Rowe sucked it into his mouth.

Noah cried out and slid deeper into Rowe's body.

It hurt, but it always did at first with toys. Rowe liked that burn, liked the feeling of fullness. There was a huge fucking difference this time, though. Noah felt so much better and when the head of his cock brushed over Rowe's prostate, he bit down on Noah's thumb and groaned.

"Oh yeah," Noah breathed. "Holy fuck." He nuzzled the back of Rowe's neck, then moved back to his tattooed shoulder. "You've done this before."

"Explore...bottom...drawer." Rowe could barely speak over the pounding of his heart, the fast pace of his breaths and the mind-blowing pleasure tearing through him.

Hoarse, strangled laughter escaped Noah as his hips picked up pace, his aim perfect as he slid over and over Rowe's prostate. He kissed Rowe's shoulder and neck, his breath hot. He bit down.

Rowe didn't care that sweat started to sting on the road rash on his back because he loved everything else about this. Every. Fucking. Thing.

"You feel so good." Noah wrapped his arms under Rowe's and clutched his shoulders, picking up the pace of his thrusts, going deep. He tilted them slightly to the side—just enough for Rowe to know what he was after even before he spoke. "Grab your dick," he huffed into Rowe's ear. "Fuck. Grab it!"

The first touch of his hand on his painfully swollen dick made him gasp and clench his ass.

Noah roared.

Rowe rubbed the back of his head on Noah's face. The power he felt, the way he made Noah lose control, it washed over him and so did a wave of tenderness. He let go of his dick and clasped the hand Noah had clutching his shoulder. He turned his head and Noah shoved deep as he came to meet his mouth.

He slowed his thrusts as they kissed, lips and tongues wet and clasping. Rowe's heart beat so fucking hard against his ribs. Noah's drying hair fell over his cheek and the scent of peppermint made him reach for his cock again. He stroked only twice before a full body shudder ripped through him and he yelled Noah's name and spilled all over his fingers.

Noah frantically reached down, rubbing his fingers over Rowe's, seeming to relish the slippery slide of Rowe's spend. He clasped their hands together, let out a groan that sounded like it started deep in his gut, his hips stuttering, losing rhythm as he clutched Rowe's body tight to him. He suddenly went still and quiet before he released a noise that made Rowe feel like he might come again.

There was nothing like feeling this man losing it all over him. Nothing.

Noah didn't let go, not even when he went soft. He didn't tie off the condom and Rowe knew he needed to. But he only held Rowe close, not speaking even as their breaths slowed to normal and the sweat dried on their bodies. When Rowe shifted into a more comfortable position against Noah, his friend went completely still and Rowe thought his heart might shatter.

"I'm not going anywhere," he whispered.

Chapter 22

By the next afternoon, the peace he'd finally felt in his bed had been blown to hell.

Glass shattered, the sound disrupting the otherwise quiet office late on a Sunday. Heavy metal and plastic crashed to the floor while the scent of burnt ozone filled the air. Still, Rowe searched his desk for something heavy to throw next. Blood pounded in his ears fueled by rage and frustration. Everything he'd built over the past several years was pulling apart at the seams. He wanted to break things. Smash glass and put enormous gaping holes in walls. He wanted a fight. Something fast and bloody. Anything to ease the building rage.

"Bad meeting?"

Rowe's head snapped up to see Noah leaning against the doorjamb. He was trying for casual, but there was no missing the tension tightening the muscles in his jaw or the narrowing of his eyes. Rowe held back his shout, limiting himself to just a teeth-clenched grunt when he saw several others poke their head into the doorway of Rowe's office, investigating the crash. He needed to watch his fucking temper in the office. Everyone didn't need to know the company was circling the goddamn drain.

Turning around to pace away from the door, Rowe shoved his hands through his hair, trying not to let Noah's whispered, "I got this" rankle him. Noah was thoughtfully calming the troops—something he couldn't possibly do at that moment. He only turned back around when the door thudded closed. Fuck, he needed to get back in control.

Noah strolled farther into the office, closing the distance between them, and for the first time Rowe didn't feel the need to immediately backpedal, keeping that comfortable barrier of empty space between them. He watched the other man move so smoothly, remembering the hard muscles that covered his taller frame, now hidden beneath a thick cream cable-knit sweater and green cargo pants. Rowe was actually disappointed when Noah chose to sit on the edge of Rowe's desk, propping one foot up on his empty chair rather than close the last few feet still separating them.

To hell with it. He was already in a bad mood. What the fuck did it matter what happened in the office anymore?

Rowe took two large strides so that he stood directly between Noah's legs. The man had barely enough time to straighten before Rowe slid one hand behind his head and clenched his fingers tightly in his long, soft hair. He covered Noah's mouth with his own, tongue plunging inside as Noah gave a muffled moan. Strong hands gripped Rowe's hips, pulling him another inch closer so that Rowe's chest bumped against Noah's.

Anger gave way to hunger as Noah let Rowe devour his mouth. His tongue swept over every inch of him, memorizing his taste, his feel. But it wasn't enough. God, it was like being a teenager again. Everything felt so new and fucking wonderful, but it was more, too. He wanted to possess Noah, mark him. Wanted the world to know that this man was his.

Noah's hand slid up from his waist and cupped his jaw, slowly gentling the kiss until they both pulled away panting, foreheads pressed together.

"You know, there are cheaper ways than trashing your flat-screen TV to get my attention," Noah teased as Rowe pulled back another inch to clearly see his face. He smiled at Rowe, but there was no missing the worry in his eyes.

The world and the shitstorm they were surfing through came rushing back. Rowe groaned and paced away from Noah. The kiss had been great for a momentary distraction, but his earlier rage returned with a vengeance. If Noah was smart, he'd get the fuck away from him as quickly as possible. His life was a disaster and Noah didn't deserve to get sucked in.

"What's going on, Ward?"

"Two fucking clients canceled contracts today!" he exploded, no longer able to hold back the words. "They've been with me since almost the beginning, but they've heard about the bullshit with Lucas and the Lyntons. That's on top of the three others who've left this past week. And then Wendy warned me that she's been struggling to hold onto two others!" he continued, mentioning the employee who dealt with most new clients when it came to determining their individual needs.

"People are scared—" Noah started.

"No shit they're scared! I look like the fucking angel of death. I've lost my wife, two of Lucas's businesses have burned to the ground, one employee has been killed, and I don't even want to think about the number of times Andrei or I have been shot at over the past year."

He dropped his arms loose at his sides, his hands flopping against his jeans. The urge to throw something twitched through him, but he didn't. What he really wanted to do was march down to Jagger's house and blow the fucker up along with anyone inside, but there was no way in hell he'd get close to the place before Jagger's security mowed him down. And even if he did kill Jagger, he wasn't one hundred percent sure that would end all this shit. He just couldn't see a way out of this mess.

"I'm tired of being on the losing end of this, and I don't know what to do next," he softly admitted.

Noah pushed back to his feet, shoving his hands into his pockets before he wandered back around the desk, putting the large piece of furniture between them. Rowe looked at Noah, arching one eyebrow at him in question. This didn't look reassuring.

"I've talked to Andrei and I've looked at your security system," Noah carefully said. Rowe's defenses automatically went up. Whatever this was, it wasn't going to be good, but Noah was his best friend, his lover. He trusted this man with his life…and as he was coming to accept, also with his heart. He'd hear him out. "It's good."

"Damn straight it's good. Just not good enough. Someone has found a way around it."

Noah paused and licked his lips. "What if they didn't need to find a way around it?"

"What do you mean?"

"What if they didn't need to find a way around your security system because they had someone on the inside helping them shut it down?"

"No!" Rowe instantly barked. "No! Fuck no!" he repeated because Noah's words were a swift kick to the gut. Just the thought that someone within his company had betrayed him made him want to vomit. He knew these people, counted them as family. Most of them had been with him for years, believed in what they were building together. No one would betray their family like that.

"Just listen to me—"

Rowe rushed around the desk and got in Noah's face. "No, you don't know these people like I do. I know this idea has been rattling around in your head for a while now and it's not what's happening here. They wouldn't do that."

Noah shoved Rowe back a step. "And you need to think!" Noah snarled. "You'd rather get yourself killed than pull your head out of the goddamn sand. I know these people and this business mean the world to you, but there's more going on and you have to face it."

Clenching his fists at his sides, Rowe stalked away from Noah rather than give in to the temptation of slugging him. He couldn't think about it. Wouldn't consider it. No one would do that...but it made sense. These were damn arsonists. There was no way they could hack his system. He'd hired some of the best white-hat hackers to crack his security system and they all came up with nothing. There was only one way in and that was if someone was letting them in.

"For just one minute," Noah started again, his voice lower and calm, "don't think about the people. Think like the sneaky bastard that you are. How would you get in?"

Rowe took several deep breaths, his fists opening and closing at his sides, as he tried to push aside the rage to think clearly. "If I couldn't hack the system, I'd get myself someone on the inside," he grudgingly admitted. "Bribe or maybe threaten. Make them crack. Give them no choice."

"How do you know—"

"Because that's not what's happened here!" Rowe snapped before Noah could continue. "There are only a couple people who would have the kind of access you're talking and they would *never* crack. Never!"

Noah looked away from him, but not before Rowe caught the sadness filling his bright blue eyes. He walked over and pulled open the door to reveal Gidget standing on the other side, her hand raised as if she was about to knock but she was frozen. Tears cut wide tracks down her cheeks, her breathing coming in shallow pants.

"I-I'm so sorry, Rowe," she said in a soft trembling voice that threatened to knock his legs out from beneath him.

Rowe stumbled over to his chair and dropped heavily into it, but instantly wondered if he should have gone straight to the private bathroom at the back of his office. His stomach roiled, threatening to send all the bile up his throat and out. Not Gidget. *Never Gidget.* She couldn't…wouldn't….

He forced his head up to see Noah firmly grab her arm and pull her into the office before shouting for Andrei over his shoulder. Rowe didn't know why Noah was calling for Andrei, but it was for the best. He couldn't think, his thoughts lost in a swirling vortex of horror and rage and betrayal.

Andrei strolled in a couple of seconds later. He opened his mouth to say something, but the words apparently got lodged in his throat upon seeing Gidget seated in front of Rowe, her face tear-streaked and her body folded in as small as possible.

"What's going on?" Andrei demanded the second Noah closed the door behind him.

Rowe met Noah's gaze over Andrei's shoulder and scraped up what little voice he could find. "She's been disabling the security systems for the arsonists."

The change in Andrei was instantaneous. Fury spilled over his dark features and he growled, taking a step toward Gidget. Noah grabbed his arm and held on when Andrei tried to shake him off. "Fucking bitch!" Andrei roared. "Lucas could have died last night! Because of you, George is dead! Rowe, Ian, Snow—they were almost killed because of you!" His shouting continued but he'd mindlessly switched to Romanian. It was no less violent and ugly even if Rowe couldn't understand it. The only thing Rowe could make out occasionally was Lucas's name.

And he couldn't blame Andrei's rage. The second he realized that their problems were because of Gidget, his mind flew back over the past year to the first break in the security system...at Snow's house. Could Snow have been killed by Gratton because of her? Was Melissa dead because of Gidget? His mind instantly skated from the question, cringing and trembling at the thought. No, Gratton killed Mel. Gidget couldn't have caused that.

"I'm sorry! I never wanted this to happen. I didn't have a choice. They took Eric! They took my son!"

Everyone stopped. The only sound in the room was Gidget's loud sobs and Andrei's heavy breathing.

Very slowly, Noah released Andrei. Tension still vibrated in the man's body but he stepped back, putting his shoulder against the door and folding his arms over his chest. He'd listen, but Rowe wasn't sure he wouldn't still consider strangling the woman.

Noah took up position between Andrei and Gidget in case Andrei didn't like what she had to say and his temper got the better of him.

"What happened?" Rowe demanded, forcing the words past the lump in his throat. He still couldn't move. Struggled to even look at the woman who had become like a sister to him. She was the sunshine brightening the office every day that he walked in. She was a little bit of mischief and sweetness. And now she'd stabbed them all in the back.

"They took Eric, grabbed him when he was walking home from school. Just two days before the party at The Warehouse." Her voice wavered and she clenched her hands together until her knuckles turned white. "Said...said if I gave them the b-blueprint and the security codes, they'd let him go unharmed. If I didn't, they'd give him over to Jagger."

Rowe fell back in his chair, his stomach clenching. For a moment, he couldn't breathe. Eric was only eight and just like his mother, all smiles and playful laughter. An innocent little boy who should never be anywhere near a pedophile like Jagger.

"I didn't know what they had planned," she whispered.

"Why...why didn't you come to me?" Rowe asked when he could find his voice again.

Gidget lifted wide eyes to Rowe's face, blazing now with anger rather than sadness. "I know who Jagger is. You think after months of digging through police files, Fed records, victim interviews and video that I don't know what that man does to boys? You think I-I-I don't know what a-a sick fuck he is?" She pushed to her feet on shaking legs and towered over Rowe. "He's got my son! He's had my son for almost a month. What if you couldn't get him back?"

What little energy she'd found left her and she collapsed back into the chair, broken sobs wracking her slender frame. No one moved. She'd been trapped and while a part of him hated her for sacrificing him and his friends, he could understand her desperation. He couldn't say with any certainty that he wouldn't have made the same damn decision if their roles were reversed and it made him sick.

"I...I never wanted to hurt anyone. Never wanted..." she started but her voice faded almost immediately.

"That's why you gave them Snow's old house," Noah interjected, his voice gentle but firm. "And the Lyntons but with the wrong date for the party. You were doing what you could to protect Rowe and the others."

She nodded. "I thought if you caught them, you could get Eric."

"But we've remained a step behind them," Rowe groaned, scrubbing his hand over his face. He hated it, but this was the missing piece. It was like the fog was finally clearing from his thoughts and he could feel the gears kicking forward in his brain. He could work with this, make a plan to bring this nightmare to an end.

He lifted his eyes to Gidget and frowned, his chest hurting. He could understand why she acted as she had, but he wasn't sure he could bring himself to forgive her.

"You've been in contact with them for a month. What have you learned?"

She shrugged. "Not much. There are at least two of them. They know the area well. I've never caught sight of them on surveillance cameras like we did when we tried to track Gratton. They use disposable phones and pay for things with cash. They're low tech."

Rowe pushed to his feet and restlessly walked away from his desk to the back of his office. "You've got nothing? Not even a name or partial fingerprint?"

"Nothing. They're ghosts. Good with fires."

"But since you're all still alive…" Andrei said.

Rowe shook his head, smirking at the man still leaning against the door. "*We're* all still alive," he corrected. "With you attached to Lucas's hip, I'm sure you're a target now too."

Noah snorted and what little lightness that had crept back into Rowe's chest was instantly snuffed out as he looked at the man who was too quickly growing in importance in his life. Noah was attached to Rowe's hip, making him a target now. Noah must have had the same exact thought, because he just grinned wide and flipped Rowe off.

"Not going fucking anywhere so let's just move on."

"Since we're all still alive," Andrei started again, "they'll be in contact again."

"And you're going to record fucking everything," Rowe said. He walked over to his desk and leaned forward, pressing both of his hands against the surface so that he was now eye level with Gidget. "You hear me, Jen?" She flinched when he used her real name, but Rowe couldn't use the other name. That was a nickname for a friend. He wasn't sure what she was now. Wasn't even sure what he was going to do with her. "You record everything and you let Quinn crawl through it, analyze every bit of it."

She nodded. "I will. I've recorded every call. Got every email and text. Everything."

"Good. You will give it all over to Quinn. He gets full access to your computers, your phone, tablet, every fucking electronic you touch."

"Of course. Anything. Will you get Eric back? Please, Rowe—"

"Shut it!" Rowe snapped and then looked over at Andrei who straightened from the wall. "Sven free?"

Andrei shook his head. "He's on Ian. With Royce."

"Fuck. Who do we have free?"

"Dominic."

"Good. Assign him to her. She is never left alone. Not even to go to the bathroom. She doesn't touch any computer or cellphone, doesn't send a single message or answer a call without Dominic *and* Quinn present. You got me?"

"Got it, boss."

"Go get both and put them in her office before coming to get her."

Andrei darted out of Rowe's office. When the door was shut again, Rowe leaned against the desk again so he could look her in the eye. "Andrei is going to take you to your office and explain the situation to Dominic and Quinn, but no one else. You get one chance to cough up all the information that you've collected and what you've handed over to these fuckers. If you fuck me over one more time, I swear you are going to wish I handed you directly over to the cops. I don't care if you are a single mother. Do you understand me?"

Gidget nodded, fresh tears slipping down her face.

"Say it!" he snarled.

"I understand."

"I will get Eric back, I swear to you. And if anyone has harmed a hair on his head, I will make every last one of them pay."

"Thank you. Thank you so much."

Rowe straightened and took a step back. His anger had left him and now he just felt hollowed out. "When this is all over, we're both going to need to do some soul searching. You and Eric never should have been put in danger like this, and I am very sorry about that." He closed his eyes and shook his head before looking at her again. "But you never should have stabbed me in the back. I…I don't know where we go from here. Not sure we can."

A brief knock was their only warning before Andrei stepped inside, his face an expressionless mask. "They're in her office."

Rowe quickly repeated to Andrei the same instructions he'd given to Gidget. Once Dominic and Quinn were settled with Gidget, Andrei would go to Lucas and keep him safe. He would also send over protection for both Snow and Jude. There was no doubt the doc and the paramedic would bitch, but he was done with this shit.

"Wait," Noah said as Andrei started to escort Gidget from Rowe's office, halting them both. "Have you given them any other places recently that haven't gone up in flames yet?"

Gidget cringed, her shoulders hunching as if she were trying to become a smaller target. "They wanted Ward Security, but I told them there are too many layers of security. One person can't get through it all. So...so I gave them the address to your house." She looked over her shoulder at Rowe. "Your old house in Hyde Park."

"No..." he whispered, staggering back a step. Mel. Everything of his life with his wife was still at that house. If the house went up in flames, he'd lose everything that was her.

Chapter 23

Rowe wasn't listening. Noah had tried to convince Rowe to call the cops during the entire twenty-minute drive across town to the quiet, tree-lined neighborhood, but he flat-out refused. George's death. The threat to his friends and business. Gidget's betrayal and the dark questions surrounding her son. It all culminated to a single-minded focus: Catch the arsonists.

Not that Noah could blame him. He was ready to walk in with guns blazing, cutting down the pair if it meant bringing Rowe some peace. The problem was that Rowe wasn't thinking clearly any longer and that made it far too easy for one of them to get killed.

It wasn't until Rowe slowed the truck, parking it in on the street in front a quaint two-story house with dark brown shutters and dark red front door that Noah grew worried about what would happen to Rowe when he walked back inside that house. Would he lose himself to the memories of his wife?

Checking the glock holstered at his side, Noah slid out of the truck and followed close on Rowe's heels as they briskly walked up the narrow sidewalk, the cracks filled in with weeds. The lawn was overgrown and the bushes along the front of the house needed to be trimmed back.

"How long has it been since you were last here?" Noah asked as Rowe paused at the front steps.

"Few months," he bit out. He quickly motioned to the left. "You go around that side. I'll go the other way. Check for signs of any kind of accelerants or cut wires."

Noah nodded and quickly started around the house, running his hand over the rough brick, pausing here and there to check for any indication that someone might have crushed the nearby vegetation underfoot. But there was no sign that any intruder had stepped onto the property.

"Nothing," he said as he met Rowe in the backyard. It was a medium-sized grassy area with a tall wooden privacy fence that had been stained a honey brown. The dogs must have loved running around here.

"Maybe we beat them," he mumbled, but he didn't sound particularly convinced. He pulled a key out of his pocket and handed it to Noah. "Go in through the front door. I'll go through the back."

Noah took the key and started back the way he'd come, but Rowe grabbed his arm, stopping him sharply. "Keep your eyes open."

A ghost of a smile drifted across Noah's lips but didn't linger. Rowe's concern was nice, but it wasn't enough to plow through the tension digging deep lines through Rowe's handsome face. The strain hanging in the air was a palpable thing, weighing down on them until Noah could barely draw in a full breath. The other man was hanging on by a thread and Noah was praying that he could hold it together a little bit longer.

Bounding up the front stairs, Noah used the key Rowe had given him and slipped silently into the house. At the same time, he heard another door open and close at the back of the house, announcing Rowe's entrance. Noah stopped in the doorway to the living room and the air rushed out of his lungs as if he'd been punched hard in the gut. With a shaking hand, he reached out and braced himself on the edge of the pocket door, trying to hold himself up when his knees wanted to collapse.

Ian had warned him that the house was a mausoleum, but this…this was not what he'd been expecting.

A harsh, bitter laugh escaped him, echoing through the silence and he blinked back the sudden sting of tears. He'd been an idiot. A fucking idiot.

Before him lay not an empty room with shining hardwood floors and bare walls, but a house—*no, a home*—filled with furniture, rugs, lamps, books, pictures, and various knickknacks. Magazines were scattered across the coffee table, a multi-colored afghan was thrown over the back of the couch, and a pair of women's running shoes sat beside one of the chairs. It was an entire life put on hold. Waiting.

"Hey! See anything?" Rowe barked, snapping Noah's horror-filled gaze up to his harsh face.

"Too much," he forced out past the lump in his throat.

"What are you talking about?"

"What the fuck, Rowe?" His companion made a face of confusion and Noah just threw his arms out to encompass the entire room, the entire house. "Is this your way of moving on?" He stepped a little farther into the room, anger putting him on stronger footing so that he could face his friend.

"It's a long process." Rowe started to turn away but Noah's sharp voice stopped him.

"Made even longer if you never start."

"I moved out—"

"You fucking ran!" Noah shouted back. "You couldn't face living here, surrounded by all her things and the memories. But instead of packing up her things and trying to move on with your life, you closed the door and left. Instead of grieving and dealing with the pain, you put everything on hold—"

"I didn't…"

"You did! You know you did!" Noah shoved one hand violently through his hair, pushing it out of his eyes. "Look around you. It's like you're waiting for her to walk through that front door right now so you can pick up where you left off."

"Fuck you! You don't know what it's like."

"No, I don't know what it's like to lose someone you love to death. But I know what it's like to lose someone you love."

Rowe charged across the few feet separating them and grabbed the front of Noah's coat, giving him a quick shake. "I had everything with her! Our life was perfect. And then in the blink of an eye, it was all gone. I didn't get to say goodbye. Didn't get to tell her that I loved her. Nothing. Just fucking gone. It's not fair. I wasn't ready…" Harsh sobs choked Rowe as his fists twisted in Noah's coat.

Wrapping his arms tightly around him, Noah pulled Rowe in against his chest, tears spilling down his own cheeks as Rowe's pain cut through him. He never wanted this for his friend. Rowe was a good man who deserved to be happy. He shouldn't have lost his wife. Shouldn't have been standing in a home that once held a lifetime of dreams but now just represented a life that would never be. There should have been barking dogs, summer cookouts, and the shouts of children echoing off walls smeared with little, careless handprints.

Rowe snuffled loudly as his crying stopped and his hands loosened where they clutched Noah's coat. Noah closed his burning eyes, no longer able to look at the living room surrounding him. He'd been stupid to hope, to think that even for a second he had a shot with this man. Last night had been perfect. It felt like the start of something more, but when he opened his eyes, he saw the truth. For Rowe, there would only ever be room for Mel in his heart and the knowledge hurt so damn bad he could barely breathe. No matter how it felt like things were changing between them, Noah knew he was just going to be a quick fuck, a physical release.

"You're right."

Noah stiffened. Those were not the words he'd expected to hear out Rowe's mouth. He froze, not sure what to say or what Rowe was even talking about. He just held him, his heart breaking for the man.

"I can't let go. Every time I try...I just feel like I'm never going to be happy again, but I know she'd fucking smack me if she saw this. Mel would be so pissed that I didn't pack up her stuff. That...that I hurt you."

"Rowe..." His name rumbled up Noah's throat in a rough moan, his hands tightening around Rowe's bowed shoulders. He wanted to deny it, but it would have been a lie.

"I'm sorry. Never wanted to hurt you."

"I know, but if you don't try to move on, how will you ever find love again?"

Rowe released Noah and took a step backward, his sparkling green eyes staring wide and almost frightened at Noah. It was a word they'd never used, at least not seriously, but things had changed between them over the past couple weeks, and the word held a new weight to it. Noah swallowed hard and forced a smile on his lips that just wouldn't stick. He could make a joke or turn his comment into something generic about moving on and being happy, but Noah was fucking tired of bottling things up when it came to this man.

"You can't really be surprised," Noah said. He swallowed again against the lump in his throat that was making it nearly impossible to talk, but he had to finally say the words or risk drowning. "Yeah, I love you. I fell in love with you years ago, but I told myself that it wasn't real because I knew you could never love me back the same way. You're insane, protective, and have the biggest fucking heart I've ever seen. I came here convinced I could handle just being your friend and that it hadn't actually been love." Noah laughed, pressing the heels of his palms into his eyes so he didn't have to look at Rowe's face any longer. "Man, I was so fucking wrong. Getting to know the person you've become screwed me. I live for your smile and your laugh. I love you even though you never clean up the jelly you smear on the counter every time you make a PB&J. I love that you use different voices for each of the dogs when you're talking to them and I don't think you even notice."

Noah dropped his hands and blinked, clearing his vision to take in Rowe's absolutely thunderstruck expression. Apparently he was surprised.

"Look, I don't expect you to return any kind of feelings. Never have. But I want you to love someone like that. Just get so lost in that person and have that person be utterly lost in everything about you. But you have to let go of all…this. You have to move on so you can love someone and be happy again. Please."

Rowe stepped forward, his fingers lightly clasping the edges of his coat before he dropped his forehead against Noah's shoulder. Noah's eyes fell closed when Rowe breathed his name in a ragged sigh. God, Rowe was killing him. If he reached down, he was sure he could slide his hand into his chest and wrap his fingers around the shredded remains of his heart. But he'd stay. He'd stay until Rowe was safe and then he'd drink for a fucking week just to be numb for a little while.

"It's okay, Ward."

"No, I…I—"

Above them, a board creaked loudly and they froze, not even breathing. In a flash, it all came back to them. They'd come to his old house looking for a pair of arsonists and there was a very good chance that they weren't alone like they'd originally thought.

They broke apart without a sound, pulling their guns from their holsters. Noah fell a step behind Rowe as he led the way out of the living room and to the staircase back in the foyer.

They really didn't have much in the way of the element of surprise, considering their shouting just minutes ago. Noah could only hope that the arsonists were trapped up on the second floor. If they were lucky, he and Rowe could put an end to the threat today and then...fuck, he didn't even know. Leave? It would make things easier on Rowe, but would either of them actually be happier for it?

Noah tightened his grip on the gun and clenched his teeth. Never mind. He needed to keep his mind on the task and that was protecting Rowe no matter what. His eyes swept quickly over the first floor one last time. He could see part of the living room and the dining room through the opposite entry. The far end of the hall held the entrance to what looked like a small kitchen.

Putting his shoulder against the wall, he followed Rowe silently up the stairs, putting his feet in the same place as Rowe. The man had lived in this old house for several years. He'd know where all the damn creaky boards were. Dozens of pictures lined the wall going up the stairs. Noah tried not to look at them, but he still caught glimpses of Rowe with his wife. There were others of Rowe with Snow, Lucas, and Ian—the family that had loved Rowe for so long. Maybe leaving wouldn't be such a bad idea. Rowe obviously had people who would be there for him.

The stairs ended in a narrow hallway that split to the left and the right. Rowe paused, balanced cat-like on the balls of his feet, straining to hear another sound to indicate which way they should go. Just as Noah was about to give up, there was a soft sound like cloth rubbing on cloth to the left. Rowe rocked forward when there was a second sound to the right, a creak of the floorboards under a foot. Both arsonists were up there.

With a sharp nod, Rowe motioned for Noah to take the left while Rowe turned toward the right. Noah paused on the stairs long enough to watch Rowe turn and slowly walk down the hall, his gun raised. The man moved like a ghost, silent and frightening as hell. He would have preferred to stay with Rowe, protecting the man's back, but it was better this way, smarter. They could take both fuckers down now.

Moving as silently as possible down the hall, Noah paused just before two doors. The one on the right was partially open and there was enough sunlight bouncing through the house to reveal that it was an empty bathroom. He shifted his stance, praying that the floor didn't groan under his weight as he moved to the other doorway and silently pushed the door open a little farther.

The bedroom was sparsely decorated with a mattress and box spring on a metal frame, but no blankets. There was a small, upright bureau that looked a little battered and old. This had likely been a spare bedroom. And kneeling on the blue and gray braided oval run was a slender figure in a black hoodie. Around the figure on the hardwood floor and rug were mason jars filled with a clear liquid Noah didn't believe for a second was water.

He drew a breath to speak when a crash echoed from the other end of the hall. Noah's gaze jerked away from his target for a second to look down the hall where Rowe had disappeared, and when he looked back, his heart skipped a beat. The figure had turned, but he wasn't staring into the face of the angry young man they'd encountered at You Are Toast.

A young woman stared back at him with dark, hate-filled eyes. He hesitated, rocking back a half-step in shock. The other arsonist was a woman? The pause was enough for her to finish swinging around. Lifting her arm, she flung the contents of one of the jars onto Noah. He barely managed to get his free hand up to shield his eyes as the cold, almost gel-like liquid splashed across his chest, face and hair. A sharp chemical smell assaulted his nose and his heart rate picked up. He was covered in a highly flammable substance in a house they had been setting up to burn.

Gunfire echoed through the house, but Noah couldn't be sure if it was Rowe's gun or the other arsonist. The woman must have had the same thought because she cried out before slamming into Noah as he lowered his arm again. She knocked him into the opposite wall before running toward the gunfire. They both knew Noah couldn't use his gun without risking setting himself on fire. Dropping his gun, Noah lunged after her. His heavier body knocked her over, but instead of falling forward, she stumbled to her right. Her head struck the railing to the stairs hard before she tumbled down the stairs to the first floor.

Noah stood at the head of the stairs, unsure of whether to check her unmoving body or go after Rowe. Fuck, he hoped she wasn't dead.

More gunfire had Noah starting for the other end of the second floor, but he didn't get far. The punk they encountered at the Internet café ran out of the room and dove into the one directly across, while Rowe leaped into the hallway toward him, knocking Noah to the floor. An angry roar bellowed through the house as flames shot from the doorway Rowe had been in just a second earlier.

Rowe started to push to his feet and paused, his nose wrinkling as he looked at Noah. He leaned close again and took a sniff before his eyes widened huge. "Oh fuck," he breathed before he was jumping to his feet and pulling at Noah. "You gotta get the fuck out of here!"

"The kid—" Noah started to say, pointing to the other room that was visible now that the wall of flames had receded slightly. Smoke was fast filling the hall and the temperature had spiked so that they were both starting to sweat.

"Fuck the kid! You're not getting killed in here!" Rowe snarled, shoving Noah toward the stairs as soon as he gained his feet.

Noah wanted to argue. They were so fucking close to having both of them, but he knew Rowe. The man wouldn't leave Noah's side until he was safely out of the burning building and no longer at risk of bursting into flames himself. Growling in frustration, Noah charged down the stairs, Rowe at his heels, pausing only to kneel at the woman's side. Two fingers pressed to her neck revealed that she was still alive, just knocked out.

"We'll put her in the truck," Rowe said.

Above them, the sound of shattering glass echoed above the crackle of the flames.

"He's trying to get out through a window at the back of the house," Noah said. "Go!"

"But—"

"I've got her. Go!"

With a grunt, Rowe turned and ran back toward the door he'd used in the kitchen while Noah scooped up the woman's limp frame and tossed her over his shoulder. He quickly carried her to the truck. The street was empty for a cold Sunday afternoon, but he worried that neighbors were looking out their windows, watching him. He tossed the woman across the back bench and located some zip-ties in a small tool box. He quickly bound her hands and ankles then tossed a blanket over her to hide her from view even though the tinted windows helped to conceal her.

Slamming the door shut, he snagged his phone out of his back pocket and quickly dialed 9-1-1, giving the dispatcher the address for the fire as he started back across the lawn. He had just ended the call when the other side of the second floor exploded in flames, sending shards of glass and wood shooting across the yard. Noah ducked, shielding his face and body as best he could. Kneeling on the ground, he tried to breathe but his lungs refused to work. Where the fuck was Rowe?

Rowe flinched against the wave of heat that washed over him as he cut around the side of the house. The other fucker was already gone. By the time, he'd gotten out the back door and spotted him, the pyro was climbing the fence at the rear of his property and into the next yard. From their earlier experience in Peaselburg, he knew there was no point in following. The bastard was too damn fast. Didn't matter. They already had his accomplice. They'd lean on her until she finally gave up where they could find Eric and her partner.

As he reached the front yard, he found Noah starting toward the house. His coat and shirt were still stained with the accelerant and his beautiful hair was damp and matted down from it as well. He was a walking torch just waiting for a stray spark or a bit of hot ash to fall on him. Swallowing back a lump of fear, Rowe ran across the yard, grabbing Noah roughly by the shoulders before he could take another step closer to the house.

"Are you okay?" Noah demanded. His wide eyes swept over Rowe, searching for some injury and Rowe couldn't help but do the same. Other than the accelerant, Noah looked fine if a little pale.

"I'm good. You?"

"Yeah, I called 9-1-1 and—"

Whatever he intended to say was cut off by the sharp squeal of tires. They both turned to find a black Mercedes stop sharply behind Rowe's truck. Both Andrei and Lucas jumped out of the vehicle and rushed over to them. Before either of them could speak, Rowe pulled his keys out of his pocket and threw them at Andrei, who easily caught them.

"I've got a guest in my truck. You and Noah take her to storage. We'll follow soon."

If Andrei found anything weird about what Rowe said, it never showed on his face. He just nodded and started for the truck, keys fisted in one hand.

"No, I'm staying with you," Noah growled.

"Keegan, you need to go. There's a utility sink there. You can wash that shit off you."

"I'm not fucking leaving you. Not while that bastard is still out there!"

Tightening his hands in Noah's coat, he shoved him backward until he was pressed against the trunk of an old maple tree. "No! You need to get that shit off you now. I—I—I can't even think straight knowing that you could so easily catch fire and there's nothing I could do to save you."

Noah's eyes drifted over Rowe's shoulder and Rowe could see the flames reflected back in his glassy blue eyes. "But..."

"Baby, look at me," Rowe said, his own voice growing wobbly. He swallowed hard when Noah looked down at him, fear and pain etched deeply in his handsome face. "There is nothing in that house more important than your life. It's just stuff. I don't need stuff. I need you. Please, go with Andrei. He'll keep you safe for me."

Noah nodded jerkily, his expression stunned. Rowe would take it for now. They would have to deal with things later. A lot of things, but for now he could breathe knowing that Noah was away from the fire and safe. He watched Andrei and Noah drive off in one direction while the sound of sirens echoed from another.

Turning back to the house, he blinked back tears to see flames now eating up both the first and second floors. He was vaguely aware that neighbors were now coming out onto their lawns to watch the fire from a safe distance, but it didn't matter. Everything that was Mel's was now gone. Clothes, shoes, makeup, pictures, her mugs…everything. He hadn't been strong enough to take any of her things to the other house, always telling himself that one day he'd be able to pack up her stuff. Now it was too late.

The thought of losing all those mementos hurt, but the pain seemed smaller under the fear of losing Noah.

Lucas wrapped his arm around Rowe's slumped shoulders and drew him in close as they watched the fire destroy the past.

"I'm so sorry, Rowan."

He nodded, blinking back tears. "I'm sorry about Shiver."

Lucas grunted, his thumb moving slowly back and forth over Rowe's shoulder. "It's like you said. It's just stuff. Nothing is more important than keeping those you love safe. And from what I just heard, sounds like you have another."

"You weirded out?"

"Weirded out? No. I am surprised, though. But we have a lot to talk about and I want to hear it from the beginning."

A small smile tugged at the corner of Rowe's mouth. He wrapped his right arm around Lucas's back and pulled him closer, resting his head against his shoulder. Fucking Lucas. He didn't know where he'd be without Lucas, Snow, and Ian. And there wasn't a day that went by that he wasn't grateful that he didn't have to face the answer to that question. Now he had Noah. Sure, things were still really fucked up and Rowe didn't know what the hell he was doing, but losing Noah wasn't an option. Smelling that accelerant on him had sent such profound terror through Rowe, he knew without a doubt what he wanted now.

But the first thing they needed to do was get a handle on the arsonists. That was okay. For the first time in nearly a month, they had an ace in the hole.

"You got a plan?" Lucas asked.

"The start of one. You and Snow want to help?"

Lucas chuckled darkly and an evil grin spread across his face. "Try to stop us."

Chapter 24

Two fucking hours later.

Rowe was ready to murder the first person to look at him wrong and he just hoped it was one of the arsonists making his life hell. The fire department had gotten the fire under control relatively quickly, but the entire house was gone. There was nothing to save.

The police had been intent on questioning both him and Lucas, not that he could really blame them. His house had gone up, two of Lucas's businesses, another of Rowe's client's home and Snow's old residence. The common link? Ward Security. Or particularly, Rowan Ward.

Thank God Lucas had thought to call Sarah Carlton on his way to Rowe's. She'd appeared minutes after the cops and had been quick to protect them from any uncomfortable questions. Rowe had to admit that even though he'd always felt uneasy about the lithe blonde shark, he appreciated having her on his side.

But that nonsense was over for now. The cops were following their leads, and he was free to follow what they had without prying eyes. The pre-fab warehouse he had built was in the middle of nowhere in Indiana, about a half-hour drive northwest of Ward Security. But in truth, it wasn't linked to Ward Security. Hell, he'd been careful to keep it out of his own name. He kept more of his sneaky shit and even some illegal toys out here.

As Lucas parked the Mercedes, Rowe took quick note that not only was his truck present but so were Snow's Lexus and Ian's Volt. Didn't matter. There was only one person in that warehouse that he was interested in laying eyes on.

The main room was brightly lit and open, with ample room to fit a few SUVs in the area, but it was empty except for a small woman tied to a chair and blindfolded. Andrei towered over her, his arms folded over his broad chest, his handsome face a cold mask of rage. The simmering anger wasn't like Andrei, but then he'd been pretty damn angry ever since Shiver went up in flames, endangering Lucas. The bodyguard wasn't handling it well.

Snow stood back, his arms wrapped around Jude's chest. The paramedic didn't look good, but then the man had been completely straight and narrow before he met Snow. Rowe wished he could have told Snow not to bring his partner or even told Snow not to come, but he knew neither was an option. If Jude was going to make a relationship work with the doc, then he needed to know all of Snow's past…even the ugly parts. It was just unfortunate that this ugly part kept leaking into the present.

Ian stood alone, his face pale and haunted as he kept his eyes locked on the bound woman. Rowe wanted to ask him about that look, but there was something else he needed to do first if he was going to stop the trembling in his limbs and clear the clutter from his brain.

Noah pushed to his feet from where he'd been sitting on the stairs leading the lone office on the second floor. He was shirtless and his hair was still wet from where he'd washed that accelerant from his hair. Worry cleared from his blue eyes as Rowe drew closer, but his expression was pinched and tense from the cold. There wasn't much heat to be had in the warehouse.

"Ward," Snow growled.

"In a minute," he snapped back, not detouring from his path directly to Noah. He needed to hear his voice, touch him, and reassure himself that Noah was whole and safe.

"Fuck that!"

"Ash!" Lucas's voice was like a whip crack snapping across the room and for a second, no one breathed. No one could stop a room like Lucas could and Rowe was just glad that it was to his advantage for once. "Give him a minute."

Rowe cleared his throat, his hands balled into fists at his sides to keep from reaching out to grab Noah. "I think I've got a sweatshirt in the office you can wear."

Noah stepped away from the stairs, letting Rowe lead the way up. "Gotta be warmer than all the Kevlar I found."

Rowe immediately went to a small closet at the back of the office, shuffling through a couple old black T-shirts until he came to a heavier black sweater he used in some of his secret black ops shit that would send Lucas through the fucking roof if he knew. The sweater would likely fit Noah. The man might have a couple inches on him, but they were about the same width across.

The sound of the door to the office closing caused Rowe's fingers to tighten in the thick threads before he turned back to find Noah standing on the other side of the small office, staring down at the floor. His wet hair hung forward, hiding most of his face, but Rowe could easily imagine him frowning or chewing on his bottom lip as he carefully weighed his words.

"Look, Ward, I'm sorry about the house. Could they save…"

"No."

Noah flinched at the single word and Rowe cursed himself. He didn't know what to say. He was doing this wrong.

"I'm sorry. Fuck," Noah whispered on a heavy exhale. "I'm sorry I ever opened my mouth. I shouldn't …I shouldn't have said anything. It's none of my business what you do. If I had paid attention to why we were there in the first place, maybe we could have stopped both of them. Saved the house."

To hell with talking.

Dropping the sweater in the empty chair behind the desk, Rowe closed the distance between them in four long strides. He captured Noah's face in both hands and pulled him forward, opening his mouth over Noah's. A sharp gasp left Noah, sucking in Rowe's exhale just before their lips met in a searing kiss. Their tongues tangled, Rowe dominating him until the other man moaned and melted, his arms wrapping tightly around Rowe.

Rowe wanted this. He wanted Noah in his arms all the time. He wanted all of his moans, laughs, and smiles. He even wanted Noah shouting and pulling at his hair because Rowe was driving him insane. He wanted him barefoot and shirtless on the couch, snuggled between the dogs with a guitar in his lap on a Saturday.

And as he kissed Noah in that moment, he knew he'd come too fucking close to losing one more moment of that because he was still holding on to the past. Rowe would never stop loving Mel, but his wife was gone and their life together was over. He was getting another shot to have something too damn amazing to pass up. A third shot if he wanted to be completely honest because he could have had this with Noah before.

Breaking off the kiss, Rowe grabbed Noah by the arms and maneuvered him until the man was seated on the edge of the empty desk. Noah blinked wide blue eyes at him, his lips already swollen from the kiss, as Rowe stepped between his knees so he could look him directly in the eyes. He reached up and ran some of the strands of Noah's hair through his fingers. It was cool and damp, but not the same silky texture he was accustomed to when he used the shampoo at home.

"No peppermint," he murmured, talking to himself.

"Had to make do with some old soap I found."

Rowe licked his lips and finally met Noah's questioning gaze. Yeah, it was no wonder the man was confused. He was throwing so many mixed signals he was stunned Noah was even still there, rather than telling him to fuck off. "Maybe…maybe I like you smelling like peppermint and my soap. And maybe I like the idea of you having the right to tell me when I'm fucking up my life."

A hand tightened ever so slightly on his waist and Noah's breathing stuttered. "Anything else you like?"

"I like you in my house. And in my bed. I like you talking to my friends over dinner and playing with the dogs. I like you in every inch of my life."

"Does this mean you're going to tell me how I'm fucking up my life?"

A smirk lifted one corner of Rowe's mouth. "Like you could fucking stop me."

"True."

"I love you, Noah. Love you so damn much. You can't leave, but you've gotta know that I'm not an easy person to be with. I'm cranky and stubborn and my temper is too damn short—"

Noah's laugh cut him off. "I know you, Ward."

Rowe pushed on, shaking his head. "I've changed since we were in the Rangers. I—"

He stopped Rowe again, brushing his thumb over Rowe's lower lip. "And I know you. When I told you that I loved you, I wasn't talking about the cocky son of a bitch I met in the Army. I was talking about the man standing in front of me right now. I love you and I'm not going anywhere."

"Thank fucking Christ," Rowe muttered before pulling Noah closer for another kiss.

Unfortunately, the kiss was cut short by shouts and clapping that sounded like they were coming from just outside the door. Rowe and Noah broke apart to find Snow, Jude, Ian, and Lucas all crowded around the window in the upper half of the door to the office. The quartet laughed and clapped, making it clear they had been watching the show the entire time. Even through the door, they could hear Lucas calling down to Andrei, who'd been stuck watching their prisoner, that they were kissing. *Lovely.*

"Guess we better get back to work," Noah murmured.

Rowe looked at Noah and a slow smile split his face. "You know, for the first time in long time, I really don't want to."

A chuckle rumbled from Noah as he wrapped both his arms and legs around Rowe, drawing him in so that he was wrapped in a cocoon of Noah. "That's okay. When we're done with work, I'm going to fuck you so long and so hard the only word you're going to know is my name."

"I'm gonna hold you to that," he murmured, his lips brushing against Noah's before stealing one last quick kiss.

Noah released Rowe and he leaned back over the desk to grab up the sweater while Rowe turned back to the door to find his friends watching him with stupid grins on their faces. Oh, yeah…they were loving every second of this. Not that he could blame them. Since Mel's death, he'd pretty much crawled into the ground next to her and had been content to stay there for the rest of his life. And even before her death, he'd worked hard to suppress the side of him that noticed men like Noah.

"Shut up!" he said as soon as he opened the door, but he was met with more laughter. Of course, he was struggling to contain his own smile.

"You know, declarations of love should be done in private." Lucas winked. "But I enjoyed that too much. Mel would be happy for you," he finished softly.

Snow snorted, a wicked grin spreading across his face. "Hell, she'd want to video every second of it."

"I'm happy for you," Ian said, hugging Rowe. "Even if I am a little jealous."

"Jealous?"

"Well, he is so damn sexy. Nice abs."

"Very," Jude added with a little sigh and a wink at Rowe. Snow wrapped an arm around Jude's waist and pulled him close so he could pinch his ass. Rowe didn't buy Jude's comment for a second, and neither did the doc.

"While I appreciate the attention to my abs," Noah started, coming up behind Rowe, "maybe we should deal with our prisoner first."

"Yeah, her brother must be going crazy about now," Ian muttered. He started toward the stairs but Rowe clapped a hand on his shoulder, halting him.

"Brother? You know these two? How?"

Ian leveled a grim look on Rowe. "Take a wild guess," he said before heading back down to the first floor.

Jagger. Of course.

The laughter disappeared in a blink and they filed down the metal stairs to the first floor where Andrei was still hovering over the woman bound and blindfolded. Rowe grabbed a metal folding chair and loudly dragged it across the concrete before slamming the legs down in front of the woman. She jumped at the noise, but otherwise made no other sound or movement. Rowe turned the chair backward and straddled it, resting his arms on the back of the chair as he faced her. With a nod, Andrei removed the blindfold and stepped back.

She squinted and blinked, trying to get her eyes to adjust to the bright overhead light, giving Rowe a chance to look her over. She was slender like her brother, with a narrow oval face and angular features. Her brown eyes looked too large for her face and her mouth was pinched. She probably would have been prettier if she smiled. Of course, considering that she and her brother were trying to kill his friends, he wasn't sure anything could make this woman look pretty to him.

"What the fuck do you want?" she demanded after Rowe sat watching her for a couple minutes without saying a word.

"Who hired you?"

"Fuck you! I'm not saying a goddamn word to you!"

"What were you hired to do?"

"Fuck you!"

This was pretty much what he'd expected, but he had interesting ways of making a person crack. Rowe straightened and scratched his chin. "You see, I thought if you had some useful information, I might bother to keep you alive, but I've got other ways to get the info I need."

Her loud laugh echoed through the room, brittle and forced. "You don't know dick and you don't have shit for sources. You think I'm scared of you? You're fucking nothing. Nothing!"

"Her name is Hanna," Ian announced.

There was no missing the way the young woman stiffened at Ian's soft voice. Her breathing became rapid little breaths. She jerked in her seat, trying to look around to see the speaker, but Andrei clamped a hand down on her shoulder, keeping her locked in place.

But she didn't have to move. Ian walked around to stand just behind Rowe, who twisted to keep an eye on his friend. The young man stood stiff, his arms crossed tightly over his chest, but his eyes remained locked on the woman.

"Her brother's name is Kyle. They both arrived at Jagger's a few months before…before I left."

"Bastard," Hanna snarled at Ian. She pulled against her bindings and Andrei's grip as if she planned to launch herself at Ian. And Rowe could believe it. Hatred blazed in her eyes and flushed her once pale face.

"Jagger wanted them both?" Lucas questioned from across the room.

Ian shook his head. "No, he had no interest in Hanna."

"Shut up, traitor!" She screamed. "Shut up! Shut up!"

"From what I saw, Kyle listened to Hanna. If she was kept happy and safe, then Kyle did what he was told." Ian's voice broke.

"Shut up!" she continued, her voice moving higher in pitch and more desperate.

"Gag her!" Rowe shouted.

"Don't!" Ian said, putting up a hand as Andrei grabbed the blindfold that had been wrapped around her eyes with his free hand. "They were young. Younger than me when I was taken to Jagger. I…they were alone and…"

Rowe suddenly stood and grabbed Ian by the shoulders, his own hands shaking. He wanted to kill Jagger. He wanted to drag the man out of his fancy house on the north side of town, strip him nude, and crucify him in the middle of Fountain Square before peeling every inch of flesh off the bastard. And then he would work over every fuckstick that he employed.

Over the years, he told himself that it was enough that they'd gotten Ian out and given him a better, safer life. But the knowledge that it hadn't been—that they should have burned Jagger down—hit him like a stab to the chest. Here he stood, looking into the eyes of a warped and battered human being who hadn't escaped Jagger and his men. Getting Ian out hadn't been enough. Trying to sabotage Jagger behind the scenes hadn't been enough.

"Breathe, Rowe," Ian said calmly.

Rowe nodded absently and carefully walked him over to Lucas, who wasn't looking too good either following their brief stroll down memory lane. He had a feeling both Lucas and Snow were feeling the same as him—ready to murder Jagger and torch his entire compound. But Ian didn't need them losing their minds over this.

"So, Jagger hired you," Rowe said loudly, trying to get their thoughts back on the right track again even as he delivered Ian into Lucas's arms. Ian dutifully leaned against Lucas as if seeking comfort, but he knew it was Lucas who needed the reassurance that Ian was safe as he wrapped arms around the younger man. A glance across the room revealed Snow holding Jude in a death grip, his face pale and features strained.

When Rowe started back to his chair, he found Noah now seated in front of Hanna, a wide, charming grin on his face as if the man hadn't a care in the world and that holding women prisoner in the middle of the country was a common occurrence. That eased him. Seeing the man use his brain and his killer charm when Rowe was too mired in the past.

"Jagger hired you and your brother to kill Rowe, Snow, Lucas, and Ian," Noah started and then stopped. He stared at

Hanna long moments, then sucked in a sharp breath at something he saw. "Not Ian," he corrected, his grin growing wider.

"Fuck you!" she snarled.

"You're not supposed to kill Ian. Just the other three…possibly even their boyfriends," he revised. Rowe hung back, watching Noah's intent focus on the woman's face, reading each little tick and twitch as a tell. Admiration, pride and a fierce stab of pure love surged through him. The man was incredible. And fuck, there was no way in hell he was playing poker against him ever again.

"You don't know shit." Hanna laughed, but she didn't sound nearly as confident as she had earlier.

"I know you almost killed Ian at the new nightclub. I know that could have gotten you in a shitload of trouble if he wasn't on the hit list. If maybe Ian was still a favorite…" He paused, reading something that Rowe couldn't see but he was happy to let the man work his magic. "And that failure at the first nightclub, that would have brought attention down on you. Making you reckless and desperate."

"Whatever. Like you know anything about starting fires."

Every nuance in her tone said Noah was hitting pay dirt.

Noah shrugged, his grin staying light and carefree. "You're right. I don't know shit about starting fires." Reaching into his back pocket, he pulled out a smartphone and held it up in front of Hanna. "But I am damn good at guessing security codes on phones. Particularly when people don't bother to clean off their screens."

To prove his point, he tapped a few numbers and the lock screen disappeared, giving him access to the phone. "I noticed there are only two numbers in your phone and one of those numbers has been calling you almost constantly since you fell into our care. I'm gonna guess that's your brother. Shall we call him? Tell him you're safe?"

Rowe walked to stand behind Noah, just in time to see Hanna pale. Interesting.

"Leave him out of this. You wanna deal? Then you deal with me."

"But that's the problem," Rowe said. He stood over her, his hands on his hips. "We've got you, but you're not what we want at all."

"What do you want? I can't start any fire if I'm here. Your place was the last one I had on my list. You want us to leave town? Hand over Jagger? Like I can fucking do that."

"Facetime the brother," Rowe said. "And hold the screen up so he sees her face first."

With a nod, Noah did as Rowe instructed while Hanna began to curse Rowe with a new desperation. This was interesting.

Kyle answered the phone on the first ring, his frantic voice coming through and for a moment, Hanna was silent. And then she started sounding warnings.

Rowe snatched the phone out of Noah's hand. "Gag her. I want to talk to my new friend."

As Hanna fell silent, Rowe turned the phone so that Kyle saw only his face. The kid—or young man since he looked to be in his early twenties—was a mess. Thin and pale, his eyes were red-rimmed and puffy. His dark hair stood up in all directions as if he'd been pulling at it.

"Where the hell are you? If you hurt her, I will kill you all! I will burn down this entire city!"

Rowe forced a smile, trying to ignore the little pangs of guilt cutting sharply through his chest. When he looked at Kyle, he saw a shadow of Ian and it hurt. He could easily imagine that Hanna had been the one thing to get him through those weeks and months and years with Jagger. She's probably tried to keep him together and sane…or at least somewhat sane. And now Rowe stood between Kyle and the one thing that had probably kept him balanced and breathing.

"Had a little chat with your sister," Rowe started, cutting off Kyle's rant. "I get the impression that you're not our fire starter. In fact, I bet you can't even light a cigarette without her help."

"Fuck—"

"But that's not your job, is it? It's your job to protect her."

Kyle was completely silent, but he didn't need to say a word. His face crumbled and he rapidly blinked back tears. It was written on his face. He felt guilty for his sister's capture. Blamed himself.

"You want your sister back?"

"What do you want?" His voice was low and sullen.

"Eric Eccelston."

"The kid?"

"Yeah, Jennifer Eccelston's son. I want him alive and unharmed in twenty-four hours."

"That's it? We'll make a swap—the kid for my sister?"

Rowe grinned and Kyle actually cringed away from the phone. "I want the kid, unharmed, and I want you and your sister to leave the Cincinnati area forever."

Kyle sucked on his lower lip, looking more than a little disbelieving. "You'd let us leave?"

"I want Jagger, not you. You and Hanna leave quietly and we'll forget about this."

The young man glared at Rowe for several seconds before sucking in a ragged deep breath. "Fine. Midnight tomorrow at 1034 Boron. Just you and Hanna. I'll come alone with the kid." He then ended the call.

It was for the best. Rowe paused as he was sliding Hanna's phone into his back pocket. The address sent a chill down his spine. It was familiar. Too familiar but he couldn't recall why.

"Why there?" Lucas snapped, his voice echoing in the large building. "Why would he pick *that* location?"

Rowe's eyes jumped up to look at his friend. Deep lines dug into his face and he couldn't take his gaze off of Andrei, who was watching his lover with a mix of confusion and concern.

And then it hit him why the address was so damn familiar. He, Lucas, and Snow had been there before. But things hadn't ended so well. They'd crossed a line in that building…to save Andrei.

Chapter 25

Rowe flinched against the cold wind as it rushed in through the open garage doors, rustling stray bits of trash before rushing back out of the building. Hanna sat with her legs crossed on the rough concrete floor in front of him, her arms bound behind her back. She'd been quiet since they'd struck the deal to make the swap, and Rowe could only hope that she'd stick to their agreement. That's not to say that he didn't have a couple tricks up his sleeve.

He looked around the abandoned factory, his eyes skirting away from a heavy metal door tucked off to his right near the front of the building. He never expected to be back. Everything had gone almost according to plan that night. They'd all gotten out alive, but Andrei had come close to dying. Too damn close.

The wind rushed in again and Rowe reached up, touching the earpiece resting in his ear. "Snow White in place with the Apple," Rowe said in a low voice. "Everyone check in."

"Doc in place. Road is clear," Snow came back immediately from his position on the top of the building just a bit down the empty block.

"Sneezy in place. Momma bird is waiting in the nest," Jude replied in a tone that managed to convey both amusement and fear. Again, Rowe worried that he shouldn't be here. Jude had taken up a position hidden in the offices. His job was to look over Eric, check his health when they got him and keep the little boy safe. Snow was not happy about Jude's presence, but the paramedic had demanded to come along, immediately countering that someone would need to check over the child and Snow would be too busy protecting Rowe's back. Rowe almost pitied the doc when it came to arguing with his man. Jude had a sort of commanding personality that made arguing hard. Snow, as tough and difficult as he was, didn't stand a chance.

"Bashful in place with his babysitter," Ian grumbled over the earpiece. "I hate my code name. Just for the record."

"Dopey in place with eyes on Bashful and the road," Andrei said with a hint of a smile in his voice. Ian was the other one who demanded to be present for the hand off. Rowe wasn't surprised. Hanna and Kyle were from his past and if Jagger was involved, Ian wanted to be there. Of course, that didn't mean Rowe was going to let him anywhere near the danger. He'd stationed Ian and Andrei at the opposite end of the road from Snow in a dark car hidden deep in the shadows of another abandoned building. He didn't want Andrei or Ian near the drop spot.

"Happy in place," Noah said sharp and clear. He had settled in the tall grasses to the left of the building.

Silence stretched for several seconds before Lucas's growl could finally be heard. "You're an asshole. Is this you getting even?"

Fighting back a laugh, Rowe made a noise in the back of his throat, mimicking the sound of static. "I'm sorry. Who was that? You're breaking up." He looked down to find Hanna staring up at him like he'd lost his mind. He just grinned back at her.

"Grumpy in place, motherfucker," Lucas replied and Rowe cackled. He thought he could also hear Snow snickering over the earpiece.

This was not their first op together. Hell, it wasn't even their twentieth. They'd taken up the habit of whoever took the lead on the op getting to choose the code names. He and Lucas had felt a certain pleasure in screwing each other over in the past several, particularly since they'd discovered the joy in using fairy tale themes. This was what the freaking grumpy ass millionaire got for making him the Blue fucking Fairy when they'd rescued Andrei.

"Everything clear from my view," Lucas continued, ignoring him.

Rowe frowned, trying to tamp down his own anxiety. He would have preferred to have Lucas at the sniper position instead of Snow, but ever since Kyle had given the address, Lucas had become increasingly visibly upset. He and Andrei had nearly come to blows over Andrei taking part in this operation and his focus had grown more fragmented with each passing hour. Rowe had stationed Lucas several yards behind the building to keep an eye out for anyone who might try to sneak up on them from that direction. Luckily, Lucas hadn't argued. Rowe was just hoping that his friend realized that this place was fucking with him too badly to take point as usual.

"Eyes open everyone," Rowe said, glancing one last time at Hanna before checking his watch. It had just turned midnight. "Should I ask if your brother is the punctual type?" Hanna didn't look up at him or answer. Well, he did have her gagged again. She knew that Rowe had ample backup despite her brother's demand that he appear alone with Hanna. He didn't need her giving away his friends too early.

"Got a car," Andrei announced, breaking the silence.

"How many?"

"Just the driver. I don't see a kid."

"Could be lying down in the backseat," Ian suggested.

"Or the trunk," Snow chimed in.

"Nice, Doc," Jude grumbled.

"Cut the chatter," Rowe snapped. This was the last time boyfriends were allowed on an op. "Grumpy and Doc, eyes?"

"Clear," Lucas immediately replied.

"Clear," Snow followed.

Rowe didn't know if he should feel relieved or disappointed that Kyle had come alone to the meeting. But then, he was beginning to feel that while Jagger had hired these two to kill him and his friends, they weren't acting with Jagger's full support. He shouldn't have been surprised. Jagger was undoubtedly being watched closely by the feds and the cops. They'd come close to nailing the fucker to the wall with their recent case. There was no way the cops were walking away from Jagger when they could practically smell the blood in the water.

The late-model sedan pulled up to the front of the open garage doors and stopped, the headlights splashing across him and Hanna. Rowe made a show of pulling his gun from its holster at his back and putting it to the back of Hanna's head.

"Hold positions until the baby bird is spotted," Rowe said softly.

Kyle left the car running as he threw open the driver's side door and stepped out. His breath fogged in the bitter night air, his hair shifting slightly as the wind picked up. He immediately pointed a gun at Rowe. Even across the distance with the lights nearly blinding him, he could see the end of the gun shaking wildly.

"Give me my sister!" Kyle shouted.

"Where's the kid?" Rowe replied calmly. "Give me the boy and I won't put a bullet in the back of her skull."

Kyle seemed to hesitate in indecision for a second before cursing to himself. Still trying to keep the gun pointed on Rowe, he stepped back and pulled open the rear door. He reached in and pulled out a small figure. Frog-marching the kid to the front of car so that he was standing in the headlights, Rowe finally drew in a deep breath of relief. The little boy's face was lined with fear, but he otherwise looked fine.

Rowe swallowed back the lump that had grown in his throat at the sight of Eric standing there. He couldn't wait to get him into the waiting arms of his mother so this nightmare could finally end...at least for her.

"See! He's fine. We never hurt him. Never gave him to Jagger. What about my sister?"

"She's fine."

"I want to hear her say it."

Reaching down, Rowe pulled the gag out of her mouth.

"He didn't come alone! He's got all his friends here!" Hanna immediately started shouting, but Rowe had expected that. What he didn't expect was to actually see Kyle's shoulders relax as soon as his sister started talking.

"Are you okay?" he asked, but already some of the frantic tension had left his voice.

"Yes, I'm fucking fine," she snapped.

"Cool. What do you want me to do?"

Hanna groaned and dropped her head, shaking it.

"Send the boy over to me," Rowe said.

Kyle's hand twisted in Eric's shirt and he stiffened. It was like he had forgotten for a moment that Rowe was even there. "What about Hanna?"

"She's safe. You're both safe so long as I get the boy back. Send him over and you'll get Hanna."

Rowe held his breath, waiting for Hanna to start shouting something to contradict his order, but she sat silent on the ground, still shaking her head.

With a shove, he sent Eric running toward Rowe. At the same time, Lucas and Noah stepped around the building from opposite directions, closing in on Kyle with their guns aimed at his head. Rowe focused on the little boy. Tucking his gun into the pocket of his hoodie, he knelt down and held his arms out to him. The smaller body crashed into him and wrapped thin arms around his neck. Eric knew him. He and his mother had come over for cookouts. They'd hung out in the office when his mom was working. All the guys in the office knew and loved Eric. A shuddering breath escaped him as he held him close. He was safe.

"Are you okay?" Rowe whispered, choking on the tears of relief he was holding back.

Eric nodded against his shoulder. "Where's my mom? I want my mom."

"We're going to get her, I promise." Rowe brushed a kiss across the top of his head. "Do you remember my friend, Dr. Snow?" Eric nodded, tightly clutching Rowe's hoodie. "Good. Well, his very nice boyfriend Jude is in that office over there and he has your mom on the phone. Can you go wait with Jude and talk to your mom?"

Eric gave another nod before he darted off toward the open door with the light shining from the interior office.

"Sneezy has the baby bird," Jude said over the earpiece a couple second later, indicating that he had Eric safely in the office.

"There! You have the kid! I want my sister back!" Kyle shouted.

Rowe pushed back to his feet and resumed his spot behind Hanna. "Put your gun down, Kyle."

Kyle shook his head. "I don't think so."

The pyro shuffled his feet, but kept his gun down. Still, Rowe would have preferred it out of his hand completely. "Why here?" he asked.

Kyle flinched but thankfully kept his weapon down. "What?"

"Why did you pick this location for the meet?"

"Because...because it's artistic." He laughed, a thready, broken sound that resembled a wounded animal. "Don't you get it?"

Rowe blinked, trying to follow Kyle's train of thought but he was lost. This rundown, abandoned factory in the middle of a declining town in Kentucky was artistic? Maybe if you were into ghetto trash.

"This is where it all started," Kyle continued. "It was supposed to be this grand piece that made everything better. You and your stupid friends were supposed to die in that fire in Price Hill because that Vallois bitch was never supposed to get that property. And then we were going to kidnap Ian and bring him here. We were going to wrap him in a big red bow and hand him over to Jagger. And...and everything was going to be right again. Ian wasn't even supposed to be at that stupid club." He raised the gun again.

Ian's gasp of horror was nearly drowned out by Hanna's low, evil laughter.

"You still don't fucking get it, do you?" she said. "You don't get why Jagger hired us at all."

"What are you talking about?" Rowe asked, his stomach sinking as pieces of the puzzle starting fitting together in a terrifying picture.

"You killed Jagger's son. Chris Green was Jagger's kid—one nobody knew about, not even the feds. Jagger knows it was you fucks who made him disappear and he wants you dead."

"No..." Lucas's haunted whisper slipped through his ear before he shouted it again. "No!" Lucas took a step forward, his gun still pointed at Kyle's head, but Kyle didn't seem to notice. His eyes were locked on his sister and Rowe. "Chris Green had nothing to do with Jagger. He was no one. Just some punk property investor trying to kill me, kill Andrei. He killed other people!"

Rowe watched his friend starting to unravel as everything suddenly made sense. Chris Green had threatened Lucas and nearly killed Andrei. Lucas had lost it. Andrei meant everything to him and he couldn't deal with the idea of someone threatening Andrei or the rest of his family, so he'd killed Chris Green rather than risk the man coming after them again...and finally succeeding. They'd thought that was the end of it, but Green's disappearance didn't go unnoticed by apparently...his father. Now their old enemy was out to get the blood he never got when they'd bought Ian from him.

Fuck, the domino effect of that one act hit him.

If Lucas hadn't killed Green, Mel wouldn't have been killed.

Snow wouldn't have been nearly killed by Gratton.

Ian wouldn't have been nearly kidnapped by Gratton.

Lucas's businesses wouldn't have been burned down.

Rowe's business wouldn't have been shredded by the fires.

And an innocent child wouldn't have been kidnapped.

Over the earpiece, he could hear Andrei trying to talk to Lucas, but the man wasn't listening. Andrei was hurrying to the drop spot with Ian, but Rowe didn't think the presence of Andrei would help this time.

"Doc, you need to get here now!" Rowe shouted as he grabbed Hanna roughly by the arm and pulled her to her feet. Sliding his knife off his belt, he quickly cut the ties binding her wrists behind her back. He'd watched Lucas reach Snow on so many occasions when the doc sunk into a dark place. He was praying that Snow could help Lucas now. Noah still had his gun trained on Kyle, but Lucas had dropped his arm. This was bad. Real bad.

"Nearly there," Snow immediately came back.

Rowe shoved Hanna at Kyle. "Get out of here."

Hanna walked quickly over to Kyle, who dropped his gun down to his side, oblivious to the chaos he'd created. His eyes were locked only on his sister. When she was finally standing at his side, trying to pull him into the car, he lifted his confused gaze to Rowe again.

"I don't get it. You're just going to let us go?"

"You promised to leave Cincinnati and never come back."

His brow furrowed and he looked at his sister for a second before looking back at Rowe. "Yeah, but..."

"You can go home, Kyle Fogle."

Kyle stepped away from his sister and actually approached Rowe, stepping a little into the shadows of the factory. Behind them, Snow and Andrei reached Lucas at roughly the same time, but they kept their distance from the man. He had his gun pointed again at Kyle, but his hands were shaking. Noah stepped behind the car, moving out of Lucas's shot, though Rowe was pretty sure they were all praying that nothing set Lucas off. They didn't need more deaths.

"What did you say?"

"You could always go home, Kyle Fogle," Rowe repeated, soft and even.

"He's lying, Kyle." Hanna snarled. "He doesn't know shit. Now get in the car."

Kyle jerked at her tone, but he didn't move.

Rowe took a cautious step forward. "I know your names are Kyle and Hanna Fogle. Your parents are Linda and Mark Fogle. You were born in Boise, Idaho."

"How?" Kyle murmured and even Hanna stopped trying to pull Kyle back toward the car and turned a shocked expression his way.

"Facial recognition software. We got a picture of you off the computer and it matched an old picture from a missing poster," Rowe explained. "Your parents are still looking for you. They want you to come home."

"No!" Hanna screamed, pointing at Rowe. "You don't know what you're talking about. You don't know—"

"I talked to them, Kyle. Talked to your mom. They want you both to come home." He didn't add that he'd bounced the call through a shitload of channels and masked his voice—that he'd never told the parents his name.

"Home?" Kyle's voice broke on that single word.

Hanna was growing more frantic with each word Rowe spoke. "No, we can't!"

"I can put you on a plane tonight. You'll be back home with your parents by morning. This will be put behind you forever. You can move on with your lives and never have to think about Jagger again."

Kyle looked at his sister, a smile starting to spread across his lips. "You hear that? We can go home."

Hanna smacked Kyle hard across the cheek, snapping his head around and knocking him off balance so that his thigh slammed into the side of the car. "It's a lie and you know it! We can't go home. We can never go home. You think they're going to want you after what Jagger did to you. What all those men did to you. You're broken and dirty. I'm all you've got. I'm the only one who will protect you and keep you safe. Mom and Dad don't want you. Not like you are now."

Rowe's heart just shattered. Hanna had been just as traumatized as her brother.

Kyle's eyes darted from Rowe to Hanna and back again, indecision and pain twisting up his features. "But…but I just want to go home."

"I told them about Jagger, Kyle." Rowe kept his voice steady, his gaze mostly on Hanna, who grew increasingly more agitated by the way she shook and twisted her head side to side. "I told them what happened and they still want you."

"Lies! He doesn't know!" Hanna shouted.

"He's not lying." Ian's voice cut through Hanna's desperate shouts, drawing all eyes to him. Ian walked around the car so that he was now standing on the driver's side. Noah moved closer to Ian so that he could easily shield the other man if something went horribly wrong. "I've told Rowe what it's like with Jagger. What life was like at his compound. He wouldn't lie about this. He told your parents and they still want you. Don't turn your back on that."

Kyle looked back at Hanna and Rowe could see the horror changing to rage. He cursed himself under his breath. He should have been more adamant about Kyle dropping his gun before he released his sister. Every interaction with the kid pointed to the fact that he wasn't particularly stable. Neither of them were. Rowe had hoped that the news of their parents would give them hope, give them a new start. But something niggled in the back of his brain about Hanna. She'd been there, known what was being done to her brother. God only knew what was done to her during their time with Jagger.

"You're the one who lied," Kyle growled, turning toward his sister. His hand tightened around the gun that he'd begun to swing around as his voice lifted to a roar of pain. "We could have gone home. You didn't want to call them. Didn't want to tell them what we saw and what we did. You were scared. I just wanted to go home."

"You know we couldn't! Everything I did, I did for us so we could survive. You didn't want to leave Jagger. You didn't want to try to live without that filth. He sucked you in and made you believe—" she broke off, lips twisted. "But I gave us a second chance, a purpose. Mom and Dad wouldn't have understood."

Kyle rocked back, scratching the side of his head with the gun. Tears slipped down his cheeks.

"Kyle..." Rowe started in a slow, even voice. He took one step closer to the pair and then another. He was too far away to try to make a grab for the gun. Noah was covering Ian and Andrei and Snow had their hands full with Lucas.

"No!" he roared, pointing the gun at Hanna. "You always blamed me. Hated me. You were ashamed. Didn't want to try!" He suddenly screamed and squeezed off three quick rounds, each bullet slamming into Hanna's chest at pointblank range. Rowe jerked back, his heart stopping for a second as he watched Noah immediately snatch up Ian and roll him to the asphalt, using his own body as a shield.

The silence was deafening after the shots were fired. Kyle stumbled back, the gun hanging limp in his hand at his side. A choked, ragged cry broke from the young man's throat as he stared at his sister's lifeless body, her blood spreading across the ground. He collapsed on the ground as if his legs had suddenly given out underneath him.

Noah slowly allowed Ian back to his feet, but kept a hand on his shoulder as if he was preparing to tuck him back under him again.

"Kyle...oh God, Kyle," Ian whispered.

Rowe started to charge toward Kyle when the young man's hand tightened around the gun and he lifted it again. Rowe's breath stuttered as he reached for the gun tucked in the pocket of his hoodie.

Kyle looked at Ian. His trembling lips jerked in a ghost of smile for just a heartbeat. "I just wanted to go home," he murmured and then pressed the muzzle of the gun to his head.

Rowe sucked in a breath to shout, but it was already too late. Kyle pulled the trigger and ended his life.

Ian cried out, lurching toward Kyle, but Noah was already grabbing him, gently wrapping him up in his arms as he sobbed.

Fuck, this wasn't supposed to be how this went down. He'd honestly thought he could get through this night with no one getting hurt. Hell, he'd hoped he could actually get the siblings on the plane and back home to their parents.

"Snow White! I hear shots! What's going on? Doc? Somebody?"

Rowe jerked when he realized that he'd been staring at the two bodies, his thoughts scattered. Jude's frantic voice was coming over the earpiece.

"We're safe, but we gotta get moving. Sneezy, stay put. I'm sending two your way to escort you out," Rowe quickly said, shutting down all emotions until he could get his family out of this nightmare. The shots had undoubtedly been heard and someone somewhere had called the cops. They'd made sure not to leave a trace of their presence and they couldn't be caught there. Trying to explain it all would be a mess that no one would believe. The cops would find the siblings. What they deduced would be up to them.

Marching over to where Snow, Lucas, and Andrei stood, Rowe clenched his teeth to see the dead stare in Lucas's eyes. This was bad. He'd never seen Lucas shut down like this.

"Snow, Andrei, get Lucas home now!" Rowe snapped. No point in keeping with the code names now. Everything had gone to hell. "Ian, Noah, and I will escort Jude and Eric back to Gidget."

He started to look around for Noah, but his gaze once again caught on the lifeless bodies of Kyle and Hanna. It wasn't supposed to go down like this. They were supposed to go home, get some help, and try to live happy, as normal as possible lives surrounded by people who loved them. They weren't supposed to be dead outside an abandoned factory in the middle of nowhere Kentucky for some clueless cops to find.

Were all the kids that had been touched by Jagger headed for this same horrible end?

Except for Ian. They'd saved Ian. But was it enough? No, it hadn't been.

"Rowe!"

His head snapped up to find Noah standing in front of him. Cold but gentle hands came up and cupped his cheeks, wiping away tears he didn't even realize were there.

"Andrei and the others are heading to the car. We need to get out of here," Noah said, but Rowe still couldn't get himself to move. It wasn't just the death of the Fogle kids fucking up his brain. Everything had started right here just over a year ago. If they done something different...

"What happened, Rowe? Tell me what happened that night with Green."

"Green kidnapped Andrei, nearly killed him. We rescued him right here," Rowe said, waving one hand at the factory. "Green attacked Lucas and Lucas knocked him out. But we knew it wasn't enough. We should have taken it to the cops, but we were afraid that he'd get off and then strike again. He was a murderer. Didn't want to take the risk that he'd actually kill Andrei or Snow or me. I...I didn't want him to kill Lucas. So Lucas shot him and we incinerated the body."

"Rowe...do you blame Lucas? For Mel?"

Rowe stepped out of Noah's touch and rubbed a hand roughly over his face to try to get his brain functioning again. "I can't...because I was there with him. He might have pulled the trigger, but I didn't try to talk him out of it. I just kept thinking that if it had been Mel who'd been kidnapped, I wouldn't have stopped with a bullet to the brainpan. And we...we didn't know."

"But if he hadn't, Mel would be here."

Rowe stepped forward, getting in Noah's face. "And you wouldn't be. Mel's gone. I will never stop loving her, but she's gone. Wasting time on what ifs will just drive you crazy. Trust me, I spent the better part of a year playing that game. I've got you now and I am not letting you go. You got that?"

A smile lifted one corner of Noah's mouth. "Love you."

"Love you too. Now let's get out of here. I've got some friends who are a fucking mess right now. Including an employee who should never have had to pick between her son and me. We've got to make some plans. The shit is definitely not done hitting the fan."

Chapter 26

"Ian, please, tell me there's something I can do. Something I can help with," Noah pleaded for the third time in the past hour. The handsome man with the wide blue eyes flashed his most charming smile and Ian could only shake his head. He was struggling to deal with allowing someone to take care of him...at least when it came to food. Ian had trained the others that when it came to cooking, he was best left alone in the kitchen. It centered him like nothing could. Noah was hovering and Ian was struggling to not let it annoy him when the man was only trying to be useful. Of course, he could still hear Rowe snickering from the next room as if he were waiting for Ian to start beating Noah back with an oven mitt.

Glancing around him, Ian frowned. The rolls had just come out of the oven and he was about to carve the turkey. Everything was settled. Outwardly anyway. More than a week had passed since the nightmare that had occurred in Kentucky. He still felt horrible about leaving the bodies of the twins like that and knew his friends suffered the same guilt—despite the fact that they'd tried to kill them and had destroyed so much. They'd been victims and Ian kept seeing them and the others he'd left behind every time he closed his eyes at night.

So, he'd worked hard on this holiday. Worked hard to make everything feel as normal as possible. The only thing still off was that they were still waiting for Lucas and Andrei. Last year, Andrei had brought his parents, which had been an amazing amount of fun, but Andrei had called two days ago saying that his mother was recovering from the flu and wouldn't be coming this year.

This year's Thanksgiving was also quieter without Mel's presence. It was the first major holiday without her and they were all feeling her absence. Ian had trouble getting out of bed this morning—one of his favorite days of the year—knowing that he wouldn't be seeing her smiling face across from him at the table.

Noah had been alternating between sticking close to Rowe when he attempted to drift off alone and giving him space when Snow or Jude were entertaining him. For the first time since Ian had met the man, he seemed uneasy and anxious.

"I've got it under control," Ian said. "We're nearly ready to eat. If you want to do something, you can text Andrei or Lucas and find out where the hell they are. If they're any later, food is going to start getting cold and Lucas knows bet—"

The sound of the front door opening and closing cut off Ian's rant and he breathed a sigh of relief. They were finally here. Stepping around the island in the middle of the kitchen, Ian walked toward the foyer to greet the missing couple but his heart skipped a beat. There was only Andrei standing there, looking worn and lost. Dark shadows underlined his eyes and his hair hung limp around his face.

"Lucas—" Ian started.

"Isn't coming," Andrei finished and then cleared his throat. He didn't look up at Ian, keeping his hands shoved into his pockets. Ian could hear the others come up behind him, their voices suddenly dying off when they noticed Andrei standing there alone. "He called this morning and said that he wouldn't be able to make it back today because of work. He thinks he might be back in town tomorrow night, but since he has to be in Geneva next Monday, he might just stay over."

"That's fucking bullshit," Rowe snarled. "What the hell does he think he's doing?"

"He has never missed a holiday," Ian murmured.

Snow heaved a heavy sigh and Ian looked over his shoulder to see the surgeon push a hand through his hair. "This is Lucas's form of dealing with shit—he doesn't. He buries himself in work until he doesn't feel anything anymore."

"I'm...I'm thinking about moving out," Andrei admitted, lifting his red-rimmed eyes for the first time. Ian started to talk him out of it, but Andrei shook his head. "He's barely been home since that night in Covington. The day after he jumped on a plane to Seattle. Then it was London and Madrid. Next week is

Geneva. He's avoiding me, can't even stand to look at me. I'm not running him out of his own home."

Rowe reached around Ian and tightly grabbed Andrei's shoulder, giving it a shake. "You're not going anywhere. You belong in the penthouse with him. You belong with him."

Andrei shuddered, squeezing his eyes shut. "I think I've already lost him."

"You haven't," Snow said. "We'll drag him home and knock some sense into him if we have to, but you're not leaving."

Rowe smirked over at Snow. "Why do I get the feeling you're looking forward to delivering a little tough love?"

Snow grinned back. "Certainly not because he's beaten me with it over the past few decades."

Noah helped Andrei shed his winter coat and they followed Ian into the kitchen with the intent of helping him get everything served. The group had fallen silent, the weight of two missing members heavy among them.

"This is my fault," Andrei whispered, the words cutting through Ian. "If-if I had just been more careful. Hadn't been so stupid and just watched my back..."

Ian's hands tightened around the ceramic platter for a second before he gave in to his temper and smashed it against the floor. When he spun around, everyone was staring at him with a stunned expression, mouths hanging open. Good. He wanted their full attention.

"Enough! We're done playing the fucking blame game. Andrei, you feel guilty for getting kidnapped and pushing Lucas into being reckless. Lucas is drowning in guilt, because he thinks what he did led to all this recent hell, including Mel's death. Rowe has undoubtedly twisted the events in his head to feel guilty about Mel. Snow probably feels guilty for attacking Gratton all those year ago."

"Nope," Snow interjected and just flashed him a wicked grin. "Just guilty about not killing him the first time we met him."

"Whatever," Ian said with a roll of his eyes. "You want to get technical? This is my fault. If Snow, Lucas, and Rowe had never met me years ago, had never tried to help me, then Jagger would never have entered your world. But you know what? Fuck it! I love my life. And I love my family. And this entire shitstorm comes down to one man: Boris Jagger."

Ian suddenly swung around to face Snow, poking him in the chest. "You want to get Lucas back here? You call him and tell him I'm going after Jagger. We are done with this bullshit and we are bringing Jagger down for what he's done to this family and other families."

Rowe's smile grew and he loudly clapped Andrei on the back before looking over at Snow. "I like this plan."

"Of course, you do. It's mayhem and chaos." Jude snickered.

Noah slung an arm around Rowe, drawing him close. "Can I ask a question?" he said, lifting his hand as if in school. "Before we go storming the castle, can we eat first? Because that turkey smells really fucking good."

Ian blushed while the others finally laughed, the tension finally breaking in the room. He turned back toward the stove when something crunched under his feet. "Oh fuck."

"What?" Snow demanded, his hand landing on Ian's shoulder.

"That was my favorite platter," Ian said softly, looking at the broken fragments scattered across the kitchen floor.

Snow hugged him close, pressing a kiss to the top of his head. "I'll get Lucas to buy you the most expensive platter you can find."

"He's gonna have to do something to make up for not being here today."

Tiny snowflakes swirled in front of the headlights as Rowe drove himself and Noah home from Ian's. It was too early for snow in Cincinnati and while it hadn't been particularly warm recently, the white stuff wasn't going to stick. But it was a sign. This was going to be a bad winter. Which only reminded him of that line Noah had been repeating endlessly since he finally got Rowe to start watching *Game of Thrones* with him. He snickered softly to himself, flipping on the high beams as they headed farther from the city lights and into the winding countryside.

"What was that for?" Noah asked, breaking the silence for the first time since they'd gotten into the truck. He'd been too quiet since leaving Ian's. At first, Rowe had thought he might just be slipping into a food coma, but this felt different, heavier.

"Just thinking about the snow and winter."

"You know, I never asked, but…how bad are the winters here?"

Rowe snorted. "Thinking about heading back to Alabama now?"

"Nope, just wondering if I should invest in more long johns."

"It wouldn't hurt. Some are mild. Lots of rain and little snow."

"And others?"

"Shit-ton of ice with a nice layer of snow."

"Lovely," Noah mumbled and then fell silent again.

Rowe opened his mouth to ask about Alabama winters when they came around a turn to find a small herd of deer standing at the side of the road and coming down out of the woods. As he pressed the brakes, his right hand automatically shot out, pressing to Noah's chest to hold him back in his seat. Even through the sweater Noah was wearing, he could feel the brisk thump of his heart under his fingertips, the warmth of his body. As the car stopped, the deer shot across the road and into the woods on the other side.

Noah's slightly chilled fingers slid across the top of his hand, dragging his gaze from the deer as they disappeared in the darkness. "I'm sorry."

"For what?"

"I'm sorry that Mel wasn't there today."

A crooked smile drifted across Rowe's lips for a second and he patted his hand on Noah's chest before returning it to the wheel. He resumed their drive back home, his speed a little slower after being reminded that the deer were out.

"I miss her, but it was a good day. And if there's a life after this, I think she would have been at dinner, watching over us, laughing too."

Rowe glanced over to see Noah staring out the window, his face reflected in the black glass to reveal a grim expression. This wasn't like Noah, but then Lucas's absence and Jagger's shadow had created a somber tone today. More than once Rowe had caught Snow watching Andrei and muttering that he planned to beat some sense into Lucas. He was pretty sure each of them had snuck off at some time in the evening and tried to call Lucas, but he was willing to bet they all got the same answer that he'd gotten—silence.

"Sometimes I feel guilty…for being happy with you."

Rowe nearly slammed on the brakes, but he caught himself in time. He'd never expected to hear those words. "Why?"

"If she hadn't died, we wouldn't be together. I wouldn't be happy like this. Never would have had a shot. But she did…and it just doesn't seem fair."

Rowe almost breathed a sigh of relief as he turned into their subdivision. He couldn't have this conversation with Noah while he was stuck driving. He remained silent another minute as they rode down the street and finally pulled into the driveway. Throwing the truck into park, Rowe immediately turned in his seat so that he could face the man who had brought him back to life.

"No, it's not fair, but life isn't fair. If Mel were here right now, I know that she'd smack you for being an idiot and then kiss you for making me so damn happy." Rowe reached up and cupped the side of Noah's face, smiling. "I wish you could have met her. She would have loved you."

"I did meet her. Once. Sort of."

Rowe jerked back a little in surprise. "When?"

"You were skyping me a few years ago. It was near Christmas. She came in and peered over your shoulder. Said I had nice eyes."

Looking into those hypnotic blue eyes, Rowe had to agree with his wife. "She also said that she picked the wrong damn Ranger, but that was Mel. Always teasing and laughing."

"I'm glad you found her."

"And I'm glad you gave me a second chance." Rowe leaned in and gently kissed Noah, slowly exploring the softness of his lips, reveling in the fact that Noah was his and he could sink into his warmth and laughter anytime he wanted. He just needed to make sure that Noah understood that he wasn't going anywhere.

He broke off the kiss before it could continue and bumped his forehead against Noah's. "Let's get inside where it's warm."

Noah nodded and slid out of the truck, while Rowe turned off the engine and grabbed the giant bag of leftovers from the backseat.

"Is Ian worried about us being able to feed ourselves?" Noah asked as he unlocked the door.

"Are you really complaining about getting Ian's food to take home?"

"Nope," he said with a wide grin as he led the way into the house.

They took a moment to give attention to the dogs who were excited about their return and the smell of food. It was as Noah was taking off his coat that he noticed him take a thick yellow envelope out of his pocket.

"What's that?"

Noah paused, his hand tightening around the envelope so that the paper crinkled. "After your other house burned, I asked Ian and Snow if they had any pictures of your wife. I thought…when you're ready…we could put them up around the house."

Rowe dropped the bag of food on the table and grabbed Noah in a searing kiss because there was no way he could speak past the lump in his throat or hide the tears burning in his eyes. Noah melted against him, kissing him back as if he was the only thing that mattered in the world.

"Tomorrow," Rowe said, his voice rough with emotion. "Tomorrow, we'll go out and get some frames."

Noah chuckled. "Babe, tomorrow is Black Friday."

"Oh fuck," he whispered, feeling his stomach drop in panic. There was no way in hell he was heading out in that madness. "Okay, we're going online tomorrow and ordering some frames. And then we watch college football and fuck."

"Did anyone ever tell you that you say the sexiest things?"

"Only my mom."

Noah shoved Rowe away, laughing hard. "Sick perv."

Rowe backpedaled, grabbing up the bag of food again. "Go put on some comfortable clothes while I shove this in the fridge. I'm too full of Ian's food to struggle with stripping you out of difficult stuff like belts and things with buttons."

Noah's warm laughter echoed down the hall as he walked toward the guest bedroom. They were sleeping together every night now, but Noah continued to keep his clothes in the other room as if he wanted to give Rowe some space. Yeah, that was changing whether Noah wanted it to or not.

"Holy fuck!" Noah shouted, his voice carrying enough to bring the dogs rushing to his side.

Rowe smiled and gave up trying to shove the last container in his full fridge. Shedding his coat and throwing it over the back of the kitchen chair, Rowe walked down the hall and leaned against the doorjamb. Noah stood in the center of the room, both hands shoved into his hair, pushing it back from his face so that Rowe could see the tears sparkling in his eyes, which he couldn't take off the upright piano.

"You like it?"

"How?" was all he could manage.

"I happen to have some large, strong men who work for me. While at dinner, they stopped by and moved the bed to the basement and the piano in here."

Noah gave a choked laugh as he looked around the changed room, what Rowe was now thinking of as the music room. He'd found a refurbished upright piano just a few days ago and arranged for Sven and Dominic to pick it up and bring it to the house. They met with Royce, who helped to move the piano and remove the bed. Noah's acoustic guitar was also on a stand in the corner. The guys even left a fresh stack of music sheets on the top of the piano.

"You made your people work on a holiday?"

"Hell no. I just said that anyone who helped would get some of Ian's leftovers from Thanksgiving." Noah's laugh was a little freer this time and Rowe stepped into the room. He moved behind Noah and wrapped his arms around his waist, soaking in the man's natural warmth, the soft hint of peppermint. "You'll quickly learn that Ian's food is worth a lot on the black market."

"I see."

"You never answered my question. Do you like it?"

"God yes!" Noah reached out with trembling fingers, running them over the keys which released a discordant sound.

Rowe winced. "Sorry about that. I've got a guy coming on Monday to tune it. I know it's not fancy and new, but I thought it would work for now. Then maybe in a few years…we get a bigger place and maybe a better piano—"

Noah turned and kissed him, gripping him hard so that their bodies were pressed tightly together from knees to lips. Air couldn't even slip between them and that's how Rowe wanted it to stay. He would never be able to get enough of Noah.

"It's fucking perfect, Rowe. I love it. Thank you so much," Noah said between kisses. "How…how did you even know?"

A soft chuckle rumbled up Rowe's chest. "You talked about playing your grandmother's when you were a kid."

"Yeah, but that was years ago, when we were Rangers."

"And you couldn't get one then because you were moving about. Never felt settled."

"Yeah, but—"

"I want you to be settled here with me. I want this to be your home. *Our* home." Rowe pulled away from Noah enough to look him in the eyes, his smile falling. "I know I'm asking you to stay when things in my life are about to go to hell in a big way with Jagger, but…just stay with me. Be with me."

Noah lifted his hand to the side of Rowe's face, his thumb rubbing across his lower lip, sending an exciting frisson down his spine. "Bring on Jagger and any other madness you can cook up. You're mine now. I'm not going anywhere."

Don't miss out on Ian's book!

DEVOUR

Coming Spring 2017!

About the Authors

Jocelynn Drake is the author of the *New York Times* bestselling Dark Days series and the Asylum Tales. When she's not working on a new novel or arguing with her characters, she can be found shouting at the TV while playing video games, lost in the warm embrace of a good book, or just concocting ways to torment her fellow D&D gamers. (She's an evil DM.) Jocelynn loves Bruce Wayne, Ezio Auditore, travel, tattoos, explosions, fast cars, and Anthony Bourdain (but only when he's feeling really cranky). For more information about Jocelynn's world, check out www.JocelynnDrake.com.

Rinda Elliott is an author who loves unusual stories and credits growing up in a family of curious life-lovers who moved all over the country. Books and movies full of fantasy, science fiction, and romance kept them amused, especially in some of the stranger places. For years, she tried to separate her darker side with her humorous and romantic one. She published short fiction, but things really started happening when she gave in and mixed it up. When not lost in fiction, she loves making wine, collecting music, gaming, and spending time with her husband and two children.

She is the author of the Beri O'Dell urban fantasy series, the YA Sister of Fate Trilogy, and the paranormal romance Brothers Bernaux Trilogy. She also writes erotic fiction as Dani Worth. She can be found at RindaElliott.com. She's represented by Miriam Kriss at the Irene Goodman Agency.

Jocelynn and Rinda can be found at: www.DrakeandElliott.com

Or you can sign up for their newsletter on the website to stay up to date on all upcoming books and news.

They are found on Facebook as Drake and Elliott and on Twitter as @drakeandelliott.

And don't miss out on all the sneak peeks and speculation at the Facebook Group, Unbreakable Readers.

Made in the USA
San Bernardino, CA
02 January 2019